# MONGOL MOON

NOVEL
LLC
PLOTS

# MONGOL MOON

## MARK SIBLEY

NOVEL
LLC
PLOTS

For Dad,
I think you'd love that I wrote a story.

For all the Watch Standers,
in uniform and otherwise, that keep us safe.
Thank you.

# ONE

November, 1979
Tehran, Iran
Javad Shir-Del

There was a chill in the air for November, but the city seemed close to boiling. The streets were filled with thousands of people supporting the growing revolution against the Shah. There was a restlessness about them now, more than ever, and they had a passion the likes he'd never seen before.

Javad Shir-Del was eighteen years old. His parents were middle class Iranians who kept their allegiances close, but he knew they hated the Shah with his corruption and extravagance. They didn't really care for the Ayatollah either. Two sides of the same coin, his father was fond of saying. Javad and his family were good Muslims, but not what you would call devout. But times, it seemed, were changing. The family attended prayers. His parents, himself, and his younger sister Sara, who was turning sixteen that year, prayed at the required times during the day when they heard the Adhan or call to prayer. However, under the Shah, the religiousness was relaxed, informal.

Earlier that year the Morality Police had appeared on the streets, filling the vacuum of the Shah's waning power. They were formed by the Ayatollah's followers to ensure all faithful Muslims attended prayers and conformed to the strict tenets of the Koran. Women were required to cover their heads in public and it was becoming even more strict. He had to accompany his sister when in public or the roving teams of Morality Police would stop her on the street to question her. Some women caught in public without a male family member or husband had been beaten with batons, the same fate if they weren't suitably covered. Many women had taken to wearing the full burka. It was unsettling to Javad, and he was anxious as to the outcome.

1

His thoughts drifted to his supper conversation with his father the previous evening.

*"The Shah of Persia in 1259 thought his lands were invincible. Even though the reports he received from Asia and Europe were grim, the Shah had nearly impenetrable mountains to block the Mongol's advance."* His father spoke with a passion for relaying this knowledge that drew Javad, as fascinated with military strategy as he was.

The Mongolian Empire was his father's life's work at the University, and he brought it alive in the retelling. Javad ate his food every evening, listening with interest, while his sister, Sara, would nod along at his father's diatribes on the Silk Road, Genghis Khan, and the myriad battles and military campaigns. When it came to how the Mongols conquered Persia in the middle of the 13th Century, Javad's interest was piqued. These supper conversations had been going on for years, and he loved them. It was when he and his father truly bonded with this common interest.

*"How would the Mongols do it?"* He had heard it all before, but was always happy to hear it again. His father was a gentle man of slight build with a full, graying beard. He was completely consumed by the history that he taught. His mother, on the other hand, was the one who ran their home. She was constantly after Javad and Sara to focus on their studies and to tidy up around their flat before any fun was had. She was as much a taskmaster as she was warm and loving.

*"Ah, you will be a great strategist I think, Javad. A future in the Shah's military is what you have ahead of you. But, for now, the Mongols never invaded a region without first knowing everything there was to know about it. It took up to a year, at times, to gather all the information they needed: enemy weaknesses, troop strength, garrison locations, food and water dispositions, fortifications and population, and what it was they produced. It was all critical to the Mongol's success."*

*"Why would the Mongols need to know about food and water and how the population lived?"* Javad's questions were more to keep his father focused on the military aspects, which he enjoyed more, but if he didn't ask probing questions, his father would ramble on to other less interesting aspects, and then he wouldn't be able to get him back on track.

"*Excellent question, my son. Excellent, for if the Mongols could deny their enemy of their food and water or even disrupt the production of what it was they relied on for livelihood, perhaps they needn't fight at all. However, most of the time, they did fight. On one occasion that I know of, a small complement of Mongols conquered a much larger garrison at a city in the north near the mountains, which would today be somewhere in eastern Afghanistan.*" His father was now deep into the telling. Javad loved the conversations in which his father told him about specific battles or invasions that the main histories forgot or just discarded. His father continued.

"*This Mongol leader had only five thousand men with him, mostly cavalry. They couldn't hope to breach the walls of the town, so they camped on the other side of the mountain range for the winter, while he sent some of his more savvy men into the town disguised as traders and craftsmen, which had been their employment before military service. Over the winter these men gained the trust of the people and military garrison, which was twice his own. They were not the only travelers that over-wintered in the town. Travelers were a common thing, and they were few of many. However, when the first thaw arrived and spring had sprung in the valley, one of these men reported back to the Mongol leader on everything from troop strength, illnesses, where the town got their food and water supply, and other general goings on.*"

"*So the Mongols knew everything there was to know about their enemy, but their enemy knew next to nothing about the Mongol force camped on the other side of the mountain range?*" Javad focused his father again.

"*Exactly. Exactly. You have the way of it. So then the Mongols began a campaign to cut off their water from the river that flowed down the mountain by diverting it, so that it no longer flowed into the town. At the same time, they killed the farmers that surrounded the town under the cover of one night. They also cut off the roads to the town. They did all this very quickly. The opposing military leader sent out several columns of men on foot and horseback to find out what was occurring in his valley. None returned. Had he sent his force out as one, he could have overpowered the Mongols, but the smaller groups were easily slaughtered one at a time. So, when it came time to finally confront the enemy, the Mongols chose to announce their presence by surrounding the town in the middle of the night under a full moon with torches lit, two to a man, with bonfires alight as well.*

*"So the Mongols had taken away the town's means of survival, reduced their fighting force, and were now making it look like they had more numbers than they had? All under a full moon for effect?" Javad asked as he leaned forward, nearly on the edge of his seat.*

*"Precisely. The two forces were now evenly matched, and the Mongols would win that contest, or the town could stay behind the walls and die of thirst. If it is land you seek, you must remove the inhabitants from that land. The easiest way to do that is to deny them food and water and even shelter. They will leave if they can or they will die where they stand. They were terrified and knew they were defeated, so they threw open the gates; the Mongols occupied the town. They then slaughtered every last man, woman, and child, save for one small group who they instructed to go to the next town, and tell them this story. If the next town surrendered, they would all be spared." His father was really deep into the story.*

*"Did it work, father?"*

*"Unknown to the Mongol leader, the small group they let go told a far more horrifying story to the next town. Of course, they told of the slaughter and occupation. What they also wove into their telling was that the Mongols had come under a full moon and nothing could stop them—they were invincible. As the story passed around, the telling evolved into the Mongols coming with the moon and when it was full, they couldn't be defeated. That is how the legend of the Mongol Moon began, and it served the Mongols well in their continued conquests in Persia."*

*His father ended as he realized the food on his plate was cold and they both chuckled as Javad's was cold as well.*

Javad smiled and contemplated the present and the past as he sat at the window of their modest three-room flat in north Tehran. He ate breakfast, consisting of what fresh fruit and bread was on hand from the local market. His sister, Sara, was getting ready in her room to go out with her friends. They were to be chaperoned by Javad and his best friend, Ahmed. He slept on a fold out futon in the main room so that the Princess could have her own room. In Farsi, Sara means Princess and she acted the part, spoiled constantly by their parents. It seemed more so that morning. She was set on going out into the streets that day. Sara and her friends wanted to be part of the demonstrations against the Shah. Javad's father, who worked as a professor of

Asian and Islamic History at the University of Tehran, just blocks from their flat, wanted them to stay out of those crowds, but Javad had promised to go with them. His father agreed reluctantly. Sara always got her way with their father. His mother, on the other hand, had given Javad strict instructions that they stay away from trouble and not get close to the demonstrations, but only watch from a safe distance. Women were being arrested for the most minor of infractions, based on the whims of the Morality Police. They also heard reports of women being beaten or worse.

The Morality Police seemed to be everywhere, and one of those groups was led by a particularly loathsome young man named Hafez, not much older than himself. His family lived nearby and was of a poorer and more religious strata of the surrounding area near the university. Javad had some run-ins with Hafez growing up, including that morning at the market when he was out getting fruit and bread for breakfast. Hafez was a particularly foul person, and he recalled the interaction.

*"How's your sister?" A voice whispered in his ear when he stopped to select a loaf of freshly baked bread.*

*Javad spun to find Hafez and a couple of his Morality Police stooges standing behind him. They blocked his way.*

*"No business of yours, Hafez. Let me pass." He spoke to the elder Hafez, but older only by a couple of years. He approached, but Hafez placed his right hand on Javad's chest to block him.*

*"Everything is my business, little Lion Cub. You should be careful out here alone in the streets. Your friend isn't here to protect you this time, is he?" Hafez said, squared face to face with Javad. Hafez's horrid breath made Javad turn his head. Did the man not brush his teeth?*

*"Look, he won't even look me in the eyes!" Hafez said to his comrades, while still looking intently at Javad. His hand was still on Javad's chest when a shadow blocked the morning sun.*

*"Is there a problem here?" A deep voice boomed as Javad looked to the side and was relieved to see his towering friend, Ahmed, standing a few feet away. He hadn't seen him approach with the mass of people in the market even though he was taller than all of them. Hafez removed his hand from Javad's chest and spun with his comrades to face Ahmed.*

*"Ah, to the rescue again, Ahmed? When will you let the little Lion Cub learn to fend for himself?"* As Hafez spoke, Javad moved toward Ahmed. His towering friend moved closer to Hafez, blocking the path between them.

*"You have more to say, Hafez? You don't have enough men with you, I think."* His words spit out in a whisper. Hafez looked up at Ahmed and then back to Javad with a sneer.

*"Ha! We'll see you soon enough, little Lion Cub."*

Hafez and his goons turned to join the throngs of market goers, then, looking back over his shoulder, Hafez yelled, *"Say hello to your pretty sister, Javad!"*

Ahmed took a long, menacing step toward Hafez, who quickly disappeared into the crowd. Javad relaxed as Ahmed turned to him.

*"What did you say to get that bastard riled up, Javad?"* Ahmed asked with a smile.

*"Did you smell the man's breath? He must eat dogshit for breakfast."*

*"You good now? See you in an hour for our chaperone duties?"*

*"Yes, thank you, my friend. An hour it is."*

With that they parted company and Javad returned to his family's flat with his gathered food.

It didn't help that Hafez had some twisted interest in his sister. She had not returned his unwanted advances over the previous few months, and at one point his father had to tell Hafez to stay away. It didn't stop him from lurking around though. He was a thorn in Javad's side. He hoped they wouldn't run into him today while they were out in the city. He wouldn't have agreed to go, but Ahmed was tagging along with his sister, Yasmin, who was friends with Sara. He wouldn't pass up an opportunity to be around Yasmin. She and Sara went everywhere together and he went wherever his sister went, when she went out, unless their father was with her.

Restlessness, it seemed, was in the blood of the young in Tehran, and God help him, he thrived on the unknown of it. He'd promised his mother that he'd keep the girls safe and well away from the more problematic streets, and by that he meant Ahmed would keep them safe. His father said the Shah's days were numbered. Change was coming, and he wanted to witness it like many others of his age, although others that he knew were out in the demonstrations against the Shah. His father warned him most were ignorant of what would replace the Shah. One tyrant for another, was his father's saying.

A knock on the door startled Javad out of his thoughts. He opened it to see the towering figure of Ahmed. He was easily six inches taller than Javad's five-foot eleven frame, with broad shoulders and rippling muscles under his shirt.

"Al-salam u alaykum!" Javad grinned, beckoning in his old friend with the Farsi greeting, which translated to peace be upon you.

"You big oaf. Come in. Bring the herd. Good to see you again this morning."

Ahmed stepped into the flat ushering in three more of his party, all girls the same age as Sara, including Ahmed's sister Yasmin. She was beautiful. He didn't think his friend knew of his feelings. It was more than a childish crush. He thought about Yasmin throughout each day. The vision of her wouldn't leave him be. It consumed him to the point he had pestered Sara about her for weeks. He was unsure if he should first ask his friend for advice and possibly his permission to ask Yasmin out for coffee or if he should just ask her first. He was conflicted.

Yasmin and the other two girls, who were nowhere near as captivating to him, moved past Javad and Ahmed and proceeded to the back of the flat disappearing into Sara's room. They removed their head scarves as they went, but not before Javad met Yasmin's gaze. She smiled at him, her teeth just apart and mostly covered by her lips. He stared, dumbfounded. Her round eyes had a hazel tint and were set in a face of perfect, almond skin. Surprised at the sudden attention, he smiled back as she turned away. He kept smiling at the back of her head, long brown hair swaying side to side, as she followed the others down the hallway.

Ahmed responded with 'and upon you be peace' in Farsi, "Wa alaykum al-salam! You seem to be getting smaller, Javad, my friend, and stop staring at my sister like a lost puppy."

He backhanded Javad lightly in the chest to bring him out of his obvious stupor. Javad snapped out of his trance. His friend always horsed around. Sometimes it was a huge bear hug, sometimes a friendly punch or slap on the back.

"I wasn't looking at her like a puppy!" Javad feigned insult.

"Ah, but you were looking at her," Ahmed responded with a large smile.

"I wasn't…" Javad started.

"Chilly today, but I think not so much in the streets, Lion Cub." Ahmed changed the subject abruptly.

Javad's last name meant lion's heart or brave in Farsi. Again, making it the diminutive Lion Cub was his way of poking at Javad. Always poking with the intent of evoking a response. Javad knew better than to physically react to Ahmed's bait. Ahmed was a rock. A boulder even. They were a good combination as they were. Each complemented the other. Javad's strength was in his quick wit and quicker thinking. Ahmed was all muscle and action. He had gotten Javad out of more than one predicament that his mouth had gotten him, or them, into.

"I was just thinking there was a chill in the air." Javad responded. There was an interruption from the kitchen doorway; his mother's voice snapped behind him.

"Javad! Stop staring at Yasmin like a puppy."

His mother, who they all called Bibi, emerged from the small kitchen and smiled mischievously at Ahmed, wagging her finger. This played out the same way every time Ahmed came over to the flat. Ahmed was warmly welcomed by Javad's mother as if he was her own son, and, in fact, it was nearly the case. They had been friends for so long, and Ahmed's parents passed away when Ahmed was only seven from a particularly nasty influenza strain. Ever since his parent's passing, Ahmed had lived with his aunt and uncle, but they were quite old. He actually took care of them in his older years instead of the other way around these days. Javad helped with their care as well. It was like they both had two families as it all felt so close emotionally. They were all family.

"Keep these girls safe out there, Ahmed. Don't let Javad's mouth get all of you in trouble with those morality fools."

Javad's mother was looking at Ahmed as the four girls emerged from their lair in the back, donning colorful head scarves over lengths of brown and black curls and long flowing locks. They looked as if they were going to a local celebration instead of a civil march against the Shah. Javad watched his mother kiss Sara's forehead, tucking wisps of her long hair back under the bright red head scarf to Sara's irritation. Then his mother ordered Sara,

Yasmin, and the others to pay attention to Javad, stay close to Ahmed, and above all, to stay together.

They would have their hands full, Javad thought, shaking his head in mock derision at the gaggle of girls. Ahmed shooed them through the door of the flat into the rabbit warren of concrete and asphalt alleyways and narrow streets that ran through and around the buildings and tenements that was Tehran. The cloudless sky allowed the morning sun to illuminate them. The slight warmth provided was welcome. A beautiful morning. The last one Javad would experience, at least in his youth.

An hour or so later, the six of them were secreted in the mouth of a dead-end alleyway that contained a few small shops, watching throngs of demonstrators march towards the University of Tehran some blocks away. There were hundreds of men in their late teens and early twenties in the street. Such was how the demonstrations against the Shah usually began. They all marched from different points to the University, then as a group, marched toward some government building or the Shah's palace. It was nearly like a parade, but with the prospect of violence.

All the protestors were clad in black or gray, some with helmets, many with hoods or bandanas covering their faces from the nose down. Some carried batons and other implements of the mob. There were chants of "Death to the Shah!" and "Death to the USA!" These hundreds were joining thousands of men, and even some women. Those women were fully covered head to toe in burkas, while others only wore the hijab or chador over their clothes. They marched east on a wide thoroughfare with buildings and tenements on either side.

Ahmed slapped him on the shoulder, and Javad turned his head. Several lines of police blocked the protestor's path about a hundred yards away. They were armed with batons, shields, and helmets. There were vehicles behind them. The police had positioned themselves between the approaching protestors and the larger group at the University. The police weren't moving. Javad saw a lone object with smoke trailing from it rise from the lines of demonstrators. It landed just in front of the police line. The object hit the street and shattered spreading liquid which instantly caught fire with a whoosh. It expanded into a fireball.

"Molotov cocktail!" yelled Ahmed in Javad's ear. Sara, behind Javad with the other girls, strained to see around Ahmed's protective cover. They were a good distance away, but the fire didn't sit well with Javad. The police line was moving as one against the protestors. The police clashed with the protestors, beating many of them with batons. Several on both sides were knocked to the ground, starting an all-out melee.

CRACK! Then another. Then staccato pops.

Demonstrators throughout the crowd went down. Javad glimpsed one black clad body lying motionless on the street, blood pulsing in a stream from a head wound. The police were shooting the protestors.

Screams rose from the mass of people in the street. Another firebomb exploded among the police line engulfing several officers. Their comrades attempted to pull them free of the fires. Other groups of police drug protestors back toward their lines while beating them with clubs and batons. It was madness. Javad hadn't expected such behavior. They were not witnessing one of the peaceful demonstrations that had been occurring. They were in the midst of a riot, and they had no business here.

Javad grabbed Ahmed's arm to get his attention. "We have to move! Get the girls out of here!"

Ahmed nodded sternly and led the way to the edge of the street, using the wall of a building as a guide. They moved away from the chaos just as a handful of canisters of teargas hurtled through the air, spewing their noxious fumes and smoke. Javad yelled for Ahmed to move faster. Ahmed saw the smoke and picked up his already quick pace. The girls followed, Javad brought up the rear. It was slow-going against the flow as the crowds were moving in the opposite direction. Ahmed used his considerable mass to carve a path through the oncoming crowd. It seemed like it took them forever to reach the first side street, which Ahmed turned left on, and immediately they were out of it. The group stopped for a moment to catch their collective breath. Javad looked down the narrow street. He motioned for Ahmed to move toward the first cross-street or alleyway.

They'd walked maybe twenty yards when a group of six or seven men spilled into the street in front of them. They were all clad in black, a couple of them carrying Kalashnikov rifles, more commonly known as AK-47s. Ahmed moved to the side of the street; Javad and the girls followed. The group of men moved past, faces covered, clubs and batons at the ready, as another larger group of demonstrators emerged at a cross-street further down. The crowd was coming toward them. This group also passed uneventfully, although Ahmed nodded to one of the men with a rifle, and he nodded back. They seemed more intent on getting to the main street than harassing the group.

"Ahmed," Javad grabbed his friend's arm and motioned to the first street on the right. "Take that street and let's get away from this. That was too close. We need to get out of here."

Javad pointed at the group of protesters that was pouring into the mouth of the street they were on. The acrid smoke from the teargas and fires was following them.

Ahmed nodded and led the group down the first street on the right. It was very loud in the narrow back streets. Others, like them, were trying to escape the mayhem; some were trying to join it. As they moved into the narrow alley-like street, they were confronted with another mass of demonstrators moving toward them. Javad found himself pushed up against the wall of the alley next to his friend. The girls had been separated and were on the other side of the alley with the mass of people moving between them. They chanted and moved fast. Some of them yelled at Javad and Ahmed, while others pumped their fists and sticks in the air, obscuring Javad's view of the girls. Teargas wafted into the alleyway. Javad tried to force his way across the street, but he was pushed back. He covered his mouth and nose with his hands, but the gas seeped into his eyes, and it burned. Ahmed couldn't get through the crowd either. There were hundreds of people all shouting and working themselves into a frenzy and moving as one mass in the chaos. Javad yelled for his sister; Ahmed yelled for Yasmin. Their calls were of no use.

Javad frantically looked up and down the street. It was hard to see with his stinging eyes. Once the crowd thinned slightly, they moved across. The girls were gone. Ahmed grabbed his shoulder.

"You go down that cross street, and I'll go to the main street to see if I can spot them over the crowd."

Ahmed pushed Javad toward a small alley and he started to run. Javad had to find them before someone else did: The Morality Police...or worse. The once crowded street was eerily empty, a light, lingering smoke swirled as he ran through.

It seemed an eternity as he ran from street to street in the twisting and turning alleyways. He heard a distant scream. Where was he? How far had he run? Where was it coming from? He stopped, listened intently. He recognized it, assumed a direction, and started running again. He followed the sound, stopped, listened. Every muscle in his body was tense. Sweat dripped from his short dark hair.

"*Javad!*"

There! Ahead, down this alley.

He ran and looked up at movement he caught out of the corner of his eyes. An old woman in a dark hijab sitting on a balcony motioned to him, and pointing frantically around the corner. She was old and bent, only her eyes showing through the hijab. She stood with effort, leaning on the balcony for support, and pointed a gnarled finger in the direction she wanted him to go. She said nothing, but her eyes were wide with concern. He waved a hurried thanks to her and darted around the corner and onto another narrow street. He stopped. It was empty. He strained. Listened. He heard men laughing, females screaming. Down the alley, a door was cracked open to a dark entrance hall of an apartment block. He slowly pushed the door open.

On the floor about ten feet away was Sara, stripped bare. Yasmin lay on the floor next to her seemingly unconscious, but still clothed. The other two girls were against the opposite wall, huddled together and sobbing. He took it all in for a split second, then realized they were not alone. Something hit him in the side of the head, hard. He hit the floor. The salty taste of blood flooded his mouth. He heard that deep, guttural laughing again, then everything went black.

Eventually, he came to, and managed to slightly open his right eye. His head throbbed. His sight was blurry, but he could make out his sister's visage a few feet away. There was a dark mass on top of Sara. He couldn't make out the form, but it was moving. Other sounds came to him. Sobbing. Tortured crying. He would have nightmares about these sounds the rest of his life—as well as the abrupt silence that followed.

"Finish what you are doing and shut that whore up!" It was a voice he didn't recognize, but the next voice he did.

"I'm done with her. No time for this fun anyway. You see, Javad. This is the punishment for unclean whores who are caught in the streets without their brothers."

It was Hafez. He was on top of Sara. Allah be merciful! What was happening? What had he done to her?

Then he saw the knife in Hafez's hand. He focused on the shiny glint of steel that came to a sharp point; the handle was hidden in a dark brown hand. The steel had a dragon engraved on the length of it.

He was helpless. He couldn't move. The pain. He tried. Nothing. Hafez ran the knife across Sara's throat while he locked eyes with Javad. A wicked smile stretched across Hafez's face, but it was his dark eyes that would haunt Javad. There was no soul in there. How could there be? Sara's scream bubbled. He heard gurgling and saw blood flow from her neck as she gasped for breath. She feebly grasped at her neck, her eyes filled with terror as she turned toward Javad.

"No! No!" Was all Javad could manage in his rage.

There was a clang on the floor next to him. The knife. Through his tear blurred vision, he saw the silver dragon blade covered in blood; the pool growing beneath Sara slowly approached Javad. The men scrambled away down the hallway away from a booming voice he recognized.

"Ahmed! Please get to her, Ahmed." Tears puddled on the cold slab floor beneath his cheek. Hands on his shoulder, strong hands.

"Ahmed! Please save her!" The last thing he remembered before the black returned was Sara's eyes. The darkness returned and it would follow him the rest of his life.

# TWO

Gale Washington's work space was cluttered. He'd read somewhere on social media that a cluttered desk was a sign of genius. He wasn't so sure about that. He didn't feel like a genius. He was tired. There were so many reports coming in that he couldn't keep up. In front of him was a report from Canadian intelligence on failing crops in northeastern China. The report was stale—a couple of years old. What did this information mean now? He thought to himself as he spun slightly back and forth in his swivel chair. His hands occupied themselves with a stress ball, squeezing it in one hand then the other, then bouncing it off the thinly carpeted floor. If crops were failing a couple of years back, what was their status now? It wasn't even his area of expertise, but they floated intel around his team here for what they called "new eyes" to piece disparate pieces of information and data together to aggregate into a common intelligence picture.

He was the senior intelligence watch officer for this combined team of staff and analysts from several three-letter agencies and the military. He was the only contractor in the place. He'd worked on this specific contract for years as the contract switched from company to company and back again. The beltway bandit defense firms battled for the contracts, but the staff remained mostly the same. It worked for him. He was able to follow his wife around the country on her duty stations, but his work remained stable in this contract. He was in demand. He was pulling a double shift to cover ahead for time off over the holidays. It was a couple of days before Christmas and he was due to get out of here soon.

He was supposed to pick up his daughter, Layla, from the gym shortly.

He was proud of her. A senior in high school and one of the best rowers on the East Coast. She had been offered crew scholarships to several colleges and universities, but she hadn't made up her mind yet. She was always in the gym with her boatmates from her four-person crew boat. That was a misnomer though, because they actually had five people in the boat. The fifth was their coxswain. This particular coxswain he knew. Alex was a smaller, very loud and larger than life version of Layla, who was known to start yelling obscenities at her boat in Russian when she got frustrated with them. It was more than amusing to watch. Alex lived a few houses down from them.

Slowly, he turned the pages of the wheat intel as he thought about Layla. His mind drifted to his wife, Joey, who at this moment, was literally drifting over the East Coast of the United States at four and a half miles per second, at around 279 miles up. On a good, clear night, he and Layla would sit outside and wait for the International Space Station to fly by. It was visible to the naked eye and the fastest moving object up there. Sometimes they could even video chat with her as she streaked by their house, rather than just watching and waving. They had a call with her tonight, which he and Layla were looking forward to.

Joey was the current Commander of the ISS and crew of three, including her. They would see her in person soon enough as her mission was coming to an end in January when they'd be relieved by the next crew. It had been a long year and even though they spoke and emailed regularly, the time apart was taking its toll. He missed her being there, missed her touch, her laugh, her presence around their house in a small neighborhood west of D.C. near where the Blue Ridge Mountains started making their presence felt, but close enough to commute in every day. The fusion center was about ten miles east of their home and twenty miles further on to D.C. He just missed her sitting on the couch on a Sunday by the window reading one of her novels. They could sit there reading together without saying anything. It felt complete.

But more than his needs, Layla needed her mom back. There were girl things and boy things Layla needed her mom for. It wasn't his area of expertise, and although he thought he did okay, he probably wasn't as good as he thought he was. Chinese wheat failures and girl things—both were boggling to him.

He did have a great deal of experience in satellites and tracking them and their characteristics. He'd been recruited out of college for his ability to put together incredibly different pieces of information to form a conclusion. He'd done some intense work early in his career that had made a difference, or so he was told. He didn't know what difference that was. He wasn't cleared for that level, but he felt some satisfaction.

The last few years had been harder though. He was still good at putting data together, but it seemed that no one was listening now. This chain of command, which ran the fusion center he now sat in, seemed more focused on chasing terrorists around every corner and being politically correct than acknowledging the serious nature of his current work. His theories were considered outliers at best. Crazy and to be ignored at worst. He'd gotten so rutted in his work recently, with no real excitement or action, that he'd been seeking excitement at the casino. Blackjack was his game and he'd gone overboard. He'd won a bunch early on, but then, as all gamblers do, he lost it all and then some. He wasn't looking forward to telling his wife about it when she got back.

He looked up at the array of three flat-screen computer monitors he had in front of him. The left was for email. The other two had images of satellite tracks overlaid on a world map. There were several he was particularly interested in. Well, two specifically, KMS 3-2 and KMS 4. He couldn't pronounce their North Korean names in full, Kwangmyongsong 3-2 and 4, so he stuck to the acronyms and numbers. They were launched by the DPRK in 2012 and 2016 respectively. The North Koreans stated that they were for weather data collection. However, he and others in the community thought they were for a far more sinister purpose. The prevailing wisdom was these two satellites were tests to perfect the North's capability to put a satellite in orbit with a small nuclear weapon onboard, which they could then detonate over the United States creating an EMP blast or Electro-Magnetic Pulse. A nuclear detonation at the altitude of these two satellites, which was approximately three hundred miles up on average, just above the ISS and Joey, was the perfect altitude to create an EMP and fry all electronics in the U.S. thereby sending America back to the 1800s in seconds with little hope of recovery. But that was before the new deal was reached between the NoKo's, China, and the U.S. Now it looked like things were normalizing on the Korean peninsula. One big happy family. What this wheat intel had to do with the satellites, was a head scratcher. Probably nothing.

"Those satellites blow up yet?" Gale swiveled in his chair to face his boss, Dennis. He was standing next to Gale staring at the screen on Gale's desk where the NoKo satellites were slowly moving across the map in real-time.

"What's up, Boss?" Gale asked, knowing what was coming.

"Let's have a chat in my office, Gale." Dennis said quietly and walked toward his office.

Gale followed and once the door was shut behind him, he took the seat in front of the desk that Dennis sat behind.

"Two things, Gale. Neither are great. First, your five-year security clearance re-investigation came back. When did you start gambling? Does Joey know?"

Gale sighed. "Been about a year. The new casino opened up and I love blackjack. It crept up on me and before I knew it, it had gotten out of hand. I've stopped now. Joey doesn't know yet. Wasn't going to tell her while she was on mission. She doesn't need that. Will tell her when she gets back though," Gale explained.

"It's over though, right?"

"Absolutely, Dennis." Gale replied, somewhat indignant.

"How much are you down?"

"About twenty thousand."

"Damn, Gale! What were you thinking? I had to burn a good deal of capital for them to let you keep your clearance, which is the good news. The bad news is you're being transferred out of the center. I was able to get you a seat at one of the DHS Ops Centers starting in January."

"What? Why?"

"It wasn't the clearance issue, Gale. The General wanted you out. He doesn't like your attitude or the fact you openly argued with him in his staff briefing a couple of weeks ago. Insubordination was the word he used when he chewed my ass."

"Oh for fuck's sake, Dennis?" Gale was hot now. "The General wasn't listening to my recommendations. He's just biding his time until retirement. We both know this!"

"Gale, you called him unenlightened in front of his entire staff. What did you expect to happen?"

"He is unenlightened, Dennis!"

"Be that as it may, you can't yell at a three-star general in front of his entire staff, calling him names, and expect no retribution."

"Dennis, we have a ton of risks and threats here and I listed them out more clearly than anyone else has. If an EMP goes off over the U.S. we'll be back in the 1800's. No power, no phones, no ATM's, no cash, no Internet. Most cars will die where they are and won't restart, unless they're older models with no electronics. Oh, and all the passenger planes will drop like bricks. The NoKo's and Chinese are up to something. The Iranians are working with the NoKo's. The Russians are playing nice, but moving men and equipment west toward Europe under the guise of exercises. Not unusual, but concerning, given the rest of it. We know these countries are helping each other, Dennis, regardless of the deal that's in place now!"

Gale stopped talking and looked out the office window onto the Ops Center where some of the analysts closer to Dennis' office were looking over at them through the window. He'd been steadily raising his voice until he was yelling at the end. What did it matter now. No one cared. The complacency was infuriating.

"Look, Gale, it's done. I'm truly sorry. You'll be on the roster here until first week of January, but take your time off around the holidays. You've earned that. After the holidays I'll call you with your next post and where and when to report. I'm still working that out. I want to get you in with some good people. Jumping through hoops and bureaucracy. You know the drill, but you're still here until your vacation starts on Christmas Eve. For what it's worth, I agree with you on most of your assessments, I just don't have the ability to push it to the places where it will get the attention you think it needs. Your passion for this stuff is commendable. Your mouth, however, shot you in the foot. Try to remember that going forward, Gale."

"The general is a moron, Dennis." Gale said.

"Gale, I get it. I really do. But, no one is interested in this doom and gloom stuff you come up with all the time. Take a break over the holidays and get your mind reset. The peace deal with the NoKo's is a good thing.

Stop looking for bad things under every rock, man. You've got too many devils dancing in your head."

"Okay, well, I suppose I'll finish out my shift here and get going then. I'll make sure my current analysis work gets to the right people in the center." Gale stood and left the office, leaving Dennis rubbing his eyes. The General was a moron…and an asshole.

A couple of hours later, Gale thought he'd wasted enough time. He closed the classified intelligence report and returned it to the safe that he had next to his workstation. He had let the other analysts know where his assessments were on the systems and what he had in his safe. He had to go get Layla from the gym, head home and get ready for their call with Joey. He logged off his system and shut it all down. The satellite tracks disappeared on his flat screen and turned into a screen saver of a white beach with blue water and an umbrella. This was where he wanted to be with his girls right now, not in the middle of winter and the pile of crap that was now weighing him down. There would be plenty of time for vacations away from all the worry after Joey came back to Earth next month. He couldn't wait to see her, he thought, as he donned his jacket and grabbed his backpack, throwing it over his right shoulder and headed for the door with a wave to the duty officer in the back of the operations center. He left through the glass door of the ops floor and then through a series of doors, getting to the exterior hallway, the lobby, and finally out of the squat, one-story building out into the diminishing December light.

# THREE

Early December
In Orbit
The Kangaroo's Court

The task was critical, Joey thought as she watched Pasha. At least that's what Pasha had told her prior to beginning this insanity. He had to get it just right or suffer catastrophic mission failure. Only slightly amused, Joey tolerated Pasha's *mission* as the large cosmonaut floated inside Harmony, the internal passageway of the International Space Station, approaching one unsuspecting Tavis Kinley, the European Space Agency Astronaut. The doctor, of the DVM and PhD variety, was tethered to the wall in his sleeping bag at the far end of the berthing node. He was snoring—lips slightly parted with saliva floating an inch from his red-haired chin.

"That's nasty," Joey Washington, ISS Commander, said from her workstation, as she pointed at the spittle. God, two more months of this.

"Shoosh!" Pasha whispered.

He didn't want her to wake up the easily agitated doctor before the mission was ready to go.

Joey was at her personal workstation preparing to video chat with Gale and Layla, her husband and teenage daughter back home. She was flipped upside down in relation to Pasha and the floating Scotsman. She took Pasha's shooshing in stride. He wasn't a verbose talker, although fluent in English. He said no more than what was necessary to relay his points. She didn't know if that was due to his military background or his upbringing, but it worked for him. She watched him contort his arms so that he could get into the right position to deploy the shaving cream between the good doctor's face and his floating hand. Tavis liked to sleep with at least one arm out of the bag. Pasha had formed a sort of bubble around the sleeping doctor with a plastic trash bag to catch the eventual splatter of shaving cream. It was her one condition of the *mission*. They couldn't have shaving cream balls getting into sensitive gear. Tavis was going to be extra agitated, caught in his sleeping bag and a plastic bubble, with shaving cream on his face, just woken, and having to clean it all. Maybe Pasha would help, but probably not.

Tavis was an odd addition to the space program. A Veterinarian and Anthrozoologist. In his previous life, he'd been a member of the United Kingdom's Special Boat Service, or SBS, and served several tours in Afghanistan early in the war. He'd seen combat. Lost friends. He told her that he wanted to do something as different from the military as possible. He preferred animals to humans most of the time as humans were just plain mean. Surveying the scene in front of her, she couldn't argue Tavis' point.

Her Russian friend had successfully deployed the shaving cream. A big blob of it floated in a somewhat stationary spot, occupying the space between Tavis' hand and face. She thought the Russian's massive hands would spell disaster for this spectacle, but Pasha had pulled it off, a huge smile on his broad, flat face. He was a good-natured man. What they considered the station's "father" for this mission. Usually, a female flight member, if there was one, would end up as the official station mom, but this mission's female was her, and that just wasn't her way. She was a woman, but she didn't have that particular mom mentality about her, except with her daughter. Even then, she was away so often, she felt the guilt of not being more of a mom to Layla. Especially now, in Layla's teenage years.

Joey preferred to be all business up here, and while she loved being a mom to her daughter, she had no interest in mothering grown men on the ISS. She'd been a fighter pilot during the war. Flown F-18 Super Hornets off the Truman and Lincoln. She'd seen her share of combat, but it was different from the air, different from what Tavis had gone through on the ground. She dropped her ordinance on the bad guys, but hadn't seen their faces, like Tavis.

She missed it. Not the bomb dropping. She missed being one with the plane and the feeling of being shot off the deck of the carrier. It was a rush each and every time. She smiled to herself. Suddenly, her daughter's face popped up on her monitor and Joey was snapped out of her memories as Layla's excited voice was clear over the system's speakers.

"Mom! Howdy."

She could see Layla but the connection speed was slow, so Layla's mouth didn't move in time with her voice and her face was somewhat contorted. Joey enunciated her response as clear as possible so her daughter would understand her through the wonky connection.

"Hey, baby girl! I see you, but your face is frozen."

Still one eye on Pasha, Joey watched him use the end of one of the many cables that hung from the walls to lightly touch the doctor's face. Tavis, still unconscious, moved his hand to scratch his face, catching the blob of shaving cream with his hand and smashed it to his face, causing smaller blobs of shaving cream to go spinning into the plastic bag. One little white blob succeeded in its escape and floated toward her slowly, wobbling in the air—she tracked it as it closed in on her. The blob, about an inch in diameter, was nearly a perfect ball.

"You great Russian Bastard!" Tavis yelled in a deep Scottish brogue.

He was still cocooned in his sleeping bag failing miserably to free himself with his shaving cream covered hand, large plastic cocoon around his tethered sleeping birth. Joey surveyed the scene in front of her. Pasha was gone. She heard his deep bellowing laugh from the Destiny module, which was connected to Harmony. He was pulling himself along the wall, grabbing anything he could to retreat to the Russian Orbital Segment for his physical safety. His laugh was getting fainter, but still clear, and it was contagious and she felt her stomach bounce as he laughed. She turned her attention back to her daughter, while deftly plucking the ball of the white, menthol fluff out of the air as it drifted between her face and her laptop listening to the Scotsman yell obscenities that she couldn't quite make out through the brogue.

"What the hecky decky is going on up there, Mom?" Layla said, her face still frozen.

"Cosmonaut Pasha is fascinated with Inspector Clouseau and Cato from those Pink Panther movies. They've been at it for a month or so and getting fairly punchy up in here."

She heard Tavis yell that he was going to blow Pasha out of the airlock. Layla giggled and Joey rolled her eyes with feigned effort. She could tell when the doctor was really agitated as his R's were really rolling.

"Tavis! Shaving cream control! Get it all before you begin your pursuit. Copy?"

"Aye, copy that, Commander, but fer da record, bite ma bawsack, Arsepiece! Imma coomin fe ya, ya fookin' Ruskie! Fookin' bollacks…"

As the yelling subsided to mumbling, Joey could hear the vacuum nozzle sucking up the bits of liquid. He'd have to suck up his face as well. At least Pasha was nice enough to leave the vac's hose close by. Points to Pasha.

"Love the hair, Mom. What did he just say?" Layla said, referring to her explosion of brown hair and lighter brown highlights which normally sat shoulder length. It was now free floating around her head. She forgot to put it in a ponytail. The highlights were grown out. No stylists in orbit. She'd take care of it first thing when she got home.

"Yeah, anti-gravity head. Don't you worry about what Astronaut Kinley said. Where's your father?" Joey asked, shooting a glare at Tavis, who had just made his clean, if sticky exit from the bag he was now squishing down to a tight ball to place in the refuse bin.

"Here, Roo." The picture jumped again slightly and there was Gale's face, frozen. His eyes were halfway shut. He looked like a stoner.

"There's something wacky with the video, Commander," Gale said. "We'll have to make do with voice only. All we can see is a frozen you and a little white blob."

Apparently, their view had frozen just prior to her plucking the menthol ball from the air.

"Sorry Mister. You get to look at a ball of shaving cream. Don't ask," Joey said.

Her husband liked to use her aviator call-sign sometimes because of how she got it. He was always messing with her. She loved getting shot off a carrier, but landings were another story altogether. They were the toughest maneuvers a naval pilot had to accomplish. On her first tour as a nugget she came in for her first carrier landing and bounced the plane so hard off the deck that she missed all four arrester cables and had to go around and try again. She finally got her nerves under control later that tour and was landing sans bounce. She even caught the number three arrester cable more often than not, which was optimal. However, that didn't save her from the other pilots. Kangaroos hopped, or bounced, as it were. And her first name was Joey, a baby kangaroo. It fit. She was Roo. She was snapped out of her memories by Layla's face appearing on the monitor, her voice coming through the speakers.

They talked for a while about work and what Joey wanted to do when she got back to the planet in January. Fairly generic stuff. Not all communication from station to ground was private. Joey was sure that the ground monitors were not at all interested in their family chat. This was routine after so long in orbit, but Layla did get pretty emotional about Joey being gone so long. It wasn't teenage hormones that got to Layla, she wasn't really like that, kind of like Joey. Pretty solid emotionally. Her daughter was just really to the point that she needed her mom back. Gale was understanding of this. He needed her back as well. She'd been gone too long and this call was reinforcing that feeling now. She needed to be home for herself as well. She missed them so much. And she was weary of her companions up here, even though they were a tight crew, she needed to be home.

"Hello, Washingtons!" Tavis yelled as he floated past Joey, clearly having pushed off something to gain speed.

"Goodbye Washingtons!" And he was gone.

As he floated away, she could hear him say, "Stay tuned fam! May be deres a burnin' Zvezda module come crashin' to da Earth dis very evenin' wit a wee crispy cosmonaut aboard."

Layla giggled and Gale laughed out loud.

"So," Gale said, "it's been like this for the last month or so?"

"Yes, God help me," Joey said, eyes rolling hard in their sockets. "Though, I think the doctor might be serious this time."

# FOUR

Early December
Beijing's Western Hills

"Mei! Come here."

The Minister was not happy as he bellowed from his office. Mei had never seen him like this before. She had been his personal secretary for more than a decade as he rose through the party ranks. He was reading about the current wheat forecast and crop yields from the North China Plain again. It was Minister Level - Eyes Only, but she knew it was bad. In her position she had access to most of the reports that crossed his desk. China would hit famine level yields next year. Too many people. Too much alteration of the land for quick victories. Fix the water crisis and the food crisis looms. Fix the housing crisis and the job crisis looms. The damned fixes broke more of the country than they'd helped solve. China was running out of time. No—they were out of time now! They were a couple of years away from becoming the North Koreans. They were feeding them as well. That was where they were headed. She entered his expansive office.

Standing just inside the large teak doors, she waited for her boss to acknowledge her. She thought about the stress he was under, which translated to stress upon her. The last year had been draining. She wasn't privy to all his activities, but she knew enough to worry. The Agriculture Minister was hardly ever invited to full Committee meetings and he had been to many this past year. She supposed that feeding the people had finally become a strategic priority for the pig-headed Politburo. The Minister sat behind his desk, small for the size of the office. Several lamps sat dark on the desktop. The large windows behind him let in enough natural light. The Minister finally noticed her.

"Have you read this report, Mei? Terrible! The North Plain has almost completely failed. Yields down dramatically from last year. Forecasts are shot. I will not be the one responsible for another famine that kills tens of millions of my countrymen!"

"I've seen the report, Comrade Minister. Is there nothing the South can do to make up for the loss?"

"Bah!" He was incensed. "We are tapped out. We've done almost all that can be done."

"What about our Canadian partners? They seemed open to negotiations for more wheat during the talks last month? What about the Americans?"

He looked at her for a moment. Actually, she thought he looked through her as if he was thinking of something totally different. He changed the subject abruptly.

"I wanted to remind you that I'll be leaving early today for my wife's birthday. Also, and more importantly, I'll be away on Committee business tomorrow. I won't need you to accompany me. Thank you as always, Mei. That will be all."

"Yes Minister."

Mei scurried back to her small office to clear the Minister's calendar for the next day. She sat contemplating the abnormal changes in the Minister's schedule this past year. It had only gotten more hectic as the end of the year approached. The randomness of these Committee meetings. By Committee she meant the Politburo Standing Committee chaired by the President. The Agriculture Ministry was not part of this council per the Chinese Constitution, so why was he attending and so often. Perhaps she should make an effort to report this anomaly.

Mei was tall for a Chinese woman. Five foot six with black hair and a broad face. She was unremarkable in appearance and could easily go unnoticed in a room full of people. She was the proverbial fly on the wall. A great attribute for an intelligence asset. She was spying on her own country, which would carry the heaviest of penalties if she were caught. The state security apparatus saw everything, or thought they did. She was good. No one paid attention to the Agriculture Ministry anyway. There were no secret operations here. Just food, land, and water.

She contemplated that last thought. Food, land, and water. Only the main reasons nations had gone to war over the centuries, besides religion. Before there were nations, there were tribes, fighting over the same resources and ideals. As long as there had been humans, they had fought over these things. It's why the Canadians had recruited her in the first place. The Chinese didn't pay as much attention to the Canadians as they did, say, the Americans. It was a short-sighted view. China and Canada had many reasons to discuss trade deals and many opportunities to meet. Wheat in particular was a hot topic of discussion. These meetings were when she had her chance to drop information in her hotel room. Her handler would come in days after the talks and retrieve it from wherever she'd hidden it. Most recently during the talks in Canada last month.

She had a good life and was well compensated. She needed for nothing. Nothing except Shan. Her lover was a captain in the PLA. She hadn't seen or heard from him in well over a month. He said they'd be together soon, but there was training he was required to take part in. The secret kind.

Odd aggregate thoughts wove impossible visions in her mind. Should she report secret training as well? No. Shan was hers alone. No country or compulsion would twist the loyalty and love he'd shone her. Her early life hadn't been ideal and she relished what she had now.

She was an only daughter of parents under the infamous one-child policy. While her father had truly loved her, she remembered him fondly and with aching loss, her mother had wanted a son. Mei was seven when her father died. Her mother, aloof and cruel to her memory, was not the kind of woman that should have had children at all. At least a boy would have been something for her to be proud of. A daughter was not. She wanted to remarry and have a son. The only way to do that was to give Mei to her father's brother, who had no children of his own. Mei resented and hated her mother and she projected that hatred onto the State.

It wasn't that her uncle was unkind to her. It was a hard life as a farmer and she was just another set of hands for him to use. Afterall, it's where she learned about agriculture and got her to where she was now. However, her determination to do whatever she could to undermine her government consumed her. She had no doubt that at some point she'd be caught and tortured by the security services. She was also under no illusion that her information was staying with the Canadians. Which was the whole point. The Canadians, she hoped, shared all intelligence, but specifically hers, with the Americans. She didn't know for sure, but she hoped.

❈ ❈ ❈

The next morning, deep underneath the western hills outside of Beijing, the Politburo was meeting. The complex was massive. It was where the top Chinese leadership would convene in the event of a nuclear war or other monumental situation that threatened the Chinese government.

The Agriculture Minister was on the subway that took him from central Beijing to a line which connected directly to the complex. It was heavily guarded and free from the prying eyes of the ever-present reconnaissance satellites of the U.S. and their allies, as well as the Russians. Although the Russians helped to build the first part of this complex back in the 1950s, they still weren't trusted. Over the years it had been expanded into the large, but claustrophobic bunker complex that it was today.

The Minister had his briefing in his case. Mei had put it all together for him. He wished she could have accompanied him during these meetings, but it was strictly Minister level and above. She always kept him organized, he thought, as the train pulled into his destination. He was the only one in the car. The lights were dim and there were none of the signs or advertisements for cigarettes, food, or services that were common on regular subway cars in the city. None were really needed for this one, he supposed. The train stopped with a lurch and the doors opened onto another dimly lit platform. Couldn't they spend the money to provide adequate lighting?

A lower level male officer in a crisp uniform stepped forward from the shadows and asked the Minister to follow him to a bank of elevators. There seemed to be no-where else to go from here. He followed the officer into one of the open cars and it began its descent. Either it was a long way down or the elevator was very slow. There was no "ding" for each floor passed, so he had no concept of how deep into the mountain complex they were going. It wasn't his first time here, though. He just hated being here. It was tomb-like and he began to sweat with anticipation, or was it anxiety?

The car stopped abruptly and the doors opened. The officer motioned for him to proceed down the long, now very well lit, hallway to the end where he could see more guards. Heavily armed guards. He walked briskly with his slim, leather case under his left arm, pulling a badge from his trouser pocket and presenting it to the guard sitting at a desk. The other guards studied him intently, while the desk guard looked at his ID and then back to him. He looked up from the guard to the metal door behind the desk and the other guards in the hallway. The desk guard picked up a phone and spoke into the handset and replaced it in its cradle. The phone itself looked to be decades old, red, and had no buttons or the old rotary dialer. It was just an old, red, box shape with a handset. The guard held out the badge to the Minister while looking down at a sheet of paper in front of him with a list of names on it.

The Minister retrieved his badge as one of the other guards stepped forward and held out his hand without speaking. He stared blankly at him for a moment until he remembered his mobile phone. He handed it to the guard, who then handed it to the guard behind him, turned back to the Minister, and gestured for him to raise his arms so he could search him. The guard was not gentle. He ran his hands along the Minister's legs and arms and then up under his crotch. The Minister's discomfort clearly wasn't a concern. Not only was the young soldier violating his person, he wouldn't stop looking directly into the Minister's eyes while he groped around. It was unnerving and maybe that was the point. The man smelled as well. The body odor was nearly overwhelming. He hadn't been searched prior to this and it irritated him, but not to the point of complaining to the guards. No, not to the guards. Not to anyone. The Minister was not a boat rocker.

The guard took a device that the Minister had seen at airports and ran it up and down his front and back, emitting little squeaks here and there when it hovered over his belt buckle and his party pin, which they asked him to remove as well. It was put in a box with his phone. As he was being subjected to this search he noticed a long line of dress shoes lined up on the floor against the wall to his right. There were at least a dozen pairs, all black, like his. The guard stepped back and told him to remove his shoes. The Minister opened his mouth to object, but the words didn't come. He did as instructed and placed his shoes at the end of the line of lonely pairs. He picked up his case and started toward the metal door when the guard who had patted him down stopped him as if he hadn't seen the case and gestured for the Minister to open it, which he did. The guard took the case, put it on the desk, swung it around so the Minister could remove what he needed, which he did, then closed the case and handed it to another guard, who put it on a rack with other cases. The guards finally parted and motioned him forward to the door, sans case.

Abruptly, there was the clank of bolts moving. It happened every time, but it always made him jump inside. The door swung open and he hurried through before the door closed on him. It wouldn't, his nerves were just at an end.

It was a different world on this side of the door. Concrete replaced with wood paneled walls and carpeted floors. He stood in a long anteroom with desks in a row along one side occupied with more military officers, or lower level soldiers, he couldn't tell. He'd never served in the military. One of these officer/soldiers stood and motioned him to the closest of several double doors on his right. He noticed this person had no footwear either. He nodded and went through into a cacophony of discussion. There were generals in uniform at one end of the room and other ministers at the other end. Not one had any ribbons or medals on their jackets and he quickly glanced down. No shoes. At the head of the long mahogany table that occupied the middle of the room was the Boss. The Chairman of the Communist Party of the People's Republic of China. He couldn't see his feet, but he assumed he had his shoes. Perhaps. It was surreal.

He waited to be acknowledged by the Chairman before taking his seat, as was customary. While he waited he looked around the large room. There were televisions on the walls displaying news from around the world and a large world map on the far wall with other maps just as large on the wall on either side depicting the South China Sea, the United States, and the China-India border among others. These maps were new.

"Minister. Join us," the Chairman said as the voices in the room died off quickly.

"Thank you, Chairman."

The Minister laid his red folder with Most Secret stamped across the front on the table and sat. He removed one sheet of paper from the folder, also classified Most Secret across the top and bottom of the page.

"Are you prepared to brief us on the status of our food supplies, Minister?" the Chairman asked.

The question focused his thoughts away from the comfort of the chair and the physical violations he'd just experienced. The Minister took a deep breath through his nose and exhaled through his mouth, calming his nerves.

"I am, Chairman, Ministers, Generals. As you know, the crop yields for the northwest have been in decline for a number of years and this year will be worse than feared. The land has been overused and, due to the extension of the cold climate this year, planting started late. Also, major flooding of the Yellow and Yangtze rivers this past spring was of major impact. The lasting cold created ice dams up river on both, which were not identified in time. When they broke, millions of acres flooded on both river plains with great loss of life and land even with our rescue and recovery efforts.

"Whose fault is this river flooding, Minister?" the Deputy Chairman accused with an icy stare.

The Minister and Deputy Chairman locked eyes for what seemed to be an eternity, which was broken by the soft words of the Chairman.

"We are not here to place blame for acts of nature. We are here to finalize a decision with regard to the coming year." the Chairman said softly, but firmly.

The Deputy Chairman broke eye contact with the Minister, and looked down at his notes as the Chairman continued.

"Is your part of the plan still on track, Deputy Chairman? It seems as though the Agriculture Minister's plans are useless if the ground we seek is irradiated for decades. Let's focus on that for a minute." The Chairman seemed uncustomarily agitated to the Minister.

"Chairman, I can assure you that all our nuclear engineers, generators, and fuel trucks are procured, pre-placed, and ready to intercede at all generating plants. We have even hardened the engines of all transports so that only one part will need to be replaced to return them to working order afterward, so they can arrive at each of their destinations promptly." The Deputy Chairman stated confidently.

"There are ninety-eight in the United States and one hundred and fifty in Europe. Between us and the Russians, we are positive that we can restore backup power for enough time to restore grid power to each before they meltdown?"

"Indeed, Chairman! We have, along with the Russians, have been pre-placing equipment and replacement parts for over two years now under the guise of shell companies. We have thousands of men and material in and around these generating plants, all with specific tasks to complete when it starts. It has become one of the largest logistical achievements ever attempted in history." The Deputy Chairman continued, his delivery of the words sliding into arrogance.

"Attempted?"

"Chairman, we will succeed, as we must!"

"Indeed, Deputy Chairman. The entire operation will be in peril if you fail." The Chairman leaned toward his deputy and continued, "That won't be the only thing in peril if you aren't successful, Deputy Chairman." The Deputy Chairman only nodded curtly. That was the first time the Minister had ever heard the Chairman threaten death for failure. He felt an involuntary shiver run through his body.

"Minister, continue please."

"Thank you, Chairman. Our efforts for the coming year will enable us to expand our food sources and eventually alleviate our resource constraints here in the northwest as we begin to move parts of the population elsewhere. Preventative action is necessary for the benefit, even the survival, of the Chinese people in the out years."

He finished his assessment and recommendations, sliding his briefing sheet back in the folder and waited, looking down the table at the Chairman.

"Minister, thank you for your report," the Chairman said. "How are the plans progressing regarding the pre-positioning of equipment and resources?"

Clearly the question was meant for the Generals. However, another man in a suit halfway down the table just across from the Minister spoke.

"We are still in process of moving the equipment. There have been no issues. None are expected. Men and material will be in place and ready for implementation at the appointed time."

The man was middle aged, and seemed to be overweight, but the Minister couldn't quite tell as he was seated. He had black hair somewhat longer than the rest of this group. It was slicked back on top and pulled to a pony tail. It reached his shoulder blades. He had a high hair line. It was almost as if the man's hair was trying to escape his forehead and hide in the back. He amused himself with the thought. Thick glasses with heavy black frames and a rumpled black suit completed his look. The man had never been at one of these meetings that he could recall. If he had been he'd never spoken, so the Minister was at a loss for his identity. Perhaps he was part of the intelligence directorate. That made sense. Regardless, the man paid the Minister no attention, so he would pay the man none. This was a safe course of action in this room.

As he pondered the mysterious man, other questions were asked and answered around the table. Status of Chinese emigration to North America, not just to the US, but to Canada and Mexico as well. Well above prior years. Normally about 1.7 million Chinese visited the US annually. The last two years the number had gone up substantially and many of those had extended their stays, whether it be for studies or visiting family. Some had started businesses in the U.S. and been granted extended work visas. There were literally millions of Chinese—loyal Chinese, in America right now. Many of the new Chinese immigrants to North America were not there for tourism, vacation, education, or business ventures, although these were their stated reasons upon entry. It fascinated the Minister that China could, for all intents and purposes, invade the United States without any conflict. The reverse could never happen. Not here. Everyone was watched and followed. The West was so open and inviting. Driven by their Capitalist system. As long as you had money to spend, you were welcomed in with open arms. All was going well, it seemed.

As the man spoke at length, the Minister's eyes fell to the open folder in front of the man. It was upside down to him, but he could clearly see the words at the top of the page it was open to. They were big, bold red words: *Mongol Moon.*

The Deputy Chairman asked the mystery man about the status of their North Korean friends, but did so with clear derision. The answer was that the North Koreans were fully on board, but were very nervous and had to be constantly reassured. His Iranian counterpart, however, was being extremely helpful with the North Korean's concerns. The Iranian was a tremendous asset. As he spoke, he turned his head left and right from the Chairman and his deputy at one end to the Generals at the other end. As he did so, his pony tail whipped from side to side. The Minister thought the man had to be very important to be allowed in this meeting with a pony tail. It was unprofessional, at least to the Minister's sensibilities.

There was the distinct chance, the man continued, that the Americans would figure this out after the fact and strike the hermit state. This was, the Minister knew, all to the plan, but they had to play along until then. Hopefully, they'd be free of the parasitic country in the end. The crop issues that were plaguing China were more serious in North Korea. The only way to get them to play along was to get the West to provide massive amounts of food, which in turn required the North Koreans to denuclearize. Which they were in the process of doing under the auspices of the United Nations, China, Russia, and the United States with inspectors digging through all the nuclear facilities in North Korea. They were turning over all nuclear weapons developed from highly enriched uranium. They didn't find any plutonium during any of the inspections, because there was no plutonium in the country. Not any longer.

All eyes were on North Korea. Hopefully, they held up their end of the bargain. There was even talk of signing of a final peace treaty with South Korea to officially end the Korean War. This would never happen, but it was being offered for more concessions. The West just had to keep their eyes on the bright, shiny object that was being floated in front of them. The American president, John Anderson, was touting his peace accomplishments on social media and at his rallies. He wasn't the normal political operator. He was a populist. Their efforts relied, in part, on President Anderson being himself and doing things his predecessors had been incapable of doing. It was amazing to observe their efforts coming to fruition with the West following along like a puppy chasing a treat.

"Minister, your people are ready to take over their new roles and duties as soon as it is practical?" He was jogged back to the conversation in the room at the Deputy Chairman's question.

"Yes, Sir. They are aware of the reorganization that will be occurring in the near future. However, they do not know the details. They only know they will have new roles and will be moving with their families when the time comes. We'll ensure the next year will be one of new and historic production for our people."

That was a bit thick, he thought, but this was a heady situation. It seemed to go over well, though.

"Thank you, Minister. Your work has not gone unnoticed. Your role overseeing our new production strategy will be very rewarding. That I can promise you."

As the Deputy Chairman finished, the Minister only nodded smartly to him and the Chairman sitting to his left at the table head. He was filled with pride.

"Good. It is set then." The Chairman's voice commanded attention and the end of conversation. "Our decision must be unanimous. All of you have had adequate time to voice your concerns and have at length; however, the time for action is upon us. With the Minister's agriculture report and the assessment from the Intelligence Directorate concluded along with the rest of the reports we've heard this morning regarding our military readiness, it is time for a final vote. All in favor must raise their hand. We shall all be remembered for our part in the long and glorious history of our country."

The Minister, taken in the moment, looked around the table. Every single person had his hand up. Are we really doing this? It truly was historic. Everyone was looking at him. He hadn't put up his hand. He quickly thrust his right hand into the air and the Chairman nodded.

"So it is decided. May the next year and beyond be historical and glorious for China and the Chinese people. But know this gentlemen, failure at any juncture could be catastrophic. When we are successful, we will have rid ourselves of multiple problems both near and far. We will have ushered in a new dynasty for China. Our long gambit is finally coming to its conclusion. Continue with your preparations and I wish us all luck. We are concluded."

The Minister rose with the rest and headed out to the anteroom where there were refreshments. He did not partake, but instead, headed back through the heavy door, retrieved his pin, phone, and slipped on his shoes under the heavy stare of the guards. He made his way to the train, desperate to get back to some semblance of normalcy before the world was changed forever. He didn't believe in a God, but thought he should ask someone to look after them in this endeavor. It truly would be historic.

# FIVE

Two Weeks Before Christmas
Lonny

The Port of Long Beach sprawled over more than ten square miles of cranes, docks, container storage, and buildings. One of the largest ports for container ships in the world and the second largest in the United States. About ninety percent of the shipments that come through the port are from China, Hong Kong, Japan and South Korea. It shares space with the Port of Los Angeles, which it competes with.

Five days a week, Lonny sat at the port exit monitoring the images from the scanning equipment as the trucks came through. He was good at his job and proud of it. The port never stopped operations and ninety percent of the seven million containers that came into the port annually got scanned, either here where Lonny sat in his booth or at one of the other port exits. Lonny had the highest anomaly identification rate. When he spotted something odd or outright obvious, he alerted the Command and Control Center by radio. Customs and Border Patrol agents would check out the truck in question and instruct the driver to pull his truck out of line for physical inspection. No one questioned his skills with the equipment.

· Today was a momentous day for Lonny because, after today all the stress would be gone. The sleepless nights would hopefully be a thing of the past. His family in West Virginia was doing well now. His father had passed away two years ago, taking with him the insurance from his coal mining job. Lonny's mother was a diabetic and suffering from early stages of Alzheimers. His brother, Larry, did what he could to care for her, but the medical bills had piled up and become unmanageable. That is until Lonny's luck changed. He was approached one night about eighteen months ago while he sat at the bar after his shift had ended. He'd just gotten off the phone with the family back home. Things were getting bad. His mother was deteriorating and his brother was a wreck. What money he could send home wasn't enough anymore. He was into his fifth beer when a young woman took the stool next to him. She was Asian and stunning with long black hair reaching down to the middle of her back. She smiled at him and introduced herself in perfect English.

"Hi!" she said enthusiastically with a big smile. She was gorgeous. He couldn't believe that she was talking to him. He smiled back and they began talking. As the night wore on and the drinks flowed, they got more friendly. She laughed at his horrible jokes and had rested her hand on his thigh. He'd taken her hand almost involuntarily and she let him as her eyes settled into his. He knew he wasn't overly good looking, but his mind only glanced by that thought as he held her hand.

The next morning when she left his small, rent-controlled, one-room apartment between Los Angeles and Anaheim, she promised to call him. And she did. Tori, short for Victoria, was the daughter of Chinese immigrants. Her parents owned a convenience store up in San Francisco somewhere. She'd told him, but he couldn't remember now. She was in LA auditioning for parts in TV shows or commercials or whatever she had told him last night. He was still kind of fuzzy on the details as he rubbed his face with both hands, still laying in bed. She had a day job that paid her bills. Some kind of account manager for an overseas manufacturer of medical equipment or something. The details escaped him as he drifted back into blissful sleep.

Over the last few months they became close, seeing each other several times a week. She often stayed at his apartment. Never hers. He didn't care as long as he could see her. He was falling for her. Not only was she beautiful, but she listened intently when he talked of his family and his mother's challenges. She was sympathetic when he railed about the insurance company. She held him after one particularly rough call with his brother. Lonny's mom didn't want to talk to some stranger on the phone. His mom was forgetting who he was. That was a rough night. They were running out of money for her care and he was in a state of mental disarray.

The next day was when she became his savior. She called him on his mobile while he was at work, which she'd never done before. Her voice was excited. "Babe, I think I have a way you can help your mother."

"Hold on a sec, Sweetie." Lonny asked one of the other guards to take his spot so he could take the call outside. Lonny stepped out the door into the bright, midday California sun with the phone to his ear.

"Okay, I can talk now. What's going on, Sweetie?"

Tori explained that her company was having difficulty getting some of their equipment into the country. Due to the contentious trade ties between the US and China, their shipments were sitting in port in China and weren't able to be brought in. She said these sets of diagnostic medical devices were sorely needed in the U.S. Her company would be willing to pay Lonny under the table a lot of money to clear their shipments when he was on shift. If he could screen them through, it would be good for the patients that needed this equipment and good for him financially. She said it would be enough money to pay for the care his mother needed and more.

That seemed so long ago. His eyes refocused on the screens in front of him. Here was the same bright orange truck cab coming into the scanners. They said this was the final delivery. He was glad. He was risking everything. His job, his security clearance, possibly his freedom. It was worth it for his mom. The truck came through the scanners. What he saw was the same set up. Several long cylinders stacked on their brackets. Tori said they disguised the equipment inside the cylinders this way just in case. There was always a big round, flat piece at the front of the container that seemed out of place, but Tori said that those were CAT scan machines. He knew what CAT scan machines were. His mom had needed several scans done with those things.

There was a very long line of trucks behind this one. He pushed the button to raise the metal arm blocking the exit. This signaled to the driver and the two Customs and Border Patrol agents standing feet from the truck that it was good to go. The driver moved out without incident.

He was done!

He couldn't wait to see Tori tonight and get the final payment, which was supposed to include a bonus. Though he really just wanted to see Tori more than anything. His family was doing much better with the cash that had come in from these shipments. Twenty-five thousand dollars cash for each delivery, straight to Lonny and then much of it sent to his brother. Larry had been able to hire a part-time, in-home nurse and covered the costs of all the prescriptions and doctor's visits for his mom. He hoped the medical equipment was going to do some good. There had been a dozen deliveries over about twelve months. He hoped he had helped someone.

# SIX

Late December
South China Sea

The island was a gleaming, distant spec in the blue expanse. One of those magical islands the Chinese military built out of nothing, or almost nothing: Fiery Cross Reef. Major Tang had limited information why the People's Liberation Army Air Force wanted his flight of two H-6K Heavy Bombers deployed to the island at the southern end of the South China Sea. It'd been explained as force projection, although he was certain he'd find out more upon arrival. He wasn't sure they could land their heavy bombers on that ridiculously small airstrip anyway. His co-pilot dropped the landing gear and extended the flaps, increasing the drag on the plane, slowing it even more, as Tang focused on guiding the large bomber onto the short runway. It was built to suit fighter jets and smaller aircraft. Not the one he was flying or the one right behind him, but it was the only land they had. Landing was a foregone conclusion. They didn't have enough fuel to return to base in Southern Mainland China, or divert anywhere else.

*Thud.*

The bomber touched down harder than he liked He brought the nose gear down and engaged the air brakes and thrust reversers, which threw Tang and his co-pilot tight against their harnesses. The bomber quickly slowed to the point he could engage the actual brakes without them burning up. The H-6K shuddered violently as they fought the forward momentum. The bomber finally slowed to a roll at the extreme opposite end of the runway. They'd used the whole damn thing and now had to get out of the way of the second bomber coming in behind them. There was nothing left of the island in front of them. His headgear was soaked and his hands were sweaty.

*Full stop.*

The voice in his headset ordered them to turn slowly off to the left to make way for Captain Liu's plane, which was coming in a little hotter than he thought he should, right behind him. He gave over the controls to his co-pilot and laid back on the head rest as they taxied back to the middle of the island.

He glanced through the cockpit window at the stunning blue water as the second bomber landed. The beautiful view was interrupted on the other side of the plane by the concrete tarmac and low buildings. The structures and paved areas had been constructed along with most of the actual island over several years. When the military had begun reclaiming the island from the sea, only a fraction of the island was actually above sea-level. Now it was a fully operational air base on one side with a small port for supply ships on the other.

There were soldiers and airmen everywhere, but none near his plane except for an airman with paddles guiding them to a spot on the tarmac. He felt his plane stop as his co-pilot applied the brakes. Captain Liu's bomber pulled next to his. There were no palm trees or green of any kind as Tang scanned from right to left through the cockpit windows. There was only sand and concrete surrounded by the endless blue expanse. It was oddly serene and sad at the same time. He unstrapped from the seat, which was tight and getting out was something of a contortionist's trick. The bomber was utilitarian in design and comfort wasn't a priority.

As Tang, his co-pilot, and two other crewmen exited the aircraft onto the brownish-gray concrete, he was immediately caressed by a cool breeze. Year round, the island's temperature was somewhere between seventy-five and eighty-five degrees Fahrenheit. The tropical air, filled with the salty scent of the sea, passed around his still sweaty, close-cropped hair. Tang felt suddenly comfortable and relaxed after the tense flight and landing. He raised a hand to shade his eyes from the intense sunlight and scanned ahead. A door opened on what looked like the main building about fifty yards away. Shimmering people stepped out. They appeared to be officers through the heat coming off the tarmac. Tang and his crew, now joined by Captain Liu and his crew, headed in their direction. As they approached the building, he felt Liu come up next to him.

"Major, what are we doing here? All this secrecy is getting on my nerves.

I couldn't even call my wife before we left and then radio silence all the way here. What the hell is going on?"

"I honestly couldn't tell you, Captain." They were about halfway to the building now. "I was instructed not to talk with anyone prior to leaving home as well, but that's going to be my first question for these three."

Still looking at Liu, he tilted his head in the direction of the officers now just a few feet away. He caught his breath. There were a lot of stars on these uniforms. He immediately came to attention and saluted the three men. He heard his crews do the same behind him.

"Major Tang!" one man said loudly.

There were two stars on his shoulders signifying the rank of Major General. What the hell are we into here?

"Welcome to Fiery Cross Reef, Major." The General returned the salute. "At ease, Major. You and your crews could do with some rest, but first, I'm sure you're wondering what you're doing here. Follow me. We'll get you briefed and answer what questions we can, which are probably many. But I can tell you that you are now part of the Indian Ocean Strike Group until further notice."

"Yes General. We look forward to whatever the mission is, Sir."

"I like your enthusiasm. It's why you were selected."

They filed through the doors into the darker building, a sharp contrast to the brightness outside. The General led them to a briefing room about halfway down a long hallway. Tang couldn't help but notice the large map on the opposite wall indicating what appeared to be their area of operations from where they were in the Spratly Islands in the South China Sea to Australia and out into the Indian Ocean. There were two points highlighted on the map with arrows from where they were. One point was the extreme Northwest corner of Australia and the other point on the map was a tiny island in the center of the Indian Ocean: Diego Garcia. He took a deep breath. Diego Garcia was a key U.S. military base used as a refueling and re-arming base for bombers, submarines, and special operations forces. He didn't know what the target—was that the right word here?—was in the northwest tip of Australia yet, but there was no mistaking what this was any longer.

* * *

Zhanjiang was one of more than a hundred major Chinese ports and it sat on the southernmost area of Guangdong Province in Southern China. With a population of over seven million and a modern skyline, it was one of the most desired cities to live in throughout China. A bustling industrial port, regularly visited by cruise ships, it provided the People's Liberation Army a good cover to move the mass of civilian and military men and women, gear and vehicles from the area's transportation hubs. They moved in phases to the port.

American satellites, ever overhead, had a good view of daily operations and movements. The PLA had erected new warehouses next to the docks a year earlier with wide, covered ramps and gangways to shield the loading of people and gear onto either cruise ships or massive container ships. Both types of vessels were common here, as they were in most Chinese ports. Some docking next to the warehouses shouldn't call unwanted attention. Most of the ships had already left port. There were only two left. They had been redesigned to look like they were stacked full of normal cargo containers.

On the inside was a different picture. There were several companies worth of main battle tanks on the lower level, parked with their turrets and main guns pointed to the rear of each tank body in transport configuration. The ramps and decks above the tanks were packed with armored personnel carriers and other vehicles used to move troops and materiel. Men were busy tying them down to the decks, secure for the trip, wherever that was.

Captain Zhou still didn't know where he and his regiment were going. Wherever it was, they were going quietly and were going to fight once they got there. Rumors were rampant. Some talk pointed toward the Philippines and others Japan, but most were focused on Taiwan. He actually thought Taiwan was the more likely mission. Settle that thorn once and for all, he thought. The full briefing wouldn't happen until they were at sea and all communications were fully and confidently locked down. The last two armored divisions here in Southern China were loading on these ships. He and his men were preparing for whatever it was they were going to go do. Wherever they were going to do it. They were ready. It was time.

The People's Liberation Army hadn't seen major combat in decades. They all wanted to be part of history. His thoughts drifted to his wife and newborn son as he sat on the hood of his command vehicle on a middle deck. He looked down through the steel grates that held his heavily armored vehicle. He took a last drag on his smoke and dropped in on the grate as he jumped down and squashed it out, the glowing remnants floating down onto the top of the camouflaged behemoth below him.

Would he see his family again, Zhou thought hopefully. They were bringing enough men and firepower to take on even the Americans. And win! But it couldn't be the Americans, so all of this was just overkill. They'd be back in a year or less, he thought. The Americans crept back into his tired mind again. No, that was ridiculous. The PLA and the Politburo couldn't be that stupid, could they? Of course not! No, Taiwan was their mission. He was as positive of this as he was that he loved his wife and son. He went to find his Executive Officer and ensure that the rest of the Company was squared away prior to departure.

# SEVEN

"The bar is open! Come on over and cop a squat with us."

Their neighbor Robert waved enthusiastically beckoning Gale and Layla to the fire pit down the pipestem to the left of Gale's house that he and his partner, Lou, had going in their driveway. Gale and Layla had come outside on their own driveway to try to spot the ISS flying overhead. It was dark with a crisp feel to the cold air. It wasn't deep winter cold yet, but they still needed good coats and gloves. Layla had her ear muffs on and waved back to Robert, bouncing her way to the fire, Gale slowly walked behind with a wave of his own.

Their little piece of the larger neighborhood was peaceful. There's was the only cul-de-sac on this side of a stream and nature area close to the main highway. The rest of the very large neighborhood was on the other side of the stream and trees by at least a hundred yards. The end of the cul-de-sac emptied onto the main neighborhood road that went left to the rest of the single-family homes, townhouses, and apartment blocks, along with a couple of small shops, restaurants, a bar, and gas station. To the right, that road led out to the main highway with more neighborhoods on the other side. Further up the highway to the west was the ridge road that paralleled the neighborhood road with a bridge over the highway, which led out west over the small mountain to the upper Shenandoah Valley. The highway led east from here to D.C. some thirty miles distant. The ridge road sat slightly higher in elevation. Over the mature trees that stood taller than the houses, he could see the blinking lights on the two water towers that gravity fed water to the whole neighborhood. They were lucky in their seclusion. The only sounds were the constant vehicle traffic on the road and the planes coming and going overhead from Dulles Airport.

As Gale approached the group illuminated by the crackling orange glow, he took them in. Lou was his normal serious self—he had a dark beer in one hand and an iron fire poker in the other, jabbing at the crackling logs. Robert was regaling Lou and one of their other neighbors, Floyd, with sordid stories from the club scene in Washington D.C., San Diego, and New York City. Some of it not was not safe for Layla's ears, but he kept it clean. It was a crazy time in Robert's life that he didn't fully remember. Lou just rolled his eyes at as Robert jumped from story to story. He'd heard them all before.

Gale ended up with a beer in his hand. Robert handed a soda to Layla warning her, "Don't do what we did, Darling. Keep it on the narrow path 'cause you've got scholarships to think about."

"Speak for yourself there, dear. What do you mean, we did?" Lou said quietly, flashing a rare smile for Layla.

Layla laughed with Robert, who seemed to always be laughing at something, including any joke he told himself. Floyd had a Guinness in his hand and the Wookie on his lap. Not carrying his sidearm tonight, apparently. Then Gale remembered the potatoes he had promised Floyd. He still had what seemed like a ton of them in burlap sacks in the basement from what he had grown this year. He was saving some of them for planting in the spring. He hoped they lasted that long. They should, he thought. Joey and Layla made fun of his gardening. He was fully into it now, although he had started several years back growing everything from tomatoes and cucumbers to beans and corn. This year was potatoes.

"I'll be right back. Floyd I owe you some tubers from my fall harvest." He looked at Lou. "Don't let Robert corrupt my daughter in the thirty seconds I'm gone, please, and don't let the Wookie eat her."

"She's in good hands Gale," Lou said. Gale gave the group a quick survey as he got up.

Floyd was smiling down at the tiny dog in his lap which looked to be going in and out of slumber. Floyd scratched hard at the spot just in front of Chewie's tail where he knew she couldn't reach. The rat-dog slowly rolled over on Floyd's lap presenting her round, fat tummy. Didn't look like the thing was in any hurry to jump down and eat a human any time soon. The little monster's favorite pastime was biting any man, except Floyd, on the foot or calf with the one fang she had left.

He jogged across the stem and was back quickly with a burlap sack full of red and Yukon potatoes. He put it down next to Floyd's chair and said, "There's like forty in there, Floyd. I've got more if anyone else wants some. It was a bumper crop this year."

"Are you and the lovely Layla here coming to our Christmas Eve party, Gale? I want some of those taters for dinner." Robert was the cruise director of their little part of the neighborhood. "Some of the others will be stopping by. If not for dinner then for pre-dinner cocktails at least."

Robert gestured to the other homes on the stem and out into the court. With his movement, he woke the sleeping beast under his chair. Robert and Lou also had a dog—an overly plump Pug named Christopher. The thing was a mess. Old, neurotic, pretty barky at just about everyone, but not a mean bone in his rotund body. Christopher kept one protruding eyeball on Chewie at all times, unless he was sleeping, which was frequently. They were adversaries of a sort. It was not uncommon for the two diminutive energy balls to stand on either side of the pipestem that separated Floyd's property from Robert and Lou's and bark and growl at each other for hours. There really was a great vibe here. They'd been lucky to find such a good place for Layla to finish high school.

There were seven houses in their court here. The pipestem was a shared driveway separating Floyd's house from Robert and Lou's. To the right of Robert and Lou's house was Mimi and her husband. Now their seventies, they had come to the U.S. at the end of the Vietnam war. Her husband fought for the South in the war and had saved her just before he evacuated from Saigon. They'd been together ever since. Floyd had fought there as well.

Mimi was the neighborhood mom. She did have twin sons of her own, both Marines now. Brooke, the older twin's very pregnant wife had come up from Camp Lejeune a couple weeks ago to help Mimi care for her husband in his final days. He had a lung disease that had crept up on him last year. They'd made the decision to keep him at home until the end. It was sad, but Mimi wouldn't hear of any hugs or sympathy for her, always smiling and talking up her sons. Gale's house was next to her's.

Across from Gale on the court was Sara's house. She was the teenaged niece of Ahmed, an older Iranian man, along with her Grandmother, Bibi. They'd moved in six months ago and Layla and Sara had become fast friends. On the other side of Sara's house was Susan. She was a veterinarian and going through a nasty divorce. Luckily they had no kids together. She did have a teenaged son, Dallas, from her first marriage, who she'd sent to live with her first husband. But not before Dallas and Layla had grown close. They were constantly on the phone with each other. The house next to theirs was where Alex and her parents lived and speak of the devil.

"Wash!" Alex screamed.

She popped out of her front door and bounded to the pipestem. Layla jumped up, and the two met in the middle of the narrow, communal driveway. Alex jumped onto Layla like a little monkey. She was Layla's Coxswain for her four boat on the crew team. As diminutive as Alex was, her voice was large and she was definitely in charge. Alex was short for Alexandra. Her family was second generation Russian, and Alex had a habit of screaming at her boat mates in Russian when she got frustrated with them, or so Layla frequently relayed to him. He believed her, as Alex had a habit of swearing in Russian so the adults couldn't understand what she was saying. But Lou spoke some Russian and had let him in on his secret once.

"Pops! What's up?" Alex called to Gale as she came over and gave him a bear hug. She looked around the group and said, "What's up, fabulous neighbors?" Alex usually said whatever was in her head, no filter.

Robert jumped up and gave her a hug. "Planning our holiday party, my Dear. You and your parents are joining us, right?"

"Wouldn't miss it for the world, Ethyl!"

Ethyl was Robert's club name back in the day, and he made the mistake of telling the girls. As the conversation returned to what it had been, Alex started to eyeball Christopher, and the pug knew it. He was hiding under Robert's chair, growling, one eyeball on her and one on Chewie. Alex got down on her knees and hands and reached under the chair, grabbing the neurotic pug by one front leg and pulling him out against his wishes. Alex let go briefly to reposition herself into a cross-legged sitting position. That was Christopher's chance to escape. The pug turned corkscrew tail and darted, in his significant dotage, up the driveway to the front door of Robert and Lou's house. Once on the stoop, he turned and barked at Alex.

"Come back here, Christopher! Now!"

He didn't move. His mouth open, his tongue hung low, panting like he'd just run a marathon. Alex jumped up and jogged up the driveway. The pug jumped into the front bushes and laid down in the mulch.

"Come here, fat-body, and snuggle me!" Alex pleaded.

"You won't get him out, dear. He doesn't like Russians," Lou said quietly in the direction of the standoff, right side of his mouth hitched up in a half smile.

Gale was amused and thought about what it must be like for Alex's parents. Eric and Ana. They were an amiable couple and contained the bubbly, blond Alex as well as they could, he guessed. It was strange to him though that although they both had jet black hair while Alex was blond. Just a passing thought. He wasn't a geneticist. He spoke with Eric regularly when they saw each other, but Ana was more stand-offish. He was a financial guy at some firm nearby and she was a nuclear engineer and taught at one of the universities closer to D.C.

"But Mr. Lou, he needs to love me. Russians need love too. Specifically this one, with that round thing under the bushes laying in the dirt. I must have him," Alex said. She was like a predator stalking her prey. "Snuggle time fat-body!"

Just then, headlights appeared at the end of the court. It was an early model minivan that belonged to Ahmed. As it slowed at their driveway, Layla saw Sara wave at them from the front passenger seat and she waved back.

"Alex! Sara's home, drop the drooler, come on."

Alex had just popped up triumphantly from the bushes with a now fully snuggled Christopher in her arms, and they were rubbing noses and exchanging kisses and licks. Victorious, she plopped the pug down onto Robert's lap, and both of the girls took off at a brisk walk to see Sara. Gale watched as Ahmed got out and walked to the mailbox to check the mail. Robert was dealing with a very confused and jacked-up pug, and Chewie was all tense, staring straight at Ahmed, with a barely discernable growl.

The girls got to the van as Sara exited the passenger side. The three of them hugged and started chatting. Ahmed walked back to the van. Gale studied him. He was a large man and around sixty years old, bald, but with a full, dark, but graying beard. Ahmed wasn't large in an overweight way, but in a towering, muscular way. Gale noticed his slight limp and hadn't had the chance to ask him what happened, or thought it would be rude to inquire, so he hadn't.

"Come in soon, Sara." Her uncle said as he waived to the group. Gale waived back, as did Floyd. Lou didn't seem to pay any attention to him at all, but Robert stared and slowly raised his right hand in a sort of acknowledgement. He kept staring as the minivan disappeared into the garage.

"I'm telling you, there is something strange about them," Robert said in a whisper to no one in particular.

"Here we go again. You're imagining things," Lou said softly. "They're nice people. Ahmed just keeps to himself and you're nosey. You've been on this kick since they moved in. I've spoken with him. He seems like a normal guy. He's a worker. When I shook his hand, I could tell by the feel of it. Calloused, and a very strong shake. Have you really seen him up close? The man is huge. Gentle, I think, but I wouldn't want to be on his bad side, I'm sure of that. He either worked with his hands all his life, or he was military."

"They're Iranian." Floyd spoke up then with a southern drawl. "Came over to escape the regime or some such thing. Was talking with the girl's grandmother a while back. Couldn't understand everything she was saying. Religious persecution or something like that."

"Yeah, but what does the guy do here? No one knows, do they?" Robert asked, irritated that they seemed to be ignoring him.

"I think he manages a self-storage place between here and the executive airport," Gale said, knowing Robert needed the info or he wouldn't let it go. "Layla told me all about it. Sara said they came over to start fresh. Ahmed's the older brother of Sara's mother. She passed away when she was a baby. Didn't say from what. Bibi is her paternal Grandmother. Don't know about Sara's father. Think he's still in Iran. It's all pretty confusing to me." Gale took a long pull on his beer and reached over cautiously to pet Chewie on Floyd's lap.

Lou spoke then, jabbing the logs, absently staring at the fire. "They had been in Europe for a while, first Germany and then France. Then made their way here. Ahmed mentioned that Sara really likes it here and are going to stay for as long as they can. She likes the school and her friends. Layla and Alex got her to try out for the crew team this fall and she made it, so she'll be rowing in the spring. Can't you tell they're just normal humans, Robert?" He gestured to the three girls walking back to the group, all on their phones, and giggling.

They looked over at the girls approaching and Lou shook his head. "They need to get their faces out of their phones and pay attention to the world around them or they'll miss it." Heads nodded around the fire at that.

"Mr. Floyd, what does your flag mean?" Alex asked, pointing to the two flags hanging on either side of Floyd's front door, illuminated by his porch light.

"Well, the one is the American flag and the other is the Virginia state flag. The words on it are Latin. Sic Semper Tyrannis. It means "Thus Always to Tyrants", my dear," he explained.

"Dad! Mom should be overhead!" Layla said.

It was kind of a tradition; they all hung out around the fire once a week or so, talking and laughing, waiting for Joey to fly overhead. Everyone moved out into the stem away from the firelight, heads arched to see if they could catch a glimpse of the ISS streaking past. At that moment, Lou touched Sara on the arm to get her attention.

"Sara, please extend our invitation to our Christmas Eve party to your Uncle and Grandmother. We'd love to have all of you over with us."

Alex immediately jumped in, "Yes! Sara, you let me know if I have to do any convincing. I'll come over. I'll do it. You all have to come. It'll be so much fun and the food is amazing. You have to be part of our Christmas traditions around here. Say you'll come?" Alex demanded.

Sara grabbed both of Alex's arms and with an odd, somewhat English accent, cut her off, "Alex. Alex! I will ask! Though, Uncle Ahmed doesn't like to socialize all that much, but perhaps Bibi and I can convince him. I know she would love to come. I have to warn you though, she will talk your ears off."

"That name is so cute! I love it. Can I call her Bibi too?" Alex practically screamed in Sara's face. But before Sara could respond, Alex looked up, leaving Sara exasperated.

"There!" Alex pointed to a moving object in the night sky that, if you didn't know what to look for, would appear to be a high flying airplane. Gale smiled at Sara and her attempts at dealing with Alex. He mentally wished her luck and looked up.

"Sure enough, Alex. There she is, Layla," Gale said.

They all stood and watched for a while as the ISS made its way across the sky. Layla leaned into her father and said, "I wish she was here, Daddy. I miss her. She's been gone too long. What did she say about Christmas? Are we gonna be able to video chat with her on Christmas day?"

"Yep, that's the plan, if things work out. We'll be here one way or the other."

Gale put his arm around his daughter and pulled her close, kissing the side of her head, her hair smelled like Joey's. Probably the same shampoo. "She'll be home soon, Sweetie." And with that, the ISS disappeared into the horizon. Gale was left holding Layla and thoughts of his situation crept back into his mind. At least he still had a job, but how would he tell Joey about his gambling losses? Well, he wasn't gambling any longer, but he had put thousands on the credit card in advances. She was going to be pissed. He'd have to come clean and deal with it. His mouth and his gambling. Good job, Gale. One thing at a time though. First, get Joey back on the ground and home safely. Then deal with the money thing. He watched the sky as he thought about the NoKo satellites above and the Chinese grain reports. Whatever, he thought dismissively. It was someone else's problem now.

# EIGHT

December 23
Evening
Ahmed

Ahmed walked through the garage leaving the mini-van in the driveway. It was odd, he thought. All this room. They'd never have been able to have this in Iran. He opened the inner door. Light spilled onto him. The small room, which housed the washing machine and clothes dryer, was his niece's dumping ground. Sara just tossed her school bag and jacket on the small bench. The hooks for hanging jackets were right there on the wall, empty. He shut the door and opened yet another door to the house proper.

The smell of Bibi's cooking filled the house, reminding him that he hadn't eaten all day and was absolutely starved. He snuck quietly to the family room, not wanting to do anything but close his eyes until dinner. As he sat himself down in his overlarge recliner he massaged his aching leg. The old wound hounded him to this day.

The aroma of lamb stew coming from the kitchen made him think of Javad. They'd shared these smells for years. He leaned back, closing his eyes, and he was back to that day. Herding his sister Yasmin, and her friends into Javad's family's flat. The goofy look on Javad's face when he saw Yasmin. He knew there was a connection between his friend and sister before they did. Everyone thought of him only as a large, quiet presence, but he saw most things before others did. Felt them as well. The absence of those they had lost. The absence of Javad's presence in Sara's life. The absence of Javad's presence in Bibi's life. The absence of both of their sisters. It was all inside him. A crushing weight of loss. Along with the continued responsibility he felt for his niece. The only true blood family he had left.

When Javad had come home from one of his long absences a year ago to the flat in Tehran, while Sara was at school, he'd given Ahmed a task. Javad was driven by these same demons that haunted Ahmed. He tried to get Javad to let go of the past, but it was not to be. Javad had come to him with a purpose that day. They talked quietly in the main room while Bibi busied herself in the kitchen, out of earshot. Javad had been insistent that Ahmed look after Sara and Bibi for the next few years instead of being at Javad's side. Ahmed had still technically worked for Javad within the structure of the Ministry of Intelligence. But Javad's obsession with Sara and Bibi's safety wouldn't allow Ahmed to be far from them. He became their personal protector.

What Javad had asked Ahmed to do that day made no sense to him at the time. However, Ahmed was a good soldier and Javad wasn't really *asking*. He sensed that it was an order. A mission. He was certain Javad was not telling him everything. Like an iceberg, most was hidden. Ahmed's thoughts were always local and focused on what was going on around him, while Javad's were everywhere all at once. He marveled at his friend's intellect, and was repulsed by Javad's primal side—the part that made him good at his job. He watched, over years, as a darkness took root within his childhood friend. Sara was the only light that remained. Javad's daughter came from Javad's marriage to Ahmed's sister, Yasmin.

It was why they left Iran. Something was going on back home and Javad didn't want Sara anywhere near it, but he didn't know what. Javad instructed him to find a safe place to settle down with Sara and Bibi. He provided enough money for Ahmed to do this comfortably. Javad also instructed him to prepare to survive on their own for a long time, *just to be on the safe side*, as Javad had put it. So be it. So he did it. He gathered plenty of supplies for them to survive. The date that Javad told him to be completely prepared was close. He didn't know what, if anything, would happen. There was something afoot, though. Javad was deep into some larger plan that Ahmed wasn't privy to. Regardless, Ahmed would be here for Sara and Bibi, as always.

He was more father to Sara now than Javad was, damn him. They had a good life here in this small, out of the way, neighborhood. Their neighbors were nice people and Sara had her friends. So, whatever Javad was doing, it surely couldn't affect them here. Perhaps this gathering wouldn't be a bad idea. Perhaps his neighbor, Susan, would be there as well. He knew her situation from Sara. He'd exchanged waves with her many times over the last few months, but said nothing more than a passing hello. He was too old for these feelings anyway. Ahmed rubbed his eyes and tried to clear his mind. Breathing slowly and deeply. The smell of Bibi's cooking covering him in a warm embrace.

"Hello Uncle!" Sara was right there, her usual bouncy self, staring at him.

"Hello Princess. Is dinner ready?" he said, hopefully.

"Yes. However, we have been invited to Christopher's house on Christmas Eve for dinner and neighborhood gathering. Can we go? Please?"

She was excited and knew he didn't like it when she begged him for something, but it seemed she couldn't help herself.

"You mean the dog's house? The dog is having a party?" Ahmed replied with confusion as Bibi called from the kitchen.

"We should go, Ahmed. It will be good for us to get to know our neighbors better. Make friends. They are nice people. I have no one to talk to here when you and Sara are away."

Although Ahmed had the final say in things, he knew what Bibi's words meant. She was a force to be reckoned with, much like Sara. Bibi had been there for him when first his father, and then quickly after that, his mother, had both passed away, leaving him to care for Yasmin alone. Bibi had taken them in as her own.

"Susan will be there." Bibi slid the words in quietly.

"The animal doctor? She's married. What are you getting at?" Ahmed rubbed the exhaustion from his eyes.

"Nothing at all. Just saying she will be attending the party and she's separated."

"Stop trying to play matchmaker. I'm too old for that nonsense."

He was looking up at the ceiling thinking about his female neighbor. They had talked in passing over the time they'd been there. He knew he wasn't bad looking, stayed in shape, even with his leg, but he was approaching sixty. Yes, too old for this nonsense.

Sighing heavily, "I will think on it. But not until I've eaten. Food first. Then dog parties."

He rose from his comfortable chair. Put his hands on Sara's shoulders, spun her gently, ushering her into the kitchen where Bibi was placing their plates full of stew at their normal places around the table. Tender cooked lamb in an intensely fragrant, rich and lemony herb gravy with kidney beans over rice. A loaf of freshly baked bread sat on a cutting board. The family broke pieces off with their hands to dip into the thick, sumptuous stew in front of them. This, at least, was heaven.

# NINE

Javad's sleep was fitful. The train's click, click, click along the tracks was steady and lulled him into slumber, just as the nightmares shocked him out of it. This cycle repeated itself on the long journey back from Mongolia. They were close to the end now, or the beginning, depending on one's perspective. He, however, was close to his end. The years of planning and travelling to and from Mongolia to meet with his counterparts had almost come to fruition. He was tired. Down to his marrow tired. He drifted back into sleep, where the nightmares waited for him. Click, click.

*His father had brought the crime to the local magistrate while Javad was still in the hospital, recovering from the severe head trauma from the blow to the side of his head. Ahmed and his father pleaded their case, but Hafez was well connected, his father holding high status in the religious community. The judge dismissed the abduction charge and the rest was thrown to the Sharia court, which was separate from the judicial system now, and more powerful. That court found that not only was Hafez and his crew not guilty of the killing of his sister, but that Javad and Ahmed were at fault for allowing the girls to run free without the supervision of a male relative in public. The new tribunals set up after the revolution's success against the Shah were ruthless. The outcome was crushing when Ahmed told him when he was coherent enough to understand. Hafez had been sent to serve in the Revolutionary Guard in the north of the country, while he and Ahmed were volunteered and attached to the defense of Khorramshahr in the south for the expected war with Iraq. Hafez's father was able to secure his son a relatively safe position in the north and knew that the south was probably a death sentence. So it was in the new Iran after the revolution.*

*As he lay in the hospital, recuperating from his injuries, he couldn't get that face out of his mind. He tried to picture his sister, but Hafez's face always replaced it in some kind of punishment for his failure to protect her. For weeks after he left the hospital his emotions were in constant turmoil. It didn't help that his mother was distraught and even though she cared for him tenderly in his long recovery, he could tell she was on the edge of sanity. Although she never spoke of it to him, he thought she blamed him. How could she not blame him for the death of her Sara? Her Princess. Ahmed tried to pull him out of his melancholy to no avail. It was only when on the day of their departure to the south, to what would come to be known as the City of Blood, that his thoughts focused. His determination clarified. Oh, he wasn't going to get even: he wasn't going to try. He was going to die. Finally able to apologize to his sister and wrap her in his arms. Arms that in this world hadn't been able to protect her. He would do his duty, provide his family with some semblance of honor, and then he would die in battle and see Sara again.*

Unmoving, Javad opened one eye, head turned to the window. The steppes of Kazakhstan rolled by, not concerned with the train's passing. He was tired of this landscape. Desolate and dead this time of year. He turned his head inward to the train car and shut the one eye again. Click, click.

*Javad rested there against the wall in a room on the top floor of the partially destroyed three-story building. He wiped sweat from his face with his dirt covered shirt. Ahmed was next to him, binoculars to his eyes keeping a watchful eye north. They were some of the last in the city north of the Karun River. The rest of the Iranian forces had evacuated across the bridge south and to the relative safety of Abadan. The Iraqis had attacked with artillery, airstrikes, and hundreds of tanks on September 22, 1980, just over a week ago. He and Ahmed had volunteered for this duty specifically after they'd been volunteered as cannon fodder in general. They had answered the call to prepare for the eventual Iraqi invasion and here they were. Allah be merciful, he thought to himself. They hadn't really had a choice but to volunteer.*

*He had no illusions that they would make it out of here in one piece. Their job was to direct tank and artillery fire to cover the last Iranian forces that were leaving the city. Soon, he thought. He would order his friend to make his way out and he would be the last defender of the City of Blood. So many had already died. Thousands on both sides. For what? Two insane dictators leading insane armies and fighting this insane war over what? Religion? Land? Oil? He would do his duty and in the end hopefully earn some redemption in heaven.*

*He and Ahmed had proven themselves as able soldiers. They'd come to be relied on by their commander, Major Saladin. They were his eyes up here and had provided key intelligence in Iraqi tank and troop movements, which had allowed them to repel the invaders for days even though neither side was well coordinated.*

*Suddenly, they heard footfalls in the hallway and stairs outside the flat they were ensconced in. He grabbed the AK-47 that rested against the wall next to him. Ahmed moved to the other side of the room with his weapon at the ready. There were four quick knocks at the door. It was the right number. Ahmed opened the door, while Javad trained his weapon in that direction just in case. In the doorway was Major Saladin.*

*Saladin stepped into the room, crouching directly in front of Javad so as to not offer up a target for Iraqi snipers in the fading afternoon light. Saladin placed a weathered hand on Javad's shoulder and squeezed hard, concern in his eyes.*

*"It's time to go." He said it as if it was final. "The god-forsaken Iraqi's are here in the city center. They've taken the mosque and the government building." He looked at Javad and then at Ahmed and softened his tone. "You both have done extraordinary service for Iran. You must leave with me now. I don't want to lose the two best men I have. I don't have many left."*

*"Ahmed, please see that our commander crosses the bridge safely. I'll be along behind you and provide cover." Javad said staring directly into the major's eyes, but still not moving from his resting place.*

*"No! It's time, Javad! We must go now and you will come with us," Ahmed pleaded. He grabbed Javad's sleeve, tugging hard, but Javad resisted. "Now is not the time for these heroics or for your poorly thought out martyrdom. Sara will wait a bit longer for you to say your apologies. We still have work to do." Javad couldn't know at that moment what prophetic words his friend spoke.*

*Saladin turned to look at Ahmed. "I am leaving now. Ensure you and your stubborn friend here are right behind me. That is an order." He turned and left.*

*Ahmed let go of Javad's sleeve and offered his hand. "Take it, Javad. Or I will take you."*

# Mongol Moon

*There was no pleading in his voice now, only determination. Javad looked at his friend's outstretched hand, then down to the weapon that lay across his lap. He took a deep breath and exhaled. Dust floated around his head. In that moment, alone with his mortal thoughts and his friend's resolve, he decided he didn't want to become the dust that surrounded them and took Ahmed's hand. It would not be the last time Ahmed saved him from himself.*

*The artillery shell hit with massive force. The concussion knocking the air from their lungs and depositing them across the room. Seconds later, as Javad's vision cleared, he looked back at where he had been sitting. Light poured through the dust and debris. The wall was gone. The shell must have hit below them and taken out the side of the building that had already been weakened by days of shelling.*

*"Ahmed!" Javad screamed. His friend was buried beneath the rubble of the wall, or ceiling, he couldn't tell. He crawled to his friend and began moving pieces of concrete and plaster. Ahmed winced as Javad lifted a large piece off his leg. Javad surveyed his uncovered companion. Ahmed's ankle didn't look right.*

*Ahmed grabbed his arm, "Get me up! We have to get out of here." With effort, he hefted Ahmed up as he stood on his good foot. The other dangling weirdly.*

*"Can you move? Can you walk if I get under your shoulder?" Allah be merciful, but his friend was heavy and Javad's lungs burned with each breath.*

*"I will walk out of here, dammit!" Ahmed, with Javad as a sort of unstable crutch, made their painful way out into the hallway and were met by Saladin and two other soldiers who thankfully took Ahmed from him. He straightened his battered frame now that Ahmed's weight was gone. Every bone and muscle hurt. He leaned against the remaining wall in the hallway, wracked with pain and coughing up blood, the concussion from the blast. He'd been closer than Ahmed. How was he still alive?*

*Once out, into the twilight of dirt and dust, Javad saw the bridge. It was a mess. There were craters from the shelling everywhere. An engine roared to life and he turned. In the shadow of the building was a beat up Toyota pickup.*

*"Get them in the back and let's go!" Saladin yelled as he climbed into the bed first.*

*Javad climbed into the bed of the truck behind the Major and pulled Ahmed up while the other men lifted him. His friend was in pain, he could tell, but Ahmed made no sound. The look on his face told another story. Once all were in, the driver put the pickup in gear and cranked through the gears, gaining speed as he went, swerving around large craters in the street as they quickly made the near side of the bridge over the Karun River. Javad was looking behind them from where they had just been and saw Iraqi soldiers round the corner of the building firing at them as they came. He instinctively reached up and grabbed the major, who was standing behind the cab of the truck holding onto the gear rack on top and pulled him down with all the strength he had left. Saladin came down with a thud in the bed of the truck as bullets struck the back window of the cab on the passenger side where he'd just been standing.*

*The driver swerved back and forth while racing across the bridge as fast as he could. As they neared what Javad thought was the other side of the bridge he heard gunfire from in front of them. Friendly cover fire. They'd made it across and sped through more dusty streets until they turned hard left and got cover behind some small buildings and a dike. The truck came to a quick stop.*

*Javad looked around. Ahmed gave him a thumbs up and winced in pain, squeezing his eyes shut, resting his head on the side of the truck bed. Javad felt a hand on his shoulder. Saladin was motioning for him to look towards the cab of the truck.*

*"You crazy bastard! I'd be dead if you hadn't pulled me down." Saladin was pointing to several bullet holes that had gone through the back window and the windshield. "Driver! Don't stop here, dammit! Get us to the field hospital, now!" Saladin yelled while staring at Javad with a big smile on his face.*

*"We'll get you and your comrade medical attention. After that, you report to me directly. You're both with me for the rest of this damned war."*

*Javad felt the vehicle start to move again and he laid his head back on the truck bed and slapped Ahmed's arm. We'll be okay for now, he guessed. For now. The truck rolled down the road...*

Javad started with a jolt. It was a mental jolt. If you were looking at him it would seem that he only opened his eyes slowly, although the sweat on his forehead would give up the ghosts. He looked around the train car. It was mostly empty except for the three members of his detail in seats in front and back of him and the Iranian Revolutionary Guard Corps officer across the aisle from him. They were all in civilian clothes and all younger than Javad by twenty years at least. The IRGC officer was a necessary evil on these trips to ensure continued compliance of Iran's senior-most military leaders. He knew that one of his security detail was what he called a "watcher".

He may be Iran's chief spy master now, but that didn't hold much sway around the inner workings of the entire Ministry of Intelligence apparatus. Javad's focus was external to Iran. Internally, he had almost no say as to what occurred or who they watched. Better to keep the devil he knew close. They followed him at all times. He was used to it. But more importantly, they were used to it and his routines, which he'd crafted and cultivated methodically over the last several years, just in case. The regime couldn't have their chief spy master on the loose and alone. A truly distrustful apparatus of the regime. As counter-intelligence agents, they were mediocre at best, he thought.

He rubbed the sleep from his eyes and glanced at the empty seat next to him, where only his briefcase with a leather shoulder strap sat. It had been a gift from Saladin so many years ago. He sat still and recalled the dream he just woke from. It was a recurring dream. One of many that he had regularly, but not the worst one. Saladin was long dead. His generous and honorable mentor and boss was outspoken once too often. He was purely a soldier and had refused to fire on civilians during one of the protests in Tehran years back. He'd been swept up in a purge shortly thereafter. Javad hadn't found out until months later. His blood boiled again at the thought. One more reason—ticking off the long list in his mind again.

# TEN

December 23
1:30am EST
10:00am Tehran
Javad

An hour after the train deposited him on the platform in Tehran, Javad's car pulled up to the hanger at what they were calling the Mongolian Maintenance Facility at Mehrabad International Airport. He had shed his security detail for his driver, also a watcher. His credentials had gotten him through several layers of security that surrounded that part of the airport, which included this massive hangar and outbuildings. He was exhausted from the trip back on the train from the final meeting of the Four. He'd stepped off the train and was taken by car directly to the final Supreme Council meeting where he briefed the top religious and military leaders of Iran on his trip and their allies, if he could call their partners allies. They were useful tools for him personally. Allies for the Council. They were suitably impressed, as always, with the plan and the final status.

There were two plans, actually. The plan the council saw was on track and in two days the world would be different. He cared not. That was just a means to his end. His plan, unseen, was also on track—the end of this god-forsaken regime and the liberation of the Iranian people from under its decades-long, corrupt and inept leadership. He was putting a great deal of faith in the west and their restraint for his plan to work. He had placed his faith in the West, American specifically, once before, in early 2011, during the internal protests that he had so carefully and covertly nurtured. They had betrayed his efforts with little to none of the help they had promised. The protests had ended with no impact on the regime. That betrayal cemented his path and belief that only he alone could accomplish his goal. Now the West would bear the consequences of their inaction.

They had blessed the final actions. His boss, the Minister of Intelligence, had insisted to the council that Javad's role here was done. The Minister was a corrupt and power-hungry bastard. Javad didn't care. He just hated the man. Hated them all. He was promised promotion and reward for his activities, which they thought was for the benefit of Iran and the Revolution. Let them think that. He couldn't care less for rewards or titles. His role was indeed done. Happy to bow out and be left to his own devices. He did, however, get the Minister's approval to inspect the operation for himself. He was intrigued and wanted to see what he'd only read about in the briefings. Javad would satiate his own curiosity and be free to tend to his other matter, which was waiting for him at Evin Prison.

The hanger was huge. It was constructed over two years at the very busy airport, but on the edge away from anyone's curiosity. Above the massive double hanger doors was a picture of a large moon and the words "Moon Rise Airlines" below it almost acting like the ground and the moon rising above it. It was clever, this camouflage.

His car pulled to a stop and he noticed other vehicles down the side of the hanger with some men in uniform standing by. He wasn't the only mover of parts in this endeavor. Although he knew all in the larger sense, he didn't know all in the tactical sense. The smaller details were being driven by the Revolutionary Guards. Specifically a very small subset of the Revolutionary Guards. There was a team of highly trained special forces that had been hand-picked—training for over a year and a half. As part of the Revolutionary Guards, they reported differently than he did. Everything was compartmentalized for security reasons, even from him. He couldn't run every facet of the operation even though he wanted to.

The interior of the hanger complex was impressive. He took it all in. This new airline that Iran was starting up was legitimate, at least to the industry. Decades of sanctions had left Iran bereft of new aircraft. Up until last year, when the sanctions were eased in the international deal along with North Korea and the West, they'd had to use these older 727s. They had procured two dozen of these older aircraft, in various states of disrepair. Complete overhauls on all with new exterior paint schemes and specialized interior enhancements were all done within this one hanger. The aircraft, all white with a large moon rising over a landscape on each tail, one after the next. It must have been impressive for all the planes to be in here at once, but only six left in the hangar it was still an impressive sight.

There was work being done on remaining planes. Mechanics moved around each aircraft. Air wrenches could be heard further down the line. There were pallets of gear and what looked like ammunition boxes being loaded into the cargo holds where passenger luggage would usually go. They were close. To his right was a group of men in camouflage uniforms near a side door making their way out. The door slammed and a man in a dark jacket, carrying rolled up blueprints was making his way quickly to Javad. He waved the blueprints at Javad in way of greeting.

"Salam, Director. I was told of your inspection only minutes ago," the man said to Javad as he offered his free hand.

"Salam," Javad replied, but didn't offer his hand.

He wanted to put the man off his guard. He was after as much information as he could gain here and a nervous engineer would benefit him.

"Why is there still so much activity here? Are you not on schedule, Colonel Madani?" Further unsettling the disheveled senior engineer, who was also a Colonel in the Iranian Air Force.

"Director, I assure you that we are on track. Most of the aircraft have already departed for their forward operating destinations. What you see here are only the finishing details. We're loading supplies and they will depart in the morning direct to their destinations," the Colonel replied anxiously.

Javad took a moment to recall that he was "Director" here. He assumed and shed various titles and positions as his duties and activities dictated. The colonel knew he worked for the Ministry of Intelligence. Javad knew that the Colonel's anxiety was driven by the knowledge that the ministry was so powerful that even the Colonel's superiors couldn't keep him from disappearing if he didn't meet his deadline.

"Colonel, I'd like to inspect one of the aircraft. Please show me through one." Javad had turned and stepped into the Colonel's personal space.

"Yes, Director. Please follow me." He quickly gestured to the nearest plane.

They ended up under the end of the left wing. As they moved under the plane, Javad noticed the new, glossy paint. He scanned the fuselage and found what he was looking for.

"Tell me Colonel, what are these?" he asked, knowing the answer, but wanting the details. There were four long indentations under the plane. Two on either side of the fuselage.

"Mounts for air to air missiles. They're part of the defensive countermeasures packages we've installed on each aircraft. We've also installed powerful combat radar in the nose of each plane as well as flares and chaff countermeasures. Just in case."

"In case of what, Colonel?" These planes are supposed to be covert, not bristling with missiles.

"Director, allow me to further explain, please," he said nearly breathless. "The missiles will be covered once attached to the aircraft." The Colonel pointed to pallets of what looked like half shells painted the same color as the plane. There were only a few left. "They are hardly noticeable once the covers are installed."

"And you think they'll need these?" Javad asked pointedly.

"Director, this was approved. We couldn't think of a reason not to include them, but if something were to go wrong at the last minute, we thought that they could at least have the ability to fight," the Colonel said with conviction, retrieving some backbone. It was what Javad wanted to hear.

"Rest easy, Colonel. I wanted to hear the concept from you directly. To know it was well thought out. Show me inside."

The man relaxed as Javad headed toward the stairway. Javad scanned around once inside. To the left was the flight deck. There were four seats, instead of the usual two.

"What is the configuration here, Colonel?"

"Flight crew up front. A flight engineer, and this last seat is for the countermeasures and weapons officer."

Javad walked toward the rear of the plane. It was not what he was expecting, but he was thoughtful of the design. 727s usually had three seats on each side. Here there were two larger seats to each side. By his count there was room for forty eight passengers. A new bulkhead and door just aft of the wings somewhat obscured the aft part of the plane. The aft space, he assumed, was for their precious cargo.

"This seating seams overly spacious. More passengers could have been accommodated, yes? They are not going on holiday. It's a one way trip."

"Indeed, Director. This was designed for each passenger and their gear, which is considerable. Also, taking into account the size of each group is already set, so we updated accordingly. Each aircraft has extra fuel tanks within the cargo hold to extend their operational range. About half of the planes are able to reach their destinations without refueling. The others need refueling either way. Is there a concern?" Colonel Madani's anxiety had returned.

"Very well, Colonel." Javad turned, heading back down the stairway with the Colonel still talking about seating and concerns and whatever else the man was saying. Javad had heard and seen what he had come to hear and see.

Javad stopped halfway to the hangar door and spun in place bringing the nervous and still talking Colonel up short, almost running into him. Javad reached out his hand.

"It's all very well done, Colonel. You've only hours left to full delivery of all aircraft for operations. I'm assuming the men in uniform, who were leaving when I arrived are the command element of the group taking this journey?" Changing the subject startled the Colonel.

"We'll be ready, Director. And that is correct. Head of Battalion Kabiri and his staff were familiarizing themselves with the aircraft."

"What do you think of Head of Battalion Kabiri, Colonel?" The question would make Madani uncomfortable. He was also looking for information. Kabiri was a ghost. There was no photo in his file, just scattered word of mouth details. Kabiri had good operational security, but it unsettled Javad. He had a mental itch that he couldn't scratch.

"He is a man of emotion and detail, Director. He asks many questions. Although, if I may say so, my time with you was much more…polite." Madani went silent, as he attempted to gauge Javad's reaction.

"Be at peace, Colonel. Your candor is appreciated and I will keep your thoughts to myself, unless of course the delivery is late."

Javad smiled broadly from his mouth but not his eyes. He shook Colonel Madani's hand vigorously, turned and walked out leaving the Colonel wide eyed, stammering reassurances.

The door slammed behind him as he ventured into the cold, late morning air to his waiting car. His driver opened the rear door and he entered and situated himself. Javad began to laugh deeply in the back seat. Maybe he was tired. Yes, he was tired. Exhausted actually. He missed Ahmed. He could verbally spar with Ahmed and his friend would ignore him or provide a witty retort. He missed his friend. He thought that perhaps this Kabiri would be a good mental sparring partner. He made a wreck out of the Colonel. Madani was a good man and good at his job. He'd read his file. None of it would matter in the coming days anyway. Sleep, even fitful, was required before his last appointment at Evin Prison with his guest.

# ELEVEN

December 23/24
1:30am EST
11:30pm MST
Tiger Butte, Montana
Shan Chao

Twenty-four hours after leaving Las Vegas they reached their destination. Captain Shan Chao of the People's Liberation Army Special Forces looked at the map on his phone. They were near Tiger Butte in Montana. Tiger Butte. A good omen. Tigers were powerful and focused. It had gotten progressively colder and there was fresh snow on the ground. About six inches covered everything. It was beautiful. Up the hill, beyond a stand of trees overlooking the valley below, sat a log cabin with big windows, firelight glowed within. He checked his watch, 2330hours. A figure, fully camouflaged in white, stepped out from behind a tree. He carried a long gun, also covered in white pieces of some kind of cloth or fabric. He didn't see him until he moved. His men were good, especially in the dark. Chao wondered what else he missed as he mentally berated himself. He wasn't on holiday, he was on mission. Get your head right, Captain.

The ghostly figure motioned the suburban to park in front of the cabin. He told the semi's driver to move the bright orange tractor trailer off the road into a clearing free from the tall trees that surrounded the cabin. The semi rumbled into the spot as directed. They all got out of the Suburban, snow crunching under foot. Chao headed to the cabin while his guests were getting their bags. They'd come a long way in a day and a half. He and half his team had collected the tractor trailer in Long Beach, while the other half of his team set up operations at this cabin. It'd been rented for them by persons unknown. They'd picked up the last two of their party in Las Vegas. Major

Feng and Captain Gao. Feng was in his forties, balding, overweight slightly from the looks of it, with a slimy, unkept personality. He wasn't a soldier, like Chao. He was a political officer in the People's Liberation Army. Oh, to hear him talk on the way here, Feng was a hero in his own head. He'd been places and done things, rising in rank for his apparent exploits. Chao new the type well. Connected to someone high up. Had the right political leanings, which meant he'd be a pain in Chao's ass. He hated political officers.

Captain Gao, on the other hand, was an actual soldier. She was all business. Younger than Feng. Shoulder-length black hair, round face with a wide, flat nose. She was short, even for a Chinese woman, but in shape and squared away. He'd put aside that she was a woman when they'd first spoken. He recalled it with a smile.

*They were several hours into the trip, when Chao brought out two holstered, semi-automatic pistols and handed them to Feng and Gao, who were in the back seat.*

*"You are familiar with these?" Chao asked.*

*"Of course. I've received expert rating on pistol and rifle. These are not Chinese made, Captain," Feng said as he roughly unholstered the pistol Chao had given him.*

*These types were always telling everyone of their expertise. Real soldiers didn't do that.*

*"We aren't in China, Major."*

*"I realize that, Captain," Feng snapped, adding Chao's rank to reinforce the fact that the man outranked him. "Do you expect trouble? Why do we need these when we have your team to protect us?" Feng asked, brandishing the pistol carelessly.*

*Chao remained stony. The pistol didn't have a round chambered.*

*"Isn't it better to have it and not need it, than to need it and not have it," Chao responded and looked at Gao. "Just don't shoot us," he added with a smile.*

*Feng smiled a wide, greasy smile, showing stained teeth, assuming his dig was directed at their female comrade.*

*As Chao studied Gao, he was rewarded with her obvious irritation. His mild insult was intended to convey his assumption that Political Officers and women couldn't handle firearms. He had to know who and what he was dealing with.*

*She pulled the Glock from the holster, ejected the magazine to ensure it was loaded and reinserted it in the handle. She pulled the slide back just enough to see if there was a round in the chamber, there wasn't. She racked it all the way back to chamber a round, checked again to ensure a round was chambered, then looked up and met Chao's eyes. She re-holstered the pistol, leaned her head back still looking at him and closed her eyes. Chao laugh, nodded, and looked at Feng who tried to imitate Gao. The Major fumbled with the magazine release, dropping the magazine on the floor of the vehicle. While the Major was searching for his lost magazine, Chao turned back around and shook his head slightly in disgust at the man's incompetence. He now knew who and what he was dealing with. The Major was in a foul mood the rest of the trip, but Chao didn't care, as long as Feng didn't do anything stupid.*

"Captain Gao, go check the gear," Feng ordered. "Run diagnostics without lighting it up. I want to ensure that it's operational. I will check the accommodations with Captain Chao, who's men seem to be well settled in already."

"On it," Gao replied smartly with professionalism. She turned and made her way to the semi leaving footprints in the fresh snow. She didn't seem bothered by the cold. A Soldier.

Chao watched Feng crunch his way over to the cabin's front porch where Chao and his Sergeant stood. A slight breeze hit them. Feng wasn't dressed for this. These two packed for Vegas and Feng was still wearing cotton pants, dress shoes and shirt with a light jacket. Chao was amused by the Major's discomfort, but didn't show it.

"Captain Chao, I'm assuming you have more weather appropriate clothing for us." Feng said, stepping up on the porch, wincing against the biting wind.

"Major, you do seem under dressed," Chao said dead pan, but with a slight smile. "The Sergeant here will see you inside to your room. Show you what gear we have. I'm going to make the rounds. When I return, we'll brief you and Captain Gao on our situation here. Then you can brief us regarding the contents of that truck we just hauled up here and our full mission."

"I will brief you on what you need to know, Captain," he said as Gao came bounding up the steps onto the porch, now shivering. Even soldiers get cold.

"Systems check out, Major. Please tell me there are winter clothes in there, and a fire?" She pointed somewhat frantically at the cabin door.

"Sergeant, get them settled. They're freezing off what balls they have left out here." Chao said quietly as he turned and opened the door.

As Feng pushed his way through the door in front of Gao, Chao stepped back and let Gao go in before him. She nodded to him.

The heavy cabin door closed, but Chao remained on the porch. He turned and looked out over the valley below him. His sight line went down the snow covered driveway, over the top of the semi sitting off in a clearing parallel to the narrow approach road, and down to the small town in the valley. Dim lights on tiny houses and buildings barely cut through the falling snow. That could be a problem, depending on what the Major had planned. Chao knew something momentous was afoot. He and his team wouldn't be here otherwise. The town in the valley wasn't unlike where his childhood was spent. Minus the snow and the cold. Just people living their lives.

It amazed him that they could operate this openly and unchallenged. His country was closed off and monitored. Americans trying to operate this way in China wouldn't make it an hour. They'd been in the U.S. for over a month so far, collecting gear at the myriad outdoors establishments with the funds they'd been provided by their covert contact, who himself had been in the U.S. for years. Their contact had also supplied them with a few firearms he'd purchased legally, then disappeared like spitting into the ocean. Chao set a couple of his men to inventory their new weapons that came loaded in several crates within the semi. Proper weapons with enough ammunition for whatever happened, although he hoped wouldn't need it.

Mei's image popped into his mind. He couldn't imagine he'd see her again soon. The last year had been the best of his life with her, although the last month before he got sequestered with his team for this mission, she'd become distant. Not in a physical or emotional way, but mentally she just hadn't been there. Her thoughts always drifting to work. It was hard only being together here and there when their work schedules permitted it and then only brief weekends. He imagined the smell of her perfume on the cold wind that stung his face. He'd give anything for the warmth of her touch here in this cabin, without his team, the Major, or Gao, the semi, all of it. Just the two of them by the fire, away from whatever was about to happen. He pushed the thought out and took a deep breath. He held out a hand and let the falling snow cover it for a moment as he looked down the valley at the small town. Houses and structures spaced well away from one another, muted porch lights through the snow glowed different shades of white or dull yellow. Stay down there, Chao mentally urged their American neighbors. Ten minutes later, he returned from checking on his men in their positions. He entered the cabin, anxious to see what the Major had in store for them, although his gut told him it would be unpleasant.

❄ ❄ ❄

An hour later, they were sitting in the great room of what seemed to be a charmingly rustic American cabin. There was room for the whole team: Feng, Gao, Chao, the Sergeant and ten other commandos. Most of them standing or sitting on the couches and chairs around the wood burning stove. One soldier was pouring another cup of coffee from the half empty carafe on the kitchen counter. Some of the men had mugs of the Columbian brew, while he, his Sergeant and Feng had tumblers of whiskey. Gao, the lone female, stood at one of the big front windows silently staring out into the darkness as more snow fell outside. They all listened intently as Major Feng finished detailing their mission. Chao was in disbelief. The mission would indeed be unpleasant.

"Are you fucking kidding me!" Chao blurted out.

"We're going to need more ammunition," the Sergeant said quietly into his mug. He was a short, fireplug of a man. Tattoos ran down his arms and up on his neck.

Chao ignored the Sergeant's quip and spoke to the group. "I want two-man teams from now on. No one on watch alone. Feng and Gao, stay inside or just near the cabin. Don't stray. Sergeant—full loadouts for the team. Three teams on duty around the clock," he ordered. Chao's stress level was elevated. He looked at Feng. "They'll know our exact location and come for us. We aren't going to be able to hold them off for long. Fuck the Chairman's mother, his ancestor's mothers, and their fucking cows!" Chao dumped the rest of his Jack Daniels down his throat and looked into the fire.

"Calm yourself, Captain." Feng said. It did not calm him. "The Americans won't have the ability to respond. Anyway, I've been assured that reinforcements are in country and ready to assist, when needed." Feng said, puffing out his chest. His overconfidence in plans working perfectly was aggravating to Chao. Once it started, it would go sideways. Feng pointed to the small, metal box in the corner. It was dull green, the size of a shoebox. "We have what we need in there to communicate with other teams like ours and our reinforcements. The gear is safe in the box. We don't open it until afterwards" Feng leaned forward in his chair. "Captain Chao, you don't have confidence in our force's ability to crush the Americans?" Feng stared at him with those beady eyes.

Chao returned the stare for a moment then glanced at the Sergeant who raised one eyebrow and pursed his lips. This was going to be a disaster. "To your posts. Sergeant, relieve the lookouts. Get them in here so I can give them the illustrious news," Chao said. "Everyone else, get some sleep. I have a feeling we won't have the chance soon. Get it while you still can."

Chao refilled his glass. The bitter air from the open door permeated the room as they left. It was going to be a cold, dark winter. He missed Mei more than ever. The only soft spot he had in his being was for her. Would he ever see her again, he thought, poking at the fire. He was left alone with his thoughts and his refilled whiskey glass. His eyes followed Feng as the Major went upstairs to find a bed. How he hated political officers.

# TWELVE

December 23
2:30pm EST
11:00pm Tehran
Javad

After some needed sleep, a shower, and change of clothes, Javad felt a bit more human. His driver was pulling the car through the gate at Evin Prison. It was after midnight. He wondered how his guest, Yousef, was holding up.

"Stay with the car, Mohammed. I will be a while so get some rest," he said.

He looked around by habit, not that anyone would care that he was there. The main prison was behind him. An imposing wall stood about fifty yards to his front. Between him and the wall, lit inside and out, sat a smallish, metal-roofed, cinder block building. There were no windows and only a single door. He shoved his hands in his coat pockets against the cold, his soft soled shoes crunching on the pea gravel lining the walkway. He approached the door, removed a badge from his trouser pocket and held it up to a small black box with a red LED light on it. It beeped and the light turned green. He entered. The heavy door slammed behind him.

Inside was as stark as the exterior. A single desk in the corner. The guard in uniform behind it stood and saluted. He returned the salute—within these walls he was a general. The guard remained standing as Javad opened the only other door, leading to dimly lit descending stairs. The steps turning several times before he reached the bottom. He stopped at another locked doorway. The guard on the other side slid open a slat about shoulder high and looked at him. He heard the metal workings of bolts being slid and the door opened inward and he stepped through.

"Salam, General." The guard greeted him.

"Salam, Sergeant. How is our guest this evening?"

"Per your orders, Sir. He should be ready for you after his treatments. The rest of the guest rooms are empty. You'll be alone."

"Good. Ensure that I am not disturbed. This may take a while. Have you collected the items I requested?"

"Yes, General, as requested. Last door on the right."

Javad walked the long corridor of water-stained, cinder block walls and metal doors. He had been in several of these cells over the years with different types of guests. It was cold here deep beneath the surface. Quiet. He arrived at the end of the corridor. A cart with the items sat nearby.

He was filled with morbid anticipation as he opened the heavy metal door outward. Yousef was hanging by his wrists in the middle of the barren room. The man's feet barely touched the floor. His naked body was limp, but one eye, barely open, studied Javad. The other eye was swollen shut. Javad recoiled from the stench. Bile rising in his throat. Yousef had been hanging here for some time. Dried blood streaked his bruised face. He was covered in blood from head to feet. Some of it dried and some still gleaming from fresh wounds on his arms, torso, and legs. The man had been waterboarded the first week. Then they had beat and cut on him. His orders had been specific. Keep him awake, alive, and able to speak. No one, however, was to ask him any questions. He was to be totally broken when Javad questioned him. And so it appeared this was the case.

"What…you…want of…me? I've done…n..nothing…wrong." The man sputtered at Javad with spittle and blood dribbling out of his mouth.

"Try to relax, my friend. I have only a few questions and then you will be free to go back to your family." Javad lied as he wheeled the cart into the room closing the door behind him with a deep metallic clang.

The tools arrayed on the cart were normal, everyday tools. He donned a plastic, see through rain poncho. Everyday tools. It covered his arms and body down to his knees. Javad grabbed a flathead screwdriver and a hand-held blowtorch. He clicked the button to light the torch and it sparked to life casting a dull, blue light on Yousef's face. The tool was heavy. A small propane tank at one end and the torch at the other. He turned to the man, who's one good eye went wide with fear, and he started sputtering again in protest.

Javad put the end of the flathead screwdriver into the blueish white flame for a minute while looking the man in the eye. The tip began to take on an orange glow.

"Do you not remember me, my friend?"

"Who are…you? I've done nothing…please!" The man was fully focused and twisting in the air as Javad moved closer to him, only inches from his face.

"We were younger. Much younger when we last met. You hit me with your club as I came through a doorway to save my sister from your bastard friend. Look closely with your one good eye. Do you remember me?" After a few seconds there was recognition on his bloody face.

"Wait…wait, I do, I'm sorry…so long ago, I did…did nothing to her!" He pleaded, twisting in the shackles, suspended from the ceiling.

"Shh, my friend. I have but one question for you. If you answer me truthfully, you can again be with your family in peace." Javad lied again. "Your wife. Your sons and daughter. Your grandchildren. They are waiting for you. You have a beautiful family," Javad said.

"What? I will answer. Don't hurt them. They've done nothing!" He pleaded.

"Okay, then. Let's attempt it. Where is Hafez? Where is your friend who slit my sister's throat in front of me? I want him, not you. You can live in peace if you tell me where I can find Hafez. Think carefully, my friend."

Javad put the torch between his face and the man's eye, their faces glowing in the light. Sweat dripped from the man's face from fear. Javad's from the heat.

"Hafez? I don't…" The man started to respond.

"I don't is incorrect." Javad laid the red hot tip of the screwdriver on the man's face just below his swollen eye. Flesh sizzled. Yousef jerked his head back, but Javad grabbed his sweaty mop of black hair and held it still. Yousef's screams wouldn't be heard down here. His skin smoking where the tip touched. Javad held it there for a few seconds while the man writhed.

"Now, let's try again." Javad was calm.

"I can't. What you want is a Guard's secret! They'll execute me!"

"You are with the Revolutionary Guard Commandos, yes? It was pure happenstance that I saw you in the market. A happy coincidence. For me, at least. I never forget a face. Do you know where you are?"

"Evin Prison." The man spit blood down his chest. "They will be looking for me. I've been gone too long."

Javad gave a snort and a quick belly laugh. "They won't be finding you here, my friend. No, not here. I am Ministry of Intelligence. This is my domain. No one finds anyone here. I don't care about your secrets. I want Hafez!" Javad yelled in the man's face and put the blow torch flame to the man's genitals garnering the requisite blood curdling screams.

"Let's be candid with each other. Would you rather tell me what I require and see your family again, or not? I'm prepared to make an evening of it." He moved to the side so the man could glimpse the cart's contents.

Javad pulled up the metal chair from the corner and sat in front of the hanging man. He reached onto the cart for a wooden mallet. He couldn't imagine what Yousef was thinking at the moment and didn't care. Javad guessed they'd be there a while, but he didn't have all night. This was his last chance to find Hafez. He grabbed the man's filthy, right foot with his hands in surgical gloves. He rested it on his lap, toes up and shoved the still glowing tip of the screwdriver under the toenail of the big toe. He held it there and looked up at Yousef.

"Hafez?"

The man tried to squirm, pleading with Javad that he didn't know or couldn't say. Yousef was confused at this point. A couple of hours of sleep for each twenty four that he'd been here had addled him. Sleep deprivation worked wonders on the mind. Javad shook his head slowly and pounded handle of the screwdriver with the mallet, driving it under the toenail, popping it off, the smell of searing flesh wafting up to Javad's nostrils.

"Stop. Stop! I beg you!" Javad pushed the filthy foot away and jumped up to the man's face. Eye to wild and wide eye. The man passed out then. He truly had been through more than most and held up to it. Barely. Javad took a break and waited.

\* \* \*

Two hours passed. He'd work until Yousef passed out. Wake him. Work some more. It was a vicious cycle that Javad was good at, but his patience and time were out. Javad felt weariness creep back into his mind. Torture, prolonged torture, was just as exhausting on the one doing the work as it was on the one receiving the work. He'd had enough and woke the hanging man with a slap to the face.

"Hafez?" he growled. Anger bubbling up as he yanked Yousef's greasy, blood-soaked, grey beard.

Yousef tensed for a strike, but it didn't come. Javad held him tight by the beard, eye to eye. Yousef finally broke. His body heaved with sobs, going limp again. "You promise me that I can…see my family again?"

"I give you my word, my friend. You will be with your family again."

"Hafez is commander of the special Guard's Force Commando detachment. They are…" The man coughed up blood and spit. Javad retrieved a plastic bottle of water from the cart putting it to the man's lips, tilting it up so the cool liquid passed into his bloody mouth. Yousef gulped at the water manically, then coughed again. Javad gave him a moment to recover.

"Continue, please. They are…?" He prompted. It couldn't be right. That was not who was in charge of the away force. Kabiri was in charge.

"Yes, yes, we are preparing for a secret mission from Mehrabad Airport. I don't know…they may have already left without me. Special hangar." The man stopped and drooled some more.

"How do you know about this hangar? Are you part of this mission?"

"Yes, they will be wondering what's happened to me." The man's eye rolled up and he lost consciousness.

"Hey! No, no. Wake up! Look at me!" Javad grabbed the man's head and held it steady. He was so close. Could Hafez have been that close all this time? Javad shook Yousef's head. His eye opened and refocused on Javad's face.

"My friend, your family awaits you. But first tell me again. Hafez is the commander of this mission? They are to be on passenger aircraft and fly into American cities? Is this the mission you are speaking of? Do not lie to me! Kabiri is Head of Battalion for the mission, not Hafez! Don't lie to me!" His intensity was driven by panic and he didn't care if it showed.

"Yes, yes! Hafez is Kabiri! He took the name Kabiri in the war to hide his past!"

Yousef screamed. Javad had both of Yousef's ears in a crushing grip. Javad had just become aware he was doing this and released Yousef's head from his shaking hands.

"We are supposed to be the second wave of a strike against the west. I don't know where my plane is supposed to go. I don't know which plane Hafez is on either, but he is on a plane. My family. Please. The planes may already be gone. I don't know how long I've been here. I don't know any mor…" He lost consciousness again.

Javad slumped down in the metal chair, staring at the floor. Could this be? All this time, he was so close. He had been in the hangar with him just hours ago. That's why he couldn't find him all these years. He was looking for the wrong name. Such a simple, stupid mistake. Then it dawned on him like a bolt of lightning. Hafez was alive and would be…

He stood. Purpose renewed. He looked at the man who had just delivered this news to him. Hanging there, sobbing quietly. Broken. He hadn't really lied to him when he said he'd be with his family again. Just not in the way the man thought. Javad picked up a knife from the cart. With his left hand grabbed the man's hair and gently raised his head to look into his good eye. The man looked back at him blankly.

"Thank you, my friend. You've done well. May Allah bestow peace upon you and your family."

As he finished speaking he slit the man's throat from left to right as his good eye went wide. It was just a gurgle that emerged from Yousef's open mouth. Javad ticked Yousef off his mental list. He was a dead man as soon as Javad had seen him weeks ago.

Javad turned from the hanging corpse and tossed the knife, gloves and apron on the cart. He made his way back down the long hallway to where the guard stood to greet him.

"Leave him in there for a couple of days to reflect. I have what I need. Don't enter the cell." Javad didn't want any questions before he was gone. His plan was changing in his head as he walked.

"As you wish, General. Have a good night."

Javad hurried up the stairs, through the guest house with the other guard bidding him good night as well. He was seeking the cold, fresh night air. He walked to his waiting car and got in the back seat, startling his driver, who'd been asleep.

"Sorry, Sir. It's late. Home?" the driver said rubbing sleep from his face.

"Yes, home and then you can get home to your wife, Mohammed. Hug your wife Mohammed. Family is precious and you should treat every moment with them as the last moment. Savor it."

"I will, Sir. We are expecting a baby. Just found out a few days ago. I was hesitant to say anything, as I know you prefer quiet when I drive you, but I can't contain my excitement and had to share. I hope I was not out of line?"

Javad could tell Mohammed expected a rebuke. He was normally blunt with Mohammed the watcher, but he felt some distant similarity with him tonight. Javad reached forward and squeezed Mohammed's shoulder. He envied his driver's simple life. Love his wife, drive Javad, tell his other bosses where he drove Javad, go home and love his wife. Simplicity.

"Good for you Mohammed. Cherish this time. I am happy for you and your wife."

He sat back and closed his eyes. The car moved. He had to be careful now. He was supposed to be one place tomorrow, or was it today, yes, it was today. However, with this revelation, he would need to be somewhere else entirely. His plan was abruptly altered. Just his plan changed. Not the larger plan everyone else was privy to. Everything was in motion. Swirling around him. But his focus was now a tunnel with one pinprick of light at the end. Hafez.

# THIRTEEN

Javad moved purposefully around his small flat several miles east of Evin Prison. He dug out clothes and boots that he hadn't worn in years. He'd thought he'd never need for them again, but here he was. He stripped down to his underwear and pulled on brownish gray pants, undershirt, and belt. The boots had once been black but were long since gray. He grabbed a military shirt as old as the boots. Brown with no insignia, sleeves rolled up to the elbows. It was tight, as was the waist on the pants. These were from another life. His credentials would get him as far as he needed to go, he hoped. He put on a military jacket over his shoulder holster and then wrapped a keffiyeh around his head with the ends hanging down in front of his shoulders and looked in the mirror. Tactical enough for his purposes. The keffiyeh was a large, square of brown and green cloth that served as a head and face covering. Memories knocked on his consciousness. He pushed them away.

He retrieved his .32 caliber pistol from his nightstand drawer. This pistol had a silencer that wasn't attached at the moment. He stuck the cylindrical suppressor in the pocket of his pants. It didn't so much silence the gun's action, which was quiet already, but suppressed the sound of the rounds firing. Since it was a small caliber, it was indeed nearly silent. He'd attach the silencer later. He was in a hurry. Extra magazines in a leather holder on the other side of his shoulder holster.

He felt around the top of the drawer and peeled off an old style flip phone that had been taped there. He opened it and checked the battery. Full charge.

Good. Lastly, he grabbed his short lock blade and clipped it in his pocket with the phone. Now for coffee.

He went to the main room in his flat, which he already checked for entry while he was out. He had several ways of telling if someone had been here. You could never be too careful, even someone at his rank in the Ministry. There were always watchers watching. Nothing had been disturbed though. He walked over to what amounted to a kitchen table, more of a small desk where he worked in the morning and late into the evening. There was a laptop and a small coffee maker with a clear glass carafe. It was half full of the cold, weeks old dark brew. It smelled stale. He poured it out in the sink. What he was left staring at was a small, rectangular package taped to the bottom of the inside of the carafe. He retrieved the package and laid it on the desk/table and peeled away the plastic wrapping and was rewarded with the thumb drive he'd put in there weeks prior. It was dry. Good. He put it in the breast pocket of his shirt and buttoned it to ensure it stayed put.

He smiled as he wrote a short note and folded the piece of paper in half, addressing it appropriately for the minister. Sitting back, he looked out the window at the darkness. What time was it? He needed to move and walked to the door, giving a last turn and surveyed the flat one last time. It was so empty. His daughter hadn't known this place. She'd grown up at his mother's flat after Yasmin had died. Ahmed had moved in as well to watch over them.

His path, and that of his friend, diverged a while ago. Javad loved Yasmin with all his being. Ahmed had also loved his sister. One and the same. When she died, he disconnected from his emotions and the family world he had known. He couldn't lose anything or anyone else. He had a singular purpose and it slowly grew over time until he understood it and shaped it and nurtured it. That purpose was not his daughter or Ahmed or his mother, even though they were involved now. Only as a means to keep them as safe as he could, but they didn't know that.

Ahmed was furious with him for not being there more than he was. Javad tried to be a good father and was around a good deal, but Ahmed, whose heart was bigger than any he had encountered, moved in with his mother and Sara and cared for them, while he worked his obsession. His mother wanted him around more in her old age and for Sara's sake. His friend, who said little, communicated his displeasure and disappointment of him in less verbal ways. Whenever Javad was home, Ahmed's eyes conveyed his disappointment. Ahmed made excuses for his absence for Sara's sake. His friend knew his job took him away and they were nearing sixty now, his mother eighty. Time was growing short, Ahmed would say to Javad. Sara missed her father.

Javad provided money and other resources for the three of them as his station in the government allowed. But he saw himself serving a higher purpose for good or ill. It was the course he put himself on. He and Ahmed had exchanged harsh words when Javad sent them away. He still missed his friend, in reality, his brother, terribly. Almost as much as he missed Sara. It was for their protection, he told himself. He hoped he was right.

He locked the door behind him, not that it would stop them from gaining entry and finding his note. It would be too late then. Javad made his way down onto the busy morning street. He looked at his watch. Nearly 8:00 a.m. The last plane was due to depart at 10:15 a.m. He needed a taxi. He couldn't use his driver. He knew other watchers were sure to be close. They always were. He pulled the cheap flip phone from his pocket and dialed a number from memory as he walked down the street. It rang several times.

"Hello?"

"I have a pizza delivery."

"You have the wrong number. I didn't order a pizza." The line went dead, but it was the correct response from his contact at the Indian Embassy.

Javad picked up his pace. He often walked this neighborhood in the morning and when he couldn't sleep at night. This was to ensure that if he had to escape and was followed, which he always was, his walkabouts wouldn't seem out of character. He dialed another number from memory. It rang once.

"Salam!" the male voice said.

"Salam. I need a taxi in five minutes."

"On the way." The line went dead.

Javad continued down the street, thankful he'd put these contingencies in place. He noticed the watcher out of the corner of his eye. Behind him to his left. The man was leaning against a street sign post smoking a cigarette and looking at his own phone.

Watcher.

Javad turned and walked leisurely to the next intersection and turned up the street. Normal. He ducked into a narrow, shadow filled alleyway that opened onto a small courtyard with several doors spaced around. These were homes and a small tailor shop, not yet open. Awnings jutted out over the doors, casting shadows. He flattened himself against one of the walls next to the courtyard's entrance. He mentally admonished himself for not putting the silencer on his pistol when he had the chance. He pulled the lock blade from his right pants pocket using his thumb to rotate the blade out of the handle until it clicked in place. He exhaled and listened.

If his luck held, the watcher had walked past the alleyway, searching for him on another street in vain. No time to wait any longer, he inched his way to the corner of the alleyway and slowly, with his back still on the wall, craned his neck to the right so that he could just peek around the corner to see if the way was clear.

The watcher was standing there, peering into the courtyard, his shadow-cloaked frame in stark contrast to the other end of the alleyway where the sunlight was brighter. Javad sprang. Every muscle and tendon in his old, but still spry body, moved in concert, releasing pent up energy and power. The motion was lightning quick, just as he practiced most days in his flat to keep in shape and keep his skills sharp. The watcher was surprised, frozen for a fatal second. Javad's knife slid into the front of the watcher's neck. The watcher collapsed silently backward with the force and weight of Javad on top of him. Javad slid the knife out and plunged it into the watcher's left eye socket. It was done.

Javad pulled the knife out and rolled off the corpse. He sat breathing deeply, absentmindedly wiping blood from the knife on the watcher's coat. The dead were piling up around him. He put the knife back in his pocket and grabbed the man's feet, dragging him into the courtyard around the corner.

Back on the street, he walked several more blocks, carefully checking behind him. He came to a street corner near one of the many embassies in this part of the city. A car pulled up behind him and for a second he thought that maybe more watchers had found him. He forced himself to turn. Taxi. Relief. It pulled closer. His taxi. He recognized the driver as one of his, although the driver didn't know that. He got in.

"Drive to the Beyhaghi Car Park. I have to see someone before we go to our final destination. Ensure that we are not being followed."

"Okay."

As they drove, Javad checked his clothes for blood. He was amazed there wasn't any. He also screwed on the silencer to his .32 caliber pistol. He was too old for knife fights. He put the pistol back in his shoulder holster. The sprawling car park was empty this time of morning. Javad unbuttoned his shirt pocket and pulled out the thumb drive, holding it tightly in the palm of his right hand while he scanned the lot. Movement caught his eye to his left as a man exited an older style sedan from the driver's side. Good, he was alone.

"Pull up near that car." Javad pointed in the direction of the man now standing behind the sedan. The taxi stopped several spots away and Javad got out. "Wait here. I will only be a minute."

His contact was younger than Javad, tall, with a full black beard. He was dressed casually. Javad had never met him before this. He was just a phone number that he used from time to time. They greeted each other in Farsi and Javad reached out with his right hand to shake the other's right hand and then they embraced. The thumb drive moved from Javad's hand to the other's hand while in the embrace.

"It is good to see you, my friend," the Indian said in flawless Farsi.

"You as well," Javad replied. They made small talk, gesturing around them as if discussing the weather for a minute or two and then they embraced again in farewell. All for show, just in case. This meeting was too hurried.

"It's most important that you get this to your western contacts today. You will not hear from me again," Javad said in the man's ear and stepped away, bidding him farewell.

"Mehrabad Airport," Javad told the driver. He thought about his next move. What if Hafez's—Kabiri's—plane was still at the airport? He didn't know which plane he would be on. Maybe he ends this in the next hour, or maybe something else entirely. He would know soon enough.

# FOURTEEN

Gunnery Sergeant Bao Nguyen stood outside the non-commissioned officers barracks at Fort Knox, Kentucky. A bitter wind blew across the base, or post as the Army called them. He stared down at the mobile phone in his hand with his brother's name, An. His thumb hovered over the call button on the screen. His brother was somewhere near, but Bao hadn't been to the fort before. He hadn't thought to ask An where he bunked when he arrived earlier today.

He and An were close. They'd joined the Corps together right after high school, but their paths diverged when they completed new recruit training, or Boot Camp, at Parris Island. He'd stayed at Camp Lejeune while An had been stationed at Camp Pendleton. A whole country between them. Although, at the moment, they were both at Fort Knox. An with his company of fourteen M1A1 Abrams Main Battle Tanks and Bao stopping over to visit on his way home. An's team was on a rotation to bring armor back to the Fort. Some years past, the Army had moved its Armor School to Fort Benning, Georgia, but that's a long way to go for some Reserve and National Guard units to travel with their tracks, even on trains. So they were opening up Fort Knox to armor again. The top cheese wanted to do some combined unit training between the Army and Marine tankers. An's unit got the duty.

They'd both done multiple tours in Iraq and Afghanistan. Unscathed. Much to their parent's relief. They were both training their Marines up for deployments in the Middle East in the near future. An was cross-training soldiers and Marines. That's some sorry duty, he thought.

His thumb still hovered. He was born two minutes before his twin. Being older, it was his duty to call his brother. Bao's wife, Brook, was in Northern Virginia at his parents place in the suburbs west of D.C. She'd been there a while helping his mother care for his sick dad. Pulmonary Fibrosis is what they called it. A lung disease that slowly scarred and hardened the lungs to the point of failure. He could feel tears well in his eyes. He didn't feel the cold wind any longer.

Brook left before her pregnancy kept her from traveling. She was due in a couple of weeks with their first child. Brook called him early the day before. His father was back in the hospital. He was on morphine to ease the discomfort. It hadn't registered with Bao what that meant. He just talked with his dad days before that and he seemed in good spirits. So much so that Bao hadn't changed plans to go straight home instead of here to see An before heading home for the holidays. He should have gone straight home.

His dad passed away an hour ago. A tear hit the phone's screen.

He thought of his parents then for a long, lingering moment. His dad had rescued his mother from some Viet Cong outside Saigon in the last days of the war. He was a special forces sergeant in the Army of the Republic of Vietnam. Neither of his parents ever elaborated on the details, except to say that several Cong lay dead and they'd been together ever since. Do the right thing and protect those who can't protect themselves—his dad had ingrained that in them from the time they could understand. The wind slapped his face. It was getting colder. He felt it on his skin, but that didn't bother him at the moment. He was warm inside, even through the loss. The memories were warm.

His thumb hovered. Life had abruptly changed an hour ago. Crushing sadness overcame him. He sobbed. Alone with the chill wind. He didn't want to change An's life. The longer he waited the longer his brother could remain whole.

His thumb hit the call button and he put the phone to his ear. Ringing. It was 0200hours. What a horrible way to wake up. Especially on Christmas Eve.

"Better be important," his brother's groggy voice echoed in his ear. Tears fell from Bao's eyes as he spoke.

# FIFTEEN

The transition was jarring. The car pulled off the expressway that ran next to Mehrabad International Airport and onto an access road. The expressway was nicely paved, while this access road was dirt. This was the exception rather than the rule. Dirt was prevalent. The access road circled around the airport to the other side, opposite from the terminals and passenger areas. The massive hangar loomed in the distance, doors open. They rounded the end of the main runway approaching the security perimeter. Two vehicles sat at the entrance. His driver slowed. His plan had changed and if he knew anything, it was that plans change and in that changing, danger lurked. Altered patterns attracted attention. If that was the case, this would be his first indication.

The driver stopped the taxi as a guard in military uniform, AK-47 slung around his neck and down his back, held up a hand. He approached the driver's lowered window.

"This area is closed to traffic. Turn around," he ordered. Javad rolled his window down and held out his credentials.

"My identification. I'm going to the hangar. I was here yesterday and have a final inspection to do," Javad stated gruffly, exuding as much irritation as possible.

It would lend credence to the lie. The guard took his identification, looked at it, then at Javad who was glaring at the guard. The guard quickly returned the ID.

"Proceed directly to the hangar. Go nowhere else. Hangar only."

The guard stepped back, waving them through. They made it through the inner security perimeter as well, approaching the hangar as one of the 727s was being rolled out. The taxi stopped and Javad took a deep breath. At least one plane was left. There was a lead weight in the pit of his stomach as he stepped onto the tarmac.

"Leave now. Tell no one of this ride or of me, understand?"

The driver nodded, rubbing his hands together and looking around anxiously. As soon as Javad closed the door, the taxi was moving away.

"I'm here to see the Chief Engineer. Here is my identification."

Javad pulled out the bi-fold again. He didn't need it. The guard at the side door of the hangar must have figured he had passed the perimeter security and opened the door for him without speaking. So far, so good.

He stepped into the hangar. Relief swept over him as he saw one last, bright white aircraft in the hangar. The other one moving out onto the tarmac began spinning its engines up to taxi. This one sat motionless, passenger doors open on the left side facing him with rolling stairs in place. This was it then. Javad choked down anxiety as he saw a group of men climbing the forward staircase. All but one wore camouflaged uniforms. The one he wanted wore dress shoes, slacks, shirt and tie, with a clipboard in his hands. Colonel Madani. Javad started across the mostly empty hangar floor to the chief engineer as the last commando disappeared into the plane. Passing the rear staircase leading to the open rear door, there was movement inside. He knew there would be three men in the rear compartment. These men were technicians for the cargo.

"Salam, Colonel Madani," Javad said with authority, but with a smile this time.

He had given Madani a hard time on his last visit. He wanted the man's total cooperation this time. Javad's rare smile would set the man at ease, hopefully.

The Colonel turned at the greeting and stared for a second. "Salam, Director! What are you doing here? I wasn't told to expect another inspection. We are done with the last plane. The commandos and their gear are loaded, as well as the special cargo in the rear. It's leaving in a few minutes."

"Not an inspection, Colonel. Not this time. Relax, Colonel. I am here to pass on congratulations from the highest authority."

Madani seemed to deflate as he exhaled a breath he had been holding. "I am very appreciative of the recognition, Director. We worked very diligently to accomplish this in the short time we were given. I'm glad those that hold the highest offices are happy with the work."

Javad was now standing directly in front of Madani and stood there waiting for the man to finish his irrelevant words.

"You didn't have to come all the way here to tell me this, but thank you, Director."

"Your mission is complete. Mine, however, is only beginning. I am going with this plane. Is there an empty seat?"

Madani was confused. Javad knew the man's orders. This was yet another change. Danger lurked.

"Director, I was not informed of this. As the senior authority at this facility, even I don't have the ability to allow it. Only those on this list board the plane. My orders are very clear." Madani replied carefully, tapping his clipboard with checked off names.

"No, you don't have the authority to allow it, Colonel. But I do." Javad stepped closer to the man, so close that he could smell the man's last meal. Javad continued quietly, "I have orders as well. Mine come from a higher authority than those that provided you with yours. I will be going. In this aircraft. This is all carefully planned. You don't have all the information. Need to know, Colonel."

"Director, with respect, we've planned space very carefully. There are no empty seats. There is no space."

"I don't require a seat up front. I will be traveling with the cargo. There is space in the rear, isn't there?"

"There is but it's restricted to the technicians. Even the men up front are separated from the cargo by the locked bulkhead door for security reasons."

Javad didn't respond right away but let silence and a few moments fill the meager space between them. It was an old tactic. Javad stared down the colonel. He was a good engineer, but Javad was trained to break people and so he would.

"Colonel, let us be candid. Your stellar work shouldn't be tarnished by a lack of judgement. You know me as a Director in the Ministry of Intelligence. I am also a full general. Those four stars put me a full five ranks above you,

Colonel. I know what the cargo is and vetted all the technicians. I'm going with it as my mission and orders dictate. Walk away and receive your accolades. Know that I am no longer asking."

"Of course, Director. I'm sorry, General."

"Salam, Colonel Madani. May God care for you." He said it very formally. He truly meant it. The colonel looked at him and nodded, his understanding of the situation skewed to his knowledge of it. Javad turned and climbed the stairs. He stopped at the top. A thought popped into his mind. He looked down the fuselage of the passenger plane toward the front stairs.

"Colonel, one last question."

"Yes?"

"Which aircraft is Head of Battalion Kabiri on? Just so I know where the commander is when we reach our destination? Also, what is the target destination of this aircraft?" he asked.

The colonel thought for a moment. Then waved an arm toward the plane Javad was about to board. "This is the last plane. It's target is Washington D.C.

"And Kabiri?

"Head of Battalion Kabiri is also on this plane. Salam, General." The man turned and walked away.

Javad's blood went cold. He looked down the outside of the plane's fuselage. He could end this now. Or could he? Too many variables. Would he be able to even identify him in the crowded cabin? No. He choked down bile. Breathe. He forced himself to turn and enter the rear of the plane.

There were three men sitting in seats all facing inward with their backs to the covered windows. It was brightly lit. There were several empty seats. Odd, if they had planned everything out, why were there extra seats? It didn't matter. He stepped past the man on his side and took a seat. He looked at the three men, one to his left and two across from him. They all stared at him. They were in camouflage uniforms, boots, no hats, helmets, or insignia though. All had short, dark hair and were clean shaven.

"Salam. I am going with you on orders from the highest authority. Do your jobs and ask no questions. Do you understand what I've told you?"

They nodded. Javad exhaled a long-held breath as the engines started to spin up and the door was secured. He finally noticed the large, gray cylindrical object that rested on small, rubber rollers. They were attached to a substantial looking track parallel to the fuselage. The object was secured with straps and took up most of the space between Javad and the technicians on the other side of the cabin. The pointy end facing the rear and fins toward the nose of the aircraft. He felt a sense of menace.

Its purpose was singular.

It was one of twenty-four. One for each 727. Iran didn't have the fissile material for these, even after decades of trying. That material had come from their North Korean friends. Just enough smuggled out, while the rest was given up in the landmark nuclear deal the NoKo's had made with the United States, China, and Russia. A contingency plan of sorts, he mused. A side deal he'd made with the Chinese. If things went sideways and the Americans or their allies were able to test any of the blast sites for radioactive residue, their analysis would show the plutonium had come from one of the North Korean's nuclear reactors and not Iran. Of course, it wouldn't matter in the end. Not to him. The plane lurched forward and taxied out of the hangar. They were airborne in minutes. He drifted into slumber.

*Javad knew he was dreaming because his wife, Yasmin, was talking tenderly to him about their daughter, Sara. He couldn't hear most of her words, but he could see her smiling face.*

*Yasmin. Ahmed's sister.*

*She had almost kept him from his fate. She'd brought light back into his life—for a time. His sister's murder and the long years during the war had taken their toll on him. He'd kept busy with his newly found career in the ministry of intelligence until Ahmed had invited Yasmin over to the flat that evening. They were well into their forties when they'd been married. She'd studied abroad and become a doctor in the United Kingdom and had only arrived home recently. She was as wrapped in her career as he was in his, but with the happy reconnection, driven by an amused Ahmed, they'd courted and then married.*

*His dream was hectic, changing.*

*A year after their marriage, they'd welcomed their daughter into the world. They named her Sara, in memory of his sister. He'd never been as happy as he was then, before or since.*

*His dream shifted again to a stark and dim hospital room. He was looking down at her again on the bed. Her cold hand in his. The inept doctor said there was nothing more he could do. Javad screamed as the doctor turned and left. Yasmin's body became blurry as tears welled in his eyes. Javad added another reason to his list. Ticking them off, one at a time.*

*Such a long, sorrowful list.*

# SIXTEEN

It was cold this morning. Colder than Gunnery Sergeant An Nguyen would like, but it was a chill in his bones that he felt. A terrible morning it was. Cold wrapped in sorrow starting at around 0200 hours when his brother had called to let him know their father had passed away. That was hours ago. He now stood just outside his M1A2 Abrams Main Battle Tank staring out over the fighting positions his Second Platoon, the Blackhearts, were in at the moment. They were preparing for live fire training as part of their pre-deployment activities. They were deploying in two months to Afghanistan to relieve the Marine Battalion on duty. So, the Company was here in Fort Knox. He didn't mind training with the Army. They were good tankers. Not as good as his Marines, but still badass tankers.

His emotions were getting to him now. He took a second to compose himself. Several rounds of this mental exercise had to be accomplished this morning, not for himself but for his Marines. They all knew about his father by now, but he was a leader and his Marines came first. It was his job to spin up his replacement who would be taking over for him for the next few days. He'd booked a seat with his twin brother, Bao, on the red-eye flight from Louisville International Airport to Dulles Airport in Northern Virginia tonight. He'd be home by the morning. Christmas morning.

"Your timing is horrible, Dad," he said out loud to himself.

Or maybe it wasn't. He'd at least be with his family over Christmas for a few days before returning.

"Too early in the morning to be talking to yourself Gunnery Sergeant."

An jumped as Lieutenant Nelson walked up behind him and put a hand on his shoulder. They both stood staring out over the dark firing range east of the fort, overlooking the mountains of northern Kentucky and the Salt River, with the Ohio river just north of them.

"Morning Lieutenant. Funny what days like this will do to your mental status. Shouldn't you be with your crew, Boss?" he said.

"I should be, but someone in my track crop dusted the fucking thing and I needed fresh air. Are you booked?"

"I am, Sir. Thank you. I know it's a bad time for this, but my crew is ready. They've trained hard. Who's my replacement?"

"We're going to move Sergeant Jones up in your place. He needs some time up top. I'm stealing a gunner from First Platoon. One of their tracks is out of commission at the moment. It'll give Jones a good few days of command experience and he better not fuck it up or I'll be on your ass when you get back."

"Oorah, Lieutenant!"

"Let's mount up and put rounds down range Gunny. We've got a long day and I want this platoon on target for the next hour. Then I'll have a debrief and First Sergeant Dubois will have corrective actions to go over and then we'll hit it again before chow."

"Yes, Sir!"

The Lieutenant headed to his track and An walked around his doing a last tread check prior to climbing up next to the turret where his Loader, Private First Class Milton Stewart, was keeping watch, smoking a cigarette. There was no easy or graceful way of getting up onto the tank. He stood next to it for a minute and took in his home away from home. The thing was massive and was literally nicknamed *The Beast*. Twelve feet wide and almost twenty-six feet long and if you counted the 120mm smoothbore gun it extended to thirty-two feet. Eight feet tall, including the turret, which is why it was a comedy of errors trying to get up on it. With effort, he pulled himself up.

There was also no surefire way to get into his fighting position in the Commander's hatch without tweaking his shin, or his back, or his elbow. However, it was an easier gig than his driver had, for sure. A BMW this was not, although some thought these tanks drove like one. It was all function, form be damned. Even though there was a majestic look and feel to the beast beneath him.

Power, authority, freedom.

He took one last look at the range in the distance and began the process of lowering himself into his hole. He was halfway in, going too fast, when his left hip bone hit the side of the hatch. He stifled some more than salty vocabulary and stopped to rub his side to ease the pain. Now lowered into his seat, which was comically padded, he looked around and surveyed his position. The targeting system and laser range finder provided split second adjustments to the cannon prior to the Gunner actually putting steel on target even when they were rolling at speed with the stabilized gun that remained on target when the tank beneath it moved over uneven ground.

"Alright, Stewie?" An asked his Loader.

"Ready to feed the beast Boss-man," his Loader replied in his Alabama accent, referring to the main gun and his job of feeding whatever type of rounds his commander ordered him to load.

"Roger that."

An donned his helmet. Once he was all plugged in and situated in the right side commander's seat he keyed the mic.

"Sergeant Jones, you up?"

"Up Boss. Ready when you are."

"Lance Corporal Fletcher, are you awake?" Fletch had a habit of falling asleep at the drop of a hat anywhere and anytime he could, so it was a valid question.

"Here, Gunny! Want me to spin up?" He also had a twang to his voice, not as bad as Stewie, but still there. Not Alabama, but Oklahoma.

"Okay, Fletch, start it up and move into wing position on Tank One. Let's get some heat radiating in here. Freezing my ass off."

The engine was a massive gas turbine engine that could run on multiple types of fuel and could get the heavy tank up to forty-five miles per hour or more depending on the terrain. The heater in the tank was next to worthless, but the jet engine that powered this hulking monster actually radiated heat into the crew compartment, which was nice. Until it got too hot. Then they were sweating their balls off. Opening a hatch didn't help much either. Another nice benefit of having a jet engine under him was that most of the engine sound was vented out the back of the tank. Standing to the rear it was as loud as a jet engine. If you were in front of the tank, it was much quieter.

At a distance, you could barely hear it if it was coming at you. That's where its other nickname, *Whispering Death*, came from. You barely heard the tank before it ran you over.

They were Tank Two out of the four-tank platoon. The platoon sergeant's tank was Tank Four and his wingman on the other side of the formation was Tank Three. Their tank had a third nickname, *Alice*. Their company commander had used the name in a derogatory manner over an open channel once. That was due to the fact that Fletch had gotten them in a bit of a predicament and nearly stuck as a new driver while while his crew participated in the Marine Armored Crewmember Course at Fort Benning in Georgia. An remembered it precisely.

*"Two, Six Actual. Hey, Alice! The hell are you doing in that treeline? What are you, a little woodland faerie? Get the hell outta there and rejoin formation. Now!"*

When he heard their commander over the open net, Fletch finally found his balls. With the whole crew goading him, he escaped the treeline that he wasn't supposed to be traversing in the first place. They had immediately stenciled the *Alice* on the main gun. Now it was a source of pride and Fletch was one of the most skilled drivers in the Company. *Alice* was a bitch anyway. Little Woodland Faeries had anger management issues, especially this one.

An felt the engine's power as Fletch revved the engine after about a minute. "Spinning Boss! Ready to fight!"

"Roger. Let's go, Driver, and try not to give me whiplash."

They slowly moved forward with the other three tanks into the prepared firing positions. An got great humor out of verbally jacking up his crew. He knew the tank would roll smooth as a baby's butt, as it was designed to do, but he gave Fletch shit anyway. Normality. It was still somewhat dark so they would be training on night vision for a while. An's thoughts were no longer dwelling on his father. He was fully focused on the task at hand. There would be plenty of time for memories on the flight later tonight as *Alice* rolled out into the morning twilight.

# SEVENTEEN

December 24 - 1:00pm EST
Gale Washington
December 25 - Midnight
South China Sea

Major Tang and Captain Liu sat in their H-6K Bomber ready for take-off from Fiery Cross Air Base in the South China Sea. They now knew their target was the U.S. Naval Communications Station Holt, at the northwest tip of Australia. They sat quietly in the cockpit, cruise missiles loaded, the bomber's engines spun up. Tang had 4 CJ-20 cruise missiles on external pylons under the wings. Each missile had a 500 pound high explosive warhead and a range of about 1,000 miles. He and his wingman were to fly their two aircraft to within 800 miles of northwest Australia and launch their combined eight missiles at the antenna complex, completely taking it out and, with it, the American's capability to transmit messages to their submarines worldwide. This wasn't the only antenna complex the Americans had, but it was the one he was focused on. The others were someone else's problem. Once launched, the missiles would cruise just meters above the water until popping up at the last minute to gain full GPS and visual lock on the complex. The targets were the main central antenna tower and power supply complex. There should be nothing left.

They had enough fuel to get to the missile release coordinates. Once the missiles were on their way, they would turn back, meeting up with a refueling tanker so they could fill up and get back to the island. Assuming all went according to the plan. in about eight and a half hours they'd be back on the island.

"Tiger Flight, you are mission clear. Good luck, Tiger Flight!"

The voice in his helmet sounded enthusiastic. He was not, just anxious.

He was about to start World War III. While he wasn't as enthusiastic as the voice from the tower, that didn't mean he didn't put his game face on. When they were briefed on the mission and the wider situation, he'd had momentary doubt. He joined the PLA's Air Force to protect China. Not to sneak attack the Americans. He had no fight with them. The doubt passed quickly though, knowing if he was to disobey orders, he'd be relieved of command, marched out to the water's edge, shot in the head. His body allowed to float away for the sharks to finish off. Worse than that, his family would be imprisoned or shot as well, bringing dishonor to his name. That would not be on his conscious. This thing was going to happen with or without him. He was resigned to his role in it now.

His bomber was at the end of the small island's runway. He gave his co-pilot a thumbs up and they pushed the engine throttles forward. The bomber quickly gained speed as they rolled down the runway. The end was fast approaching as he pulled back on the yoke and rotated the bomber's nose up. He adjusted course and climbed to their cruising altitude toward Australia.

❋ ❋ ❋

On the other side of the world, Gale was skinning and washing potatoes in his kitchen. His potato hoard would become a tasty mash for the shindig across the street this evening. Layla, Sara, and Alex were upstairs in Layla's room doing whatever it was that teenage girls do. He didn't have a need to know, he'd been told.

It was another clear and crisp day outside. The late afternoon sun coming in through the family room windows warmed the house. He was able to keep the thermostat down to a manageable level, even though the girls wanted to jack it up to hell's front porch. He'd told them to layer.

The whole street was coming to the party. Robert had requested a lot of mashed potatoes to go with the roast and other sides he was making. There would be free flowing booze, knowing him. Gale was looking forward to the call with Joey at 6:00 p.m. just before heading over. He missed her. He was glad Layla and her friends liked to hang at the house. It filled it up with chaos and noise. It almost made up for Joey's absence. Almost.

The phone on his hip started going off. It startled him. His ringtone was

Godzilla's roar. He dried his hands quickly and plucked the phone from its holster. "This is Gale."

"Gale? Dennis."

This couldn't be good if the director was calling him at home on Christmas Eve. And he didn't really work for Dennis anymore.

"Hey Dennis. What's up?"

"Sorry to bother you on Christmas Eve. I know you have things going on, but I need you to come in. I'm on my way as well."

"Okay, I'll start in. What's going on?" he asked, knowing that Dennis probably wouldn't be able to tell him over the phone.

"We've got comms and anomalies in your area. I need you to get in here and take a look. Probably nothing major, but it's concerning to the watch officer. That's all I can tell you until you get in."

"On the way. See you shortly."

He ended the call as he heard Dennis say goodbye. You kicked me off your team Dennis! Gale yelled in his head, looking at the phone. Then he looked down at all the potatoes on the counter and took a deep breath and exhaled. All the evening's plans cleared out of his mind. He focused on what exactly Dennis had meant by "comms and anomalies." He hadn't even showered this morning. He ran up the stairs two at a time and banged on Layla's door. It popped open immediately as if someone was going to come out just as he knocked.

"Ahh!" Alex screamed and fell to the floor, laughing hysterically.

Gale looked at Layla sitting up on her queen-sized bed. "Layla, I just got an emergency call to go into work. I don't know how long I'll be, but there are potatoes all washed on the counter. I'm gonna need you to make the mashed potatoes. Have your hysterical friend here, and Sara, help you. I'll call when I know more about when I'll be home. Hopefully I'll be able to make the call with your mom, but if I don't, tell her I said hi and then head on over to the party. I'll join you when I can."

"Roger that! We got this. Come on, Sara, bring the doofus." She said, heading downstairs with Sara, who was trying to get Alex up off the floor.

Gale quickly changed into jeans and a pullover sweatshirt and grabbed his favorite black baseball cap with an American flag on the front. As he passed Layla's room, he saw a bunch of drawings on her bed and went for a closer look. Layla didn't draw, but Alex did. These must be her work. They were all various forms of skulls and skeletons etched in black chalk. Some with paint. He'd say they were pretty dark, but all the skulls were smiling, happy skulls. She had talent, he thought, as he turned and ran down the stairs in his tennis shoes. With keys and wallet in hand, he headed out to the car hearing his daughter yell "Po-ta-toes!" He loved her humor. As he pulled out of the driveway he saw Lou walking Christopher. He slowed and rolled the window down.

"Hey, Lou! Got called into work, last minute. Hopefully, I'll be back for the party. Layla and the girls are making the mashed potatoes now. They'll be over with them later."

"No worries, Gale. We'll have them until you get back. Hope everything's okay."

"Yeah, me too. Just some nervous nellies," Gale said.

"Hey, by the way, just ran into Mama Nguyen and Brook. They're back from the funeral home making the arrangements. I'm heartbroken for them Gale but Mama's sons will be here tomorrow, An and Bao. They both got emergency leave. Too bad they couldn't be here now, but tomorrow will do. I'm gonna miss my chess games with the old Sergeant. He was a good man and raised two good men…"

"Do you think they'll be over at your place tonight?" Gale asked.

"I asked them, and while Brook hesitated, Mama jumped for it. You know her. Always wants to be in the thick. She's in there right now making some food to bring. Not even her husband's passing slows her down. I really think she needs to not be alone in that house without the Sergeant. She was her own cheerful self when I was talking with them, but I could see it wasn't in her eyes. The light was gone."

"Well, let's try to get that light back, at least for tonight. I gotta roll. Be back soon."

Lou nodded and stepped back pulling on Christopher's leash to keep the pug from getting squished.

He made it to the Ops Center in twelve minutes. There was practically no traffic. He pulled up to the gated entrance to the building's parking lot and showed his badge to the security officer in the booth.

"Working on Christmas Eve, Gale? I hope they're giving you overtime, man."

"Yeah, won't be here long, hopefully. Merry Christmas!"

Gale drove through the gate and into a parking spot close to the building's entrance. The building itself was a one story, brick structure with few windows. He got to the front door and put his badge to the reader. It beeped and he heard the door latch unlock. He walked inside to a small lobby with more guards behind thick glass.

"Merry Christmas, guys!" Gale said as he walked through the lobby to the interior locked door.

He put his badge up to another reader and opened the door onto the exterior hallway. He walked about twenty feet to yet another door, repeated the badge process, this time entering into a small vestibule and tossed his phone in one of the cubby holes along the wall. Cell phones and other electronic devices weren't allowed inside. The Operations Center for Joint Intelligence Command had representatives from most agencies and military branches. As he entered, he could tell there was more activity than would be normally on a holiday. The Ops Center was a large room encased in glass. He saw Dennis and others in the smaller, glass-encased room they called the Fish Bowl.

Dennis beat him in. It looked like the leads for each Intel area were present. Interesting. Something big was going on. The Fish Bowl was so named because everyone could see you, like fish. Dennis saw him coming and waved him in emphatically. He badged into the Fish Bowl, the heavy glass door closed slowly behind him.

"Thanks for coming in. You have to look at this."

Dennis pointed to several large monitors at the end of the room that were suspended from the ceiling. The rest of the staff in the room were looking at laptops in front of them, power and LAN cables strewn all over the corporate-like conference table. He looked up at the middle monitor and he recognized it at once. He used this daily. It was the satellite tracking system that monitored various satellites from less than friendly countries. It startled him just a bit to see two satellites highlighted on the monitor. They were the North Korean satellites.

"Why are the NoKo's up? Are they burning in after all this time?" he asked

Dennis, knowing whatever came out of North Korea was less than state of the art.

"If only. We have pings. On both of them. Simultaneously. Thoughts?"

"Really? Both at the same time?"

"Yeah. What do you make of it? Could it be a malfunction of some sort?"

"Um, they malfunctioned by turning on?"

There were several barks of laughter around the table. Dennis shot them a dirty look and silence returned.

"Well, Mr. Funny Pants, we can't figure this out. They started pinging, sending short radio transmissions, about an hour ago and it's been steady since. Communications have been restored to these two long dead North Korean satellites. On Christmas Eve. What do you make of it?"

# EIGHTEEN

The four command centers were fully staffed at this point. Deep, underground bunker complexes. Each near their capital cities. With the exception of the Russians, who were well to the east, under the Ural Mountains. The cities themselves were bustling with normal traffic, restaurants were open, markets were full of people. Except the one, which had no real restaurants, markets, or traffic. North Korea in winter was a place of misery, hunger, and poverty. Even though sanctions had been lifted partially four months ago with the nuclear deal and peace initiatives, things didn't change overnight. Beijing, Moscow, and Tehran all looked as they should, if anyone was watching. They all looked peaceful and normal, but deep in the bunkers, activity was frenetic.

It was H-Hour. One hour, the last hour, before action. The Chinese were first. It was 6:00 a.m. in Beijing on December 25. Under the watchful eyes of the Chairman, they were once again in the hidden room in the Western Hills. The officer typed on the secure, encrypted chat application on his smart phone and hit send. It said only "Khan." This was the code word for the Chinese part of the operation. It conveyed their readiness.

The aide nodded to the Chairman, who then looked around the room at the other ministers and generals, and waited.

\*\*\*

Across the Asian continent, a smart phone dinged where it lay on a small conference table in one of several bunkers here deep under the Ural Mountains fifteen-hundred miles east of Moscow. The female FSB officer picked up the phone and read the comment out loud so that all in attendance could hear. She looked to her left, where the Russian President sat quietly. She looked at the digital clock on the wall, 2:00 a.m. on December 25.

"The Chinese are ready," she said.

On his nod, she sent the Russian code word signaling their readiness.

She put the phone down and looked at the large maps on the wall opposite her above the heads of the Russian General Staff, who sat talking over final preparations. She looked again to her left and locked eyes with the President. She nodded to him and he returned the nod, emotionless. She looked back at the maps on the wall. Her husband, another FSB officer and member of the Spetznaz, was in the U.S. right now. He was with a small team in the state of Maine. They would get their go code shortly. Her eyes began to well, but she forced the tears away. Would she ever see him again? Would they ever lay on the beach together again? Would he be able to get to their daughter?

They gave her up years ago. That wasn't the right turn of phrase. Coerced from them, is more appropriate. Her and Ivan had to make hard choices about their careers and their daughter was given the best life she could have imagined with Yerik and Tatyana. They were agents in the FSB, like her, but they were covert assets. Spies. They had taken her beautiful baby girl just after she gave birth to her. They were supposed to go to the United States as a family. However, Tatyana couldn't have children and the powers that be took advantage of the situation. They said it was for the good of Russia. Over the years, her and Ivan came to deeply regret their choice. They were told they'd be given pictures and later, some contact. That had never been allowed. Now there was hope. Ivan would get to her and then she would get to them. The people in this room didn't know this, but fog of war was their advantage. Being an FSB agent, she had her own resources in Russia and beyond. When things calmed down here, she'd make her exit and begin her journey. Much of her capital had been expended to get her from here to Saint-Petersburg. Favors had been called in. She hoped when this was over they could live somewhere in peace and quiet, raise children and have grand-children, happiness and peace. A dream she put in the hands of some unpleasant people. She stared blankly at the monitors on the wall. She could also be unpleasant.

\* \* \*

The iPhone that sat on the table, probably the only iPhone in the whole country, dinged, breaking the tense silence. The North Korean woman picked it up and looked at it. It said only "Tsar." The time at the top of the phone read 7:00 a.m. She looked up at the General across from her.

"The Russians and Chinese are ready," was all she said.

The general was the top ranking official in the Operations Center deep under a mountain outside Pyongyang. Their leader was somewhere else in another bunker. She'd never met him personally. He'd been a ghost to her throughout this whole operation.

"Send our response. We are ready."

"It is done, General." They waited for the Iranians. The last piece would fall into place in moments. The general picked up the receiver to a rotary phone. She had seen the newer technology and this phone seemed as if it had been here for decades. He spoke to the satellite operations center in the north of the country.

\* \* \*

In Tehran, the Minister of Iran's Intelligence Agency, was pacing outside the room where leadership was sequestered. They were not in a bunker, but in a small wing of a mosque in central Tehran. Operations were handled out of the bunkers, but the Council desired to be in a Mosque for this. He didn't care either way. He was anxious and repeatedly glanced at the clock on the wall, which now said 1:30 a.m. They were eight and a half hours ahead of Washington here. The phone in his hand dinged. He looked down at it. On the screen in the secure app were two words, "Dear Leader." He exhaled and typed in the Iranian code word and turned to inform them of the good news. They were going to kill the Great Satan!

\* \* \*

In the Western Hills outside Beijing, the last code word was received. It said only "God is Greatest." This set in motion the last step. A broadcast message, pre-set to go to all operational units and teams around the globe. This was done via a phone call by the Chairman to the Chinese Military Command

Center that sits within the same underground complex that the Chairman and General Staff sat in now. The Chairman replaced the phone in its cradle and turned with his hands grasped together behind his back. He stood staring at the wall maps. Within thirty seconds the "GO" message would be broadcast to all operational units of all four countries and in a little less than one hour, there would be no going back. He sat heavily in his chair. Their course was set.

# NINETEEN

The two H-6K Heavy Bombers had cruised at high altitude for most of the trip to extend their range. They were fast approaching launch point for their eight cruise missiles, four on each bomber, and two under each wing, hanging maliciously, awaiting their turn to dance. A dance is what it was, Tang thought. Their dance partner just didn't know they were dancing yet. The Japanese had done this to the Americans in 1941. Ultimately, it had backfired. Major Tang was a good soldier. He followed orders. Following orders gave him the peace of mind that his family would be okay. He'd see them again. It was still crazy, though. Had the geniuses thought of everything? Would this backfire like Pearl Harbor backfired? Was America still the sleeping giant or was China the giant now? He pondered these thoughts as Captain Liu broke into his comms through his headset.

"We're thirty seconds from launch, Major," Liu said calmly.

Was he thinking the same things? He and his co-pilot had been together for over two years now, but they didn't speak about these things. You never really knew who would report conversations that questioned the decisions of the People's Liberation Army back to their political officers. He snapped back to the task at hand. They'd recently descended to just one thousand feet above the sea after they'd gotten south of Java. They couldn't risk releasing the missiles at a higher altitude. Everyone in the immediate region would pick up two blips on their radar turning into ten. There would be no warning. There were no naval ships in the area either. He'd been assured of that prior to takeoff.

"Acknowledged. Waiting on the go order."

They waited. Tang looked down at his watch, 0530 hours. It was Christmas Day here. It was 1700 hours in Washington, DC on the previous day, Christmas Eve. This was going to hurt. Not him, he thought, but the Americans.

The radio came alive in his headset just then. "The Moon has Risen over Mongolia." The message repeated twice more.

"Tiger Flight," Tang said into his microphone, "weapons free. Release, release, release."

The two bombers fired their cruise missiles one at a time until the wings were bare.

"Set course to refueling point."

Within the hour, the U.S. antenna complex wouldn't exist. Yes, this was going to hurt bad.

# TWENTY

Lt. Colonel Maxwell "Coop" Cooper, or Coyote, his call sign, had just taxied out to the runway in his F-16C loaded with wingtip Sidewinder air-to-air missiles and 20mm ammunition for the M61A1 Vulcan cannon mounted inside the fuselage to the left of the cockpit. He was heading to Langley Air Force Base in South Eastern Virginia to run Combat Air Patrol exercises with the Virginia Air National Guard. The light had long faded on the ground in central South Carolina at Shaw Air Force Base. His helmet display was lit up as he did final checklist procedures for takeoff when the tower squawked in his ears.

"Hooligan One, Tower," the voice said in his ears.

Hooligan was his flight's callsign and the "One" designated his aircraft in that flight, even though he was the only one in the flight at the moment he would get the rest of his flight at Langley.

"Tower, Hooligan One, go ahead."

"Hooligan One, we have a new mission for you. Possible commercial air-craft hijacking. You are the closest available asset. Moon Rise Airlines flight 1068, a 727 tracking from Charleston, South Carolina to Miami, Florida. Aircraft is not responding to the tower and is out of course alignment, per-forming slow turns off the Georgia coast. Once in the air, heading will be South East. Flight 1068 is at 31,000 feet, 450 knots airspeed, descending. Will vector and provide additional guidance once airborne. Cleared for takeoff. Expedite. Copy?"

"Copy, Tower."

Holy shit, he thought to himself as he pushed the throttle to full power.

The fighter literally jumped down the runway. Once airborne, he climbed nearly vertical and started his turn southeast. The bogey, or flight 1068, was well within his F-16's combat radius and he pushed the throttle to the stops eventually hitting just under Mach 2 or about 1,100 miles per hour at this altitude. He would intercept in approximately twelve minutes. He kept climbing until he reached 33,000 feet. He wanted to come in just above the target. It would be twilight at altitude by the time he intercepted.

Coyote received more information about the aircraft from Charleston Tower and now assumed that all eyes would be on him to decipher what was going on. He had never heard of Moon Rise Airlines. Apparently, it was a new joint carrier out of Iran, of all places. What were they doing here?

"Hooligan One, this is Savannah Tower."

"Go, Savannah Tower."

"Hooligan One, Moon Rise Airlines flight 1068 has ceased squawking. We see no transponder pings at this time. Copy?"

With this information, he adjusted course for intercept and switched on his target acquisition radar.

"Copy, Savannah Tower. Trying to acquire. Stand by."

The radar was fed to his helmet display. There she was. Bogey was heading southwest just off the coast. She was at ten miles and a bit lower than he was so he descended down to the bogey's altitude and closed from behind. It was pretty at ground level. He could make out the coast line by the line of lights off to his right. To the left was nothing but darkness over the ocean. There was still a soft glow of light over the western horizon.

He decreased airspeed to match the 727 at about 425 knots. They had leveled off at 28,000 feet. He came in gently just below and to the right behind the aircraft at about a quarter of a mile. No lights. None of the window shades were up. The whole plane was blacked out. He radioed in what he saw and said he would try to make contact with the cockpit visually since there was no response over the radio.

He maneuvered his fighter up and even with the cockpit. He was very close now, about twenty yards off the right side. He could see two pilots in the cockpit. The co-pilot in the right hand seat was looking out the windshield at him and his F-16. He barely made out a wave of a hand. He waved back and did a thumbs up and then a thumbs down gesture to see if they would respond.

To his surprise, the co-pilot gave what appeared to be an enthusiastic thumbs up in response and pointed to his headset and waved horizontally back and forth conveying that they had no comms. Coyote then pointed to the ground emphatically trying to relay that he wanted them to land and he then waved forward for them to follow him down. The co-pilot gave him a thumbs up again. He increased speed a bit to pull ahead of the 727 and started a slight descent and right turn hoping that they would follow him back to Savannah and land. He radioed back his situation.

Coyote was about a half mile in front of the Moon Rise Airlines 727 and leaning into his right turn when his headset squealed.

"What the hell!"

The squealing meant that a target radar had locked onto his fighter. He turned his head as far around to the right as he could in time to see part of the under fuselage break off and fall away with sparks and something else drop from where that piece had just been. Then he saw the bright flash of the rocket fuel ignite. Missile!

He jinked the fighter hard right and down and deployed flares, but at this distance he knew it wasn't enough.

"Mayday! Mayday! Mayday! Hostile has engag…"

The missile flew directly into his engine exhaust vent and exploded, breaking apart the fighter over the ocean mid-transmission.

❋ ❋ ❋

Ivan was thinking of his wife while he monitored his phone. She was somewhere in the Ural Mountains right now. Or more accurately, under them. It was surreal how they were so far apart, but so connected by this mission. They'd met during training in the FSB years back and were married shortly after graduating from what was known as "Spy School." The FSB was less sinister in reality than its predecessor, the KGB, but just as effective, he thought. His musings were interrupted by his phone's screen lighting up with the code phrase "The Moon Rises over Mongolia."

Game time.

His team's mission was to destroy an antenna complex situated on a spit of land that jutted out into the Atlantic Ocean. It was just a few miles south of the Canadian border in Northeast Maine, where he and his men sat in two, old, non-descript vans. Nova Scotia was just across the water and the wider North Atlantic Ocean. This part of Maine was very sparsely populated. His core team sat with him in the two vans at an elementary school less than a mile up the street from the antenna complex's entrance. It had the bite of Siberia outside and the wind brought the temperature down to the negatives. The second half of his team would approach the southwest coast of the little peninsula by boat, gaining access to the dock next to the complex's power supply building. Their job was to kill the power. His team's job was to knock down the main antennas.

The North Array and the South Array were both arranged in star patterns connected by wires to a very tall central antenna in the middle of each. There were four of these complexes. The U.S. uses them to send very low frequency messages to their submarines around the world. The others were in Hawaii, near Seattle, and the extreme Northwest corner of Australia. Those would be dealt with by other means or teams. This one was his. He didn't know the full plan. They just had to wait for the lights to go out and that was the signal to take out the complex. Unfortunately, they had to kill the personnel. No survivors.

He understood his mission was only a backup. Parts of this complex were hardened against EMP like the power supply building. Much of the connecting power was underground. The antenna wires should be fried when the EMP hit them, if that's what was going to happen. He assumed it was the only way all the lights die at once. That's why he was told to get these old vehicles. His job was to put this place out of commission permanently. He was an insurance policy.

Less than half an hour now. The sun had set. It was already dark on the coast. He could see lights across the water and within the complex. His boat team should have made their gradual turn toward the dock by now, slowly closing the distance. There shouldn't be too many personnel on duty here tonight. He expected a skeleton crew on Christmas Eve. Maybe six people, some armed, maybe. They'd deal with it quickly. They all had night vision goggles, their targets didn't. Darkness would be their friend this evening.

# TWENTY-ONE

December 24
5:30pm EST
3:30pm MST
Shan Chao

Chao was sitting in front of the wood burning stove, as he had most every day since they had arrived. Darkness was beginning to fall with the ever present snow outside. As beautiful as it was, he understood the gravity of what was about to happen. He couldn't appreciate the solitude of the place because of it. Gravity. Weight of his responsibility for his team and their mission. It was heavy on him. He and Gao had discussed their situation in private several times without the major and his irritating bluster.

The U.S. Minuteman III ICBM bases were located here. Gao had explained all of this during one of their chats. There were three bases, but the individual silos at each base were spread far and wide through the northern plains of the U.S. He was surprised they'd gotten this far without being confronted. Planning had begun years ago and it was something of a marvel to him.

He looked at Feng, sitting across from him. Their chairs faced each other in front of the fireplace. Gao sat in one of the window seats with a blanket wrapped around her. She liked her comfort, but she had a toughness about her. It was where she sat each day between equipment checks and meal times. She had a mug of hot tea nestled between her hands. Steam rose in the air in front of her face. She grew quieter each day and barely spoke at all now.

DING.

All this time waiting and the major hesitated to pick up the phone. Chao leaned forward and noticed Gao turn her head to stare at Feng. The major reached for it, accidentally knocking it to the floor with a thud. Feng frantically reached down for it and picked it up, turning it over to see the screen.

"The Mongolian Moon is Full."

"Is that the go order?"

"It is."

They moved outside in unison. Chao surveyed the fighting positions they set up around the truck. Their plan was good. Not great, but good. They were ready. Several commandos took up position at the back of the truck. Just a bit longer.

They stared down at the small mountain town lit up in the valley below them knowing what to look for. Feng was the only one not watching the town. Chao didn't think he could think less of the man, until Feng climbed up into the cab of the truck to get out of the blowing snow, leaving the rest of them outside. What an entitled little shit.

Chao watched the valley in the diminishing light. The people below were preparing for their holiday. He wasn't a Christian and didn't care about their holiday, but it still bothered him that shortly their world would change forever. Such is war, he thought with resignation. He walked over to check with the major when Feng threw the door open.

"Captain! My phone's dead. It's time."

"Major, get in the driver's seat and try to start the engine."

"Nothing! Truck's dead!" Feng yelled. Chao spun to survey the town. No lights.

"Sergeant! Gao! It's time!" Chao barked. They began their rehearsed tasks.

They pulled heavy metal pins from various spots on the trailer's roof, sides, and rear. Once all the pins had been pulled and discarded, the commandos entered the container from the rear. Chao and Feng stood back as Gao gave instructions. The top and one side of the container began to move slightly up and sideways. As it did, the other side fell free to the snow-covered ground. He felt the impact in his feet. The other side, with the container's roof attached, fell free to the other side.

The commandos and Gao stood around the three S-400 Russian-built surface-to-air missiles, the radar dome, and it's monitor housing. Gao activated the radar systems and elevated the missiles to vertical. Still on the trailer bed, they stood ten meters tall. Chao hoped that the other teams spread around the northern plains all had similar good luck. They were the first line of defense of the homeland if the Americans decided to retaliate. Feng was probably correct that the Americans wouldn't know.

"All systems operational!" Gao shouted from the fire control radar housing. There were several radars employed here and they could track multiple contacts and guide multiple missiles at once. They were oriented northwest toward one of the three missile farms. Each farm had up to forty-five Minuteman III Intercontinental Ballistic Missiles in individual silos. They may not even need to fire one of these missiles, but time would tell. Until that time, they would wait. Gao and Feng would take turns manning the fire control radar. Feng was actually useful for something. He was the other missile operator. Chao didn't think that anything would happen immediately, so he checked with Gao. He turned and scanned the snow covered darkness around him. His team had disappeared again into their fighting positions. They were invisible. Chao touched Feng's arm and caused the man to jump.

"Let's get warm. They are on watch. We aren't. We need to sleep. Our turn out here will come soon enough."

"Lead the way," Feng said.

Chao was already walking back up the drive to the warmth of the cabin's fire. Adrenaline rushed through him. It would be difficult to sleep.

# TWENTY-TWO

December 24
5:45pm EST
Donneker

Kim Donneker sat in his car thinking. Eyes closed. He was calm, which was odd, considering what he was about to do. He thought about his wife, Susan. He wasn't going to see her again. Was it his fault that she left him? No. She was a crazy person. Always starting fights. He didn't need the meds and the couples therapy. That was her. She brought all this. Screw her and her therapy. She was the one that jacked him up all the time to the point where he had to get out of the house and go the few blocks to the neighborhood watering hole to drink. Then he'd oversleep and be late for work. It was her fault he couldn't focus and didn't meet his sales numbers. His boss was a hardass and didn't give him a chance. He had deals in the pipeline. Not his fault they were taking their own sweet time closing, but his manager didn't care. He let his boss have it last week in front of the whole team. He was told to go home and to come back in the morning after he cooled off. That's when they pulled him into a meeting with Human Resources and fired him.

He remembered calling Susan when he got back to his little one bedroom apartment on the opposite side of the neighborhood from his house. His wife's house now. He told her what happened and asked if he could he come over to talk. She seemed to feel sorry for him, but said no. Susan said he scared her. No contact. It's what the restraining order said. No contact at all. She didn't want anything bad to happen to him or her. She sent her teenaged son, Dallas, away to Kentucky to live with his father, her first ex, months ago because she was afraid of what he'd do to Dallas in one of his rages. Her ex was some colonel or something in the Army. Screw him. She said she was sorry, but she couldn't help him or be part of his life anymore and hung up.

Bitch! After today, he'd never have to deal with her again. He was afraid what he might do to her anyway. She'd totally deserve it though. He rubbed his bandaged right hand again unconsciously. There were several holes in the walls of his apartment after his call with her that night and it really messed up his knuckles. His hand still ached.

The pain brought his mind back to the task at hand. He had brought presents, of a sort, he thought. Most employees would be out today, but he knew the sales team, including his old boss, would be there late today and hadn't left yet. His manager's very expensive car was parked in the lot. They were working on several large deals with companies overseas in China and the Middle East. They didn't care if it was Christmas Eve or not. Just another day for them.

A thought popped into his head just then—if he lived, but was wounded, how he would pay for the medical bills he'd have after this? He shook his head, took a last drag from his cigarette and tossed it out the window. Stupid. You're not going to live through this. He'd miss his buddies at the bar, though. Jimmy and Dale were always good for listening and sharing stories as they drank. He was amazed at just how many men like him were in his same situation with their wives. Jimmy had a restraining order put on him by his wife, which he broke, putting him in county jail for a month. He'd gone to pick up Jimmy at the Adult Detention Center when he got released. That was a fun night, although none of them really remembered much of it. He didn't even know how he got back to his apartment. They'd hit the booze hard.

The apartments where he lived were next to some lower end townhouses, which transitioned to higher end townhouses. After that it was all single family homes. There were strip shopping centers here and there, and coffee shops and restaurants. There was so much money here. One of the most affluent places in the U.S. Donneker and his buddies would sit at the bar weekly and discuss this over drinks. They'd talk about world events and the crazy fat man over in North Korea. What if they nuked D.C.? It was their favorite topic. He supposed people would call them tinfoil hat wearers, but what if it happened? All hell would break loose and all these rich people with their nice homes and cars would be on the same level as him, Jimmy, and Dale, just like that. The field would be even. Rich and poor. All the same, except for those who had guns. He and his buddies would have the power then.

Jimmy and Dale thought he was crazy for the crap he got into with his wife. He had a good, well-paying job. Donneker had it the best out of the three of them. He had a bunch of guns in a safe in his basement. In her basement. Shit. She wouldn't let him come get them. How he hated her. Told them as much one night when they were deep into the booze. He'd told them that if anything ever happened to him, they could have the guns, just go get them. He'd warned them not to hurt her though, if she were there. They weren't bad dudes, just rowdy. They wouldn't really do it and they thought he was crazy for suggesting it. Something would happen to him today, though. Would they even remember what he had said about his guns after drinking so much? Probably not. Although, it was about that time of day when they'd be at the bar getting good and liquored up. He put the thought out of his mind. Things to do now.

# TWENTY-THREE

December 24 - 6:00pm EST
December 25 - 8:00am - Pyongyang

It was approaching 8:00 a.m. in Pyongyang. The operations center was quiet. It was deep underground, packed with high ranking military officers with ribbons and medals too numerous to count. They all stared at the big screens on the wall. It was comical, to a point. All these officers standing around him and his computer. There were other technicians and computers, but his was the important one. The big screen on the big wall showed two satellite tracks. Both satellites were moving slowly southward. One over North America. The other over Northern Europe. Several times a week since they'd been put into orbit, their tracks coincided with the middle of the United States and the middle of Western Europe. To be exact, the locations were Junction City, Kansas, where the time was approaching 6:00 p.m. on December 24, and Stuttgart, Germany, where midnight was about to pass from Christmas Eve to Christmas Day. Nearly there.

An old phone sat on the desk with his computer. The ranking general sat next to him. The phone would ring soon and the general would answer it. The phone was grayish with a rotary number dialer. It had been made in the 1960's. His computer was another story. There was a state of the art laptop in a docking station with a keyboard and optical mouse. On the mouse pad was a picture of the North Korean flag. From this laptop he accessed a program that controlled communications to both satellites. At the moment, there were several lines of code in two dialogue boxes on his monitor. Another dialogue box was open below those two. He kept scanning the lines of code, ensuring they were correct. His supervisor stood over his left shoulder, looking at the same lines of code, squeezing his shoulder, whispering to him that they were correct. They were both sweating profusely. It wasn't warm in the room.

In the third dialogue box, one line of code with a blinking cursor at the end of it awaited the push of the enter button. His hands were in his lap so as to not mistakenly hit any button prior to being told to.

RING!

The abrasive sound of the old phone's ringer cracked the silence in the room wide open. The general didn't hesitate and picked up the handset.

"We are ready, what are your orders?"

The general listened for a moment and said quickly, "It will be done."

He set the receiver back in its cradle and looked at him, emotionless.

"Execute the mission."

He exhaled a breath that he'd been holding since the phone rang. Taking one last look at the code in all three dialogue boxes, he felt a firm squeeze on his shoulder and moved his right hand to the "Enter" key and pressed it with the tip of his middle finger. Nothing happened. He stared at the screen feeling the general's eyes on him. Then another dialogue box popped up with the message "Command Executed." He looked at the general and nodded.

The general picked up the phone's handset again and dialed three numbers on the rotary dialer. He gave whoever was on the other end of the line a command to execute his mission and hung up.

Within two minutes, another screen on the wall began to track a ballistic missile rising from its launch site in the north of the country. It passed its initial phase within one minute and gained its optimal altitude and position within five minutes. Once there, just thirty miles above the southern Sea of Japan, exactly between South Korea and Japan, the small nuclear warhead in the tip of the missile detonated.

Within seconds of the explosion, the lights and power in South Korea and Japan would die. North Korea was also well within this affected area. Due to the lack of any real electrical grid, or vehicles with computers, or any computers for that matter, North Korea would be minimally impacted.

The general had one last call to make this morning. He dialed three numbers to reach his commander at the Demilitarized Zone.

# TWENTY-FOUR

December 24
6:00pm EST
Arlington, Virginia

The Joint Air Defense Operations Center, or JADOC in military parlance, was situated in a non-descript building on Joint Base Anacostia-Bolling on Bolling Air Force Base in Washington, D.C. After September 11, 2001, JADOC was built as a combined military and civilian intelligence agency operations center to monitor and protect the air space in and around the National Capitol Region. The room was busy, even on Christmas Eve. It was fully staffed twenty-four seven and on this evening, Lieutenant Colonel Scott Hemp was the Duty Officer. He pulled up a chair behind the Air Force Sergeant that was monitoring Hooligan One's intercept of Moon Rise Airlines Flight 1068.

"Do what?" Hemp snapped at the Sergeant.

"Hooligan One is gone, Sir. He broadcast a mayday. I thought he said that he had been engaged, but it cut out."

Hemp stood up and yelled to Air Traffic Radar Operations. "You got Hooligan One on scope? Where is he?"

"Colonel, Hooligan One's no longer on radar. No signature at all except for Flight 1068, which is continuing southwest."

"All hands! Listen up! I want alert fighters up now! Who's closest?"

"Quick reaction fighters from Shaw. Rolling now. Raptors."

"Tell 'em to treat this plane as an armed Hostile. Mission is Intercept and Destroy. You read me?"

"Yes, Sir! Instructions relayed, Sir! Twenty minutes."

"Roger that. Someone pull up a fucking map. What high value targets are in their path? I want to know where they're going."

Hemp picked up one of the desk phones near him and punched the button marked NMCC. It connected him with the National Military Command Center in the basement of the Pentagon.

"Colonel, I'm on the phone with Australian Joint Operations Command." A sergeant at another set of desk stations on the other side of the room yelled. "They're telling me that they just had a cruise missile attack on NAS Holt Communications Station in northwest Australia. The base and antennas are completely destroyed, Sir.

"Colonel!" A civilian analyst sitting a couple stations away got Hemp's attention before he could respond. "If the Hostile stays on current course, they'll fly over King's Bay, Georgia. That's our only base asset currently in or near their path."

"Fucking Christ!" He growled as a voice in the phone's receiver said for the third time, "NMCC."

"Hey! Yeah, this is JADOC, give me the Duty Officer now!"

The room went pitch black. Even the monitors were out. "Really!" He said to no one in particular. "Hello?" Nothing. The line to the NMCC was dead.

"Someone figure this out. Now! The line is dead to the Pentagon. I want a situation report asap!"

Flashlights began to light up the room. Hemp could see staff trying desk phones to no avail. He pulled out his smart phone and hit the button. It didn't come on. He hit the power button on the side. Not a blink. He stood there staring down at the expensive brick in his hand.

"EMP?" the Sergeant asked.

"Holy shit! Mother fuckers!" Hemp said, knowing what that meant. Electro-magnetic pulse. Caused by a coronal mass ejection from the Sun or a nuclear explosion high above the Earth. Hemp didn't think the Sun had such nefarious timing. He had a plane down, a Navy communications station attacked on the other side of the world, and an unknown passenger plane headed toward a nuclear ballistic missile submarine base in Georgia. There wasn't anything else he could do here with no power. They had to get to their alternate location west of D.C. That site was protected under a mountain and built to survive an EMP. He laughed out loud. With dead vehicles, how would they get there?

# TWENTY-FIVE

A few hours passed and they'd run all the normal technical and theoretical scenarios they could think of. Gale rubbed his face with both hands as he thought, then asked, "What's going on in the rest of the world right now? What's the fact pattern? Sound off around the table, guys. I'm out of ideas."

The various representatives from the agencies and military provided quick status on the global goings-on. Everything was relatively quiet. Iran was quiet. The Middle East was fairly quiet at the moment. North Korea was cooperating and looked to be denuclearizing. China was still flexing its military in certain areas, like the South China Sea, but they weren't being problematic, currently. Russia was doing some military exercises, but those had been planned for a year. Gale looked at the monitor with the satellites moving slowly over a backdrop of a map of the world. That was unsettling. One NoKo satellite was coming over the middle of the U.S. while the other satellite was coming over the center of Europe. Now they're pinging. The liaison from JADOC spoke.

"So, pretty quiet except that JADOC is reporting they scrambled an F-16 from Shaw to meet up with a passenger jet that isn't responding to traffic. The aircraft is Moon Rise Airlines flight 1068 tracking from Charleston to Miami. It's out over the Atlantic at the moment, but its current flight path is putting it on course with King's Bay, Georgia. It stopped squawking and non-responsive. Possible hijacking."

"Well, that's not normal. Where did it come from prior to Charleston? Find out what you can about Moon Rise Airlines as well. Anyone ever heard of that airline? I haven't. Where does it originate from?" Gale's mind was racing now. What the hell was this thing?

Several minutes went by as everyone went to work, but as usual, Google was the winner.

The Department of Homeland Security Liaison at the far end of the table spoke up. "Hey, it looks like Moon Rise Airlines is a brand spanking new passenger carrier. Its Iranian. They just started operations earlier this year, according to the Googs. Not much else."

"What the fuck?" The JADOC Liaison, a first lieutenant from the Air Force, said louder than he probably meant to. He had a head set on with an earpiece in one ear and a microphone hanging from the headset, near his mouth. "Say again JADOC."

All eyes were on him now and the room was silent. Gale noticed a bead of sweat forming on his forehead. He was leaning forward, resting on his muscular forearms over the phone. "Roger that, will advise Operations."

"What's is it, Lieutenant?" Dennis barked.

"Sir, they lost contact with Hooligan One, the ready fighter that was on route to intercept the Moon Rise Air flight. JADOC says Hooligan One reported he got hand signals from their cockpit indicating their comms were down. But seconds later, Hooligan One sent a Mayday. They think he was engaged somehow, but unknown from what or who. Hooligan One is gone. No radar signature, no squawk, nothing. Just gone."

All the lights in the Ops Center suddenly went out. All of them. Emergency lights didn't kick on, laptops and monitors were dark, it was pitch black.

"What the hell!" Dennis yelled. "Someone get a flashlight. Use your phone lights."

Gale felt his way by memory out to the cubby area and grabbed his phone and hit the button. Nothing. He yelled across the center as he came back. "Dennis! EMP! Those two NoKo satellites, when I looked at them a minute ago, were over the central U.S. and central Europe. They just started pinging earlier out of the blue? This was planned. My phone is dead. They fucking pulsed us!"

The room was silent. Then Dennis said, "Well, now what? If we're down, we're down. I agree with Gale. This has to be an attack. Hooligan One and now this? If the whole U.S. and Europe are in the dark, we're defenseless now. We can't even alert anyone."

An ethereal voice in the dark said, "Well, this is some real pretty shit right here, isn't it? Aren't the backup generators supposed to kick on? I don't hear 'em, which means we're all just sitting in a box with nothing to do."

Gale stood thinking. He could see people moving about. Layla. She popped into his mind like a thunderclap. Shit. Joey. Holy Mother…Joey! If those satellites had nukes on board and detonated in orbit, was the ISS still there?

He opened the door to the conference room. "Everyone huddle up and listen up!"

He took up a spot right in the middle of the Ops Center. The conference room emptied and all eyes were on him. Flashlights were pointed at the ceiling to cast as much light around the room as possible.

"Look, I believe that the two NoKo satellites were armed with nuclear weapons." Murmurs and curses rose from the group. "Settle down! Listen! They just detonated them above the U.S. and probably Europe. We've lost all contact with JADOC, our phones don't work, all the lights are out and the backup generator hasn't come on. I will bet all of you that none of our vehicles will start up either. An electro-magnetic pulse kills anything with sensitive electronic parts in it. Including cars that aren't stone-aged. What this means is we all need to think about what our individual next steps are."

Dennis was beside him now. This was Gale's area of expertise. Dennis nudged him on. These people were highly trained and professional, but this was different. Several shouted questions and there were some who'd just had the gravity of the situation hit them, as it hit him minutes ago.

"Okay, listen up! We obviously can't help here, or at all. We've got no comms. Everyone here has families and that needs to be our first priority now. First things first. Let's go see if any vehicles will start, just in case I'm wrong." Gale looked at Dennis then.

"Boss, you live east near JADOC. I live west. We need someone to report what we know."

"Getting ahead of ourselves, but yeah, anyone with a working vehicle probably needs to take me to JADOC before heading home, if you're willing. If any vehicle works. I know this is quick, but the rest of us need to start walking home before night really sets in. It's cold outside, so make sure you've got enough layers and cold weather gear. Forage around the building for emergency supplies, flashlights, anything else you'd need for the walk home. Go in groups in the same direction as far as you can. Also, just to be sure, grab your phones on the way out and see if any of them still work. Any questions or suggestions?"

"Hey, can we stay here until tomorrow morning, when it's warmer?" A female voice said from the back of the group. There were probably thirty or so people in the Ops Center including the guards.

"I'll stay with you." Another voice answered. "I live up in Maryland anyway. I'll need days to walk home, unless I can find and steal a bike. Not gonna start tonight though."

"Yes!" Dennis replied through the murmurs in the room. "If you don't want to walk tonight, stay. Go in the morning. You'll be warmer in here than out there. But don't delay longer than that. If the country is power down, social order is going to deteriorate quickly. Get home asap."

The gravity of the situation settled into the room like a brick tossed in a pond. There weren't any more questions, so they moved to the lockers and cubby holes. Everyone was grabbing phones and trying to turn them on. No one had any power. All the phones were dead. They filed out to the dark parking lot, people getting out their car keys, mumbling obscenities. After another minute, they all heard the roar of an engine.

"Hot damn!" Gale got out of his car, which he knew would be totally dead, and looked over at an old jeep about fifty feet away. The Air Force lieutenant was punching up in the air out of his window. The old jeep was running. That was the key. Older vehicles didn't have all the computers and chips in them.

"Dennis!" Gale called out to his friend. "His jeep is running!"

"Get in, Sir, I'll get you to the JADOC. My family is in California. I don't have anywhere else to go but with you."

"Good deal. I hope your family's okay. Let's get going."

"Dennis, look, I'm thinking this is bigger than just the Iranians and NoKo's. That Chinese crop intel about their crop failures for the last couple of years makes sense with this now. They are running out of food. Didn't mean anything before this. I think this is bigger. Tell them that if they're still there. I've got to get home to Layla."

"Gale, I'm sure Joey's fine. They have an escape pod they can use. She'll be okay. Get to your daughter. Stay safe. I don't know what's coming next, but be ready for anything. I don't think the Marines are coming to save anyone anytime soon."

Gale nodded. They shook hands. Then they heard a weird whooshing sound above them. A large, what looked to be, 747 was gliding through the twilight air not 500 feet up. Gale didn't see any landing gear. They watched it move, transfixed, as it descended, looking like it was going to land on the main highway out toward Dulles Airport. It descended too fast and disappeared behind some buildings farther down the highway. Silence. Then they heard a crunching sounds and a fireball rose into the night.

"Ho-Lee Shit," the lieutenant said under his breath.

"No time to waste. Go!" Gale said to the lieutenant and Dennis.

They did. Quickly. The jeep moved out of the parking lot and up the side street toward the main road, but going the opposite direction, toward D.C. and Arlington, where the JADOC was located. Gale watched them until they were out of sight. He went back to his car and popped the trunk. There was his "Get Home Bag." A small backpack that had some food, socks, a knife, and other survival-type gear. He watched as the others started walking in groups in various directions, everyone wishing everyone else good luck and waving. He was the only one walking toward the trail next to the building. He started down the paved bike path headed west.

# TWENTY-SIX

December 24
6:00pm EST
Donneker

There were probably about a hundred employees still in the building when Donneker finally decided it was time to get on with it. He stepped out of his car. A scattering of cigarette butts near his boots. He was dressed in jeans and a camouflage jacket. His pistol in its holster on his right hip. He reached back into the car and pulled out his AR-15 semi-automatic rifle. It was his pride and joy, which he'd hidden from his wife, along with his pistol, when she told him she was filing the restraining order. His other weapons were in the safe in her basement still. No contact.

The AR was all black, thirty-round magazine loaded with 5.56mm ammunition. He looped the sling over his head and pulled the charging handle to chamber the first round. He had a red-dot sight on the rail on top of the rifle. There were extra magazines in pouches in the web harness he wore around his midsection with shoulder straps to take the weight off. The body armor he wore was heavy. This was only the second time he had put it on since he purchased it months ago on a whim. Hopefully, it would keep him alive long enough to accomplish what he came for. If the cops arrived before he was done, he'd deal with it.

He ran his left hand, his free hand, through his wavy dark hair and started walking toward the front doors, looking up at the sky as he went. The moon was full and there were scattered clouds. It was dark now and cold. He wondered if a storm was coming. He ran over his plan again in his mind. Enter the lobby. Deal with the security guard. Take his access badge. Then up a couple of floors and deal with the sales team. He wanted to see the look on his manager's face. Then he would handle whatever came next. Not deal with them. Kill them. Stop hiding behind words, he thought.

Security had to have seen him by now on their cameras, but nothing. No sirens. No movement. He was approaching the lobby doors when they opened. A group of people stepped out into the cold night, laughing loudly. There were five of them. He recognized his old manager as one of the group. His vision narrowed and his breathing was shallow. He stopped cold. They didn't see him yet.

That's when the lights went out. All the lights. The whole building went dark. Donneker stopped in his tracks, spooked, and looked around at the surrounding buildings. They were all dark. No street lights. What the hell? He was cloaked in darkness now. The emergency lights in the building in front of him hadn't clicked on yet. The group was standing in the open. He could hear them talking about the lights. That's when he realized he could hear them very clearly. There was no other sound. The highway was close and there were other roads as well around this building, but the normal vehicle noises weren't there. He back tracked to his car and walked around to the other side. He was confused now. This was perfect cover for him, but what the hell was going on? What should he do?

He let his eyes adjust to the darkness, and slowly, with the full moon, he began to make out the group heading to their cars. Several tried starting their vehicles, but he heard them yelling to each other that they wouldn't start. He could see clearly now. Not their faces, but their forms. They grouped back up in the middle of the parking lot looking around, talking in whispers. They still hadn't seen him. About ten minutes passed as he listened to them and tried to figure out this situation.

There was an odd sound above him. A dark shape, a plane, passed over him headed toward Dulles airport.

Donneker stood, mouth open. The plane hit the road hard. It didn't even look like the pilot was trying to land. The massive plane's nose hit first and skidded, sparks flying. Then it buckled and the whole damn thing came down and rolled snapping the left wing. He could see sparks from the metal frame sliding on the asphalt roadway. Blue and orange engulfed the whole thing and a fireball shot into the air like a mini mushroom cloud.

"Holy shit!" Donneker yelled out loud. In the distance, maybe two or three miles west, near the airport, there was another fireball. The sound reached him a second after he saw it. Damn, he thought, airplanes were falling out of sky. That's when the group came running up near him, pointing, and screaming at the fireball.

"Kim Donneker? Is that you?" His former boss had just noticed him.

The shit who'd fired him. The one he was here for. They stared at each other and the rest of the group turned to look at Donneker. He raised the rifle at the group about twenty feet from the rear of his car.

"Y'all stay right there!" Donneker said sharply as he moved sideways away from his car to get a better field of fire.

"Kim, what are you doing here? Wait! You don't need to do this, man!" His boss held both hands up in front of him.

Donneker ignored him. "You know what you did to me? Last straw, man. Last straw. You could have given me a chance. My wife's divorcing me, you heartless prick!"

"Look, it wasn't me, it was the higher-ups. Look at that. A fucking plane just crashed and all the lights are out. The cars won't start. Something bad is happening. You don't have to do this. Let us get home to our families. I'm begging you!"

Donneker took a deep breath, but kept the rifle pointed at the group. The other four were trying to get behind Donneker's boss. What the hell? This was all too much to digest. The lights and cars and the plane. Explosions by the airport. What if his boss was right? Susan would need him now, wouldn't she? Something bad happened and they were all in the same boat now, weren't they? Wasn't this good enough? He couldn't process all that had just occurred. He wanted to get home. But just to prove he was in charge, Donneker moved closer to his boss pointing the rifle at the man's head, finger on the trigger.

"You know what, we're all in the same boat. You're just like me now. You got nothing. Just like me. You better thank God this crazy shit happened or you'd all be dead."

The group stood there staring at him, one of the women whimpered with her hand over her mouth. He was about to tell them to get out of here when another explosion distracted Donneker and he glanced to look. He felt the rifle jerk away from him hard enough that he squeezed the trigger.

BOOM!

The tension on the rifle disappeared. Donneker recovered quick and realized his boss had tried to grab the rifle from him. The round took his boss in the neck and he was laying on the ground, still.

"God Dammit! You stupid mother fucker! I was letting you go!" He looked to the others.

"Go! Are you stupid? I was letting you all go! That wasn't my fault. Get outta here!"

He watched them run thinking he should just shoot them. They were witnesses. He looked down at his boss's body. A pool of liquid shimmered the moonlight. He turned away and walked the few steps back to his car. He put a hand on the trunk to steady himself, feeling suddenly nauseous. It wasn't his fault, he thought. He vomited on the ground beside his car. Several times. One hand on the fender and the other holding the rifle to his chest so he wouldn't get vomit on it. Finished, he stood straight and stared at the plane still burning brightly on the road.

Whatever had happened, it was still going on. Another explosion in the direction of the airport confirmed that thought. He was armed and still alive. Whatever was going on, he had a chance to get his life back, if that was possible. He wondered if it was like this everywhere. If so, it was going to be every man for himself. No cops. No law. Susan would have to take him back now. She would need his protection. He was going to do it too. He glanced back at the body, regret creeping into his thoughts. He would be a better husband and father. He stared at the burning wreckage up the highway. He'd walk that way. Home was on the other side. The fire would at least provide him light as he walked this first bit. How many people died in that crash? Regardless, Donneker was going to be in charge of his world now. The whole area suddenly lit up in a bright light. He shut his eyes reflexively. He ducked behind his car and opened his eyes. He slowly peeked around the trunk of his car. His mouth dropped open.

There, miles and miles away, had to be over D.C., was a tiny, glowing mushroom cloud. He just stared at it. He couldn't make out the top, but the stem of the cloud was glowing orange or yellow. He didn't know anything about nuclear explosions, but it had to be over D.C. and that was over twenty or more miles east from where he was. He forced himself to move. He ran out of the parking lot in the direction of the burning plane. He couldn't keep this pace, but the horror behind him spurred him forward. He ran until he couldn't any longer. He was well past the airplane, a 747, when he had to stop jogging. He started to walk. It would be a long walk home. To his actual home. Not the apartment he rented, but his home. As he walked, the thought of radiation and fallout terrified him, but the wind was against his face, so he figured it was blowing all that the other way. He hoped that was how it worked. He had things to do and he wasn't dead. His thoughts swirled.

# TWENTY-SEVEN

December 24
6:00pm EST
Fort Knox, Kentucky

An was cleaned up from the morning's training maneuvers and had squared his Marines away during the afternoon. He was at the Main Base Exchange for a black coffee. The drive to the Airport in Louisville to catch his late flight to Dulles was a short one. Corporal Bevins, who was driving An and his brother, was next to him and ordered a triple venti skim latte or some such goofy drink. Bao was out by the car on the phone with his wife. An gave Bevins the side-eye.

"Enjoy your millennial drink, Corporal Snowflake." An said to Bevins with all the intent in the world of shaming the poor Corporal into pouring it out and ordering a black coffee.

"It's the little things in life, Gunnery Sergeant." Bevins shot back immediately, not at all embarrassed.

He hadn't seriously thought about his parents since early this morning, but he was thinking about them now. Thirty minutes or so in the car with another few hours at the airport and then an hour flight to Dulles. He needed sleep. He and Bao had been lucky enough to get adjoining seats on the flight, so he was sure they'd talk about their dad instead of catching shut-eye. He'd been up for twelve hours already. He hoped the caffeine from the steaming black coffee would help.

Planes didn't bother him. He could sleep anywhere. It was a military thing, he supposed. He was used to grabbing winks wherever he was, even if it was on the hard ground. He slept like a baby most places. He walked out to the car and to Bao who just finished his call.

"How's everyone doing?" An asked.

Bao turned around at An's voice with wet eyes. The two brothers joined in a long hug, ended by gruff thumps on backs.

"Brook's good. Mom's a mess, though she won't show it. Brook says she puts on a brave facade. Dad's at the hospital morgue. Mom can't stand the thought of him being alone. I should've gone home with Brook. No offense, man."

"How could you know from the phone call. We'll be there soon. Sort it all out. I still can't believe he's gone."

"Yeah. Aren't we a couple of tough Marines here?"

"Oorah! Let's cowboy up and get outta town. Bevins! You ready to go? Got your Army coffee?"

"That's funny stuff, Gunnery Sergeant. All you Marines got jokes."

Bevins unlocked his old Toyota Supra. He told them he fixed it up over the last few years. An thought it was still old as crap. Silver with some rust. He hadn't fixed that and didn't really care about the looks as long as it ran well. They all got in, An put his small backpack in the hatchback while Bao squeezed himself into the backseat with some cursing. Bevins put the key in the ignition and started it up. It turned over and he revved the engine a couple times to get the juices flowing. The instruments in the dash were digital and had an orange glow to them. It was 1800 hours and their flight was at 2200 hours. Bevins started playing with the radio stations when the car cut off.

"Really?" Bevins said. He turned the key in the ignition again, but got nothing. Dead.

"The hell? Give me a sec guys."

He reached down and grabbed the lever to pop the hood. Bevins got out, kicking up dust with his boots as he went to the hood. An joined him and watched as he messed around with wires and checked a few other things, but they all seemed to be in order. An realized that something else wasn't quite right. There was no sound. Utter silence. There was always something making noise at the Fort, but not now. An looked around as Bao joined them.

"Want me to take a look?" Bao asked.

"No, man, look." An pointed.

The three of them saw some soldiers and civilians coming out of the Exchange looking around in confusion. A few checked their phones. An turned and saw vehicles on the road next to the Exchange stopped dead in the street or rolling to a silent stop. This wasn't right at all, he thought to himself.

"An? My phone had a full charge a minute ago. It's dead now." Bao kept pushing and holding the power button with no result.

"Let's get our gear and hump back to the barracks. I don't like this. Doesn't feel right at all, man."

"We're not going to make our flight, are we?"

"Hey, Marines! Don't planes make noise when they fly over? That one's just gliding?" Bevins pointed to a passenger plane that was way too low here over the Fort for approach to the airport in Louisville. They watched it glide past, miles away and out of sight.

"Let's go!" An started out toward the barracks with Bao and Bevins right behind him. "I don't think the flight's gonna happen, man. Brook's with mom and her neighbors are good people. Whatever this is, we'll sort it out and get home."

"Oh, I'm getting home, even if I have to steal your tank." Bao said. An knew he wasn't joking.

# TWENTY-EIGHT

Tanner Kinley pulled a short, fat cigar from his breast pocket and stepped out onto the port bridge wing. The cold Atlantic breeze was refreshing. He fished in his pant's pockets for his wind-resistant lighter. He pulled it out with a weathered hand. Facing aft to shield the blow torch-like flame from the lightly rushing air around him, he clicked the button and the lighter sprang to life. He held the end of the cigar to the flame for a few seconds and then brought the cigar to his lips and puffed on it a few times to get the cherry glowing. Sliding the lighter back into his pocket, he leaned against the wing rail and looked out over the ocean. The fairly calm seas were clearly visible in the full moon light. He looked up at the moon and his brother, Tavis, popped into his mind, as if he'd cross the moon, silhouetted so he could see him. He glanced at his watch. They were already ahead of schedule, making good headway at sixteen knots.

They were currently about fifty nautical miles west of the northwest tip of France on a southerly heading. Off in the darkness was Brest, France. His cargo ship, *Shark*, was enroute to Oman via the Suez Canal from Greenock, Scotland. He was headed to Sohar Port and Freezone on the extreme northern coast of Oman, just a short distance from the Strait of Hormuz. He'd departed many hours prior on this cold and calm Christmas Eve. Well, it was past midnight now, so Christmas. The Shark moved in concert with the slight swells beneath him. She was of Russian design, but about forty years old, so he supposed it was Soviet designed. That never really set well with him, but it was all his. He purchased her several years ago and overhauled it, which wasn't cheap. She purred now, though, and was a tough little cargo carrier, roughly a football pitch long with a twenty meter beam. She was a Roll-On/Roll-Off ship. She carried vehicles, usually cars and trucks, which were rolled on and off via the drop ramp in the stern of the boat. He looked back up at the moon and thought about his brother again.

Tavis was younger by five years. They'd gone different directions in the Navy, which they'd both loved. Tavis had become a naval commando in the Special Boat Service. He'd gone to Afghanistan and killed Taliban—a lot of them, while helping the Americans hunt Bin Ladin. Tanner, on the other hand, was in ports all over the world following the merchant path. On the rare occasion they saw each other over the last ten or so years, Tavis had not been keen on discussing his experiences in detail. He instead focused on his brood of offspring and getting his Doctorate in animal husbandry or veterinarian science or something to do with animals humping. Proud of his brother he was, but couldn't for his life figure out what he did for a living. It got Tavis into the European Space Program and now he was floating up there in orbit. Tanner wondered if animals humped in space. The vision of that and his brother made him laugh out loud to the sea.

The sea was calming for him. He was married to her, in a sense. He didn't have a wife and had no children, that he knew of. Living the life of a sailor was transient most of the time. He had been around the world and in most ports of call in his forty-nine years. His parents still lived in the home he and Tav had grown up in Campbeltown, Scotland. A thin spit of land jutting out on the West coast of Scotland with the Firth of Clyde to the East and the entrance to Glasgow and his home port of Greenock. It also happened to be close to where the U.K.'s Nuclear Submarine Base was at Faslane, Scotland.

He had a great network within the U.K. military due to his twenty years in the Royal Navy. He retired a decade earlier and began his own shipping business with the Shark under him. He was finishing up this last leg of a very lucrative contract with the Ministry of Defence and Oman. It was his fourth delivery. In the open hold was the last of his cargo from the Army. Then he could relax for a little while. He'd been pushing himself and his crew hard this past six months, but the payoff was worth it. Make the last payment on the boat and it would be his free and clear.

"Captain?"

"Jesus, Mary, and Joseph!" He yelled and squeezed shut his eyes. "You scared piss out of me."

"Sorry to interrupt your deep thoughts, Captain, but somethings weird with the radio."

Sammy was in his late twenties and not new to the sea, but new enough that Tanner still considered him in training, which was why Tanner was on watch with the lad.

"The radio, you say? Let's go see what this is about then."

They both moved back into the bridge, shutting the wing door behind him and letting the warmth of the dark bridge begin to warm his weathered face. Tanner's bright blue eyes took in a cursory glance around the myriad glowing dials and controls around the bridge, then came to rest on the radio gear.

"Now what's this that's got you worried, lad?"

"Well, Captain, the radio was quiet, and then all of a sudden there was a loud squawk and some static and then nothing. I mean nothing, Captain."

Tanner looked around at all the other gear. Seemed to be in working order. The radar was up and running. There were several contacts, but not close. He noted the time, 0100 hours. Tanner checked several stations that usually had routine traffic on them. Silence. The gear was in proper order, but no comms were coming in. Curious, but not overly concerning.

"Atmospherics, lad. You're jumpy is all."

Sammy was still new to this and when you're new on a boat, everything is something, until, with experience, it becomes normal and routine. Eventually, Sammy would be able to explain virtually everything that occurs on the open ocean. He put the boy's nerves at ease with some captainly words of wisdom and told him to watch his course. Sammy dutifully went back to his job and Tanner, who was still holding the smoking cigar, went back out onto the port bridge wing.

He'd been standing there, trying to remember where he was in his thoughts before Sammy's "emergency" had interrupted him. Ten minutes later, taking deep pulls on the fat cigar, Tanner looked off at the moonlit waves. There was a bright light or flash or something that lit up the eastern horizon. It was terribly bright, but whatever caused it was below the horizon. Jesus, that was bright white. He stared in that direction for a moment, trying to figure out what was. He turned, flicked his glowing cigar into the sea, and re-entered the bridge.

He went to the plot table and took his ship's bearing and plotted them on the map in front of him. What was over there?

"Captain, did you see that light?" Sammy asked, concern crept back into his voice.

"Aye. Saw it." Was all he said as his studied the map and made some rough calculations.

"Brest. The flash was over the horizon and I bet it was Brest. Sammy, what's around Brest, France? Any thoughts?"

He was grabbing for anything. Something had happened. He looked at Sammy, who shook his head.

Tanner went back out onto the bridge wing and stared East. There were no clouds. Moon was full. There was a slight, orange glow on the horizon now. Not as bright as before, but steady. He racked his brains for what seemed like minutes, but within less than a minute, the horror dawned on him.

"Jesus, Mary, and Joseph!" He said loudly to the waves and the moon. He went back inside where Sammy was rock steady at the helm.

"Captain, what's over there?"

"Brest is where the French Navy docks their Ballistic Missile Submarines, Sammy. They've had a bloody nuclear accident!"

"You mean one of their subs exploded or they were attacked?"

"Accident. Has to be. The coordinates match exactly. If it were war, lad, we'd know it." He said more to himself in reassurance. "Adjust course. Hard to port. Head toward Brest. We'll see soon enough. We're fifty miles out and we've got some time. I'm going to get on the radio and see if anyone else saw that flash. I'll check the satellite comms as well. Don't worry lad, the world's not ended, cause we're not dead. But we need to help if we can. At least try to gain some information and relay it, if possible."

"Won't there be radiation if it was a nuclear accident?"

"Aye, Sammy. However, the wind is blowing to the east, so we can get a bit closer. Any radiation or fallout would be falling inland." Tanner hoped that was right.

# TWENTY-NINE

December 24
5:55pm EST
Floyd And Chewie

"Git!" Floyd said.

As he dried himself off after a quick shower, Chewie was there under his feet trying to bite the towel. He almost stepped on her twice. The rambunctious furball quickly turned and ran out of the bathroom. After several tries, she was able to jump up on the king-sized bed and turned around wagging her tail. Her whole body seemed to vibrate as Floyd came out of the bathroom into the master bedroom he used to share with his wife, Linda, while she was still alive. They'd gotten married when he got back from Vietnam. He looked at her picture on the nightstand as he dressed for the party in blue jeans, a nice, long-sleeved button-down shirt and loafers. He ran a comb through what was left of his gray hair.

He walked out of the bedroom towards his office, which was really just one of the other three bedrooms. He walked down the hall and heard the thud of Chewie hitting the floor as she jumped from the bed to follow him. The hallway was dark and he almost stepped on her again!

"Go, you little monkey!" Floyd shooed her in front of him as he entered his office and hit the light switch.

He sat his aged frame down in his leather swivel chair. Chewie jumped up on his lap for some love. She was middle-aged for dogs and had one good fang left as the other three had fallen out during tug battles over the years. She looked up at him and her long tongue came out and licked both sides of her furry muzzle. She yawned and dropped her head, exhausted. From what he couldn't fathom.

He swiveled to his desk to check the forecast, printed them out and tacked them to the cork board, disposing of the old ones. He was a constant planner and prepper, he stuck to a routine until it became discipline. Once that happened, his discipline became routine. Everything Floyd did was for a purpose. That purpose was survival. It was the one thing, along with Malaria, that he brought back from Vietnam. And the nightmares. But this was actually useful. Malaria and nightmares were not.

He perused the forecast and smiled. It would be a white Christmas! Floyd looked at the clock on the computer screen. It was 6:00 p.m. Time for the human interaction he sorely needed, especially during the holidays. He'd drink some Guinness and talk shop with Lou and Gale.

"You ready to go play with Christopher, Chew Butts?" The dog immediately jumped down, knowing something absolutely amazing was about to happen.

All at once, he and Chewie were in pitch darkness. Floyd didn't move. It was odd. There was no light at all. His blinds were down in the office and in the other rooms as well. He let his eyes adjust to the darkness…and the silence. That was odd. Chewie was shaking on his lap. He rubbed her furry head to calm her. He left his phone in the bedroom instead of bringing it with him like he usually did. He chastised himself for not having a flashlight on his desk. He'd remedy that soon enough. Then another thought drifted into his mind while he sat there with Chewie. His computer was off. It had a battery. What in the world happened?

After a minute or so, his eyes adjusted enough to move. He walked to the window. He saw the street below in the full moonlight. It was so dark. Everything was out. He walked by memory, feeling for walls and doorways, to the master bedroom and fumbled on his nightstand for his smart phone. It didn't work either. Nothing. What the…? A dark thought crept into his consciousness. That thought grew in his mind and in consequence. He knew what this *could* be, but he'd need others to confirm it. He'd go next door and see what everyone thought.

He cautiously stepped into the hallway, toward the stairs. He got to the top with the railing on the right and the wall on the left. He'd gone up and down these stairs in the dark countless times, but not in this kind of pitch darkness. He reached for the railing, shuffling his feet to the first step. Chewie got there first. Floyd's right foot landed on the dog. Her yelp alerted him to her location and he lifted his right foot just enough to not crush her. He saved the dog, but he missed that top step. It all happened so fast that he let go of the railing and reached for the wall, his fingertips brushing it as he went. He frantically reached for the railing again, but too late. He screamed in pain when he hit the stairs and his shoulder popped out of its socket. Momentum propelled him. His feet now in the air, his head hit one of the stair risers in the middle part of the staircase at the wrong angle. Did something snap? He found himself at the bottom of the stairs.

His mind was still there, but he was trapped in it. He couldn't move anything, including his eyes. He could hear a whimper and scurrying of tiny paws and the dog was in his face. His eyes open, but unblinking, he saw her. She whimpered and barked a couple of times and then licked his face. He couldn't feel it. He could barely see her now. His last thought was that Chewie was snuggling up in a curled ball next to face. Oh, Chewie... sadness, then nothing.

# THIRTY

December 24
6:00pm EST
Joey Washington

"What the hell?" Tavis yelled. Joey spun slowly away from the cupola windows and her beautiful view of Earth to look up into the Tranquility module.

"You okay, Tav?" She yelled up into the station.

She didn't know where he was, but it sounded far. The Russian modules? Pasha really needed to stop punking him. She began to spin back towards her laptop and the view when he yelled again.

"Joey! Something's wrong out there! Where are you?"

"Cupola!" she yelled back. "What's up?"

His face appeared above her as she spun back again. "Was in Zvezda and saw a bright flash through one of the upper windows. Don't think it was near. Didn't see the actual point of the flash." He explained, voice raised, out of character.

Most of the windows in the station faced downward toward Earth. Only a few, like in the Russian modules, faced away from Earth.

"I didn't see anything, but I probably wouldn't have. I'm oriented toward the planet. We're between sun and earth, so a flash above us would be difficult to see from here. What direction did it come from?" Joey asked.

"It seemed as if it came from—"

The station lurched violently as if hit by something. They were both stationary, floating, when it happened. As the station moved, they were slammed into the module's ceiling. Tavis hit the top of the Tranquility module with the flat of his back, but Joey was facing him. Her head and torso were shot up through the hatch from the Cupola to Tranquility, but her legs were floating at an angle to her torso. Her right shin hit the side of the hatch with a crunch. She screamed in pain.

Tavis pulled her up into Tranquility, her laptop came up with her, screen smashed.

"No, I don't think…my leg hit the thing."

Joey reached down, touching the side of her right lower leg. It wasn't… right. She looked at Tav, who was now looking at her leg. The pain was terrible. She was light-headed.

"Joey. Joey!" He yelled in her face. He snapped his fingers in front of her eyes. The pain was excruciating. She made a low growl and focused on his face. Red hair. Red Beard with some gray. Blue eyes.

"Commander Washington!"

"Okay! I'm here! Leg?"

"Broken. Pasha!" he bellowed.

The sound of it wasn't something she'd heard before from him. She looked down at her leg and it surely wasn't right. Her foot and half her lower leg were at a slight angle to the rest of her leg. Shit! She didn't hear the Russian respond before she blacked out completely.

# THIRTY-ONE

Sitting in the van's driver's seat, Ivan was sweating even though the temperature outside was below freezing and felt even colder with the bitter wind. It should be close to go time. He was watching the street lights. One of them flickered off and on intermittently, which unsettled him—thinking that was it each time it flickered out. His nerves were raw. Come on, he thought, let's go. Then another thought popped into his mind. His vans were old enough that there were no electronics to burn out from the pulse. However, the second team was fast approaching by boat. They got an old boat, with an older motor. Would the boat's motors die with the lights? They should be at the dock when it happened anyway.

The street light flickered again, but this time they all went out. Complete darkness. The vans engine remained on. Good. In the distance at the antenna complex, he saw bright sparks shooting off the towering antennas and wires stretching between them.

"It's time."

They all retrieved night vision goggles from an insulated metal case and put them on. The metal box protected the goggle's electronics from the pulse that fried the antennae wires. The pulse only lasted seconds. With the goggles on, his vision was various shades of green. He put the van in drive and slowly moved toward the gate with the headlights off. The men in the back rolled down their windows, letting in the frigid night air. They were a couple hundred meters from the gatehouse. Only one guard on duty. He was armed with a pistol, but that wouldn't matter in a moment.

They rolled up to the guard shack. The guard stood outside, looking the opposite way, toward the antenna complex. He turned at the sound of the van's engine and was met with two 9mm subsonic bullets in the chest from a suppressed rifle. That still made noise, but wasn't noticeable at a distance. He didn't know if the guard was wearing a vest or not, but the second van slowed and one of his men put two more rounds in the guards head as he lay on the ground. They were active.

Ivan drove quickly. The second van peeled off to the right while Ivan drove to the left out onto the peninsula. They had four vans, but the other two sat idling with only drivers, back on the approach road. As they approached each antenna, he slowed as one man exited the sliding door, armed with a suppressed rifle and a pre-set bag of explosives. It was amazing what you could bring into a country under the international rules of diplomatic courier pouches, which weren't searched.

After he dropped the last man off, he headed to the operations building in the middle of the compound in case the boat team hadn't been able to make it to shore. It was required. He saw his second team exit the building and head toward the datacenter building near the shoreline. That building was on fire. There was an explosion at the first antenna and then the second. They all were being blown and the towers were falling outward, while his men were all gathering in the middle of the complex, clear of the blasts and falling metal.

Ivan put the van in park and got out, leaving the door open and walked the few feet to where Sergei, the boat team leader and two of his team stood, one smoking a cigarette, watching the burning datacenter. Shadows danced on their faces.

"It's done!" Sergei said in Russian, extending his right hand. Ivan shook it roughly.

"I was worried whether your boat would get to the dock before the power cut out. Seems your engines didn't die. All good it seems."

"They did die! We were close enough that we drifted in. Hit the dock pretty hard without power, but tied up fast and got to it."

Sergei smiled and raised his goggles, rubbing his sweat-covered face. Ivan raised his goggles as well to get an unobstructed view of the coast line to the south. Just minutes prior, it was brightly lit with small fishing towns and homes. It was now as if there were no coast. Only the burning buildings gave off light, which their eyes were adjusting to.

"Mother of God, Ivan. I didn't expect the darkness. What have we done?" They surveyed the destruction around them and looked down the coast. Ivan thought about the all-encompassing darkness only broken by the fires burning behind him.

"We've done our duty. Fulfilled our primary mission." Ivan didn't face Sergei.

"We've started a war, Ivan."

"It was already started. We're protecting our families and our country."

He thought of his wife, safe in a bunker, a world away. He wanted to take her away from all this, to somewhere warm. That was a dream now. Just a dream.

"We have more to do. Get your men together and loaded up into the vans. We've got a long drive ahead of us."

So many were going to die before this was over. The weight of it slammed down on him. Yes, they had more to do before this was over, but it was a different purpose now. It was a long way to Virginia.

# THIRTY-TWO

Joey's vision returned. How long had she been out. She looked around and was aware of the walls moving past her. Looking to the right, small red blobs floated past her face. That wasn't good. It was surreal. There were small droplets of blood everywhere. She didn't think it was hers, until she remembered her leg as the pain thundered back into her consciousness.

"Pasha!" She heard loud and clear in a man's voice. Tavis. Things were wrong. Badly wrong.

"Here!" she heard, but it was muffled.

"Pasha, you good?" Tavis said. "We're coming, Pasha!"

"Okay." She heard and looked down her body. Tavis was floating in front of her, dragging her through the modules.

"Bloody 'ell!" Tavis pulled her along, cussing as they went.

Tavis spun about to face her. They were near the Soyuz pod. He reached into the large first aid kit and pulled out surgical shears to cut her trouser leg open as well as a rolled up splint that hardened into a temporary cast of sorts. The lights in the Zvezda module began to flicker, but came back on. Tavis grabbed one of her hands and guided it to a hand-hold on the wall.

"Hold on to that, Joey! Tight! This is not going to be pleasant for either of us."

He looked into her eyes. She nodded, squeezed them shut, and put her other hand over her mouth, tears streaming down her cheeks.

He put the bottom of her pant leg into the shears and started cutting. He took stock of her leg and exhaled.

"Tavis. What's status?" she managed.

"Well, no bones sticking out of your skin. Good news. Bones were broken. Bad news. It's not a compound fracture, but it's broken and badly. I have to put them back in place, lass. You will scream. Try to keep your wits."

"Okay, but I meant Pasha...the station!"

"Screwed. Time to leave. Comms are shit. Integrity is questionable. Pasha's in the Soyuz. Bloody knot on his head. He'll live. Gotta splint your leg quick before I put you in. Hold tight!"

Joey nodded to him and shut her eyes. She felt him put her knee under his arm as he faced away from her and in one quick motion, Holy Sh—all went black.

When she came around again, she was in the Soyuz, strapped into her seat. Pasha was on her left, Tavis on the right. Hatch sealed. Pasha was feeling around his pockets. He was probably looking for his good luck charm. It was usually floating next to him or at least in the same module. The small, round, black and white plushy toy was filled with beans and soft stuffing. It was a panda his niece had given him years ago. He took it everywhere. She heard him sigh with relief. He pulled it out and squeezed it in one of his large hands. She wanted to squeeze it now too, even though it was probably asinine, but she didn't want to leave without the Panda ball. They needed all the luck they could get.

She was still light-headed, so Tavis and Pasha worked through the separation sequence. She looked through the single porthole. Where were they? Earth was below. She scanned the planet trying to get her bearings. They were on the dark side of the planet at the moment. She saw what she'd seen hundreds of times. That had to be Russia and down below that was the outline of India. To her left was the Middle East and the west coast of Africa. Odd. Europe should be on the horizon. Usually shinning bright with all the city lights around the Mediterranean Sea, but all was dark. Then something caught her eye to the right. They were coming up on the Indian Sub-Continent. Bright flashes on the ground. One had caught her attention, but it was followed by another. Then another in the space of a minute.

"Tavis." Pain forgotten momentarily. "Tavis!"

"What's wrong? Almost done. What happened? You okay?"

"I'm fine. Was looking at Earth. There aren't lights at all in Europe. Pitch black. I can see lights in Africa and Asia, but there were bright flashes over near India and I think Pakistan! I think this is very bad. Seeing flashes from here could only be explosions?"

"Are you sure? Nukes? The Indians and Pakis? Shit, we're outta here!" Tavis continued his rapid-fire speech. "There was an explosion. That flash I saw, I think was a nuke. Higher orbit than us. Shock wave hit us. Nuclear blast would pulse the power grids on the ground."

"Comms? Mission Control?" Joey blurted.

"Nothing came up, no time to send down. I think Houston has its own problems and Russian Mission Control hasn't said a peep. We're alone."

"Tavis, we don't have re-entry suits on. This better go perfect. No comms. Shit." She looked at both of them. They both nodded.

"Kind of has to be perfect, does it not?" Pasha squeezed the plushy until Joey thought the thing might burst.

Fist bumps all around and Tavis detached them. They waited a few minutes to orient correctly before firing the engines. Joey strained to look out the porthole to get a glimpse of anything to situate herself in any way possible. She totally forgot the pain in her leg. Her jaw dropped. There was an entire solar array missing and others were bent all to hell. Yep. Leaving. Good decision.

"Hey Tav, when you're oriented, don't wait, do it. Let's get home. Or what's left of it." She trailed off and put her head back while the pain in her leg reappeared with a vengeance. She closed her eyes and just breathed.

"Oriented. Engine start. Hold on."

Pasha, in his usual dry tone, scratching his graying beard, offered support. "Well, my friends, in three hours and thirty minutes, we'll either be on the ground or we'll be dead, or both."

# THIRTY-THREE

December 24
6:05pm EST
Javad

The seat was utilitarian and not at all comfortable. He wanted to get up and stretch, but kept looking at the long cylinder in the middle of the small, aft cabin and thought better of it. He knew his fear of this weapon was irrational, but it did give him pause. He glanced at his companions. They hadn't spoken a word to him the entire trip. When they did talk, it was in low whispers to each other. They were clearly uncomfortable that he'd joined them right before takeoff. Another change to a carefully rehearsed plan. Javad ignored them. His mind elsewhere. He'd forbidden them to alert the flight deck that he was here, intimating that less than nice things would happen to them if they did. He was polite about it, of course. Charming, even.

As if his thoughts triggered it, the green light above the rear door of the 727 turned off and the one next to it lit up in an orange-yellow color. It started a flurry of activity from the three technicians. He watched them work. The cylinder they worked on sat on small, rubber wheels on a track that would guide it out once the time came. The technicians were focused silently on their specific tasks. As one, they all stopped and stepped back from the menacing, metal weapon. Tasks complete. They took their seats again and strapped in.

The one next to him gestured for him to do the same and he anxiously fumbled with the straps until, like the others, he was bound to the seat and wall. He noticed that the others had clear goggles and face masks on with a hose attached to the front of each. They all frantically motioned for him to grab the one hanging next to his chair and put it on. He quickly did so and just in time. There was a swooshing of air in the cabin. His mask in place he donned the goggles. He wondered why, if there were only three of them, there was another mask and goggles. He looked around. There were two other seats as well, unoccupied, also with masks and goggles. They over-engineered this. Perhaps in case one or more malfunctioned. Either way, he was glad he had them.

They had to be close. He looked at his watch again. He hadn't planned on being here in this plane. With this weapon. These weapons were just part of the mission when he was in Iran. To be here within feet of one of them was unsettling. He couldn't shake the feeling which developed and morphed in his mind over the last ten hours or so. Perhaps his quest for the vengeance he so desperately wanted was ill thought out. Not only for what would happen to the innocent, but to his soul. His body shuddered at the thought. He had long ago given up any hope of salvation and focused only on the task at hand. He was tired. Down in his bones weary. Weary of possible discovery. Weary of not being discovered at all. He was exceptionally good at his game. Could he finish it though? For Sara he would. Yes, for her definitely. For both of his Saras. Wrenching his thoughts to reality, he dwelled on his predicament? He'd come this far for his family, but now he wanted to see them; Sara, Ahmed, and his mother, one last time with an ache that would not relent.

How would he get away when they landed? And, once away, these technicians would most certainly alert the commandos sitting just feet from him on the other side of the pressurized bulkhead. What would the soldiers do with that information? Would his description give him away to the one he knew? All questions soon to be answered, one way or another, as the swooshing continued.

The first thing he felt was cold. They were depressurizing the rear cabin. What he'd read in the classified reports was coming back to him now. They had to equalize the pressure in aircraft with the altitude outside before they lowered the rear door and the ramp or they could all be sucked out. The soft glow of the cabin lights was replaced with a deep red glow. He assumed it provided cover from the ground or other aircraft. Red light wasn't as visible as other light in the spectrum. The orange-yellow light above the rear door abruptly turned off and the one next to it turned a bright red. There was mechanical whining and then a clank. That had to be the rear ramp, where the stairs on this 727 used to be. The door rose up from the bottom on a hydraulic arm attached to the ceiling of the cabin. As it opened, it barely cleared the pointy tip of the weapon and then stopped. He saw nothing but darkness through the hole in the rear of the plane as the bomb began to move slowly toward the dark hole.

Then it was gone. There was no sound of its leaving. Javad stared at the small rubber wheels, still spinning on their ball bearings. The doors closed. Pressure was returned to the cabin. He followed the technicians lead and removed his goggles and oxygen mask as the cabin re-pressurized. My God! They just dropped a nuclear weapon on Washington, D.C. He turned to the window next to his right shoulder. The retrofit of the aircraft replaced the normal plastic covered pushup blind with a metal one. It was down. There were many windows in the cabin and all the blinds remained down the whole flight so no light escaped the plane. Now, he thought, what was the point? The cabin remained cloaked in dark red light. He strained against the harness holding him in his seat and reached for the metal tab at the bottom of the window blind and began to raise it. He was startled as the technician next to him grabbed his arm and pushed it away and sliding the blind back down.

"Don't do that. You'll go blind if you look. Also, the metal blinds are part of our electro-magnetic protection. The whole plane is shielded. Don't open it until I tell you it's safe to do so." The man stared at Javad, clearly irritated with him.

Of course. When it detonated, the flash could blind them. He softened and gave the man a quick nod and shrugged in innocence. Why had he wanted to watch anyway? He set the world on this course, or at least he been a key part of the whole plan, and now he wanted to watch it burn? Nero had watched Rome burn. Was he equally as insane? He couldn't process it any longer. No matter. His own personal mission wasn't insane. To the mission. Keep to that. To the end. Then, be at peace. And rest, if he was allowed.

He kept repeating this mantra in his head and he realized that during these short exchanges with the technician and his own mind, the aircraft sped up and climbed at a pretty sharp angle. Would they get caught in the blast? He knew nothing at this point. It was in Allah's hands now. And Allah was probably not as pleased with him as he used to be. He had that feeling.

As if on cue, the plane shook violently and he was thrown against his harness. The plane tilted to the side and up. After a few moments, they seemed to level off and resume a smooth course.

❈ ❈ ❈

They had climbed and flown in what he thought was a circular pattern for quite some time. He figured it was about thirty minutes from when they had dropped the weapon over D.C. They were descending. His ears were popping regularly. The red light was still on in the cabin and he gestured at the window to the technician beside him and received a nod. The others across from him raised their window blinds too. He was eager to see the outside and supposed the others were as well. They'd been sequestered in here for too long. As he looked out on this new world, what he saw surprised him. He saw nothing. It was totally dark on this side of the plane. He thought that he'd see something—a lone light in the distance maybe, but there was nothing. As his eyes focused and adjusted a bit, he noticed that there was indeed ground beneath them. Moonlight reflected off of a snaking river. He looked through the window across from him and saw a deep orange glow in the distance. Washington. There were two fires closer to them. Probably airplanes. It was why this plane was shielded. He shuddered involuntarily.

They were going to land soon. How would they do that in the dark? He hadn't really put this together yet. He read the planning documents and reports, but really only focused on his side of things. He hadn't bothered with the operations after the initial attacks as he had expected to be dead by then. He planned on being with the supreme council and telling them that he'd given them away to the West and to await their eventual nuclear retaliation. But, here he was. His primary concern now was getting out and away before the Commandos found him. There was little chance of taking Hafez here, surrounded by his men. Get to Sara and Ahmed. Warn them and assess their options from there. If he could do that, they'd stand a chance. Perhaps, after that, after his family was safe from the possibility of harm, there would be time to deal Hafez. There were too many men with him now and he desperately wanted to see Sara and Ahmed.

The wheels hit the ground. Startled, he grabbed tightly to his harness. The plane shuddered violently and the engines whined with a deafening ferocity.

As the plane braked hard he was thrown sideways against his harness. His mind raced. He had to move fast. He felt the plane lurch again. Perhaps they had gone off the runway. The front of the plane dipped, another shudder, and then they were still.

Javad hit the button to release his harness and reached into his jacket and retrieved the silenced .32. With surgical precision he shot each of the technicians twice. The only sound was the clack, clack of the pistol's slide. He ejected the nearly empty magazine and replaced it with a full one. There was still a round chambered. He looked at the technicians, all slumped in their harnesses. He felt a momentary flash of guilt. These men had just dropped a nuclear weapon, destroying a city and its inhabitants. His remorse was gone, but the irony of it stayed with him. It was his plan.

He'd exit the same way the bomb did. He didn't want to exit on the same side as the Commandos and Hafez. He pushed and held the button to open the rear door. Unsure how far down it was to the ground, he stepped through the interior door and felt his way along the ramp to the end. His eyes adjusted enough that he saw the ground below him. It was grass, not a paved runway. He stepped off the ramp hitting the ground a second later with more force than he'd expected. It was also farther than he estimated and his legs couldn't handle the force. He collapsed hard and lay on the ground. The fresh air was welcome. He hadn't expected the cold, though. It wasn't this cold in Tehran and he wasn't dressed for this. Another consequence of altered plans. The wind stabbed his face like a thousand little daggers.

"Are you ok?"

He heard the voice and then the footsteps on the frozen ground coming fast. Perfect English. His mind raced as he forced his old body up from the ground to come face to face with a man who clearly wasn't Iranian. His skin was a pale white illuminated by the red light cast from the hole he just dropped from. Javad could just make out his dark hair and white face. He acted fast. The man reached out to offer assistance.

"Yes, I am okay. Thank you."

Javad reached for the man's outstretched hand, grabbed it, and yanked it toward him while his punch landed square on the man's nose. The man fell backward and lay still on the ground. If this man was here, he was with them.

He heard voices around the side of the aircraft, but distant. Commandos. He saw buildings and a hanger in the moon-lit distance. He looked left and could just make out a tree line about a hundred yards away. He ran. The uneven, grass covered ground was difficult to run on. The wind whipped his face. He dare not look back or stop. It was dark enough and he was dressed in dark green. Only his movement would catch an eye, but they were on the other side of the plane. He ran as fast as his old legs would carry him.

Breathing heavily, he reached the treeline and disappeared into the brush. He made an effort to control his breathing and scanned the area between his spot and the plane. The totality of the darkness was welcome. He'd studied enough maps of this area since Ahmed, Sara, and his mother relocated here. All he needed was a landmark to orient him. This was a small, executive airport west of D.C. There were only a couple of them. He knew the layout of the buildings here and how they were oriented to the runway out before him. His family was relatively close. Voices and movement focused him. They were at the plane, not in the expanse between the plane and him. He smiled, turned, and vanished into the unknown woods. He was free of them.

# THIRTY-FOUR

December 24
6:05pm EST
Ahmed

"Whoa! I don't want to be a rude host, but we were fine until you two showed up."

Ahmed watched Robert chide Alex and her mom, Ana, with some laughter from the bar leaners. The music from the small, but powerful speaker connected to Robert's phone, had also stopped The firelight danced off the ten foot Christmas tree in the corner of the room, with all of its ornaments. It was beautiful. Peaceful.

"Merry Christmas to you too, Mr. Robert! Where's the fat body?" Alex was searching around the crowded family room for the pug.

"Hey! My phone died. I was texting with Dallas." Layla complained. "Ms. Susan, can you text Dallas and tell him my phone died?"

Dallas was Susan's son. He'd gone to live with his father in Kentucky while Susan and her estranged husband sorted out their divorce. That hadn't set well with Layla. They'd been dating according to Sara, who told him everything that went on with her friends, boring him to death. Teenagers.

"My phone's dead too, Layla. No worries, Sweetie, he'll understand. Let's see if they have a charger."

"He's hiding behind the bar, Alex. Ana, welcome and Merry Christmas! Where's Eric? Charger's in the kitchen, ladies." Lou multi-tasked his conversations, apparently not caring that the power had died. He told Ahmed that he loved the holidays more than any other time of the year. He was several cocktails in already and was full of holiday cheer.

"Lou, Merry Christmas to you as well!" Ana replied and gave Lou a soft hug with one arm, the other carrying a platter of appetizers for the gathering.

Lou took the platter and gestured to the hooks on the wall in the foyer for her to hang her coat. "Eric will be here shortly. He got called into work earlier today, but should be done soon." Ahmed noticed Ana didn't seem to be full of cheer like Lou and Robert.

Ahmed moved past Bibi, Mama, and Brook, who were sitting on the couch. He passed Susan at the bar, where Layla and Sara were getting soft drinks from Robert.

"I will go to see if the rest of the houses are without electricity," Ahmed said.

Leaving the warmth of the house, Ahmed stepped out onto the stoop and walked the driveway. The houses around the cul-de-sac were completely dark, except for the full moon rising in the distance, its light reflecting off a small stream he could barely make out that ran behind the houses.

He pulled out his phone and hit the button. Nothing. He pressed and held the power button on the side of the slim device hoping it would come on. He thought for a moment, then put the phone away. What have you done, Javad? This power outage wasn't right. He felt someone come up behind him.

"Well, this is dark." Lou joined Ahmed in the middle of the stem.

"Yes."

It was not only dark, but overwhelmingly silent. That was not normal at all. As they stood there staring into the darkness, there was a small bark on the chilled air.

"That would be Chewie. Let's go see if Floyd's phone is working, although I expect it's like ours."

They walked up Floyd's driveway. Chewie's barking grew louder. Lou rang the doorbell. Well, he pushed the button, but nothing happened. Power's out. Stupid. He knocked and was rewarded with a small, furry, just barely perceivable face in the window that ran the height of the door. Chewie bounced and barked, but no one answered the door. Lou banged harder without answer. Ahmed reached for the thumb latch and handle to see if it was open.

"I wouldn't do that. Floyd's usually armed. Probably stuck in a dark shower."

Lou turned and walked back down the driveway as the others came out. Robert had a flashlight. It was the only source of light other than the moon. They met on the stem, while Christopher wobbled past them and up to Floyd's door and barked at Chewie through the glass. A low rumble cut through the barking dogs and they turned in the direction of the sound.

The sky seemed wrong to Lou. The high clouds were lit up and they moved slightly away in unison from the fading eastern glow, then back again. A slight breeze blew, like the clouds and air were filling a sudden void. Then it was back to the eerily silent darkness again. No sound except for Christopher's whining and Chewie's barking.

"This is not good, Lou." Ahmed pointed east. "That was very large explosion."

"Mr. Robert, can I have the flashlight?" Layla asked taking the flashlight, joining Alex and Sara up at Floyd's front door where the anxious pug was dancing. She shined the light down where Chewie's furry face could be seen through the thin, bottom window. Then she put her face up to an upper pane of glass while shining the light through a lower one to cut the glare. Ahmed was watching this as he felt something move through the trees and them. Barely discernable. It moved through him.

Ahmed grabbed Lou's arm. "Shock wave." It was slight, but he'd felt shock waves before. He did a quick mental calculation and his breath caught, putting the cloud movements and shock wave together.

"Mr. Lou! He's on the floor!" Layla shouted. Ahmed and Lou ran to the door as Alex grabbed the thumb latch and pushed. The door swung open and Chewie shot through the opening to Christopher and they circled around each other and then darted back into the house.

"What?" Ahmed and the rest of the party crowded through the open door where Layla's light illuminated Floyd, laying awkwardly at the bottom of the stairs. Ahmed was first to Floyd. He said his name loudly with no response. Two fingers went to Floyd's neck. No pulse.

"He is gone, my friends." Ahmed said quietly. Robert took the flashlight gently from Layla, her free hand to her mouth, tears welling.

"Sara. Girls. Come with me." Bibi said in broken English

Alex was wrapped in her mother's arms, silently sobbing. Sara was with Bibi and Mama had taken charge of the shocked Layla. They all stood there in disbelief.

"Take them back to our house and get something warm in them. There is hot chocolate in the pantry. Robert, go with them and help." Lou left no room for discussion. He turned to Robert and whispered, "After you do that, get everyone into the basement. We'll be there directly. I have a bad feeling about what just happened east of here." Robert eyes widened in understanding and he ushered the rest back to his house.

Susan was now over Floyd's body, also checking for a pulse. Ahmed watched her. She was the only one here with medical training, so he supposed it was routine for her to step in. She hung her head and stood next to him. Ahmed surveyed the stairs and foyer with a flashlight.

"Probably fell down the stairs. Neck is broken." Ahmed looked to the front room off the foyer. There was a couch along the far wall and he pointed to it. "We'll move him over there."

"I can grab the shoulders if you can get the feet. Good?" Lou said to Ahmed. They gently lifted and moved in the dim light. The three of them looked down at Floyd's body. Susan crossed herself.

"It was an EMP. Knocked out the power." Ahmed didn't look away from Floyd as he spoke.

"Makes sense, but are you sure?" Lou pressed.

"Did you feel the shock wave out on the driveway? Came from the bright light to the east. I'd say that was Washington D.C. Nuclear detonation."

"What?" Susan blurted.

"Yeah, I felt it. Shock wave travels farther than blast or radiation. We are well west of D.C., so we should be okay. Fallout will be to the east. We are west about thirty miles."

"It was not a large weapon. So, probably not the Russians." Ahmed said.

"Wait. How do you all know this stuff? How do you know it wasn't a large weapon, or explosion?" Susan was frantically looking back and forth between them.

"Because we are still alive." Ahmed looked at her with a smile to reassure her. It didn't work.

Lou interjected. "Susan, can you please go back to the house and make sure Robert has everyone in the basement? We're west, but better to get below ground, even a little, for a while. We'll be right behind you. I want to look in Floyd's basement for something."

Realization hit Ahmed. Christmas Eve. Surprise attack. Couldn't be terrorists, they wouldn't have nuclear weapons or the ability to create an EMP in orbit. Another country or countries? Javad. Are you part of this? But if so, why did put you us here in the middle of it? No. He put the thought out of his head.

"We will be ok, Lou. I have supplies. We will need to do some things fairly quickly though, but not now. In the morning is soon enough. We need to stay in your basement for a while."

"I don't think any of us prepared for this? Come with me. You can tell me your thoughts while I search the basement."

"I prepared for something. I am always preparing for something. If you've seen what I've seen and done what I've done, you would also prepare." Lou stopped and shined the light at Ahmed. They stared at each other for a long moment.

"I'm sorry. I'm a bit rattled by all this, so forgive my blunt questions. Robert and I also prepared for ourselves. We have some supplies, but not necessarily for this. I've been meaning to ask you—were you military of some sort?"

"I was in the war against Iraq. I fought for years. Was wounded." He touched his leg.

"That was a long time ago. What have you been doing since? Sorry to impose, but I think we should know each other better if we are going to get everyone through this."

"Agreed. I did various things over the last couple of decades, mostly administrative duties as an assistant to an officer in Iranian Intelligence. I had disagreements with the regime and had to get my family out." Ahmed's lie was quickly replaced with a question. "And you, I feel you were also military?"

"Okay. I thought so, just from your demeanor. I was a Navy SEAL. Seems we've both seen and done things."

"Yes. A question though. You and Robert are…together? The military didn't care?" Ahmed asked awkwardly.

"We are. I came out after I left. Is this a problem for you?"

"They execute homosexuals in Iran. Was one of my disagreements with the regime. Is not a problem. Nuclear weapons will kill you as easily as they will kill me. We are all just people, Lou."

"Good. And yes, these people, our families, will need us. All of them are my family. I sense they are yours now as well. You've obviously brought Sara here to protect her, but maybe you didn't anticipate all of this?"

"Yes I did, and no, I did not anticipate this. I have a feeling that this is going to get worse, Lou. We're going to need to trust each other to survive this."

Ahmed watched Lou rummage around. It seemed that Floyd was very prepared. Lou showed him around Floyd's stash of supplies. He finally found what he was looking for. Ahmed studied the container. It was a metal trash can with a metal lid. Lou forced it open and pulled out two yellow boxes. Both had handles and a dial on the top.

"Here. You take one and I'll take the other. We'll need these for the short term. Geiger counters."

Ahmed took the yellow box by its handle. Lou flipped the switch on his and was rewarded with a squawk and beep and then silence. Good. Ahmed turned his on in the same fashion with the same results.

"These are helpful. I don't think that any fallout will come this direction though. Let's get back," Ahmed said.

He led Lou up the basement stairs and from the house. Lou closed the door. There was another rumble. Closer and sharper. No flash this time. He and Lou stopped.

"Airplanes. They're crashing. EMP knocking out their engines." Ahmed said in resignation. They continued to Lou's house to join the rest in the basement and fill them in on what they thought they'd figured out.

# THIRTY-FIVE

"General! FLASH message from the NMCC. Authenticated. Intel suggests attack imminent. More intel incoming. Posture—DEFCON TWO. Dial in several strike packages for the fields."

The duty officer rushed to get all the words out coherently. The fields referred to the Minuteman III Intercontinental Ballistic Missile complexes that were located relative to three Air Force Bases located in Montana, North Dakota, and the third field spread over the borders of Colorado, Wyoming, and Nebraska.

"Jesus Christ! Do it. Lock us down! Attack from where, who?"

"North Korea and Iran." The sergeant wiped his bald head with a handkerchief. It came away wet.

A moment later claxons began to sound throughout the complex. Out in the long tunnel to the bunker, the blast doors swung shut. The director glanced at the bank of clocks on the wall, 1608 hours. East Coast time was 1808 hours. He heard the deep clank of the blast door complete its quick closing. At that exact moment, all the monitors went blank or froze. The televisions were still on, but nothing was coming in. The rest of the monitors on their closed network inside were still functioning. However, it looked like they were dropping signals.

"Status! Contacts? Launches?" the general barked.

"No launches. Airspace is clear. However, we've lost tracking over CONUS and Europe, systems are freezing up, Sir!" another officer yelled from across the room.

"Get the NMCC on the li—"

The mountain shuddered. That's the only way he could describe it. It was subtle, but evident that the building they were in, two thousand feet beneath the granite mountain, had just swayed on its massive metal springs.

"What the hell was that? Get me SITREP on that now! Did we just take a hit?" Nothing had changed in the ops center physically, but something had moved the building.

"No incoming bogeys. Airspace clear. We've lost external monitoring. Waiting for sensor analysis now." He exchanged a haunted look with his duty officer.

"Go to DEFCON ONE. My authority. I want to see whatever intel came in before this. Do we have any comms to anywhere, God dammit?"

"NMCC is off-line. No comms. Could be the blast here."

"Do we have comms to the missile fields?"

"Affirmative! Those are green. Sensors around the mountain are indicating radiation and blast. We've been hit with a nuclear weapon. Exact location unknown."

"Any other impacts? What screwed our external networks? EMP?"

"We have no ability to determine impacts, except the one that hit us. EMP is probable. External networks would be fried after a pulse. It would blind us."

"Could they have gotten it in on the ground? Thoughts? Anyone?"

"They could have, but the EMP would have to be in orbit. Gravity bomb? Could have hit the mountain with an old fashioned gravity bomb."

"Shit." The general was in his role for among other things, his calm in crisis. He spoke calmly, "Ok, let's have that intel. We need to clarify the fact pattern and spin up a response."

He looked at his duty officer and they both knew what the other one was thinking. Their families lived in Colorado Springs. Not far enough away. The general held it in and put a hand on his duty officer's shoulder and closed his eyes for a moment in a quick prayer. He opened his eyes, and took the intel sheet from a sergeant standing next to him. He read fast. Okay, you bastards, we're gonna send you a Christmas present.

*** 

It was about thirty minutes since Chao and Feng had gone up to the cabin leaving Gao on duty surrounded by the soldiers. She was in the housing looking at the radar scope. She'd yell if there was any activity. Chao was standing on the porch with a mug of coffee. There were contacts at first. Airplanes. However, they disappeared from the radar one by one. He didn't want to think about that.

"Contact! Launching!" He heard Gao yell from the housing and then shut the small door. Chao watched his soldiers lay flat in their fighting positions.

Chao saw the truck shake as one missile left its protective tube and shot like a bullet into the sky. Gao opened the door, got out and stood on the side of the small platform. He watched with her as the missile ascended to its target, twitching left and then right, adjusting its course. It was moving much faster than the ICBM currently, but that would change fast and there was only a small window to intercept. Feng bolted through the cabin's front door, past Chao and down to the truck. Chao tossed his coffee and followed.

"How many?" Feng yelled at her.

"Only one. For now."

They all stood there watching. They couldn't see the missile any longer, but followed its exhaust trail. It was too far off now to hear the impact, but they saw the flash in the darkening sky. It was then that Chao wondered about the nuclear weapons on the ICBM. Would they detonate when they hit the ground near here? He didn't know if that was how they worked. Or did they need to arm once in their terminal stage to detonate? They would find out in a moment, wouldn't they? Gao didn't seem worried. He trusted her.

# THIRTY-SIX

December 24
7:30pm EST
Fort Knox, Kentucky

The lights had been out now for about ninety minutes. They were ready to go. Lieutenant Wu and his team, consisting of both men and women were in position. There were two hundred some odd fighters on this side of the base. Some only recently arrived, supposedly for the holidays, as couples, or to visit family in the states. Others, like himself, had been here a year or more. He'd come over on a student visa and then melted away into hiding about a month ago. Wu, like the rest, were in the People's Liberation Army.

He didn't known what his mission was when he left China. He was told, by various methods since then, to do certain things in a slow and methodical manner, so as not to attract attention. Like rent the self-storage units and with others, over time, stock them with non-perishable food, water, and other supplies. There were many self-storage units at several locations. Others were in the United States so long that they'd become permanent residents or even U.S. citizens. That was total and true dedication. However, it also served its own purpose. Over time, they were able to buy firearms. A great many firearms. The entire team was well armed. A tractor trailer had arrived at the warehouse a week ago. Buried within the crates of more non-perishable food were more crates. Those contained rocket propelled grenades and launchers, hand grenades, AK-47's, ammunition, and more.

Wu was an up and coming junior officer in the PLA Tank Corps. He was offered a new training opportunity due to his political reliability and his hatred of the capitalists. Consumerism had been creeping into China for decades now. Ruining his country. Once he'd eagerly accepted his new mission, they had shipped him, along with many other tankers, to a training facility in the middle of China, where he'd been introduced to the American M1A1 Abrams Main Battle Tank. They had several of them. They didn't say where they got them, but they were the real thing. Several countries purchased these tanks from the Americans, but weren't squeamish about getting paid to let a few go quietly. A year later, he was studying in America and now, tonight, Christmas Eve, he and his team were ready to put their extensive training to the test.

The men on this team that weren't tankers were PLA special forces. The elite of the elite of the Chinese military. Many were women, who'd come in as wives, girlfriends, or sisters of the men. It added to the force they had, without raising suspicions. These soldiers were traveling light, carrying only weapons, ammo, and their night vision goggles. They didn't need all their gear for combat. Everyone had a radio with earpieces, which they'd handed out from crates after the lights went out.

Through the goggles, Wu saw the hand signal. The soldiers around him rose from their positions in the treeline outside the base. They moved quietly toward the dark and sprawling base. Their target was a line of Abrams tanks, armored personnel carriers, and Humvees. The vehicles had their headlights on. The tanks and APCs were hardened against the pulse that knocked out the power. He learned of this during his training. The tracks looked like they were getting ready to move. That wasn't going to happen. He was told this place held half the American's gold reserves, but they weren't here for that, not yet. They were here for the tanks.

As they crept in the darkness, Wu wondered if there were any American guards. They hadn't seen any. They made their way to the road that separated them from the line of armor. When they passed one of the buildings he noticed two bodies laying by the side of it. Guards. They weren't expecting Wu's team. Why would they expect an attack here in the middle of their country? The guards weren't as alert as they should have been. The team moved as one across the road. Wu followed the female soldier in front of him and his men followed him. A column of tanks and other vehicles was already moving to his left down another base road. He counted four tanks. That was a problem. He couldn't let them get away. He'd need to deal with that shortly, although, their rear guard they'd left back down the road may try to deal with them on their own. They'd slow them down, but probably lose that battle. He'd finish it.

*** ❖ ❖

Several hours after everything went to shit, An was once again sticking half-way out of the Commander's hatch on Alice, her seventy tons of fun beneath him. His platoon of four tanks painted in desert camouflage were rolling, leaving exhaust fumes behind them. It was nothing but cold darkness ahead of them. The news they received at the stand-up briefing was horribly bad. His mind raced over it again.

*"Listen up!" the army colonel yelled as the soldiers and Marines went silent. Something happened and the rumors that swirled in the last ninety minutes were everything from alien invasion to the Russians. An and his lieutenant had already been fully briefed on their mission, but everything was moving so fast that they were having one last stand-up to ensure everyone was on the same page.*

*The colonel continued, "Okay. Best we can tell from what little intel we have is that an EMP was set off over the U.S. We don't have confirmation on that, just conjecture on our part. However, likely the only thing that could have knocked out all the power."*

*There were shocked and angry responses from the Marines around An.*

*"Hold on…it gets worse." he said softly, which was out of character for the old man. "We have zero comms with anyone. Everything is down. Power is out, as you all can see. Civilian vehicles are all mostly dead. Many of our vehicles are dead as well, with the exception of the tracks and LAVs, which were buttoned up. That said, our vehicle comms network is also down. We think the pulse fried the gear through the antennas. The good news, if there is any good news, is that the Exchange had a bunch of these short range walkie-talkies that we've passed around to track commanders. They work if you're close, not affected by the pulse. I guess cheap, plastic radios made in China still work. If this was an EMP, it was likely set off above the atmosphere. What does that mean? For those of you not up on your Electro-magnetic Pulse knowledge, it means that when it went off, via a nuclear weapon detonation, the effects are line of sight, hence the high altitude to impact as much of the U.S. as possible. However, at the edges, the effects trail off and have less of an impact. In any event, Lieutenant Nelson, Gunnery Sergeant*

*Nguyen and their Marines will be heading east to D.C. to relay our situation to whoever is still in charge, if anyone is, wherever they are. Questions before I go on?"*

*The lieutenant spoke up. "What are we likely to get into out there, Colonel? Any situational awareness east? If we're a cluster-fuck here, what's it going to be like out there? I skipped EMP class, Colonel." That last bit broke the tension and some Marines snorted.*

*"Get your giggles in now fellas. It's a fair question, Lieutenant. I skipped that class as well, but what I can tell you is it's bound to be bad. Full effects of an EMP would kill most vehicles, phones, power plants, and all electricity. It's winter. In most of the country it's gonna be cold as a witch's tit. People out there, your country men and women will be surviving on what little they have in their pantries. When that runs out they're gonna be looking for food for their kids and it's a long winter. We all have families here as well. My son, Dallas, is back at my house. We're gonna gather them all up and move them with us."*

❁ ❁ ❁

An watched the fort disappear in the distance. He turned to face the direction they were heading. He saw his gunner, helmet on, scanning left. The turret and main gun were oriented front. The other tracks had their turrets oriented out either left or right. Fletch, his driver, was running about thirty miles per hour. They were settled in for a long haul, but likely some of their vehicles wouldn't make the full trip. The tanks and light armored vehicles, or LAVs, were good to go, but Murphy always rode shotgun. If it was going to break, leak, or fall off, it was going to do it at the least opportune time. Just the way of it. Eventually, a tank would throw a track. That would suck. After several hundred miles of constant movement on paved roads, maybe not so paved roads, depending on the situation, the tracks were going to need some love.

*"Stay away from the big cities," the colonel said. "They're gonna be a mess and people are gonna want you to help them. Show the flag, tell 'em we're going to do everything we can, but don't stop. Stick to the mission. You're gonna see a lot of bad, I think, and it's only going to get worse as winter gets colder. Steer clear of anything that looks half sketchy and watch for any kind of infiltrators or fighters, especially ones that don't look like us. Mark their locations and report them when*

*you get to leadership. If you run into friendlies, and you probably will, share intel and move on. We don't know if they know what's happened here and likewise. That's your mission. Find our troops and any command elements and spread the word, Lieutenant. Understood? The rest of the brigade will head south and try to link up with the 101st near Fort Campbell. We have to get out of these known bases. We're sitting ducks."*

*"Yes Sir."*

*"As for the rest of us, within the next thirty minutes we ain't gonna be here. You can bet your asses that whoever did this knows we're here or they're dumbshits of the highest order. Lieutenant, get moving. You don't need to be here for the rest of this. Push hard. You've got the fuel trucks that the mechanics were able to get running and a couple Humvees as scouts with your Armor Platoon and LAVs. Good luck, Lieutenant, Gunny!"*

*"We'll get it done, Colonel!"*

*Nelson and An saluted. The colonel returned it with a snap. They turned and walked toward their tracks as An heard the colonel start to brief the rest of the battalion's men on their route south to Fort Campbell.*

❋ ❋ ❋

They'd stop in a few hours and he and the Lieutenant would have a quick chat, check the men, and reassess the best route once they were out of these narrow valleys. An's track was lead while the Lieutenant's tank was in the rear. They had three LAVs as well, one to the front of Alice, with one Humvee in front of the LAV running point as Bravo Four. The other two were rear guard behind the lieutenant's track. The LAV's callsigns were Bravo One, Two and Three. The tank's callsigns were Alpha One through Four and the two fuel trucks were Charlie One and Two. The maintenance crew were able to get the two older fuel trucks running and filled up. They were also hauling long trailers that were rigged to carry replacement treads, other than the pieces An had on Alice, and other necessities like ammo for the big guns. An's brother, Bao, was hooked up with one of the fire teams riding in Bravo One further back in the column. An was a tanker, but his brother was ground pounder. A grunt. Bao was more than happy to gear up and ride with the other grunts. There was no room for him in Alice anyway.

The Abrams was a drinker and they'd need those fuel trucks. The tanks had a 250-mile range, so they were going to stop a lot. Hopefully, they'd find gas stations along their route. They'd get into the actual underground fuel tanks and siphon as much as they needed, but they couldn't count on that. The scout LAV was about a quarter mile ahead with the Humvee. He started to think that after a few hundred miles in this government issued seat, as comfortable as it was for short periods, he'd want out for a good while. Right now, though, the cold night air rushing over his face was refreshing. Not too cold for this time of year, but he knew come morning, he'd think differently. At least he was heading in the right direction. Home. He'd have plenty of time to think about his father and the rest of the family in the coming days. Thirty miles an hour or so would be about two days with stops. They needed to sleep. They could switch out drivers, but he wanted Fletch in the driver's seat of his track if they ran into a situation. He stared ahead into the darkness and the silhouettes of the Kentucky mountains. He could use the night vision in his Commander's sights, but there was nothing to see. Just darkness ahead.

❋ ❋ ❋

The distinct sound of engines spinning up on the Abrams sitting outside across the motor pool's wide lot made Lieutenant Wu wince. He and his men had gotten into the tanks easily enough and taken their positions. The special forces had quietly killed the lone guard next to the line of armor. Wu trained the turret on the large garage building. The other tanks did the same. One of the soldiers had peeked into the building through a small window and signaled there were many men inside.

As one, the mass of men in the building filed out into the moonlit night about thirty yards from the line of tanks and Bradley Fighting Vehicles. A cold wind blew from the west. The silence that had returned after the Marines had moved out was replaced with the turbine engines of the tanks. Wu could see the Americans standing in front of the building. He opened up on them with the machine gun slaved to his optics on top of the turret. His gunner fired the machine gun slaved to the main gun. There was no warning as several of the other tanks opened fire with their co-axial machine guns. The Bradley's opened up with their twenty-five millimeter Bushmaster Chainguns. Rounds went through men and building, virtually cutting in half anyone standing outside or within the building. Within twenty seconds, every man in front of Wu was dead.

Silence returned. Wu surveyed the carnage before him. This was his first experience with actual combat. Bile rose in his throat and he popped quickly out of the commander's hatch of the tank that he had quietly procured only moments prior and emptied his stomach down the side of the massive turret. Wiping spit from his chin, he regained his composure and ordered his driver and three other tanks onto the road next to the motor pool. He had the rest take up defensive positions. There was prey to the east. To a tanker, other tanks were prey. He snapped at his loader to load the main gun with a sabot round. Each tank had high explosive rounds for general use or sabot rounds. Sabots were depleted uranium dart-like rounds that seared their way through tank armor, creating and spraying what was known as spall, or liquid metal, inside the tank, killing everyone inside.

❊ ❊ ❊

"Column halt. All stop."

An heard lieutenant Nelson over the ridiculous little handheld radio. All the vehicles in the column came to a stop and idled in place. An had his head sticking out of the commander's hatch. He clearly heard gunfire coming from behind them in the distance. The Fort.

"Six Actual, Five Actual. I heard gunfire, copy?" An said into the radio.

"Five, Six Actual, roger that! Stay up front with Recon and the fuel trucks. Something's up. All quiet now, but that was definitely a chaingun. We're only a couple miles into this valley complex. Bravo Two, reverse your course quick. Head back to the Fort and see what you can see. Bravo One, Alpha Two and Three, with me."

All vehicles responded affirmatively and began turning, or rotating as it were with tanks, in the road. An didn't have a great feeling about their position with the valley walls high to either side. Someone had lit something up back at the Fort and the returning silence made him uneasy. His muscles tensed. He lowered himself reflexively down in the hatch as the first Rocket Propelled Grenade, or RPG, swooshed from the left side of the valley about halfway up the side of the hill there into the second fuel truck with a blinding explosion. An reached over and grabbed the hatch handle and secured it above him.

"Gunner! Target! Dismounted enemy! Loader! Load HEAT!" An yelled all this while traversing the turret and elevating the main gun along with the co-axial machine gun to the point where he saw the RPG originate from. Stewie loaded a High-Explosive Anti-Tank round into the breach of the main gun.

"HEAT up!" Stewie yelled.

"Fire!"

"On the way," Jones said calmly.

The main gun kicked back, vibrating through the tank. The machine gun began a staccato beat. An followed his tracer rounds into the tree line up the hill about a hundred yards where the HEAT round exploded with some satisfaction. The Recon LAV had also opened fire further up the road with its chaingun, sweeping the enemy position with twenty-five millimeter cannon rounds. The intense fire of the wrecked fuel truck danced light up the valley walls, partially impairing his optics.

"Cease fire."

An couldn't quite make out the second fuel truck through the bright flames of the first, but it didn't matter. A second RPG round from the opposite side of the valley slammed into it with a deafening roar and burning fuel blanketed the middle of the valley.

"God Dammit!"

Even as the Recon vehicle lit up the new enemy position, An was swinging his main gun in that direction.

"Six, Bravo Two! Tanks in the road. We…" The transmission over the walkie-talkie cut out as An heard a main gun's report. Another explosion rolled up the valley from Bravo Two's position a second later.

"Gunner! Fire!" The main gun expelled the second HEAT round up the other side of the valley in a crunching blast taking trees with it and hopefully whoever was engaging them. Only seconds had passed since this started. An tried to quickly make sense of the landscape unfolding in front of him and in his head.

"Zombie Five Actual, Six Actual! Move! Get out of here now. That's an order! We'll fight here, whoever it is, and catch up if we can. Do not stop! You have the mission! Understood, Gunny!"

"Six, Five Actual, Roger that! Kill those bastards! Be advised. Enemy positions, both sides of the valley. We lit 'em up, but there may be more."

An was shaking from adrenaline. Several more booms echoed down the valley. The lieutenant was in the fight, but who were they fighting? Dammit! He hated this. Where was Bao? He had no time.

"Driver! Forward Fast!" Alice rolled, picking up speed toward the Recon LAV and the Humvee while watching the unfolding chaos behind them through his optics as two more RPGs shot out of the treeline behind the burning fuel trucks. An watched in horror as both projectiles hit the side of one of the LAVs.

"Recon, Five Actual. We're coming to you! Move forward up the valley! Scan the hills and watch for RPGs. Kill anything that gets in your way!"

"Five, Recon, Roger!"

Both vehicles popped smoke out of their canisters on the turrets to hide their movement from whatever was behind them.

"What are we doing, Gunny? We can't leave! We just lost half the damn column!"

Stewie was hot and rightly so. Unfortunately for him he was yelling at An right now. An was nearly blind with anger. They had just lost a dozen Marines, maybe his brother.

"You heard the Lieutenant on the radio just like the rest of us. Square your shit, Lance Corporal! We don't know what's in front of us and we can't go back. Job to do. Sucks ass, but here we are getting our shit pounded. We're following our orders and getting the hell out. Clear!"

An's blood was boiling. He took it out on Stewie. It wasn't like him to do that. He saw Jones stretch out a hand to lightly punch Stewie in the arm. Stewie returned gesture and sat his self on his perch next to the main gun and stared at the floor where the two expended shell casings were rolling back and forth with the motion of the tank now speeding at maximum clip.

What the hell had just happened? Who hit them? Was Bao in the LAV that was hit. He struggled to remember which one his brother was in as a lead weight formed in his stomach. Was his brother dead? What was he going to tell Brook, he thought, fighting back panic and tears. He felt a tap on his knee. He looked down.

"I'm sure your brother's givin' 'em hell right now," Stewie said.

"Damn right, Stewie. Damn right." They were unaware that the Battle of Fort Knox had just begun.

# THIRTY-SEVEN

December 24
9:00pm EST
December 25
7:00am - Kazakhstan
Joey Washington

The Soyuz hit the frozen Kazakhstan steppe with a thud and everything inside, including the three temporary inhabitants, lurched sideways as they tipped first one way and then the other before falling all the way over onto their side. It was not supposed to happen like that, but it was probably better for exiting the capsule. The round hatch would be above them if the Soyuz were upright, but now they were upright and facing the round hatch, horizontal to the ground. Success. She was home. Her larger home, but not her home. Gravity returned with a vengeance. The weight of it fully restraining her in her seat. Lifting her arms was a struggle. She knew that would fade, but she didn't think they had time to wait before they had to move and be active. They were at other's mercy for now, if anyone was even aware they landed.

The three of them had been in space about six months, so their recovery would be brutal. They wouldn't even be able to walk immediately, with their muscles in varying stages of atrophy. Balance would be a bitch. Returning to gravity was tough under normal circumstances, but this wasn't normal. Would anyone be coming to get them? Her leg was throbbing again, worse than before, now under the effects of gravity. There was no telling what would happen with her leg or how she would even be able to move without crutches or some kind of support. She was getting ahead of herself. One thing at a time, Commander, she thought. First thing—they were on Earth.

Done. Check. They hadn't died in space or burned up on re-entry. They were alive. What was next?

She looked at her companions and could tell they were feeling the effects as well. Dizziness, maybe some nausea, muscle fatigue. She needed to get out of this claustrophobic coffin. They had gear and supplies to survive on the grassy steppes of Kazakhstan. Enough to give their crew rescue team time to get to them, if they knew they were here. There were automatic alerts that the station and Soyuz sent to the ground in case of emergency evacuation. What if those auto alerts had been damaged? She unbuckled her harness and caught herself from falling forward. This was going to suck. Tavis and Pasha unbuckled as well. Pasha was holding his head, one eye closed.

"Pasha, okay?" she asked.

"Da. Gravity." he replied.

Tavis was the first one to reach over to the hatch from his seat, and with noticeable effort and strain, worked it open. Seconds later if fell free and a rush of freezing air slapped their faces. They all breathed deeply and Joey pulled in air through her nose, the smell of Earth on every molecule. She savored it a moment before checking "opening the hatch" off her mental checklist. Next.

"Tavis, collect up the emergency gear, I'm going outside. Pass it to me and follow. Pasha, you're after him." She began her exit process, which included not banging her broken leg on anything, or passing out.

"I should go first, Joey. Your leg," Tavis said.

"Nope. I want out now." Joey had to get out of this flying coffin. She wasn't usually claustrophobic, but she needed fresh air now.

She squeezed, crawled, and pulled herself through the hole on her stomach. Once her hands hit the lightly snow-covered grass, she rotated and let her shoulders and back rest lightly on the ground. She stayed there for a second looking up at the sky, dizzy. It was a beautiful blue with some wispy clouds. The sun was low in the east. It was morning on the Steppes. She took a deep breath. Air. Sweet, fresh air.

"You good, Joey?" Tavis said from inside the capsule.

She put her good foot down and pushed backward holding her broken leg just off the ground.

"Yeah, hold on a sec."

She squirmed gently around so she could reach the bag of gear that Tavis was holding out the hatch. She grabbed it with some effort, feeling nauseous, and put it down in the snow out of the way of the others coming out of the hatch, Tavis first. As she moved herself out of the way along the ground, her back and butt cold from contact with the dusting of snow. Tavis came out on his stomach and caught himself with his hands. His arms collapsed under him, putting his face in the snow with some profanities. He regained his senses and rolled out of the way for the Russian. Pasha came out the same way as Tavis, however, he was having a bit more trouble squeezing through the hole than they did with his big frame. He finally caught himself and pulled with his hands along the ground and rolled over, breathing deeply.

Tavis rolled over to spew his insides next to him on the ground. That was all it took. She felt the bile rise in her throat as she rolled over just in time for her insides to blanket the snow next to her.

"Oh!" Pasha said, trying to crawl away from them, the smell, and heaving sounds, but to no avail. He emptied his stomach a few feet from the others.

"Jesus, Mary, and Joseph!" the Scotsman shouted at the sky. "We're some real pretty bastards, aren't we?"

"That was fun. Hey, Merry Christmas!" Joey said dryly.

"That was...not at all fun, Commander," Pasha said, with a burp and a deep sigh.

"Now that we've collectively blown our groceries all over Kazakhstan, can we get warm? Where are the blankets?" Tavis said.

Joey grabbed the pack above her head and dragged it to the middle of the sorry-looking group. They pulled out sealed packages with blankets, ripped them open, and huddled together for warmth. The enthusiasm from being back on solid ground dissipated with every windy gust. She was having second thoughts about being outside now.

Within ten minutes they had a fire going from the fire-starting material in the gear bag. It was small and wouldn't last forever with what they had. Getting back into the capsule was an option if they didn't want to freeze to death. They put on what survival clothing was in the gear bag and the capsule, and with the small fire, they were warm enough for now. Joey surveyed the landscape. Nothing but snow covered grass land as far as the eye could see. The wind was picking up as well as she scanned the horizon. There was a speck moving out there.

"Guys. What's that out there?" As she pointed in the direction of the speck, it turned into two specks.

"Da! I see them. They are coming." Pasha said more enthusiastically than normal.

Those two specks turned into crew rescue vehicles. As they rolled up to the sparse little campsite, Joey felt a great sense of relief. Then anxiety crept in. Was the world at war? She recalled what they saw from space. They were in survival mode. Nothing else mattered, until now. The two large vehicles were bright blue with three large wheels on either side. Russian All-Terrain Vehicles. They had a large compartment in the rear with windows where they'd have warm clothes, heat, food, and water. Why no helicopters? Unusual.

"Rat teebya veedet'!" Pasha said to the group approaching. "Nice to see you" in Russian.

"Hello and welcome back!" One of the men replied in English. "Are you alright?" He continued.

"Yeah, I don't know if you've noticed, but we crashed here from outer space and its cold as a mothe…"

"We are alive. Pasha has a head wound and my leg is broken. He's fine." Joey gestured at Tavis who was about to say something inappropriate.

"Okay! We have to move fast. We will get you warmed up in the truck and tend to your injuries on our way to Karaganda. Quickly, please."

Other men had surrounded them and helped them up. Usually, there were chairs they put them in to carry. Not this time. It was warm inside, but Joey shivered for a while as the vehicles bounced over the uneven terrain. The rescue team didn't seem to care about the capsule at all. They were indeed moving quickly.

"What's happened here? Something crippled the station and we had to evacuate quickly. We saw—"

"Baikonur Cosmodrome has been evacuated. We are taking you to hospital in Karaganda to begin your recuperation." He looked cautiously at each of them in turn.

"Tell us what's going on. We saw it from orbit. All of North America and

Europe are dark and we saw bright flashes over India and Pakistan. Is it war? Did someone start a fucking war?" Tavis demanded.

"What we know…what I can tell you, is that something, probably an EMP in orbit crippled the station and knocked out electricity to America and Europe. The Indians launched a nuclear strike at Pakistan and the Pakistani's retaliated in kind. There have been other isolated nuclear incidents. All Russian military installations are being evacuated. The government is saying to stay indoors or go to a public shelter and stay there until further information is known."

"Bloody fucking 'ell!" Tavis spit out.

Pasha reached out to grab his shoulder and squeezed tightly.

"What of Moscow? Saint-Petersburg?" Pasha asked.

"We were not told of any attacks against Russia. This seems to be against NATO only, although there are reports that the North Koreans have invaded South Korea and Japan is dark. The Russian government has said it doesn't know who is to blame. Personally, I think the North Koreans are responsible for all of it. This is all we know and much of what I've told you is conjecture on our part. I understand your frustration and your concern for your families. I—we—have families in Russia and elsewhere. We can do nothing for them. We are here. As you are."

"America? Washington, D.C.? Any word?" Joey asked. She was trying to keep it together.

"I do not know, Commander. We just do not know. Nothing is working. Internet and mobile phones have been cut off by the government. No communications except what we hear from the government on emergency TV and radio. Land lines are still operating within the country. We tried to let the Russian Space Agency know you had evacuated, but we could not reach them. We found out about Baikonur on the TV. We do not know what comes next. We are in the dark."

He handed her a hot cup of tea and she took it. He offered the others the same and they took their cups and settled in. A medic was tending to Pasha's head. Another medic was removing Joey's splint.

As he worked on her leg, she thought of Gale and Layla. Dread crept in. She hoped they were safe and together. If they were, they'd be good to go, at least for a while. Now that they were on the ground, she'd get back to them. Somehow. She glanced at Pasha and Tavis. She'd do anything to get back, but they obviously couldn't just get on a plane and fly home. So many unknowns. Tavis was next to her, uncharacteristically quiet.

They were moving toward Karaganda. It was a decent sized city of about half a million people. Surely they could find a way out. There had to be a way.

# THIRTY-EIGHT

December 24
10:00pm EST
Ahmed

It was late into the night. Ahmed looked around the fire-lit room. Everyone had stayed at Lou and Robert's house as he and Lou had suggested. After hours in the basement, Ahmed and Lou went outside with the bright yellow Geiger counters and, getting no radiation readings, allowed everyone back upstairs. Robert was back behind the bar and still serving drinks to anyone that wanted one. It seemed to calm Robert's nerves. Doing normal things. They took most of the food to the basement earlier, picking at their plates of holiday fare while trying to figure out what was going on and what they were going to do.

Ahmed finished his last whiskey just before they ate, but others were deep into their drinks. Especially Mama. Bibi and Brook were consoling her at the moment. The realization that her husband's body would sit alone at the morgue, possibly forever, with the nuclear blast over D.C., was too much for the sweet old lady. Ahmed thought Layla was in the worst shape though. She was putting on a brave face, but with her mother in orbit and her father miles away, she was close to breaking. He knew what it was like without parents. His heart ached for her. He had lost his parents, but Layla had no idea if her's were alive or dead. Sara and Alex were trying to keep her occupied, but so much had happened in just a few hours, it was too much for some of them.

No one wanted to go upstairs to the bedrooms to sleep. More comfort as a group, he thought. He couldn't stop sneaking peeks at Susan. Ten years his junior. They exchanged pleasantries over the last few months as they saw each other coming and going from their homes. He thought of her often, but now wasn't the time. He had to focus on keeping his family safe, not on silly feelings. What was the point anyway? He had expected to live out his years alone, caring for Bibi and Sara and nothing more. Then the world changed. In a split second.

Susan went back over to her house to grab more blankets and to change out of her dress. Others went and returned as well in quick order, but she wasn't back yet. Ahmed decided to go check on her and perhaps grab some blankets from his house on the way. Just an excuse to talk with her again. He was amused with himself. Nuclear war, no power, middle of winter, and he was being childish. He hadn't felt anything close to this for a long time.

Ahmed slipped quietly out the front door, up the pipe stem, passing his house and up to Susan's front door. It was cracked open. He was about to call out and announce himself, but then decided against it and put his hand flat against the door and pushed. Muffled voices drifted down the stairs once he was inside. That wasn't right. All senses heightened in the darkness of the foyer. He took one step at a time, trying to minimize the creaking of the stairs. Moonlight shown in through two open doors at the rear of the hallway. A pile of blankets and a pillow lay in disarray on the floor. He was focused, however, on the closed door to the third bedroom. The voices were clearer now. Men's voices. There was a female voice mixed in, but muffled. One male voice was asking about a safe combination in an angry tone.

Ahmed crashed through the door. He saw Susan sitting in a chair across the room. There were two men. The men hesitated, surprised by Ahmed's entrance. One of them started toward him. Ahmed moved sideways, like a snake, years of training and combat kicked in, as the first man lunged at him. Ahmed caught the heavy smell of booze. The man never recovered from his mistake as Ahmed grappled the man and spun him forcefully using the his own momentum against him. He twisted the man's head around until there was an audible snap. Ahmed dropped the body and it collapsed on the floor.

The other man started for Ahmed. Susan rolled out of the chair onto the floor. Ahmed grabbed the second man as he approached. He was no match for Ahmed's strength. Even at almost sixty years old, Ahmed easily hefted the weight of the smaller man as he twisted his large frame around. The flailing man flew upside down across the room so violently that his body lodged in the drywall for a moment, then fell to the floor, immobile and silent.

"Be still. It's Ahmed," he said to Susan.

"Thank you!" she said raggedly.

Ahmed said as he sensed movement at the door and turned to meet the next attack, determined to protect this woman. He saw a glint of metal in the new arrival's hand. Knife. He tensed all his muscles and prepared to fight.

"Susan? It's Gale Washington from next door." Ahmed relaxed.

"Gale! Yes, I'm ok. Ahmed got here just in time."

"I was walking up the court and heard the commotion. Came in to see if you were alright."

"Hello, Gale. It's Ahmed, Sara's uncle, from next door."

"Good thing you were here." The two men shook hands. "Susan, who are these guys? You know them?" Gale asked, still trying to figure out what happened.

"I think they were friends of my husband. They wanted Kim's guns in his safe. I couldn't remember the combination. They were just here for the guns."

"Really? Is your husband around? Aren't you all separated?"

"I don't know where he is. I've got a restraining order against him. These assholes thought they'd get his guns. The court wouldn't let him have them after the order was filed against him."

"Well, you're safe now. Is my daughter around?"

"Oh, Gale, she's so worried about you and Joey. Any word on her?"

"No. No word. I think it's pretty bad all over." Gale said. "It was a long walk home."

"Why don't we get back to Lou's. Layla will be relieved." Ahmed ushered them from the room and the bodies closing the door. The fight had winded him. He following Gale and Susan into Lou's house. He may need another drink.

\* \* \*

"Gale!" Lou stood in the hallway beckoning them in.

"Lou, tell me Layla's here."

"Dad!" Layla ran from the large family room and crushed him in a hug.

"Thank god you're okay." He wrapped her up in his arms, squeezing tightly.

"Daddy, what happened? Where were you? Did you hear from mom? Everything is off." She sobbed into his shoulder, overcome by relief.

"There's time for that in a bit. Let your dad get warmed up by the fire. Come on in, Gale, and Robert will fix you a drink, if you need one?"

"Lou, had time to think on the way home. Is Floyd here? He's got Geiger counters in his stash in his basement. We're going to need those quick." Gale said, shedding his heavy jacket, wool hat, gloves, and scarf and the clinging Layla as they headed into the family room.

"Gale, there was an accident. We found Floyd just after the lights went out. He'd fallen down his stairs. He's dead. Broken neck. His body's on his couch in his living room. Must have fallen in the dark," Lou explained.

"What? I don't have words. Wasn't expecting that. He was the most prepared out of all of us. To end that way…"

"We got the Geiger counters though." Lou pointed to a yellow box sitting on the kitchen table. "The other one is out back on the deck. Check it every thirty minutes or so."

Robert offered Gale a beer.

"No thanks, Robert. You have coffee?"

Robert nodded and headed to the kitchen. He'd made coffee earlier from a French press and came back with a steaming mug. They all gathered around Gale by the fire, Layla next to him, not leaving his side. He proceeded to tell the group what he knew. Or, what he thought he knew.

"Is there any good news?" Robert asked from behind the bar.

"I'm afraid I don't have any, man. I think what knocked out the power was an EMP generated from a nuclear weapon detonated in orbit above the U.S. from a North Korean satellite. If I'm right, a second one went off over Europe, so the West is completely dark.

"What about the nuke that took out D.C.?" Lou asked.

"I don't think that could have been the NoKo's." Gale looked at Ahmed, choosing his next words carefully.

"Who hit D.C.?" This came from the very pregnant Brook, who was reclining on the couch, worry in her eyes. Gale knew she had to be out of her mind with concern for her husband.

"Iran," was all he said.

Everyone in the room looked at Ahmed.

"I didn't drop a bomb on D.C."

"Yeah, everyone relax. Ahmed and his family are in the dark, just like the rest of us."

This came from the diminutive, but motherly, Mama, who was sitting on the other couch patting Bibi's hand in reassurance. Her tone conveyed that she'd take offense to anyone's accusations as another knock sounded at the front door. Lou got it and found Alex's father, Eric, standing on the stoop.

"Well, everyone's showing up late! Get in here, Eric. Wait, what happened to your face? Are you okay?" Lou said.

Gale saw Eric's face. There was dried blood around Eric's mouth and smeared across one cheek.

"Was driving home and everything went dark. My car stalled, but the car in front of me slammed on the breaks and I rear-ended them. Busted my nose on the steering wheel. Had to walk the rest of the way here. My family here?"

"All here, Eric." Gale said as Ana and Alex ran to him.

"Ahmed, you and yours are part of this group." Gale said loudly. "We're in this together. Whoever did this, they're no friends of anyone in this room. We're going to need to work together to get through this. Had some time to think on the walk home. In the morning, early, we need to gather all the supplies we can from Floyd's house and mine. Wood for the fire, food, water, blankets, anything of use. So, I suggest we all try to get some sleep.

"What did I miss?" Eric said looking around the room over his wife and daughter, with one eyebrow raised.

❋ ❋ ❋

Donneker stood in his former bedroom that he shared with his estranged wife only months prior. He surveyed two bodies on the floor. Jimmy lay unconscious, but breathing. Dale was dead. The bastards came for his guns. He regretted telling them about his guns. They must have been at the bar, all liquored up by the smell of them, when the lights went out. It was a twenty minute walk. With no cars working or power anywhere and general chaos all around, they figured they could rob his house, maybe worse, with no police around. He dragged one of the pillows off the bed and knelt down over Jimmy. He placed the pillow over Jimmy's face and applied increasing pressure. There was no struggle as the last life silently slipped from him. Shooting his boss was an accident, but he wasn't at all bothered about Jimmy and Dale. He stood and dropped the pillow on the fresh corpse. Good riddance. He should have been here. He'd try to make amends with Susan tomorrow.

# THIRTY-NINE

December 25
1:00am EST
Javad

Javad stood in the living room. There was a warmth in the house even though the power had been out for nine hours. The warmth wasn't only heat. This place was filled with familiar scents and smells. There was love here. He no longer shivered. It had been a long walk, six or seven miles, through woods and then on paved roads. His memory was fairly good. He had studied this area on a map he kept at his flat. It wasn't difficult to find his way from the small airport.

He breathed in through his nose and it filled him with happier times. The smell of his mother's cooking lingered, but where were they? The house was empty, but the minivan was in the garage. Could they have driven another car? Or ridden with others somewhere? Perhaps, but not likely. Ahmed liked routine and safety in his surroundings. He walked slowly over to the bay window of the room that looked out onto the houses and what appeared to be a driveway that connected several of them. They were all dark. Where to start? Ahmed and Sara had to be somewhere close. He focused on walking distance and the age of his mother. Not far, he thought.

He peered out the slim window by the front door. No movement. There wouldn't be at this time of night. The Iranians would not come here. They were close, but their mission was to interdict any west-bound traffic on the main road. Not to patrol the surrounding neighborhoods. On the other hand, when they found the bodies he left behind in the plane, they'd know someone was here who wasn't authorized. They would hunt that person if they could. They would hunt for him. Hafez didn't know it was him, though. That was to his advantage, but this was all a new plan now. A smaller plan.

More important to him. He didn't know how the larger plan had played out once he'd set it in motion and boarded that plane. If he stayed in Iran, and if it all worked, he would be with the Supreme Council when the end came. Not knowing clawed at him. He wanted to look them in the eyes when it happened and tell them all it was his doing that ended them and their corrupt regime. To finally get justice for Sara, for Yasmin, for his father's broken heart.

He couldn't distinguish justice from vengeance anymore, but did it matter at this point? Not to him. There was only Hafez left. The last loose end. He would look into the eyes that had haunted him all these years. No matter what happened, those eyes would be truly dead when he was done with this journey. But first, he needed to find his family.

He moved outside toward the house on the left. He decided to search them one by one until he found his family or someone who knew where they were. The smell of wood smoke was in the air. Someone was around here somewhere. Javad walked across the grassy lawn, which crunched under his feet. That sensation was new to him. The grass was frozen. His breath was a cloud of tiny ice crystals in the moonlight. Everything was so quiet, he found himself creeping so as not to disturb the silence. A few snowflakes drifted whimsically on the slight wind. He grabbed the handle on the front door and pressed down with his thumb on the latch. The door opened onto a dark entryway and he stepped in closing the door behind him with a click. He looked around. The same layout as Ahmed's house. He took a step and was struck hard in the back of the head. He fell forward onto the living room floor. Blackness.

# FORTY

An intravenous line in Joey's arm provided the fluids she so desperately needed back in gravity. Tavis was in the bed next to hers and Pasha was across the room with a similar set up. They all felt better, but still weak. Joey had puked twice more, once in the truck and again when coming into the hospital. The rescue team that had plucked them from the frozen steppe had left, leaving them in the care of the doctors and nurses here at, well, she didn't really know what hospital, but it was warm and they were safe.

Safe. Were Gale and Layla safe? She couldn't get their faces out of her mind and nobody here could tell her anything new. No internet. Limited cell service. Pasha had learned the land lines were working locally after he inquired about a friend in the city. An aging male nurse had brought a phone in and plugged the line into the wall socket.

Pasha called a small, out of the way cafe down in the city center. His acquaintance, Boris the Wolf, owned the place. Boris was Russian, an oil and mineral oligarch, but the Russian government had run him out of Russia due to some seedy activities. To Pasha's surprise, Boris was there and they spoke briefly in Russian. He didn't elaborate on the wolf part.

"He will come in the morning." Pasha relayed the gist of the call in English to Joey and Tavis. "Boris has an errand to take care of first. He didn't say what and didn't want to continue to speak by phone. This is good thing that he will come. Is good thing." He closed his eyes.

"That's it?" Tavis asked.

"Da. Will give us time to rest and recuperate before."

"Before what? Did I miss something Commander?"

"I think what Pasha is trying to say is that Boris will help us get out of here in the morning."

"Da. You should rest, Doctor. Morning comes sooner than you think."

Unintelligible words fell from the Scotsman's mouth. It was the heavy brogue that materialized when he was agitated. Unfortunately, he'd been agitated for the last twelve hours or so, and Pasha wasn't helping matters. It was easier to understand Pasha with his accent and broken English. Her thoughts drifted back to her family and just how Boris the Wolf would help them get home. How scared Layla must be right now. At least she was with her father as it was Christmas Eve at home. Or was it Christmas Day there? Regardless, she took solace in the thought that they Gale and Layla were together as she drifted to sleep.

❈ ❈ ❈

Her slumber was fitful. Nightmares kept her body twitching in and out of sleep. Gale laying in a creek, the one behind their house, not moving. Layla! Her eyes shot open. She was sweating. Dream. Damn that was real. Then, there was a hand over her mouth. She panicked and struggled until she heard Pasha's deep voice.

"Joey. Easy, Joey. You're having a bad dream. We have visitors."

Pasha removed his hand from her face. The room was still dark, but there was some light from the medical equipment they were hooked up to and a dim light coming from under the door. As her eyes adjusted she made out two silhouettes. Pasha moved back to his bed. Tavis was sitting on the edge of his, rubbing his eyes.

"What time is it? Who are they?" she said suspiciously.

"It is just after midnight. I am Boris."

The shorter of the two shadows stepped forward. The other, larger shadowed figure stayed back near the door, still as a post.

"What's happening, Pasha? I thought they were coming in the morning?" Tavis asked.

"Morning has come early. Boris is here to help us get out." Pasha responded.

"Allow me, my old comrade, to explain matters. It is very exciting to meet Pasha's friends, fellow cosmonauts. Unfortunate to return to the planet in its current situation, but I'm told that is better than being dead, yes? Okay. We are taking you out now. Some clothes have been brought. Please dress. Commander, here are crutches. I will explain what I can once we are moving."

Boris gestured to the neatly folded clothes on the end of each bed. Joey hadn't seen anyone bring them in, but here they were. Pants, shirts, socks and boots. Even heavy winter coats.

"Morning did come early, didn't it?" Tavis said as he pulled on the gifted pants.

"Maybe not everything fits well. It is what we had. We must go quickly please." Boris looked down at his illuminated watch.

"Why the haste and in the middle of the night?" Joey asked, donning her own loose fitting garments and one boot, the other she handed to Tavis to carry for her. Eventually, she'd need it. She put on the extra heavy socks, stretching one over her exposed foot with some effort and discomfort. The cast they'd put on her lower leg went from her mid-thigh to her ankle. In the pockets of the heavy coat she found gloves and wool cap.

"They will come here soon to place a guard. Others will come in the morning. You will not be here if we move quickly please."

"Who will come?"

"There is war now. Two of you are from NATO countries. I've stalled them a little, but only a little. They wanted to meet you when you arrived. I knew you had left the space station the moment you detached from it. I know everything that goes on here. Please hurry. You are not the only task I have tonight."

Pasha nodded to Boris, who in turn, nodded to the other figure in the dim light. He turned, opened the door to their room and walked out into the hallway. Incandescent light flooded their room. Another man stood near the empty nurse's station along with a much younger man. With his boyish face, he looked like a teenager to Joey. He was dressed in blue jeans, tennis shoes, and a heavy jacket. His blond hair was short and he wore glasses. The older man nodded and Boris left the room with the three grounded space travelers behind him. Joey wobbled on the crutches at first, but found her balance. Not so bad. They took several turns through the hallways and came to an emergency exit. The first man went through it without stopping. No alarm sounded. He held the door for the rest of the party to come through into the night. Joey shot her hands into the coat pockets to retrieve the gloves and cap as she balanced her body on the crutches under her shoulders. Holy crap it was cold. There was a light snow falling and the wind funneled into the alleyway from the streets and buildings a block away. They followed Boris to a dark colored van as the exit door slammed shut.

The inside of the van was sparse, but warm. The driver sped off, throwing Joey back into the seat she'd barely settled into. The motion brought her dizziness back and she closed her eyes to steady herself. Boris was in the middle row bench of the van with the teenager. The other man was in the front passenger seat. Joey, Tavis, and Pasha were in the very back. He turned to them with a smile.

"Welcome to Earth!" he said with a guttural laugh. "Okay. Here is plan. I will take you to airport where we will board one of my planes. We will leave this god forsaken place. I do this for my old comrade, Pasha." He slapped Pasha on the knee roughly.

"I have never known you to do things for nothing, Boris. What do you want in return?" Pasha's eyes glinted off the passing street lights as he stared at his friend. Boris smiled

"Ah! Pasha, only a small favor, my friend. A small favor. I need a helicopter pilot."

"I don't fly any more, Boris. I'm a cosmonaut now."

"Pasha, I am a business-man, you know. There is war now. A business-man can make a lot of money in a war."

"To where? Just one flight?"

"My plane will carry cargo with us to Saint-Petersburg. The cargo needs to be ferried to where planes can't land."

"And then?"

"You and your friends may go where you wish. Where you can." Joey was about to interrupt, but Pasha squeezed her arm next to him.

"Deal."

"Good, good. This is my grandson, Valeri. He will come with us to get him away from that bastard father of his."

Boris' face turned grim and he sneered the last few words. Valeri was looking around at them one at a time and looked uncomfortable in his grandfathers' one armed hug. It was clear to Joey the boy didn't want to be here.

"Hey, weird question, but how do you two know each other?" Tavis chimed in off-hand, motioning between Pasha and Boris.

"Ah, Pasha was in my employ years ago. He also likes losing to me at chess, which is good for him, he thinks!"

"What did you do for him before, Pasha?" Joey asked pointedly, but quietly.

"He flew men and material here and there in my many helicopters. He flew me out of Russia when they came for me. It was long ago, but I repaid him by erasing his name from the computers. This allowed him to be an honest person again, with his sister and her daughter. Yes, I am proud of what you have done with your 'cleanliness' Pasha."

"Da, Da. My family. I need to get them. They are outside Saint-Petersburg."

"Da. I thought you may want to see them. I have planned for this. Must be quick though. Helicopter is waiting there for your flights. I have people in Saint-Petersburg. Is your sister still on that nice little farm next to the Aerodrome?"

"How do you remember the farm? You were never there, Boris."

"Ah, Pasha, I know all the things that need knowing. Now we do this. This is good plan, yes? Da?"

Resigned, Pasha nodded and silence returned to the van as it sped through the darkened streets. The streetlights were on, some of them, until they passed out of the city. They drove for about ten minutes with little other traffic until they approached a brightly lit airport. They pulled past the regular parking lot and small terminal building. They could see the lit runway. There was only one. It was a small, regional airport, but it seemed modern. The van pulled to a stop next to what appeared to be a hanger. They weren't going through security, it seemed.

"We are here. Follow, please."

Boris the Wolf exited the van. Once Boris and Valeri were out, Pasha paused.

"No matter what you see here, get on the plane. Ask no questions. None." And then Pasha exited. Joey looked at Tavis and he shrugged. What could they do?

Joey, Tavis and Pasha followed Boris to a rear hangar door. Through that rear door they entered into a spacious hanger. Large doors opened on the other side with a view of the runway. A Gulf Stream executive jet sat in the middle of the otherwise empty hanger. It was a little longer than a school bus. Its stairs were down and a tow cart was hooked up to the front landing gear to pull the plane out onto the tarmac. Though there was no one in it at the moment. One of Boris' men, his van driver, walked over and got in the cart. Apparently, this was really self-service here, especially at this early hour. There were other men loading packages wrapped in cellophane into the cargo hold.

"Everybody in please."

Boris offered a grand welcome gesture with one arm up the stairs. One by one, they climbed the short staircase. Joey hopped one at a time while Tavis held her crutches. Inside was cramped, all of them bent over except Joey. There were ten leather seats in the narrow cabin. As Joey took hers, she looked forward into the cockpit; two seats, only one pilot on the left. She heard the engines spin up. Boris secured the cabin door, then took the seat next to it. Valeri took a seat in the back behind them.

"My friends, we will arrive in Saint-Petersburg in about four hours," Boris said.

"Boris, do you know what's happening in the U.K…please?" Tavis asked.

"What I know of Europe is that all power is out. Glasgow and Brest were hit."

"Glasgow!?" Tavis said, eyes wide with horror.

"So, I think not Glasgow, but Faslane, just north. I misspoke. These weapons were not of strategic size. No missiles were launched. I haven't been able to find out more. There is no news on that, from either government or my sources. I do think that something else is happening. My people tell me Russia has moved troops into Eastern Europe. Many divisions along entire front. I think the Russian Government lies about their part in this."

"My wife and kids were supposed to be with my parents by now in Campbelltown. It's well west of Faslane and Glasgow, but our home's in Glasgow."

"We'll find them. We will get there." Joey assured her friend as she reached over to squeeze his arm in empathy.

"Unfortunately, the government is not allowing international flights at the moment. I have a place you can stay while Pasha is fulfilling his part of this deal. Is nice place. In the city. Pasha, your sister and niece will be meeting us at the aerodrome. They'll be my guests as well. For now, rest. You will need it, Pasha."

Boris went to the cockpit and spoke with his pilot in Russian.

Pasha leaned across the narrow isle to Joey. "You were a fighter pilot. Do you think you can fly this plane?" he whispered in her ear.

"Ha! I was and I could fly this, but I need this to do it." She patted the cast on her broken leg.

"Da. I will assist with pedals and co-pilot for you, Commander."

"Well, if I can get into the seat, it may work."

Tavis was listening in the seat in front of them. He opened a thin storage bin in front of his seat. He motioned for her to look. There were firearms in the bin. A couple of AK-47's and some pistols. Tavis looked toward the cockpit. Boris was still chatting with the pilot. He grabbed a pistol and shoved it into his waistband and shut the bin.

"Boris is transporting drugs, opium, in the hold below us. He's never far from weapons. Give me a pistol the next time you have an opportunity," Pasha said.

Tavis nodded. Joey felt her companions had things well in hand for now. She had several hours to rest and mentally prepare to fly again. Seems she'd have to get them home herself, with Pasha acting as co-pilot, who'd only flown helicopters. Great. Joey looked behind her at Valeri. He was looking back at her. He was on the same side as Pasha and Tavis, so Tavis' activities were blocked from his sight. She smiled at him and he returned it. What would they do with him? She didn't even know if he spoke English. He hadn't said a word the whole time. He turned his head to the window and closed his eyes. That was a good idea. She tried to do the same.

# FORTY-ONE

Chao was staring in disbelief at Feng. It'd been eighteen hours since the power died and they shot down the ICBM. Chao was light on sleep and he felt it. He was on edge and had no tolerance for this man's arrogance right now. Feng had unpacked the sealed metal box last night and had been inseparable from the two devices ever since. One was a smart phone and the other was a hand held satellite phone, which he had to go outside every hour to power on and see if there was any message received. The other piece of equipment was a small solar panel with hookups for both devices, so they could keep them charged. Gao was back in her usual seat by the big bay window warming up with a cup of coffee. The radar system would pick up any further launches and engage automatically. Chao was glad she was in here with them to witness this insanity.

"Those are the orders I just received, Captain. You saw the message for yourself," Feng said.

Chao thought the man's authoritative volume sounded rather whiny, but that tinge of condensation was grating on him, Gao, and the rest of the team.

"Major, I don't care what the message said. Only I command my men and I don't take orders from a message on a satellite phone, or you. You're the political officer on this mission and even though you outrank me, I'm in command tactically." Chao's voice rose as he squared up on Feng, the muscles in his back and shoulders tense, like the hair standing up on the back of a guard dog.

"Captain, do you know who is on the other end of this message? Do you?

General Command! You will follow these orders or I'll have you brought up on charges of insubordination and disobeying a direct order and shot!"

"Major Feng," Chao started and then chose his next words very carefully. "You are not in Beijing now, you are in the mountains of our adversary. Take care to ensure you're not out of your depth."

The door to the cabin flew open. "Captain, we've captured two civilians from the town."

"Lead the way, Sergeant," Chao said.

He followed the sergeant out the door and down the drive to where three of his team had two men held at gunpoint. He took them in quickly. The older man had a badge on his heavy jacket and what could only be a cowboy hat on his head, and long grey hair pulled into a ponytail. He looked like a cowboy, Chao mused. The other man, younger, was also dressed in blue jeans and heavy jacket, but no badge, baseball cap and heavy belt with holster, now empty. A shotgun, rifle, and two handguns lay on the ground behind his men.

"What's going on here? Who are y'all?" Chao understood him, although Chao's English wasn't great. He held up a hand to silence the older man, probably the town's sheriff.

"You have your orders, Captain." Feng said.

"My men and I are soldiers, Major, not murderers. I don't care what your orders are, we will not be shooting civilians here. There is no honor in this. We aren't Mongols and you aren't the Khan," Chao said loud enough for his men to hear him.

He saw Gao behind Feng, watching silently with her head cocked to one side, her mug of coffee in one hand, but no expression on her face. She had heard the orders as well. They were to execute any civilians they came across. *You couldn't take over a country for their food and resources if you still had to feed that country's people,* Feng had said. Insanity.

"I see." Was all Feng said and stepped back.

Chao turned back to the two prisoners. What to do with them. They knew he and his team were there and if they kept them, more would likely come. If he let them go, perhaps they'd stay away.

Everything happened so fast. Feng drew his pistol and pointed at the two men.

CRACK!

Chao saw the two prisoners flinch and turn, shielding themselves from a bullet that never came. Feng stood there a moment, then fell forward, pistol still gripped in his fist. Chao turned. Gao was returning her pistol to her holster.

"I also do not murder civilians, Captain." Gao said, expressionless.

They stared at each other for a moment. Chao nodded to her and she turned and walked back to the cabin with her coffee still in her other hand.

\*\*\*

Chao sat in the chair on the cabin's porch. The valley below was quiet, but he was keeping an eye for what he knew would come. He looked at the cowboy rifle in his lap. That's what he called it, at least. Lever-action. He let the two lawmen go back to their town without their weapons on their promise not to come back.

His men dumped Feng's body behind the cabin. That may or may not come back to haunt them, but that wasn't his immediate concern. Movement in the town caught his eye and he took a closer look with his binoculars.

"Look," he said and passed the binoculars to his sergeant sitting in the other porch chair.

"That didn't take long. Orders?" the tattooed soldier asked.

"Spread the word to the men. We'll have company tomorrow or the next day. More than just the lawmen this time."

"Yes, sir."

Chao watch his sergeant walk out to make the rounds. He took another look, watching the three riders heading off in different directions from the town on horses. He was in some kind of old west nightmare. They were going to get men from other towns. That's what he'd do. He could call command on the satellite phone, but he'd have to explain the situation. He disobeyed orders, but kept his honor intact. Nothing to do but wait.

# FORTY-TWO

As consciousness crept back in, Javad's first sense was a faint smell of perfume. Then he felt the pain. His head. He struggled to make sense of what happened. He was lying on his stomach, head turned to the right, resting on a very soft pillow. He blinked his eyes and instantly regretted it. A bright light filled the room and it stabbed at him. The light was coming from a window with blue curtains hanging on either side, but he could see outside. It was not full sun, but a muted, gray light. Snow was falling. He tried to move, but his arms were tied behind his back. His feet were tied together. He struggled, but he was held tight. He turned his head to the right, his face scraping across the pillow, wet with his saliva. How long had he been here?

"Who are you?"

He studied the stranger. A white man. American. Not big. Dressed in black clothing. Tactical vest with ammunition magazines in pockets across his chest. Wavy, dark hair, days old stubble on his face. Bandage on one hand. What in the name of Allah was he dealing with here? Police? Military? Javad blinked more and relaxed his body. Choose your words carefully, he said to himself.

"I am Javad." He replied in English, with an accent.

"I know your name. Who *are* you?"

The man held up Javad's identification and credentials and leaned forward in the chair. Damn. He forgot to toss those in the woods on his way here.

"I am looking for my daughter. She lives in the house next door. I arrived in the night after a long walk. My car died when the lights went out and I walked here. How long have I been here, if I may ask you?"

Javad wove falsehoods with truths. He'd give a bit of information and maybe he'd receive some information. He didn't know his captor yet. He'd always been on the other side. It was a game of sorts, but perhaps this man didn't know he was playing yet?

"You've been here since last night when you broke into my home. I didn't recognize you, and you were sneaking around, so I hit you with the butt of my rifle when you came in."

"So, you live here? You would know your neighbors next door then. My family. I am no threat to you, just trying to find my daughter. Have you seen them?" Javad asked hopefully.

"I want to know exactly who you are. This ID has the flag of Iran on it. I don't read Iranian. What does this say?"

"I'm a diplomat just trying to find my daughter. Please, if you let me go, we will have no trouble."

"Bullshit!"

The man smacked Javad in the face with the ID. A moment later, his captor sat back down and studied the ID. Javad kept an eye on him and thought about his next move. How ironic, Javad thought, and he nearly laughed out loud. He'd been in a similar position once before. A long time ago. Face down and unable to do a thing. Javad tested his restraints again. They gave a little bit, but not enough.

"What diplomat carries guns? Not one, but two pistols. And this one with a silencer." Javad turned his head to see the man had Javad's smaller pistol in his hands.

"I do. I work security at the Iranian Embassy and was on my way there when my car died and I walked here."

Javad knew it was a horrible answer. Diplomats don't carry guns unless inside their Embassy. The man didn't respond immediately, but looked out the window next to him. Javad tensed. He had talked himself into a corner.

"Tell me, Mr. Iranian Security Guard, what does your daughter look like? Who does she share the house next door with? Describe them to me. Be specific."

Javad sensed a trap, but apparently, he wasn't going to call him on the obvious security guard lie. So the game progressed. He would not make another mistake. He stared at his captor sitting in the chair, looking out the window.

No falsehoods this time. He took about a minute and described his daughter, mother, and Ahmed to the last detail. As he did so, he rolled his body so that he was laying on his side, facing the man in the chair, still staring out the window. It allowed him to work his restraints out of the man's sight.

The man had surprised him, but maybe he wasn't so good with knots. Maybe.

"Alright, maybe it is your family," his captor said. "They and the rest of their neighbors have been busy today moving things from some of the houses to another house across the pipe stem. They're armed too. The bald man you described. I haven't seen him without that AK-47 slung across his back. You must know what they're moving."

Javad listened to the man's words carefully. It had to be Ahmed, which means his daughter is close. Allah be praised! Ahmed had gathered supplies as he'd instructed him to do. That had to be it. If they were moving supplies, maybe they'd come to this house soon. He worked his wrists again. His old muscles were cramping having been locked in this position for so long.

"I can only assume they're moving supplies and having all supplies in one place is easier. If the power is out and nothing is moving, they must be getting what they need into one house. It's what I'd do," Javad said.

"So, why does the family of an Iranian diplomat have all these supplies and weapons? Did Iran attack the United States? Last night, after all the power went out and the planes crashed, there was a huge explosion east of here. Only thing that could make that kind of explosion is a nuclear weapon. As a diplomat, if that's what you really are, you should know more about this, or am I wrong?" The man loomed menacingly over him. His own silenced pistol was aimed at his head. Time to throw caution to the wind, Javad thought.

"I will tell you what I know. But first, can I know your name? If you live here, is your family alright? I truly mean no harm to you or your family."

"My name is Donneker and yes, my family is with yours, out there. Why are you so concerned about my family?

"I am on your side, Donneker. I am not actually a diplomat in the political sense. I work for Iranian intelligence."

"You're a spy!" Donneker swiftly dug the end of the pistol's silencer to

Javad's forehead. Javad tossed out truths and falsehoods as fast as he could before this man shot him in the head.

"We were trying to warn the Americans of the attack. It was the Russians, Chinese, and North Koreans! Be easy. We are on the same side. Those bastards have attacked my country as well."

The man stood there searching Javad's face for the truth. Lies and truths woven together. He was a master at this game.

"That's an interesting story," Donneker said.

The unmistakable sound of gunfire echoed in the distance.

"The hell?" Donneker stepped to the window, removing the pistol from Javad's forehead.

"What is it? What do you see?" Javad asked.

"Be quiet! Let me see what's going on here."

Donneker slowly brushed the curtains from the side of the window and peered out the slit.

"Hmm. Interesting."

Javad could barely hear the words through the panic in his head. He needed to know what was going on. His wrists were now working the bindings loose enough to free them. Once he did so, he would have a different conversation with this Donneker.

# FORTY-THREE

They were working all morning. Between that and the walk home last night, Gale was popping ibuprofen like candy. He hadn't slept much, no one had. Floyd's death weighed on everyone, but what they found stored in his basement was a godsend. Floyd truly was a lifesaver. They moved most of the supplies from Floyd's house to Lou and Robert's, because their house, or at least the large family room, was already warmed by the fire that was going all night and today.

Lou had taken charge, setting the teenagers to work. They moved the chopped wood that Floyd had stacked by his rear patio to Lou's place. The adults took inventory and moved the supplies both from Floyd's house and Ahmed's. There was enough food for several months if they rationed it carefully. There was also a portable water filter system along with all the camping supplies you'd ever need, like twenty different types of fire starters. There were also the weapons: rifles, handguns, and shotguns along with thousands of rounds of ammunition. Floyd had been serious about being prepared, fortunately for them. Then there were the ever-present Geiger counters, which were still quiet. Floyd had prepared for everything except a darkened staircase.

They assumed the nuclear blast over Washington, D.C. last night was dropping fallout to the east. They were west of the city by thirty miles.

"Dad?" Layla startled him out of his thoughts. He realized he'd been standing there in the yard staring in the direction of D.C. His daughter put her arms around him and he wrapped her in his.

"I miss mom. What do you think she's doing right now? Do you think she's okay, or…"

Gale gently stroked her hair, dotted with snowflakes. They found Floyd's weather forecast tacked above his desk. It was going to be a cold and snowy few days. This was only the first of it.

"Your mom's okay, sweetie. She's either safe up there or they've evacuated and she's back on the ground, somewhere. But she's alive and safe. We'll be together again. Not today and maybe not for a long time, but we will be eventually."

He squeezed her tight as she cried softly into his jacket.

The thought of Joey floating up there traveled to the deep pit forming in his stomach. Was she safe? The only thing he could do, and he'd do it tonight, was stand outside and look for the station to pass above them. She was smart, obviously, or she wouldn't be a damn astronaut. She was a freaking fighter pilot. She was with good people, who were like her. If anyone could get back here, it was her. He couldn't go looking for her. That was impossible now. He couldn't just call up NASA and ask them where his wife was. He closed his eyes and laid his head on top of Layla's. He didn't want to think of the alternative, so Joey had to be alive and that's how helped Layla. Stay positive for her, even though the chances were pretty slim. The feeling in the pit of his stomach deepened.

Gale whirled to the sound of staccato pops in the distance.

"What's that, Dad?"

"Sounds like gunfire. Lou! Ahmed! You hear that?" He shouted to the others.

Ahmed had put down the sealed buckets of freeze-dried food he was carrying and unslung the AK-47 from his back. Lou came out of the front door of his house where he'd been talking with Robert. Rifle at the ready.

"Coming from the main road. Toward the overpass, I think." Lou shouted back. The sound of an explosion drifted to them and made Gale's decision for him.

"Robert, get everyone inside and lets the three of us go check it out. We need to check that out. Just in case." Lou said.

"Is that smart? Someone's shooting at something." Gale didn't want to second guess Lou, but he was concerned. He'd never been in combat. Lou and Ahmed had done and seen things, killed people. Gale hadn't. He was proficient with firearms, but had never used them in anger, only at the range.

"Gale, wasn't it you last night that said we needed to know what was going on around the neighborhood. Someone's shooting out on the highway and something exploded. Don't you think we oughta know who's shooting and at what? I sure do." Lou wasn't mincing words.

Robert and Eric got the girls in the house with Bibi and Mama. Robert called from the door, "Be careful!" Lou nodded back to him with a wink. Lou's calm demeanor was calming to Gale. It was contagious.

"Look, Gale, I'll go first. We're just gonna take a look see, not get into a firefight. This snow is really coming down now so stay close."

There was more gunfire. It sounded like a machine gun, heavier than what they had and fully automatic.

"Lou, that has to be military. Civilians don't have machine guns. At least not legally." Gale said.

"Let's go."

The wind picked up and the falling snow was turning into a mini blizzard. The winter sun was failing. The houses in the distance obscured. They moved fast between Mama's house and Gale's. They came to the treeline that separated the edge of the neighborhood from the main road. Snow crunched under foot as Lou motioned for them to stop. He pointed to the road. Gale and Ahmed took a knee.

Gale scanned the snow-covered road in front of them. It was a four-lane road separated by a wide grassy area between the east and west bound lanes. There were three wrecked vehicles in front of them. One on fire, billowing thick, black smoke. Two of the vehicles were black SUVs. Suburbans probably. How were they running? The one on fire was on its side, flames coming from the passenger compartment. The other truck had skidded into the grassy area in the middle of the highway. There was smoke coming from the engine compartment, but he couldn't see flames or movement. It was the other vehicle that made Gale move.

"I know that Jeep! I know them." Gale said.

It was the Lieutenant's Jeep from the Ops Center. Had they made contact and then made their way here? But who'd been shooting at them? Gale realized the gunfire had stopped. The Jeep was facing them and he could see the windshield was torn to shreds.

"Hold on." It was Ahmed. "The vehicles, like us, are in this low point in the road. The high point is the overpass. That's probably where they took fire, but we can't see the overpass now. Too much snow and wind. If we go now, we should be concealed."

"Right. We have to see if they're still alive."

"Let's go. Quickly!"

Lou started. Gale and Ahmed followed. The obscured overpass was at least two or three hundred yards in the distance. Gale got to the jeep and looked through the fractured windshield. The lieutenant was alone, clearly dead with several bullet holes in the windshield and in his chest.

"Gale!" Lou whispered. Gale turned and saw them helping someone out the rear door of the SUV.

"Dennis! You hit?" Gale reached his boss, grabbed him by the shoulders and looked him up and down.

"Gale, what the hell? I'm okay. Banged up a bit. Took fire from the front. Bulletproof windshield didn't stop all the rounds. I was in the back with Colonel Hemp from JADOC. He's dead. Trucks were in the basement parking garage. Shielded by the concrete, so they still ran." Dennis was looking around in shock, snow starting to stick to his jacket and hair.

"We gotta move. Back to the tree line before this white out ends." Lou ordered.

"They fucking hit us hard, Gale! You were right. Should've listened." Dennis yelled as Lou was checking him out.

"Dennis. Dennis!" Lou said. "Talk quietly."

"Who hit us, Dennis?" Gale asked.

"Iranians and North Koreans. Satellites had nukes. Pulse fried everything. Dropped more nukes on D.C. Major military bases. They toasted us, Gale. Dropped nukes from fucking passenger jets."

Dennis was rambling now. Lou and Ahmed exchanged looks. Ahmed looked at the sky, closing his eyes for a moment.

"Let's get back to the house. Get him warm. He's fine physically. In shock. Move," Lou said.

They walked quietly and quickly through the bare trees. Their footprints from the walk here nearly filled in with newly fallen snow. They got halfway through the woods when Ahmed stopped and held up a hand. Two figures in camouflage blocked their way. Gale could just make out the dark patterns on their uniforms, but what was more alarming were the rifles aimed at the foursome. Ahmed put a hand on Gale's arm.

"I know the uniforms."

He yelled something in Farsi. The figure on the right yelled something back. Gale felt Ahmed's grip on his arm tighten.

Crack! Crack! BOOM! BOOM!

Ahmed pulled Gale down to the ground. The two figures dropped where they stood. What? Gale tried to process this while clumsily trying to aim his rifle in that direction. Two more figures appeared. The shorter man, dressed in dark green, walked up to the downed men. Gale watched in shock as he put another bullet, without hesitation, into each man's head, with the soft, metallic crack of a silenced pistol. It all happened so fast Gale didn't have time to be repulsed by the vicious killing. The younger man, dressed in all black, tactical clothes, Gale recognized by his wavy hair. As he approached Gale, he cradled his rifle in one arm and reached down a hand.

"Gale? Okay?" Gale took the man's hand and stood.

"Donneker! Where did you come from? Who's this?" Gale asked.

The other man walked to Ahmed, who was now on his feet. The man said something that Gale didn't understand to Ahmed. They embraced each other, talking quietly. The smell of gunpowder was strong.

"Lou? Kim Donneker." Donneker said, identifying himself to Lou.

"Kim. Holy shit. Good timing!" Lou said.

"Back to the house. Now. Before more come looking for these two. That rifle was loud," Ahmed said.

# FORTY-FOUR

Lonny had drawn the lucky shift and was off on Christmas and the week after. He'd catch a flight back home at 8:05 p.m. tonight to see his ailing mother and the rest of the family. The cash he sent them helped, but he needed to be there now. He hadn't seen his mom in a long while. He was glad that his extra-curricular activities were over now. It was a load off, but he missed Tori. He didn't understand why she broke it off or even where she was now. He had a feeling that maybe he'd been used, but the money and stress of possibly getting caught had been worth it. It was a lot of money. His last shift had ended five hours ago and he'd been heading to the airport in a taxi when the car just died. Not that they had been going anywhere as the traffic was bumper to bumper on the freeway, but all the vehicles had died. The freeway became the parking lot it had been pretending to be. Not only had the cars died, but his phone was dead.

That was an hour ago. He grabbed his backpack, which is all he ever needed as he didn't have much to pack anyway, and walked with the throngs of other confused people along the freeway. He chose the direction of his apartment. No sense in going to the airport after he witnessed several airplanes crash. Many people just stopped to stare at the black plums of roiling smoke rising from the wreckages while others had started running along the freeway in a panic. Something bad was going on and he wanted to get to his familiar surroundings. It was a long way back to the apartment.

He'd been walking for a while when he heard it. He looked up. Others around him, including his taxi driver, also looked up while they trudged along the concrete freeway. It took him a moment to realize that it wasn't one plane, but several that were spread out in a line, flying from south to north. It didn't appear that they were coming in to land, they were too high for that, but not too high. Maybe several thousand feet.

"Seven-forty-sevens," the cabbie said.

"Are you sure. I can't tell from here."

"Yes. I'm sure.

He and the cabbie stood fixed to the concrete spot they occupied and watched as the planes continued north over Los Angeles, Beverly Hills, and the Hollywood Hills, then disappeared in the sky. With nothing else to look at, he and the cabbie, along with the dwindling mass of people continued their trek.

He didn't notice it at first. Then he thought a bug had touched his face and he waived a hand to shoo it away. But as he looked at his hand, there were drops of rain on it. He looked up again. Not a cloud to be seen. He also noticed that after all the vehicles died, the ever-present exhaust and fumes from the cars on the road had cleared and he couldn't smell it anymore. That was actually nice after living in this smog filled city. Refreshing. Now he smelled a faint fruity odor. He rubbed the sparse, wet droplets on his hands and then sniffed them. There it was. Fruity. That was really weird. He took out a handkerchief from his back pocket and wiped his nose, which started to run. The cabbie stumbled next to him.

"Hey, you alright?"

Lonny knelt next to the cabbie who was face down. He shook the man lightly and he coughed. He turned the cabbie over and the man vomited all over Lonny's hands and arms.

"Shit, man!"

Lonny recoiled in shock and looked around for help from other people walking by. To his surprise, several other people were on the ground throwing up. A woman a few yards away was gasping, laying on her back, her arms were raised, but twitching. Her hands were bent at the wrists with her fingers contorted. His mouth hung open as he watched her struggle. He tried to close his mouth, but couldn't. He sat from his kneeling position and realized there was drool hanging from his chin. His saliva and the mucus from his nose was combining with the cabbie's vomit on his hands. It got harder to catch his breath and his vision narrowed so that he could only see the cabbie on the concrete in front of him.

He would be late for his flight, if the man didn't get the car started. Lonny tried to wipe the various liquids on his pants, but his arms wouldn't cooperate. He stared at the cabbie, who was now choking on his own vomit, arms waving uncontrollably. Lonny was angry now. He wasn't going to see his mother if the man didn't get him to the airport. He fell over on his side and vomited towards the cabbie. That will teach you, Lonny thought. Why was he laying here? His vision was blurry and the cabbie was just a blob lying next to him. Lonny's body started to twitch violently. What was left of his disconnected consciousness was thinking about his poor mother spending Christmas without him and he without her. It was ok, he thought, as the synapses in his brain fired erratically, altering his morbid reality. He and the cabbie just needed to rest a moment, then they'd get to the airport. He hoped he had a window seat.

# FORTY-FIVE

December 25 - 7:00pm EST
December 26 - 2:00am Saint-Petersburg, Russia
Joey Washington

Four hours later, they approached Saint-Petersburg. Joey was amazed they hadn't been forced to land somewhere by now, what with the world supposedly at war and Russia invading Europe. It was surreal. Their plan could work. Tavis said there was an airport out on the spit, it's what they called the peninsula in the far west of Scotland where his parents lived. That would be their next destination, if they could pull this off. Pasha overheard the pilot and Boris talking about being refueled when they landed. She was fairly certain that she could take off, fly, and land this thing without mishap. If everything went perfectly. She looked down with amusement at Tavis, who was attempting to regain his strength by doing pushups on the cabin's deck between the plush seats. Valeri watched him with interest.

The young man wasn't very chatty, but what few words he did say, he said with near perfect English and a slight accent. She wondered how much of their plan he overheard, if any. She saw some of Boris in his face as well as an apparently day old bruise on the side of his cheekbone. His father's doing, he said. There was no love lost there, but she sensed a great deal of regret from him. His mom had died in an accident. His father was involved, he said. He had to live with him after that, but the father was restrained, most of the time, under threat by Boris, as well as his own chain of command, it seemed. They saved his sorry ass, but allowed this to continue for years. Anger welled inside her. She felt a deep sadness for Valeri, or Val, as he liked to be called.

"Landing," the pilot said through the open cockpit door, just in time for the plane to bounce off the runway, which caught Tavis in mid pushup and smashed his face and body to the floor of the cabin.

"Bloody 'ell!" Tavis growled. Joey suppressed a laugh, as did Val.

It was a sparse little airport, more of an airstrip. The sun was up now and it was overcast as she looked out the window on the left side of the plane. The pilot rolled the plane to a stop and Boris opened the cabin door, lowering the stairs. Boris went down, followed by the pilot who began waving a fuel truck over.

"Last stop. Ah, here is my man with your family, Pasha."

Two women got out of the SUV and Pasha went to meet them, wrapping them in his arms. The fuel truck driver hooked up a hose to the plane.

"I'm going to go stretch my legs, see what you need to in the cockpit. This is gonna happen fast, when it does." Tavis said to her as Val rose and went to the lavatory in the rear.

Joey stuck her head into the cockpit. It was very current. She scanned the instrument panel. Found all the right gauges and switches. She'd been able to ask the pilot to show her around the cockpit about an hour before landing. He spoke pretty good English. She told him she hadn't flown in years since the Navy, but was always interested in these types of planes. He'd been very accommodating. She heard the sound of a bolt being racked behind her and turned in surprise. Tavis had one of the AK-47's in his hands. He leaned it next to the open door as some low rumbles caught their attention.

"That is the war. It is far off. Come now. We will go to my place," Boris yelled from outside.

His mobile phone rang. He listened to whoever was on the other end and started yelling. The pilot and fuel technician finished with the hose and started rolling it back to the truck.

Joey stood in the door of the plane as there were more rumbles. Pasha had walked over and introduced his sister, Galina, and his niece, Nina to Tavis and Joey.

"Artillery," Tavis said as a matter of fact.

"What's west of here? Estonia?" Joey asked, making a mental note where the war was.

"Yes," Pasha replied.

"This is bad."

"Aye, bad indeed. We'll need to go around that," Tavis said quietly.

"We need to get out over water. Gulf of Finland to the Baltic, cross parts of Sweden and Norway without getting ourselves shot down. Then south into Scotland, also without getting exploded. Don't know if the U.K. is shooting down Russian planes or not."

"My men are late with the truck." Boris had come up behind them. "All of you can go in the SUV, while Pasha and I wait for the truck and my men to unload the cargo and go."

"Go!" Tavis yelled.

He pulled the pistol from his waistband and pointed it at Boris. Pasha pulled his own pistol Tavis had provided him before landing and pointed it at the SUV driver.

"I'm sorry to do this, but we need to get home. We're leaving." Tavis said, as Joey scrambled into the left seat in the cockpit and methodically started the engines.

"I think this is a mistake. Pasha, you made a deal! Valeri! Where is my grandson?" Boris yelled as they all took their seats, Pasha pushed Galina and Nina into the plane.

"I am sorry, Boris," Pasha yelled back. The SUV driver aimed his pistol at Pasha. Val appeared in the doorway behind Pasha. Joey had the engines spun up now and was listening to the back and forth.

"Don't shoot, you fool. You'll hit Valeri." Boris yelled at his driver.

Pasha closed the door.

"You're with us now, Val."

"Good. Anywhere but here."

"Pasha! I need you up here!" She broke the splint above the knee so she could bend her leg for the pedals. It hurt like a bitch. As Pasha climbed into the co-pilot seat, she pushed the throttles forward, propelling the light jet down the taxiway.

"Go, Joey! Go! We're all strapped in. Get us the bloody 'ell outta here!" Tavis yelled.

Joey was having some success with the pedals. Her left foot was fine. The right foot was the challenge. She couldn't put pressure on the right pedal with her toes or the ball of her foot. The pain shot up her leg, as she used already stressed and possibly ripped tendons. She could use her right heel to put pressure on the right pedal and that was working for now. Pasha played with the radar scope that had been installed by Boris, which was up and to his right out of the way. Joey showed him where the transponder was and told him to switch it off so that they wouldn't ping out their position. They'd show up on radar, though. Joey pushed the throttles all the way forward at the end of the runway and in moments they were airborne again. The last thing she saw as she rolled down the runway was Boris on his phone gesturing wildly. She had his plane, his drugs, and his grandson. She was in control now. Finally.

Pasha spoke quickly, "Two things, Commander. Either the radar is broken. Is not likely. Or, there is heavy jamming in the area. This is likely and seems to be from everywhere, which is also likely. If Russia is indeed moving into Europe, then they are moving into Finland as well. Which is right there."

He pointed north. They were quickly out over the Gulf of Finland and Joey was keeping it low. Five thousand feet. She started a slow left turn to the northwest, which put them on track to go just south of Helsinki and over the coast of Finland. If they could stay on course, she'd mentally worked out, it would put them, without incident, on Tavis' spit in two and a half hours. They'd collect his family, refuel, and start the cross-Atlantic flight. They'd be on fumes when they reached Virginia. As if Murphy was on cue, a very loud Russian voice commandeered her and Pasha's headsets.

"Gulf Stream aircraft, Gulf Stream aircraft, this is Russian Combat Air Patrol. You are not authorized to exit Russian airspace. You will reverse course and follow my lead to Saint Petersburg and land for inspection or we will shoot you down. Acknowledge."

Pasha interpreted for her and her heart sank. This was a quick trip. Joey looked out her left window and there he was. Shit. MIG-31. They didn't travel alone, so there was probably one on her six as well. They were done.

"I can't outrun MIGs, Pasha. I can't outmaneuver them in this thing. It's not a fighter. We need to do what they say or they'll splash us."

"Hey, we got Russians!" Tavis said to no one in particular from the cabin. "There's a MIG next to us!"

"Yeah, we see 'em."

"Finland is there! It is right there! I will not go back. Go back and they will shoot us. Either Boris will or the FSB will. It's now or never, Commander!"

Pasha pointed toward the faint line in the distance that separated the Gulf waters and the land further beyond. They looked at each other and nodded their heads in agreement. The only way was to hit the deck, and fast. She was just about to put the jet into a dive, when the MIG to her left, the pilot still yelling in her headset in words she couldn't understand, disintegrated.

"What the..."

She pushed the controls hard forward and pushed the throttles to the stop forcing the jet down, narrowly missing the F-18 Hornet that shot past her. She banked hard right, screaming out loud as the pain in her leg exploded when she pushed the right pedal. It matched the screaming coming from the cabin behind her. She reversed her turn and brought the plane to horizontal just a few hundred feet above the grey, choppy waters. All she could do now was run. She was pushing five hundred knots and the jet was shaking. She was so focused on what she was doing that when Pasha grabbed her right arm, she jumped. Looking over at him, he wasn't looking at her, but out his side window. It was the most beautiful sight she had ever seen. A Hornet flew next to them. The pilot with a thumbs up. She could clearly see the white circle on the side with the blue ring in the middle of it.

"Finns in Hornets!"

Her and Pasha both returned the thumbs up. There was more Russian through the headset. Pasha engaged in a short back and forth with them as the Hornet peeled up and away to the right. She watch him go as he was replaced by a second Hornet. Wingman. They splashed those MIGs for us!

"I told them who we were and where we're going. He said it was good we left Saint-Petersburg when we did. He didn't elaborate further."

"Good luck, Astronautti!" a female voice said. She looked back out the window and it was a female wingman that gave a thumbs up and peeled away after the other Hornet.

"Don't mess with a woman in a fighter jet, Pasha!" She swung her right arm over and punched Pasha in the left shoulder and laughed out loud.

"Yes, apparently, there are no Russian fighters over all of Scandinavia at the moment. They are not doing so well here, I think. At least that is what he told me. He also said they would relay us to Swedish forces so we won't have any issues, hopefully."

"Nice." Joey pulled back a bit on the throttle and started a pull on the stick. She wanted to climb to a more fuel friendly altitude.

"Hey! Bloody 'ell's going on up there? You done tossin' us about? Fuckin' Russian's a helicopter pilot, fer God's sake! Take the controls, Commander."

She explained the situation rather curtly and he settled down a bit. Soon, they were cruising at thirty-five thousand feet. She relaxed and rubbed her face and her eyes. Okay, two hours and they'd be on the spit.

"Pasha, are you good here for a few minutes?"

"Da, think so. Where are you going?"

"I have to pee."

"Oh, da, da."

Joey unstrapped and dragged herself from the cockpit. She stood up and stretched, surveying the passengers. Tavis started to say something, but she held up a hand and walked past him and the others to the lavatory at the rear. Once inside, she knelt down and threw up in the toilet. Just once, nothing else. God, that was close. After a minute hanging there above the toilet, she remembered she had to pee. She settled that and splashed water on her face. Then the plane lurched and quickly righted. She emerged from the lavatory and hopped toward the cockpit.

"Helicopter pilot, Commander!" Tavis said as she passed him, his arms outstretched to the cockpit. She turned to him and put a hand on his shoulder.

"Tee, we're two hours from you seeing your family again. Relax and close your eyes. We have a clear air corridor to Scotland. You'll be home soon."

"Aye, thanks for that. But you do know he's never flown a bloody plane, right?"

She rolled her eyes and worked her way painfully back into the pilot's seat.

"Tee, I need a couple ibuprofen. Please!"

A hand with two pills appeared in front of her and she took them, gratefully. It was Pasha's turn to hit the head and grab a couple of water bottles from the small galley. She adjusted course slightly and rested her hands on her thighs picking at strands of the cast that were sticking up. Be home soon guys, she said to her family in her head. Next step.

# FORTY-SIX

An and his Marines had rounded Charleston, West Virginia to the north, staying on Route Sixty-four until they'd found it fully blocked with dead cars and trucks as they neared the small city. Some massive fires burned downtown. Skirting the cities and larger towns was a wise move, he thought. The roads were eerily quiet except for infrequent groups of people walking one way or the other. They told them to find shelter at one of the many small towns that they had passed. That advice seemed more of a safe bet than the larger towns or cities. The dead cars bothered him, though.

They were running down a two-lane country road with fairly flat terrain on either side. He could see a light in the distance on the left that looked like a small fire. There was a structure next to it. He reached down to rub a thumb into his left calf to try to get rid of the cramp that had been at it for the last few miles. They should probably stop soon to stretch legs and muscles and walk around Alice and check her tracks. The trip had been mostly uneventful with several stops to refuel at abandoned gas stations. They took a longer rest stop so the vehicle crews could sleep while the Humvee and LAV riders pulled security around the vehicles. An was surprised they hadn't had a breakdown yet. Abrams were hell on mechanics. Eventually, something would break somewhere on the tank. He patted Alice on the top of the turret with affection. *Stay with me, you little woodland faerie. Stay with me.* He glanced at his watch. It was 1930 hours on Christmas Day and darkness had descended in West Virginia . Twenty-four hours since they'd left the fort and his brother. With Alice only doing thirty-five to forty miles per hour it was slow going. The little, plastic radio cracked to life.

"Zombie Six, Recon. Over." An was now Six—Platoon Commander. Or what was left of the platoon after the ambush in the valley. The LAV was Recon out to their front with the Humvee bringing up the rear. Zombie was the callsign the colonel had given to their unit. He wondered if they were still alive back at the Fort. Was Bao alive? His brother's chances seemed slight to him, but if anyone could get out of that shit, it was Bao.

"Recon, Six Actual, Go." An looked through the night vision optics built into his commanders position and scanned ahead.

"Six, we have a clown blocking the road about thirty yards in front of us. We've stopped."

"Recon, Six Actual. Did you say a clown? You have a clown? Like a circus clown?"

An scanned the right side of their position as he replied. His loader, Stewie, was doing the same on the left. The tank was riding fifty yards behind the LAV with no lights. The driver, Fletch, was using his night vision built into his driver's position.

"Affirmative on a single individual standing in the middle of the road in our lights. It's dressed up like a circus clown. Just standing there looking at us kind of swaying back and forth. Over."

"Driver stop. Stewie get on your gun. Sergeant Buford, you have eyes on this clown?"

Each vehicle had a walkie talkie, but so did Buford and the fire team Sergeant, who stayed below in the LAV. The tank came to a stop as Stewie moved the safety to the off position on the M240 Machine Gun attached to his position atop the turret. An looked through his night vision. There was indeed a freaking clown standing in the middle of the road. They were in banjo country, dead of winter, middle of the apocalypse, with a fucking clown in their way.

※ ※ ※

"Six Actual, Buford. I've got the clown scoped. There's a gas station on the left just past the clown and a small church up the road fifty yards beyond that on the right. Small fire burning out front. No other movement."

Buford looked through his day scope with his night vision affixed on the front. He laid the cheap radio down to the left of the rifle without taking his eye off the clown in the distance. The actual gunner had switched places with him a while ago and was down below with the rest of the fire team. Buford's M40A5 Marine Corps issued sniper rifle was based on the civilian Remington 700 rifle commonly used for hunting. This one, however was heavily modified. It was bolt-action, but had a ten-round magazine and was fitted with a suppressor. That quieted the sound of the explosion of the cartridge as the round left the end of the barrel. It did not suppress the sound of the bullet breaking the sound barrier. He steadied the rifle with its bi-pod just under the front end of the gun frame and settled himself in the hatch. He controlled his breathing, while his right eye was lit up green by the night vision scope. Buford's senses were heightened and sharp.

"Roger that, hold tight. If he makes any sudden moves, drop him. Recon, see what he wants. Tell him to move his ass out of the way." An ordered.

"Aye Six. I hate clowns. Hate 'em. I had an incident when I was a kid. Never quite shook it." Buford said into the little walkie-talkie.

"You need someone to hold your hand, Corporal?" Buford heard over the radio.

"I had...an incident!"

The commander of the LAV in the hatch to Buford's right yelled out to the person, or clown, or whatever, to move. The clown didn't move except to continue swaying.

"Six, Recon. It's just standing there in our headlights. Got a big clown wig on, face paint, clown outfit. Don't see any weapons. Hands are hidden in pockets. Can't tell exactly, but something dark is smeared all over the front of his costume. Didn't respond to my orders. There's also movement now by the church, but can't tell what. Could just be shadows from the fire," the LAV commander relayed to An.

"Roger that, Recon. Use extreme caution." Buford heard Six reply.

Buford had the reticle in the scope centered on the clown's chest. Actually, it looked like he'd hit one of the frilly puff balls hanging in a vertical line down the dude's clown suit if he fired right now. His breathing slowed.

"Hey, Buford?" A voice called from inside the LAV. "Is there more than one clown out there? Do they look insane?"

"Don't." Another voice from below.

"'Cause you know what that is, right?"

"Stop it!"

"Insane Clown Posse, Dawg! I'm here all week."

"I hate you all," Buford said. Laughter drifted up with the sounds of someone getting an arm punch.

"Come on, that was funny, Buford," the LAV Commander said quietly from his perch next to him.

The clown quickly pulled his hands out of his pockets. There was a glint from something he pointed in their direction.

CRACK!

Buford blinked enough to avoid the flash of the gunshot. The bullet ricocheted off the front of the LAV. Buford was reflexive. His right finger slowly moved from being straight out along the side of the rifle's frame to gently squeezing the trigger. The rifle recoiled into his shoulder and the round hit the clown dead center, dropping it where it stood.

"Six Actual, Buford. Clown's down."

Buford racked the next round into the chamber. His trigger finger moved back to resting on the side of the frame. His eye never moved from the corpse on the pavement. That actually didn't feel bad at all. Fucking clowns. He felt a light hand on his shoulder from the LAV Commander.

"Righteous shot, Buford."

And that was how Buford got his nickname. Sometime later, they started referring to him as the Clown Eradication Unit. It wasn't an exact match, it came out as CEU or as they pronounced it "CUE," which was followed by "Cue Ball." Buford was known as Cue Ball from that moment on.

"Recon, Six, roll up on that church, dismount your fire team and check it out. We'll move up to overwatch. Zombie Three, stay on my ass. Heads on a swivel," An said.

"Roger, Six."

The LAV moved slowly up the road, careful to go around the corpse. Buford had his reticle on the church and scanned from the back of the building to the front. The light from the bonfire in the field next to the church danced, casting shadows along the side. As the LAV came to a stop in front of the church, the four Marines piled out of the back and took up defensive positions, eyes and M-4's scanning side to side looking for targets. Buford kept his rifle pointed at the front door of the church as he heard the rumble of the tank's treads on the pavement moving into position behind them. He hoped they went around the corpse. That stuff gets in the treads and—

"Movement right, treeline!"

Buford didn't move his rifle, but turned to look as the turret swiveled slightly to cover with its chaingun.

"Come out or we will shoot you!" The Marines were slowly moving into the field to the right of the church, their shadows dancing in the firelight. Two figures rushed from the treeline at the nearest Marine with reports of gunshots. There was a flurry of gunfire from the M-4's as both figures went down. The fire team sergeant was closest and stepped over to check them.

"Everyone good?" Sergeant Simmons asked. "More clowns. What the fuck's going on?"

They heard a loud bang and a round ricocheted off the LAV's turret next to Buford. He put his eye back on the reticle to see a fourth figure in costume standing in the open church door aiming a handgun at the LAV. He stood, unfortunately for him, in the center of Buford's sight. He flew backwards through the church door. Buford racked another round, the spent casing flying off to the right trailing smoke in the chill air.

❀ ❀ ❀

"Clear the church!" An shouted from his hatch as Alice moved closer.

The four-man fire team went in the front door one by one, stepping over the corpse in the entryway. An heard some of them yell "clear" repeatedly, until a single shot rang out.

"Clear. We found one more in here. He's shot, but alive."

"Drag is ass out here, Sergeant. By the fire." An yelled down over the engines of the tank and LAV.

"You're gonna want to see this, Gunny."

An jumped down from his perch atop Alice, M-4 at the ready, and walked past two Marines dragging the wounded clown out next to the fire. He followed the sergeant Simmons into the church. His blood ran cold. He came back outside and walked over to the clown, who was being tended to by the corpsman who was securing a tourniquet to the clown's upper arm, just under his shoulder. Each of his arms outstretched on the ground while

Marines stepped on each wrist. The clown was moaning in pain. It looked up at An and smiled.

"Bullet nicked the artery in his arm. He's lost a lot of blood. I stopped it for now, but—"

"Step off," An said, interrupting the corpsman. Malice dripped from each word, as the Marines and corpsman moved away.

"You and your...friends did this?" An asked it. Wasn't a human to him.

"Take me to the cops, if you can find any. It's the apocalypse, baby! You fuc—"

An knelt hard on its face with one knee, reached down and pulled the tourniquet off and tossed it to his corpsman. He rose and looked around at his Marines as the clown bled out.

"We'll need the tourniquet. He won't make it. Toss these bodies in the woods. We don't have time to bury those people in the church. Burn it. I don't want anyone else looking for a house of worship and seeing that." He turned and climbed up on Alice leaving the Marines to torch the church. A pyre of sorts for its permanent inhabitants inside. It was all An could do for them.

Soon, they were rolling down the two-lane road. An looked back at the church, engulfed in flames, his anger replaced with sorrow. It was Christmas. His thoughts traveled to his parents, to Bao and Brook. Those people in the church. They had to move faster. Surely it wouldn't be like this everywhere. Not yet. There was a new urgency to his focus. He would never forget the church. He knew that. He was not altogether comfortable that he basically executed that bastard, but it was what it was. They couldn't have treated him and left him there and they weren't bringing him. Out of the question.

He had seen similar guys on deployment, without the clown get-ups, but they had rules of engagement there. War had civility and justice to an extent. This was new territory. There was no longer any civility. They were the justice now. As wrong as he thought that was, it was the new way of things and he would proceed accordingly. He felt a relief. Was it relief, or something else? He stowed that. His father had taught them to always protect the weak and help when they could. He could do neither back there, so justice it was. Now justice was rolling down a country road in the middle of West Virginia.

# FORTY-SEVEN

December 25
8:00pm EST
Gale Washington

Washington, D.C.
Norfolk, Virginia
San Diego
Pearl Harbor
Kings Bay, Georgia
Fort Benning, Georgia
Whiteman, Air Force Base
Bangor, Washington
Barksdale, Air Force Base, Louisiana
Cheyenne Mountain
Faslane, Scotland
Brest, France
Jim Creek Naval Radio Station, Washington
VLF transmitter in Lualualei, Hawaii
Fort Bliss, Texas
Fort Hood, Texas
Tinker Air Force Base, Oklahoma
Offutt Air Force Base, Nebraska
Fort Campbell, Kentucky
Fort Bragg, North Carolina
Patuxent Naval Air Station, Maryland
Elmendorf Air Force Base, Anchorage, Alaska
Fort Wainwright, Fairbanks, Alaska
Guam

They sat around the fire-lit family room listening in shocked silence as Javad, this newcomer, listed off the places that were hit with nuclear weapons. The fire cracked and popped as Javad revealed the entire plan, or at least what parts he knew of from his part in it. Robert was behind the bar emptying the last from a bottle of vodka into his glass. He was the most relaxed person in the room. Donneker and his estranged wife, Susan were on opposite sides of the room. She avoided eye contact with her recently returned husband, even though he tried to apologize. She didn't want to hear it and had slapped him in the face in front of everyone. Donneker had shrunk down into his chair and hadn't moved since.

Ahmed stood in the corner like a tiger ready to pounce. He was hard to read at the moment. Eric and Ana were at the bar. Eric had been looking into his untouched drink the whole time, his back squarely to Javad and his story. Ana seemed to study Javad intently, hanging on his every word. She didn't seem upset. It was odd. Dennis sat in the kitchen silently, a blanket wrapped around him. He'd come out of his earlier shock a bit.

Gale had sent the girls to the basement at Ana's request when Javad started talking. It was clear they didn't need to hear this horrifying plan. Or did they? It was hard to know how to protect the teenage girls in all this. It was already scary enough for them without hearing the rest. Bibi and Mimi were together on the couch with the very pregnant Brook, who was glaring at Javad. She was in the most precarious situation. The group would help her, of course. There was still no word from her husband, and she was close to giving birth in this new and uncertain world. He was terrified for Joey, not knowing. He figured it was the same for Brook.

It had been hard to separate Sara from Javad. She hadn't seen her father in almost a year. Gale was still having trouble thinking of the slight sixty year old as Sara's father. Ahmed was all he knew in that position. Once they assured Sara that Javad wasn't going anywhere, they were able to get the girls downstairs and Javad told his story. It was Brook that spoke first, after Javad finished.

"You...you did this?" Her voice was pure rage as she spat out the words. "You were in the plane that dropped that bomb on D.C.? My husband could be...he was supposed to be on a plane home." Her voice cracked as she fell silent. Tears welled in her eyes, but they never wavered from Javad.

"So the Russians, Chinese, NoKo's and Iran? Iranians. That's who you shot earlier in the snow?" Lou asked, turning from the front window as he spoke.

"Yes. To all your questions." Javad replied as Lou started to laugh.

"What?" Gale asked.

"That list doesn't include the major Marine Corps bases. They didn't touch the Marines." Lou kept laughing.

Gale took Lou's point, although he wasn't as amused as Lou. He turned back to Javad. He imagined the man hadn't planned on telling anyone this story, let alone the people in this room, who'd been intimately affected.

"So that's what happened to our ICBM's then. Shot down during launch from inside the U.S. Can't communicate with our subs. Those two North Korean satellites—everything's gone." Dennis looked down at the floor.

"You were right, Gale. You were right, and we all ignored you. My God."

"We can still get you to Mt. Weather, Dennis. We can all go. Now that we know. It's staffed year-'round." Gale said. "Mt. Weather is thirty minutes west of here by car. Underground bunker complex. One of those undisclosed locations. Pretty secure from nukes, although it sounds like the worst is over. By that I mean no more nuclear explosions. There's still the aftermath. That's going to be permanent."

"The Iranian commandos are going to come looking for their friends sooner or later. They are between us and Mt. Weather. They had to have heard those gunshots. I'd do some recon if I were them. Sounds and looks like they're well-armed and here to stay," Lou said.

"You've killed all of us!" Ahmed lunged across the room. He grabbed Javad's jacket and threw him up against the wall, the chair crashing against the fireplace hearth.

"It was going to happen anyway! I only took advantage." Javad said. Gale couldn't let anything happen to Javad. He needed to tell his story to whatever command authority was left. America's counter-strike, whatever it was, wouldn't hit the right targets if they were still in the dark. They wouldn't take his word for it. He needed Javad.

"You arrogant little shit! All these years. I've protected you. Your family. You lied to me!" Ahmed screamed in Javad's face, then dragged him across the wall to the corner and slammed him into it, dropping him like a sack of apples. Javad collapsed on the floor in the corner from the sudden drop, but quickly recovered. He stared at Ahmed.

"I thought I could control it. They were going to do it anyway. This way I could get you, Sara, and Bibi away."

"How is this *safe*, Javad? How is this *away?*"

"Because our home, our country will be gone soon, if it's not already. I've made sure of it. They won't be able to take anything from anyone again." Javad said defiantly.

Gale sensed there was a history between these two, but there was no time for it now. He was still coming to grips with the two dead men in the snow, while sorting out all that had been said here. He'd never seen people shot. The sounds of the rifle and suppressed pistol Javad used, unnerved him. He couldn't get it out of his head. Gale focused on Ahmed. He approached him slowly and touched his shoulder to get his attention.

"Ahmed, whatever happened before this, it's in the past. We need everyone now. We have to figure out how to get to Mt. Weather. With Javad."

"I need to think," Ahmed said as he walked to the back door.

Eric got up from the bar and squeezed Ana's arm. He went to the basement door and called for Alex to come up.

"We're going back to our house. Frankly, I don't feel comfortable here with these two men. Don't care if they saved you all, Gale. This man here started world war three."

Gale's first thought was Eric's nose was in really bad shape. The bleeding had stopped a while ago, but it was clearly crooked and broken. His second thought was they needed to stay together. He was about to say so when Alex entered the room.

As Eric turned to leave, Javad asked loudly, "How's your nose?"

"It's fine." Eric tensed and straightened, but kept walking, following Ana and Alex to the front door.

"I know you. I saw your face. I never forget a face. Especially one I've punched."

"What is this?" Ahmed said to Javad.

"I don't know what this is. I was in a car accident. Never seen this man before tonight." Eric said as he handed Alex her jacket, waiving off her protests. She didn't want to leave her friends.

"You've been trying to hide your face from my view all evening. I was wondering how the pilots were going to land our plane after the lights went out. You lit the runway for them, didn't you? When I dropped to the ground from the back of the plane, you were there to help me up. Nice of you. I had to get away, so I hit you and ran. Got a good look at you first, though."

Gale noticed Lou had stepped away from the window with his rifle. Javad hadn't moved from the corner and Ahmed had stopped at the back door. They couldn't see around the corner of the family room to the foyer. Robert reached below the bar top. The movement was quick, but not from who they were all watching.

"Put the rifle down, Lou." Ana said, pulling a pistol from her jacket and pointed it at him. He slowly lowered the rifle to the carpeted floor and let it drop.

"Mom! What's going on?" Alex pleaded.

"Quiet, Alex!"

"We are leaving now. That's what this is. Us leaving." Eric had his own pistol out, pointed at the others.

"Son of a bitch. They're Russians. I mean you all are Russian, but like spies!" Robert was incredulous, still behind the bar.

Eric returned Gale's glare, his smirk contorted on his busted face as reached behind him to open the door. He stepped through into the blowing snow. Ana was dragging Alex by her arm, not yet to the door. No one in the group moved. Alex was clearly innocent of this. Just a kid. Gale rolled his eyes. Who the hell were all his neighbors?

Gunfire ripped the foyer and family room as pieces of drywall and splinters from the front door littered the floor. Gale took cover in the kitchen behind the refrigerator. Robert ducked behind the bar.

"Cover!" Lou screamed from the front room. Ahmed pulled Brook and Susan to the floor. Javad yanked Bibi and Mimi into the corner with him. Drywall dust was in Gale's eyes, but he saw Javad move in a crouch toward the corner of the hallway, grandmothers on the floor behind him. He pointed his pistol around the corner and emptied the magazine through the open front door. Instead of reloading it, he dropped it and pulled a another pistol from its holster. He aimed and fired, repeatedly.

"Who's shooting at us! Javad! Stop shooting, you'll hit Alex!" Gale screamed. There was debris all over. Dust floated in the firelight. Deafening booms from the front room and shattering glass, told him Lou was returning fire.

Donneker wiggled past Gale on the floor into the kitchen. He fired his rifle through the walkway to the dining room past Lou through the wrecked bay window. The muzzle flashes blinded Gale, but the sound and concussion from the rifles in the enclosed space was organ crushing. Gale saw that Lou had Alex and Ana on the floor behind him. He thought Alex was screaming. Alive.

Layla! The basement door was in the line of fire in the hallway. He moved on his stomach with his rifle in front of him. Layla and Sara were safe as long as they stayed down there. He looked through the open front door. Whoever was out there wasn't in his line of sight. He reached up and grabbed the doorknob and opened it slightly.

"Layla! Stay down there. Stay down!" He yelled between gunshots. He could barely hear himself. He didn't hear a response, but he slammed the door shut and aimed his rifle out the front door and waited. Nothing moved outside.

Something kicked his foot. Ahmed stood there, AK-47 in one hand, seemingly unconcerned about the bullets popping through the house. Gale was dumbstruck.

"We're going out the back. Keep them occupied. Don't shoot us," Ahmed said.

Then he and Javad were gone. Brook and Susan were on the floor by the fireplace, face down with hands over their ears. If they were making noise, he couldn't hear it. Robert was behind the bar, hunched down, shotgun pointed over Gale's head at the front door. Focused.

Keep them occupied? Gale said to himself. A bullet whizzed through the wall above him. Pieces of drywall on him. He aimed his rifle out the front door and squeezed the trigger. Nothing happened. He was confused for a second. Safety was on. Dammit! He didn't have a target anyway. Others were firing so they would keep whoever it was occupied. He didn't want to shoot at what he couldn't see. He didn't see Eric out front. He saw nothing.

"Lou!" Gale yelled.

"Here!"

"Ahmed and Javad went out the back to go around. Don't shoot them!"

"Sure! I'll try not to!"

Bullets stopped hitting the house.

"Cease fire!" Lou yelled.

It was quiet inside. Two shots thundered outside. Then more. Fully automatic staccato followed. Then silence. Gale was straining to hear anything. He looked over at Alex and Ana on the floor in the front room behind Lou. He could see Alex's body heaving up and down. She had one hand on her mom's back. Ana was still. Shit! Lou turned around and put a hand on Alex's leg.

BOOM!

A figure in camouflage appeared in the front door and flew backwards. Gale turned and saw Robert behind the bar rack another round into his shotgun.

Silence.

"Gale! Lou! It's Ahmed. We're coming in. It's done."

Ahmed's form filled the front door. He looked down at Gale and nodded.

"How many out there?" Lou asked.

"Five. I think. Four are dead. By the tracks in the snow, one ran before we could get him. Good news. We now have automatic weapons. Lou, can you help Javad collect the weapons, ammunition and any grenades from the dead.

"On it. Gale, get Susan. She's a vet. Need her here for Ana."

Gale turned to get Susan as he got up from the floor, but she was already past him and kneeling next to Ana and Alex, who was crying hysterically. Sound slowly returned to Gale. He regretted it. He moved to Alex and pulled her away from her mom and sat with her on the floor in the family room, rocking her back and forth.

"It's okay, Alex. Easy." He said into her hair. Then he yelled, "Ahmed! Robert! Basement. Layla and Sara!"

"I'll check 'em." Robert went down.

"Gale." It was Donneker.

"Yeah." Gale replied, rocking Alex.

"Dennis is dead. Took a bullet in the chest. No pulse."

"Dammit, Dennis!" Gale looked at the ceiling, then shut his eyes, still holding Alex.

"Ahmed! I need a tourniquet! Quickly! Something. She has a pulse, but it's faint. Hit in the leg. Lots of blood. Nicked an artery." Susan pointed to the kitchen where the medical bag they got from Floyd's house was sitting on the counter.

Ahmed returned with the bag and a flashlight on the floor next to Susan. Right there on the bag's handle attached with a rubber band was what they needed. He yanked it off and handed it to Susan. With some effort, she got the tourniquet, a canvas belt, around and up Ana's leg to the top of her thigh. She cinched it tight and then used the plastic wand that came with it to turn it tighter until it wouldn't tighten further, then secured it.

"Flashlight!" Susan yelled and Ahmed shined the light on the wound in Ana's thigh. Susan ripped the pant leg apart.

"I'm going outside. She knows her stuff." Donneker said.

"Gale, girls are alright. Shaken and crying, but good. Layla was asking after Alex." Robert stopped and surveyed the scene in the room.

"I'm a goddamn vet, not a medical doctor. I don't know," Susan said under her breath. Then louder, "Alex, I'm going to do everything I can for your mom, okay Sweetie? Hang in there."

"Ahmed," Gale whispered. Ahmed looked at him. "They know where we are. You said one got away. They're gonna come back. We have to get everyone out of here. Go—"

"Go where, Gale? Snow, cold, cars dead. We have wounded, the girls, and elderly women. At least here we are defending known ground. If they come back, we'll be ready for them. I've done this before, my friend. Besides, do you hear that?" Ahmed gestured in the air toward the highway.

Gale's hearing was still crap, so he hadn't heard it at first. Distant gunfire.

"Where's that coming from?"

"We heard it while we were outside after the fight. You Americans don't like people invading your country. I think our friends are being occupied by other residents around the area. We have time, I think." It was the first time all evening he'd seen Ahmed smile.

\* \* \*

Lou was helping Javad drag the last dead commando through the snow. They aligned the bodies on the side of Mimi's house, out of the way. Snow was still coming down. If it kept up like this, their tracks would be gone soon. He saw Donneker at the top of the pipe stem by his house keeping an eye on the cul-de-sac and the road leading out of the neighborhood. Good. Javad was kneeling next to Eric's body.

"What are you doing? We should move him as well. If for nothing else, so Alex doesn't see him like that. Spy or not." Lou said as Javad roughly searched Eric's clothes.

"Looking for this." Javad pulled out a smart phone.

"Phones are dead. What's the point?"

Javad pushed the power button and the screen illuminated.

"Not this one. It's locked, though." Javad studied the phone. He grabbed the dead man's hand and put Eric's thumb on the button on the front of the phone. The screen changed.

"How is that possible?" Lou asked.

"Like you said. Spy. He knew what was coming. Needed communication. I want to know with whom he was communicating." Javad turned to Lou. "I almost gave Ahmed one of these to keep protected until after. I didn't. I wasn't supposed to be here."

Javad walked back to the house as he studied the phone. Lou looked down at Eric's body. Damn. Poor Alex. It was still her father. Still her loss. He grabbed Eric's feet and dragged him to the others and left him there, unceremoniously. Screw it. His feelings were getting thin. Probably for the best. They'd all need to harden up to get through this.

# FORTY-EIGHT

She was exhausted, but the landscape below was beautiful as she craned her neck to the left. The early morning sun shone the deep greens of the patchwork land against the brilliant blue of the waters surrounding the spit they were flying down. They skirted north of Glasgow without incident. They weren't sure about radiation from the nuclear blast that hit Faslane, just north of Glasgow, but east of the end of the spit. Tavis had outlined the small, but long enough airstrip near his hometown where they were planning to land. Tavis's red-bearded face had been perched over her right shoulder for the last fifteen minutes and she sensed the tension and anticipation. They still didn't know if his wife and children had made it out to the family home, but they were hopeful.

"Go strap in, Tee."

"Not on your life. Here I stand."

"Fine."

The strip was out in front of her. She lowered the flaps and adjusted the plane's attitude against the cross wind coming off the sea that separated this farthest piece of Scotland from Ireland. Pasha hadn't really had to help her at all. Aside from the leg, she was good and it felt great to fly again, even if it wasn't in a Super Hornet. So much had occurred over the last thirty-six hours, who knew, maybe she'd be flying fighters again when she got back home. She doubted it, but she also was still supposed to be in orbit right now, so who the hell knew. Focus! The jet bounced on the end of the runway and Tavis cracked his head on the door frame to the cockpit.

"Mother…!" Stifling the rest of what was about to fall out of his mouth

"Warned ya."

She set the nose gear down and slowed the plane on the shorter-than-expected runway. She applied the brakes hard and they came to a stop with mere feet to spare before the grass. She let up on the brakes and turned the aircraft around to taxi to an open space next to what looked like some kind of terminal or operations building. She heard the cabin door open. When she got to the door, Tavis was on his hands and knees actually kissing the ground. Scottish.

"Get up off the ground and state your business!"

They hadn't noticed the golf cart roll up with two older gentlemen under the canopy both pointing long, double-barreled shotguns. Joey saw Pasha put his hand on the handle of the pistol still in the small of his back.

"Easy lads! Its Tavis Kinley come home from outer space!"

He rose and turned toward the two men who alternated pointing their shotguns at him and then those at the cabin door. To Joey, they seemed… wobbly.

"Tavis Kinley? Tavis Kinley himself?" Oh they were indeed in the drink. Had to be. Slurred as their words were, or it could be the brogue, but for sure had been drinking and this early in the morning. Scottish.

"Aye! Now lower those things before I've got a dozen holes in me, bleedin' out on this fine Scottish runway." Tavis walked over to the men and embraced them for a long second.

"Alfie! Owen! But you're a sight for sore eyes. Oh, and the pubs open this time of the morning, is it?"

"Well Tav, we heard the Russians were coming, so we thought, whiskey for the rounds. Been a long, cold night. Only whiskey can warm the bones," Alfie said as he waved his arm in a big arc to indicate they were indeed doing the rounds, in their golf cart, with shotguns. Amazing.

"Aye, they may be comin', but not quite yet. Ya seen the elder Kinley's? They at the house? Did my wife and kids get there?"

"Aye lad, it's on the rounds. Warm fire, food to fortify a man for the hard work that's about this morning. Haven't seen the family yet, but not much is moving. Need a lift? The cart's runnin'," said Owen.

"Need the cart, Gentlemen. Woulda ya mind?"

"Not in the slightest. Not going that way. Headin' o'er da pub fer refills."

"Tell your Ma and Da we send our blessin's and we'll be over fer breakfast." Owen smacked Alfie on the arm as they hoisted their shotguns over their shoulders and wobbled away to the pub.

"We're going to need to refuel the jet, Tee," Joey said as four of them squeezed into the cart's front and rear seats. Val and Nina stood on the rear bumper and held onto the roof.

"Later. We need food and I need to see what news there is of my family. See what my parents know."

Joey was in the front passenger seat. Tavis turned the key and the thing started right up. The old cart revved and rolled as he turned so as not to lose anyone.

They pulled up to a quaint little cottage on the shore. They got some odd looks as they drove through the seaside town and Tavis waved at people as they passed. He stopped the cart in the drive and jumped out, jogging up to the front door, throwing it open.

"Ma! Da? Ya here?" he bellowed, as Joey wobbled behind him.

She saw who had to be his parents come out of a small kitchen into the main living area off the entrance way. There was a fire going in an old stone fireplace. She and the rest bundled in after him, shutting the door against the cold sea breeze.

"My God, its Tavis!" his mother screamed and embraced him. His father came over and put his hand on Tavis' shoulder.

"Son, 'ow in the great bloody 'ell d'you get here? We were in fits about you up there."

Their course was set. Joey watched Tavis standing at the window staring out at the wind whipping the bay's waves against the slim beach. She went over again in her head what Tavis' dad had relayed to them. Tee's wife had phoned his parents on Christmas Eve that they'd be coming in the morning. Christmas morning. When Tavis heard that, he freaked out. It meant they were still in Glasgow. His dad said that Faslane had been hit. He didn't know with what, but they saw it over the horizon, glowing. His dad quickly followed-up with information that his wife and kids were staying overnight with her sister in Lochgilphead at the top of the spit. So they weren't here, but they should be well north and west of Faslane. Tavis yelled at his dad that he should have started with that. Tavis relaxed a bit then. He could get to them. This changed everything.

There was much talk within the group about who was going and who was staying. Tavis had decided the matter finally, even though he'd been grateful for their offers. With a few good hours of sleep, Joey and the group would take the plane to the U.S. Tavis was going to stay behind. He would crash for a few hours, while his dad gathered supplies for him, and head north in the cart. Nothing else around here was working. He wanted to go straight away, but she talked him into sleeping first. She knew he needed sleep. Hell, it wasn't even a day ago they'd landed in the Soyuz. In Kazakhstan! He needed rest. They all did. She was sure, though, that when they left in the plane, Tavis wouldn't wait. He'd just deal with the after affects he was feeling from gravity and go find his family. Or, he'd die trying.

She looked around the room. Everyone had a plate of eggs, bacon, sausage, toast with butter and jam, and a pile of baked beans. Val and Nina were already asleep and Pasha was settling in. Joey was offered Tee's old room to stretch out and get real sleep. She was the one that need to fly the plane, so it was mandatory that she rest uninterrupted for a few hours. His dad took the cart to round up one or two of the ground crew, maybe one of the local pilots. He knew them all and needed help to get the plane refueled while they were sleeping.

Tee's mom was speaking with Galina about their ordeal, Pasha translating where it was needed, for Tee's mom, who was enthralled with the tale. Exhaustion was quickly taking her, she felt it in her bones. Especially the one that was broken. She'd taken some pain killers, so the edge was off for now. She hobbled back to her room and collapsed on the bed.

&#10047; &#10047; &#10047;

With mugs of hot coffee or hot chocolate in them and a few hours of desperately needed sleep, they made their way back to the plane. Joey and Tavis said their goodbyes. The sun was up high, gliding slowly across the mid-Scottish morning towards Ireland.

"Take care, Tee. I left our destination on a pad of paper in your parent's kitchen. Just in case." Her emotions were wrecked, but not visible.

"It's been my distinct pleasure, Commander. When I find them and get them home here, I will make what plans I can. The war hasn't reached here on the spit yet, but I'm sure things will get much worse before it gets better. I hope we'll have the good fortune to meet again. Take care of this great, bloody Russian," he said as Pasha came over and bear hugged him.

"Will miss you, my friend. Find your family. If they can be found, you are the one to find them. Das Vedanya," he said, shaking Tee's hand.

"Don't let him fly the plane, Joey. Helicopter pilot!" Tavis yelled as he got in the cart. Joey and Pasha boarded the plane after the others. She watched through the door's window as Tavis sped back to the house by the shore.

They watched him drive away as the engines spun up. Looked at each other and then back to the instruments. Strapped in, she taxied the plane to the end of the runway and punched it. The jet gained speed and launched off the end of the runway and over the beach. The small town got smaller as they gained altitude. Before they were in the clouds, she saw a small, cargo ship fighting the waves into the town's bay. They must have been out to sea when the pulse hit. So, boats were coming home now. Ships far enough out at sea wouldn't have been affected by the EMPs, necessarily. There was hope. Not much, but some. They climbed out over the water with Ireland coming up in front of them. They had just enough fuel for the East Coast. She mentally checked things off her list. Next task. Home. If it was there.

# FORTY-NINE

All planes in the air during the attack had either landed or crashed. They hadn't seen it, but they'd come across it on the road. When the sun came up on Christmas morning, there was black smoke in the distance. They'd approached one pillar of smoke to investigate and saw the wreckage of a large passenger plane. There were no survivors that they could find. He guessed it was like this all over the country. Thousands of planes were in the air at any one time. He shuddered.

"Got the chills, Gunny?"

Staff Sergeant Simmons had ghosted him on his right. Steam rose from the coffee cup in his hands, M-4 slung tight to his chest. Simmons was all muscle. Without his helmet, his freshly shaved black head glinted in what was left of the afternoon light.

"Jesus! Scared the shit out of me. Was just thinking about what all those people must have gone through. You know, in the planes, right after it happened. Sent chills through me."

"Yeah, thought about that too. This some crazy shit, Gunny."

They were all exhausted. It had been two days since they left the fort on a stop and go affair. The church stayed with him, unfortunately. He looked out over the small airstrip in the middle of the Virginia countryside. A hot cup of black coffee warmed his hands as he took in the overcast sky. When they arrived this morning for a rest, the grass was covered in crystalline frost the sun hadn't melted yet. That was gone now, but it looked like there was weather moving. It was just below freezing. A thermostat hung just outside the door to the hangar where the vehicles were parked. They'd run security in teams of two on rotating shifts throughout the morning and into the afternoon so everyone could grab some shut eye.

The small complex had been empty and locked up. They'd helped themselves to fuel. The vending machines inside the ops building provided snacks and drinks. The coffee makers were electric, so they built a fire and rigged up a pot to boil water. Manually filtering the water through the coffee grounds into another pot so there was plenty of liquid heaven. Marines found a way. Especially for coffee. There were also a bunch of power drinks in the vending machines. Marines ran on caffeine, but man could he go for a beer. Later, when they got home. There were a couple of others in the team that had family around the D.C. area and he'd make the best effort he could to get to them as well. Only fair.

They came through the mountains and the lower Shenandoah Valley, near Harrisonburg and east across the Virginia countryside to Route Fifteen. That had taken them west of Lake Anna, where the North Anna 1 and 2 Nuclear reactors were located. If they hadn't melted down by now, they would soon, but all that would go east, hopefully, and not where they were headed.

"How are the guys?" An asked.

"Gettin' caffeinated, Gunny. Zero contact around the airport. What's the plan?" He took a long sip of his coffee.

"Well, I was looking at the map earlier. We've got some more of this county-style travel for the next twenty clicks and then we start getting into more populated areas in the western suburbs of D.C. Only thing we need to worry about is a correctional facility about five clicks up the road. Don't know if those facilities are still locked down or if all hell's broken loose. This is Virginia. Everyone's armed. Gun shops and ranges everywhere. If those prisoners got out, could be interesting."

"Roger that. We still headed to your mom's place?"

They talked about this on the road. He was going to get his family. He had to get to Brook and his mom. He still didn't know what to tell them. His brother could be dead, or wounded, or they could be a mile behind them now. He just didn't know.

"It's on the way to D.C., Staff Sergeant."

"Hey, Gunny, good with me and the men. No one's gonna hold it against you. Most of 'em would want to get their families too, if we were this close.

As you said, it's on the way. We're with you. Sure your brother made it and they're kicking someone's ass right now."

"Thanks. But home is on the way to where? Quantico is east of us, but we can't go past the nuke plant at Lake Anna. We don't know what's happened to it, but if it melts, Quantico is toast. We need to get to D.C. or Mt. Weather. Both are in range today after we get my family. Someone should know what's going on and get us into the fight, whoever we're fighting."

"Oorah," Simmons replied, then cocked his head. "Gunny, hear that? What is that?" Simmons was looking around now, searching for the sound.

They were both silent. Then, the crisp morning air brought the slight sound of an engine to their ears.

"There, plane!" Simmons pointed low into the sky.

"That doesn't look good," An said dryly, taking a sip of his coffee.

The plane approached the end of the runway, gear down, but trailing black smoke from the right engine. The plane wobbled back and forth. There was minimal wind, so there must be something wrong and not just the engine. More Marines joined them and An heard the hangar door open to his right. He glanced to see the LAV pull out with its turret mounted chaingun traversing to track the plane. Just in case, he thought. Good. Never know, especially now. The plane bounced on the runway and settled on all three wheels. When it stopped it didn't taxi. He saw the stairs hit the ground on the other side.

"Go see who we have, Staff Sergeant. Head on a swivel, take two men. We'll cover you from here."

"Hey, Gunny, I didn't know we were expecting company," one of his Marines shouted.

"Go put on some makeup. You gonna scare our guests," another Marine popped off.

The back and forth continued behind An as he took another sip. He didn't care what was happening, he was going to finish his hot coffee. As he listened to the banter, he watched his guys have a brief conversation with a woman on a crutch. Her bouncy hair pulled back in a pony tail. Simmons escorted five people, including the hair-bouncer, from the plane to where he stood. There was one very large man, another woman and two teenagers. Simmons walked ahead and got to An first.

"You ain't gonna believe this shit, Gunny," was all the time he had before bouncy-hair hobbled up on one crutch. She eyed him up and down and then surveyed his troops.

"You in charge, Gunny?" The bouncy-haired woman said with some authority that surprised him. She also recognized his rank on his uniform. Interesting.

"I am. That was some landing. Gunnery Sergeant An Nguyen." An dismissed her initially. He assumed the man standing next to her was the pilot and in charge. He reached out his hand to him. The man's hand engulfed his.

"I'm Pasha. Yes, she has some issues with landing, but otherwise it was good flight."

"Gunny, this is Commander Joey Washington. Formerly of the International Space Station." Simmons cut in quickly before An could make any more of an ass of himself.

"U.S. Navy Commander Joey Washington." She did not hold out her hand, but something clicked in his head and he couldn't believe it.

"What's your callsign, Commander?"

"Roo, like Kangaroo. Why?"

"Commander, I believe you live on the same street as my parents just north of here. With your husband and daughter?"

"Nguyen? Mama is your mom?"

"Yes Ma'am! Good to see you again, Commander. We met a couple of years ago at a neighborhood block party." Now shaking hands.

"Wow, small world, Gunny! Where you headed?"

"Home for starters. Need a lift?"

"Roger that! What's your situation here? What have you seen? Where you coming from?"

"First off, what happened to your aircraft?" They all turned to look at the plane. The engine was still smoking.

"We were going to land further north at the small executive airport near home, but as we came in for a pass we saw three 727s at one end of the runway. We took some fire from the ground. Don't know who it was, but they put a hole in my engine. We headed for Dulles, but all the runways were blocked with aircraft and we took fire from someone on the ground there as well.

"Really? They were shooting at you?" An said as Simmons gave a low whistle.

"Yeah. Shot at us. So, we headed south and found this strip. Just in time, too. Good thing I fly small aircraft around here when I'm home. I remembered this one down here. We were on fumes.

"Where did you come from, Commander, seeing as how two days ago you were in outer space?" Simmons chimed in.

"Landed in Kazakhstan. Had to evacuate the station. Some kind of nuclear weapon detonated in orbit above us. Damaged the station. Had to bug out. We also saw what looked like flashes on the ground around the Indian Sub-Continent and Pakistan. Nukes have been used and it's not isolated. We found out on our trip, nukes were dropped in Europe and here in the U.S. You all know where?"

They walked to the hangar to get in from the chill afternoon air.

"We haven't heard of nukes here, Commander. At least not from Kentucky to here. How'd you get out? Of Kazakhstan, I mean?" An asked.

"I know a man. He will be unhappy about his plane." Pasha said. The plane on the runway was now showing signs of fire from the engine compartment. An turned to see liquid pooling on the ground below the right wing.

"Pasha's friend got us to Saint-Petersburg. Long story, but we stole the plane and flew to Scotland. It's not good. When we were on the ground in Saint-Petersburg, we heard fighting, artillery, over the border in Estonia. Big guns. But the good news is that the Finns, at least, are fighting back. Saved our asses over Helsinki. Splashed a pair of Russian MIGs chasing us. Faslane, Scotland was nuked. It's where the Brits keep their ballistic missile subs. Don't know about any other places. That's us. What about you all?"

"Coming from Kentucky. Fort Knox. We had orders to get east to D.C. or somewhere east, to share intel. The Fort got attacked from the ground as we were heading out. Got separated from the rest of our column. Don't know who hit the Fort, but I'll tell you this much, everything is out. No power. No phones. Only vehicles running are the older ones. Electronics, I suspect."

"Yeah, Christmas sucked this year." Simmons yelled over his shoulder as he stood with Pasha watching the plane burn out on the tarmac. The fuel leaking from the wing tank had ignited. Black smoke was billowing into the sky.

"So, Gunny, you got room for five more? We'll be home in two hours if we book it." Joey was getting anxious.

"Roger that. Mount up. Time to go. Simmons will get you squared away. We'll split you up between the Humvee and LAV. It'll be cramped, Commander, but we'll manage it."

"Perfect. And just call me Joey, or Roo, if you prefer, Gunny. I'm too tired for rank and chain of command. Thanks for accommodating us."

"Pleasure, Roo. That's your callsign, right?"

"Yep."

"Appropriate since you bounced that thing like a marsupial," An said, as they watched the fully engulfed executive jet collapse on the concrete.

# FIFTY

December 26
3:15pm EST
Gale Washington

Gale stood next to the fireplace. Light filtered in through the blinds and curtains. The group had been awake late into the night. The adults took turns keeping watch. One by the bay window. They nailed up a thick comforter to keep the cold air from coming through several shattered panes of glass. One person was in Ahmed's house where they could keep an eye on the road coming in.

Ana had died from her wounds early in the morning. Alex was distraught. Layla and Sara took her downstairs. They finally got the girls, even Alex, to go to sleep in the basement. It wasn't too cold down there. They had all the blankets. He'd just checked on them. It was dark, except for the campfire lamp they got from Floyd's. The three girls were all curled up together. Only Layla was awake and put her finger to her lips so he wouldn't wake Alex. They moved Ana's body outside with the others hours ago. But not before Javad had found another working smart phone in her jacket pocket.

The old Iranian was sitting at the kitchen table with two phones in front of him. Lou was next to him, speaking softly. Robert was on the couch, snoring loudly. Mama was at the bay window taking her turn at watch. She insisted it would take her mind off of her own grief. She still had two sons out there somewhere. Part of him thought she was waiting for them to roll up the driveway. He thought the same about Joey, although he knew better. Ahmed was across the street on his watch. Everyone else was below trying to get some sleep.

All the emotion that he'd been holding at bay for two days surged. He slid down the wall and sat next to the hearth with his arms on his knees, head buried, and let tears flow. Sounds of gunfire intermingled with visions. Joey. Layla. Alex. Dennis. Eric. Ana. Blood. Bodies. Death. How was he going to keep Layla safe? How would she survive if he got killed? These men— Ahmed, Javad, Lou, even Donneker and Robert. They were hard. Harder than him. Hardened by war. By things they'd done. By their own loss. This was all new to him. Hopelessness turned to anger. He'd been right! He'd seen it. He'd put it together for them and no one listened. They deserved this. Their complacency staggered him. Did they think that just because it was the twenty-first century that human nature and evil only existed in pockets in remote places? That another world war was impossible?

He was no angel. He'd gambled away money his family needed. Ha! Didn't need that now. One problem solved, replaced by a thousand more. He'd rather have the one problem and have to face Joey.

A warm body snuggled next to him. He lifted his head to see Layla sitting next to him. He put his arm around her. Layla rested her head quietly on his knees as he wrapped her up. No matter what, he'd protect her. Somehow. They sat together for a while. He wiped his wet face. No more of that.

"Gale." He opened his eyes and looked up.

"What's up?" Lou was in front of them.

"We've got an idea. A plan. It's not great. But it's something. Layla, we're going to need Alex.

❋ ❋ ❋

Lou, Javad, and Alex were sitting at the kitchen table. Alex had the pug snuggled in her arms. Her eyes red. Gale stood in the kitchen. Layla was sitting quietly by the fireplace with her dead phone next to her, listening to Sara argue with Ahmed in the front room. Something about showing her how to shoot a rifle. They all wanted to help. Gale had taught Layla how to shoot. She knew her way around weapons, but Gale was unsure about it now. This was different than the range. Hell, he tried to pull the trigger last night and failed.

Donneker had replaced Ahmed across the pipestem. Susan and Bibi were in the basement asleep with Chewie watching over them. Robert was still asleep on the couch, unmoved by the activity around him. The fire was roaring, dumping what heat didn't go up the chimney into the room.

"Alex, I know you've been through too much for someone your age. But my Russian is rusty, so we need you to help us here, okay? This was your father's," Lou said. He pointed to the phone on the table in front of her and Javad. He continued, "It's been altered. Looks like a regular phone, but thicker. Your mother had one as well. They were hardened against the pulse that took everything else out. Seems they can communicate directly with at least one other phone. The person on the other end has been sending texts in Russian to this phone for the last hour. From what I can tell, whoever is sending these texts, is coming here to meet up with your parents. They're requesting confirmation of your parent's location. They're still hours away from the sound of it."

"What do you want me to do?" Alex asked, her head on Christopher's furry body. She sounded exhausted.

"Good for you, Alex. This is the plan. There are still Iranians out there somewhere, but there are Russians as well, apparently. We need you to tell them, in Russian, that we—sorry, your parents, are at your house. Tell them to come in on the highway out there where the overpass is."

"You want me to bring more bad guys here? I don't understand," Alex said.

"Alex, there are too many Iranians. We need to try to even the odds. If the Iranians see vehicles on the road, they may attack them. That's their mission here. To block this corridor out of D.C. They won't know who's in the vehicles. Perhaps, in this snow storm, the fog of war will be our friend," Javad explained.

"Do you think these Russians will kill the commandos?" Alex said, staring coldly at Javad, who nodded. Gale couldn't tell if she was angry at him, as most of the group was, or just wanted the Iranians dead.

"Here, Alex, I've written out exactly what you should tell them. Type this in exactly, but in Russian."

Alex read the words, written in English, on the pad. She took a deep breath and plopped the pug on the floor. Christopher bounced over to the couch and jumped up on Robert, snuggling into him. "Give me the phone."

Ahmed stepped into the kitchen as Sara stormed downstairs. Gale felt the man's struggle. These girls were thrust into this, as they all were, but they're just kids. Gale felt the same way about Layla, although she hadn't asked for a weapon yet. Sara had, and Ahmed had rebuffed her. Sara thought he was treating her like a child, but weren't still that…children? They shouldn't need to have weapons. Eventually, they'd all need to be able to defend themselves. Eventually.

# FIFTY-ONE

An was on edge. They were on the road for fifteen minutes and found a town in front of them on the main route. They found a smaller, winding road so they didn't have to deal with it.

Fletch slammed on the brakes. He looked to see why he stopped. The Humvee was stopped right in front of them forcing Fletch to brake the tank hard. A kid, not more than five or six stood in the road. Not one, but two kids, the other one much younger and the older one holding the younger one's hand and carrying something in her other arm. Before he could say or do anything, the Commander was out of the Humvee with her crutches.

"Sergeant!" Joey yelled.

"Dammit Roo, wait!" An watched as the Marines from the Humvee joined the wobbling Joey while An signaled to the LAV behind them to set security. He climbed down from Alice and caught up to Roo.

"Sergeant, get the corpsman and blankets if we have any. Let's get them in the Humvee." She had enveloped the younger child, a boy, in her arms. He was freezing and started to cry. Snot was caked around his nose and his eyes were red. He took one look at the older child and immediately scooped her up in his arms. She was nearly lifeless and cold. She weighed nothing to him. The bundle in her arms was wrapped tightly in a small, thin blanket. He turned and rushed them back to the Humvee's heated interior.

"Corpsman up!" Simmons shouted.

The team's corpsman climbed into the Humvee's back seat with the children and Joey, who had gotten in on the other side with the little boy. What the hell, they weren't dressed for this weather. The corpsman asked Simmons to help them in the back as he climbed out with the bundle. He took the small figure and put it gently down on the now empty driver's seat. Buford was now out front on the road with his rifle scanning ahead.

"Staff Sergeant, they have severe frostbite, we need to get them warm. Some of the guys have coffee and hot chocolate still in the LAV. Get some."

Simmons was wrapping another blanket around the little girl's legs and feet, which only had socks and slippers on them. Joey was doing the same for the little boy.

"Sweetie, you're safe now. We have you. You're safe. Why are you out here in the cold, baby girl?" Joey asked.

"Mommy told us to hide, but they were going to find us." the little girl said between sobs and shivers.

"It's alright, Sweetie. What's your name?"

"Carly."

"What's your name, little man?"

"Stevie," the little boy stuttered.

Pasha appeared with a covered cup of hot chocolate and handed it to Joey who gave each of them a couple of sips of the warm liquid.

"Carly, who were you carrying? What is her name?"

"Gracie. My little sister. Stevie is my little brother."

"You are such a brave little girl for protecting them. What happened? Where is your home? Who was after you?"

"How are we doing, Corporal?" An asked.

"The bad men came. They were everywhere. Mommy woke us up and told us to hide, but they were everywhere, so we ran away. Gracie was crying forever, but I finally got her to go to sleep a little bit ago."

She sobbed again and shivered uncontrollably. Pasha fished around in his jacket and pulled out the Panda Ball. He offered the fluffy little toy to Carly, hoping to distract her from the horror she'd just been through.

"Describe your house, little one. Do you know the address?" An asked Carly.

"It's blue with a garden."

"What the hell is this, Gunny?" Simmons had come up from the rear. The Marine looked like the face of death as he stared at the little pink bundle.

"All I can think of is that correctional facility got opened up and the inmates got out and got to the town. It's only a mile back with the prison on the other side of that. Explains the smoke and the fires."

Carly was still sobbing, even with the Panda Ball squeezed in her little hands. Her brother snuggled next to her with Joey next to him, her arm around them both. An looked at the baby and then reached in the door frame and scooped up Carly, bundled up in blankets, and held her tight to him. She sobbed into his chest through his body armor, her tiny body shuddering with each sob. He gently passed Carly to Pasha's waiting arms, who climbed into the back of the Humvee with her and settled in with Joey and her little brother. An nodded to him and shut the door.

"Sergeant Simmons, pull the team together. Corpsman, bring the baby and follow me."

"Circle up!" An was enraged.

"We doin' this, Boss?" Simmons asked enthusiastically.

"Oh, we're doing this, Sergeant. Marines, our mission was to get to D.C. and find out what we could and pass on intel. We were to avoid populated areas where we could, like we did with that town back there. However, these little kids we just found in the road were out here in the cold, probably all night and today, and the tiniest one of them didn't make it."

"Apparently, some evil mother fuckers got to that town last night, probably from that jail we skirted. That's why these kids spent the night in the cold and that, Marines, is why this little baby girl named Gracie is dead."

"Rules of Engagement?" Simmons asked.

"We're going in hot. Sort 'em quick, friendly from bad. Prosecute with extreme prejudice. Let's see if we can rescue their parents, if there's anyone left to rescue. Simmons, detail two men to stay with the kids and our guests. The rest of you, mount up. Be prepared to clear structures, door to door. Head on a swivel, Sergeant. I'm going to roll in first with the track and secure the other end of the town. It doesn't look like more than a half dozen houses and some other buildings. I want to keep an eye on that prison while we're here so we don't get surprised."

When they started, it was going to be loud and if there were any more prisoners at that facility, he didn't want them getting curious. An walked back to the Humvee with the Corpsman and opened the back hatch where the Corpsman laid the baby down gently. They'd find her mom and dad and if they were alive, give them some closure, and if not, bury them together. Either way, they'd be together again. Pasha was out of the Humvee now with his AK-47.

"We're going into that town and sort it. I'm leaving two men here for security. You're part of that security. You handle one of those before?" An looked at the fully automatic rifle in the Russian's large hands.

"Da. I am familiar with this. Go sort it, as you say. We will be here. They will be safe."

# FIFTY-TWO

December 26
3:50pm EST
An Nguyen

The tank rumbled through the small town. Devoid of life. There was no one about. Once he got to the other end past the last small building, which seemed to be a community bank, he stopped in the middle of the road. The sun had disappeared behind the gray clouds rolling in. Snow flakes, thick and wet, hit the turret. He stood in the commander's hatch with his binoculars, while his gunner traversed the turret scanning the fields to the correctional facility.

He looked back as the LAV rolled in and stopped in the middle of town. The six Marines dismounted and broke into two fire teams. They approached the small buildings and houses along the narrow street. It reminded him of an old western movie, but without the horses. Turning back to the fields, he could see in the distance some structures a couple miles off. That was the prison. They hadn't seen any one that looked like convicts yet, or anyone at all for that matter.

All the power goes out and you're trapped in a prison cell, guards leave and you're just there, starving to death, 'cause no one's gonna come and let you out. How's that for hell? He'd rather die out here under the open sky than rot away in darkness like a caged animal. He snapped back to reality when he saw Simmons look his way and wave. He gave him a thumbs up to let him know that he had this direction covered. That's when all hell broke loose.

The door to the house in front of Simmons opened and An put the binoculars to his eyes to get a better look. The man that walked out was clearly not a resident of this small, country town. The man froze outside the doorway and stared at Simmons, who aimed his M-4 at the man's chest. The prisoner turned and tried to jump back through the doorway. He he didn't make it. Simmons and the Corporal standing next to him shot the man multiple times taking no chances. He dropped where he was, but the window next to the doorway exploded outward and the corporal was flung backwards. The old house was shredded when they ceased. There was no return fire. He looked closer at the house through the binoculars. It was blue. There was indeed a garden on the side of it. Dammit.

"Corpsman!"

"Driver, back us up to the LAV. Gunner, stay on the prison. Loader, cover our guys."

As the tank stopped on the opposite side of the street from the LAV, An could see the corporal's gear hanging off his armor plate carrier. It was shredded, hit with buckshot from whoever had blown out the window. The corpsman was working on him. There was buckshot that hit just above his armor and the corporal was unconscious. Simmons stood and surveyed the street. The other men were moving into other buildings and houses. Shots rang out up the street, but muffled. Contact! More of these bastards. Two Marines came out of the shredded, blue house in front of Simmons with an all clear, but dragging another of these prisoners with them.

"Any civilians?"

"One female, Gunny. Deceased. Seems they had a party in there, but not the kind you want to go to. More prisoners too. Look like gang bangers, Gunny. They are no longer with us except this one, barely."

"Gunny, we found the civilians. This way. It's not good."

"Simmons, interrogate that prisoner. I want to know what went on here and who's left in that jail."

"Lead the way. Driver reverse slowly down the street."

An jumped down from the tank when it stopped. He knew what he was going to see before he rounded the back corner of the house. The smell. He was still shocked when he saw it. In the back yard were the town's residents. About twenty or thirty of them, he couldn't tell exactly. They were all piled on top of each other.

"What the absolute fuck!" An turned on his heels and walked back to the street. There was nothing to do for them and he didn't need to stare at the pile longer than a second, nor did he want to. He gave Simmons the round up signal with his right arm. They were getting out of here, and quickly.

Movement caught his eye out across the fields toward the prison as he climbed back up to his hatch. He grabbed the binoculars and took a better look. Well, that can't be good. A bunch of vehicles, pickup trucks and a van, were moving. How were those vehicles running? They all seemed to be older, dirty, and banged up. Anything was possible, he guessed, but there were a lot of men in those trucks. Guess we woke up the neighborhood. Simmons and the LAV pulled up.

"Corporal's alive, Gunny. The Corpsman patched him up. He's conscious. Armor caught most of the blast and buckshot. He'll make it. That prisoner we talked to said the jail is full of gang-bangers. Last day or so, they got old cars from the farms around here. Newer cars were dead. He said they own this area now and his bosses would get payback. Gang thing I suppose. Eye for an eye or some such bullshit. All good here?"

"No. We've got multiple vehicles coming in from the prison. Looks like he was right about his bosses wanting payback." An pointed in that direction. The crack of gunfire up the road where they left the commander, got his attention.

"Shit! Go!" An yelled as the LAV sped away toward the gunfire. He climbed down into his hatch. They should have all come into the town together. Dumb. He let his emotions dictate his actions this time. Stupid. Now we've got bad guys behind us and god knows what in front of us.

\* \* \*

Joey was in the back seat with the bundled up kids. The boy was asleep on her lap. Carly was leaning against her with the Panda Ball. Pasha's good luck charm had served them well so far. He was very particular about the plushy. It had warmed her heart that he instantly offered it up to the little girl. Joey looked through the windshield. Pasha, Galina, and Nina were standing in front of the Humvee with Val. She could hear them talking in Russian when they all turned and looked up the road, away from the town.

The road bent to the right and out of sight with thick, but bare trees lining both sides of the two-lane blacktop with a well-worn double yellow line down the middle. She craned her neck around the passenger seat to see what they were looking at. She put her arm instinctively around Carly and pulled her close in to her side. She winced as the movement tweaked her leg. Her peripheral sight caught a Marine standing guard between them and the town. He was walking slowly up the side of the Humvee, M-4 pointed up the road.

Gunfire split the quiet and the little boy in her lap jumped awake. She saw Pasha through the windshield wrap his arms around the other three and spin them so that she could see his face. His frame sheltering them all between him and the Humvee's hood, AK-47 gripped uselessly in one hand. Galina and Nina screamed. Then there was blood on the windshield obscuring her view. She pushed both children as flat as she could on the back seat with her on top of them. She looked at her own AK-47 resting on its butt, upright between the front seats. She reached for it rounds shattered the windshield.

"Shh, baby girl. It'll be okay."

She heard the cracks of M-4s interrupted by cracks and booms of other weapons that she didn't recognize. Eventually the M-4s stopped and there was a final boom. Silence. Adrenaline pulsed through her. That wasn't good. She reached for the AK-47 and pulled it over to her as she slid the two crying kids to the floor of the Humvee. She racked a round into the chamber and a round ejected from the weapon. It was already racked. She looked up to the left side window to see a man with a shaved head covered with tattoos looking at her, smiling. Not a Marine. He reached for the door handle. He didn't see the weapon in her hands and she braced for a fight. The door swung open and she heard the staccato bark of a machine gun. The man flew sideways toward the front of the vehicle. She sat up, rifle at the ready and peaked out the open door to see the LAV roll up and around the Humvee, machine gun on the roof turret still firing on something ahead of them.

There were Marines all around the vehicle. Several yelled for a corpsman. That snapped her back to the bundles on the floor. The adrenaline started to leave her and she shook. She sat there rocking the kids. She watched and listened to the Marines; they were safe now.

"Are you good, Commander? The kids?" Simmons said from the open door.

"Yeah. The others?"

"The boy and girl seem to be ok, but in shock. The girl's mother didn't make it. The Corpsman is working on Pasha now, but it doesn't look good, Commander."

She set the two kids up on one of the backseats. Carly still had the Panda Ball clutched in her tiny hands.

"Stay here, I'll be right back. You're safe. These men will protect you."

She opened the door on the other side and exited, not even feeling her leg as she hopped to the front of the vehicle.

"A bullet entered through his back but didn't go all the way through. He shielded the kids with his body. They're probably alive because of him. He'll be okay, I think. If we can get the bullet out."

"Pasha! Can you hear me? Stay with us, Pasha!" He was blurry from her tears. There was no hospital, no help. The would wasn't pulsing blood, so that was good. His hand tightened around hers.

"Keep them safe. Keep them all…" His grip loosened and his eyes closed. The corpsman checked for a pulse.

"He's passed out. We have to get him more help than I can give him."

"Pasha!" She bent over him, her forehead touching his, her tears dropped over his face. Don't leave me now. A hand gently touched her shoulder.

"We have to go. There's more on the way from the prison," An said.

"Sergeant! Put these two Marines in one of the trucks. I'm not leaving them for these people. The Russian lady stays here. We don't have room."

"No! We will not be leaving any of my people here to rot, Gunny! Is that understood!" She was inches from his face.

"We don't have the space and we have to move. I don't know what kind of force is coming up on us but I don't intend to lose any more Marines here."

"Gunny, I know I said I was too tired for the chain of command at the airstrip, but I'm taking command now. We'll be taking our dead with us. Make room." Joey's voice got quieter as she inched closer to his face.

"Your Marines and Galina are dead and Pasha may die because you decided to cowboy up and kill bad guys. Police up *our* people and make room. We're going home. All of us. Together. Are we clear?" Her rage flowed from her eyes as they stared at each other. An reluctantly stepped away.

"Sergeant, put the dead in one of the trucks up the road if they still run. Detail a driver. We're moving out. Provide the Commander with an M-4 and extra magazines. Commander, stow that AK in the Humvee, that M-4 is your friend now. The little kids will ride with Simmons, Pasha, and the Corpsman in the Humvee with the Commander. It'll be tight, but squeeze in. Humvee on point, then me and the track, then the truck with the LAV bringing up the rear. The two teenagers will ride in the LAV. If those shits from the prison get anywhere close to us, you light 'em up. Understood?" He got an affirmative and they got busy getting going.

# FIFTY-THREE

December 26
An Nguyen

They were rolling down another two-lane road in the Virginia countryside. They were passing neighborhoods now. Suburbs. On the last stretch of straight road, An glimpsed behind them. That wasn't good.

"Zombie Actual, Buford."

"Go Buford." The LAV was behind them half a click keeping an eye out for their followers.

"These guys are still back here. And we have another problem. With snow falling heavier now, your tracks are visible in the road. They'll be able to follow us without being too close."

"Buford, high tail it up here!"

An checked the road behind them. Damn. These guys didn't have to see them to know where they were going. An looked at the snow-covered road. The tank's treads left all the bread crumbs they'd need to find them. He knew what they were after, or at least what he'd be after. Who wouldn't want a battle tank in the middle of this chaos? They were waiting for the right moment, staying well back. He didn't know how far back they were, but they were there. If those bastards thought they could surprise him, they were wrong.

"All vehicles, Zombie Actual. We need to deal with our followers from the prison. We're not going to lead them to where we're going. After we round the next bend in the road, we'll stop and deploy for an ambush."

Soon, they halted after a ninety degree turn in the road. The snow was coming down hard and the failing light would help. Fletch had backed Alice off the road behind a stand of evergreens, while the LAV was off to the other side of the road in the bend next to a late model, very expensive looking, sports car that was dead on the side of the road. His fire team was deployed in the woods, concealed. It was a good spot.

An popped up out of the hatch and saw Commander Washington hobbling over to stand next to the tank. She looked up at An.

"Gunny, we're all at the end of our capacity here. I'm sorry for your Marines. They're deaths were not your fault. Nor was Galina's. My intent wasn't to dress you down in front of your men." He thought for a moment then spoke.

"You're right, Commander. We should have kept going, or I should have brought you all into town with us. Emotion got the better of me. It won't happen again. That I can promise you. You're in command. Do you approve of my plan here?"

"It's a good plan. They need to be dealt with. We'll see you in the hood, Gunny."

"Roger that, Commander. Be with you all directly." An saluted. Joey returned it and rejoined the others.

An watched the pickup truck and Humvee move down the road toward home.

"Simmons, Six Actual."

"Simmons, go Six."

"The Commander knows where to go. We're nearly there anyway. Take care of them and check on my mom when you get there. This shouldn't take long. We'll be there shortly."

"Roger that. See you for chow, Boss."

"Hey, Gunny, you think your mom can make us some tacos after this? I want tacos." Fletch said from his hole in the front of the tank.

"Shut it, Fletch. Ain't no tacos in the apocalypse." Jones said and kicked the metal grate door between his left foot and the driver's compartment.

An ignored his them and clipped the radio to his chest gear and sank down into his hole, securing the hatch above him. Tacos actually sounded good. Focus. He had a full field of vision through his optics. Night vision and infra-red. He settled in. What he wanted to do was take Alice and barrel down the road toward the oncoming vehicles, dealing death and destruction as he went. But this was the perfect ambush spot, so here they sat. The main gun was aimed toward the curve. By the time these bastards saw Alice it would be too late. Buford had his rifle set up on the hood of the dead sports car tracking through the trees to where the road disappeared around several bends about three-hundred yards away. The LAV was behind Buford's spot at the car, concealed by more evergreens. The fire team was deployed in a long line out into the woods parallel to the road. The only sound was the whine of the tank's engine, which also provided warmth in the turret.

"Loader, HEAT," An ordered.

Stewie swiveled to face the rear of the turret and pulled a HEAT round from the ammo box and seated it in the breach.

"HEAT up!"

"Gunner, we're going to hit the first vehicle on my command. We don't have a clear shot through the trees to the last vehicle."

"First vehicle, copy."

"Recon, Six Actual."

"Go Six."

"When they come, hit the last vehicle with your chain gun and work your way up the line. We'll hit the first vehicle when they come around the bend."

"Roger that, Six."

An leaned into his sights and slowly swiveled the optics package that was slaved to the fifty caliber machine gun above him on top of the turret. The turret remained still with the main gun aimed at the bend. Buford was ghost still. The snow was coming straight down. No wind. An elevated his sights to track the line of Marines in the woods. The hum of the turbine engine was the only sound. Soon Alice, he patted the inside of the turret. An thought of the tank as the fifth member of his crew.

"Zombie Six, Buford." The sniper came over the radio. "I got vehicles moving up the road. I count eight. I say again, eight vehicles. Pickup trucks and a couple of jeeps and old sedans. I can see men in the beds. I see weapons. Over."

"Roger. Buford, target the drivers of the middle vehicles first."

"Tracking."

An didn't traverse the turret to follow the trucks. They'd be in his sights in a moment.

"Get some, Alice, Get some." An heard Stewie chant quietly from his seat below him. His loader always got chatty just before action. He leaned into his sights again. There they were. The first vehicle was a pickup.

"Gunner! Pickup truck. Range - sixty yards. Fire!"

"On the way!" Jones yelled back.

The recoil shook the tank and the boom of the 120mm gun hit An in the gut. He was always awed by the power of the main gun. There was no other sensation like it. He was rewarded instantly with the spectacular explosion of the pickup truck through his sights. He heard the staccato pops of the LAV's chain gun muffled through the tank's armor.

"Loader! Load HEAT!" An ordered.

Stewie went through his motions again. "HEAT up!"

"Gunner, second car. Fire!"

"On the way!"

The main gun repeated its action as the round hit the engine block and detonated somewhere under the vehicle sending it sideways. An swiveled his sights to the right and down the line of vehicles. The sound of gunfire was incessant. Jones was firing his machine gun slaved to the main gun, lighting up the next vehicle in the line. The convicts had no chance once Alice was let loose. Exactly how he preferred it. She was a bitch.

✱ ✱ ✱

Donneker was in his own house again, near the bay window. The same bay window that all these cookie-cutter houses had in the front room. He was standing watch. Two vehicles turned into the cul-de-sac, lighting up the houses and lawns with their headlights. They didn't think the Iranians had vehicles, so maybe someone else? Friendlies? He opened the front door and cautiously walked out onto the front lawn, his rifle at the ready. One of the vehicles was a Humvee. That was a good sign. He watched as people got out of the Humvee on the other side and one of them went hobbling up to the Washington's door on what appeared to be one crutch.

"Stop there! United States Marines! Lower your weapon or I will shoot you!" Donneker saw a figure in fatigues walking toward him from the pickup truck, rifle pointed at him. Damn! Didn't even see him.

"Hold on! I live here!" Donneker yelled back and lowered his rifle, letting it hang from the harness and raised his arms above his head. As he did, two other Marines approached him from the Humvee with weapons aimed at him.

"Where's Gale Washington? Is he here?" This came from the wobbly, short figure on Gale's front stoop. He was about to respond when rapid gunfire echoed from the highway.

＊ ＊ ＊

They were standing back from the big window. Gale had ushered the girls downstairs with Mama, Bibi, and the dogs to be safe. Robert had been on watch after his long nap on the couch. He'd alerted them to the vehicles in the court. The rest were in various spots around the main floor, ready as they could be for anything. Robert was near the front door with his shotgun. Javad and Ahmed were kneeling with weapons near Robert in the front room. Gale and Lou were in the family room watching the front door down the hallway to the foyer and keeping an eye out back.

"I don't like this, Gale. First the booms and machine gun fire in the distance, and now these vehicles."

"That one is Humvee," Robert said from his vantage point.

"The Iranians don't have Humvees. I don't know where they'd get one." Javad said as gunfire erupted from the direction of the main road.

"That's on the highway. Looks like our Russians may have showed up. Gale, can you see what's going on toward the road out back? Stay low. I don't like all our attention on the court anyway," Lou said.

"On it. I'll let you know in a minute."

Gale stepped out back on the deck. As he closed the door behind him, he crouched to the railing that had three inches of snow on it. There were a good fifty or sixty yards of woods between him and the main road. The trees were bare for the most part and it was eerily dark. He scanned the woods when then the gunfire started again. There flashes out on the road. Whoever was out there, Russians or not, was returning fire from vehicles on the road. Between bursts of fire, he could hear voices from the court, but couldn't make out what they were saying. He didn't know how anyone could see a target in this thick, falling snow. There was no wind though. The silence returned and he squinted to see the road. A fire burned and he saw moving shapes silhouetted against the light. Shit. They were moving this way. That's when he saw several figures halfway between him and the road step out from behind trees. He couldn't tell if they were facing him or the road.

\* \* \*

"Okay, everyone, there's someone running to the door. Several more are following. Looks like Donneker is with them. There are little kids, as well," Robert said as he opened the front door.

Ahmed could see past him through the bay window. Donneker was bringing up the rear, lit up by the headlights of the Humvee.

"Lou! Ahmed!" Gale said in a whisper.

"Here. See anything?"

"They shot up some vehicles on the road. That was the gunfire. We've got a bigger problem. There are men in the woods. Don't know how many, but there are also people coming this way from the road."

"Christ!" Lou said as Robert stepped away from the open front door. There was a hulking man on the stoop. No one said a word for a second.

"I'm Sergeant Simmons, U.S. Marines. Looking for Gale Washington."

"I'm Gale Washington."

"Gale!" Joey pushed her way past the Marine and hopped down the hallway towards him.

"Holy shit! Joey! What the hell? How'd you get here?"

"Oh God. Long story. I was so worried I'd never see you again. Where's Layla? She okay?"

"She's safe downstairs. Jesus, thought I lost you, love," he wrapped her tight in his arms. As they stood there the rest of the group filed into the foyer and Robert shut the front door.

"I don't know who all of you are, but get these kids downstairs. We've got problems, Marine. I hope there are more of you?" Lou said.

"Layla!" Joey called out as she navigated the dark stairs that were partially lit with flickering light below.

"Mom!" Gale's heart was full as his wife and daughter found each other at the bottom of the stairs. He moved aside briefly to let the others down.

"Mama, Bibi? You awake down here?" Gale asked around the corner.

"We're here. Oh my god, Joey! You've come home." Mama was wrapped up with Layla and Joey.

"Mama, your son, An, is on his way. He was with us, but stopped to deal with something. He'll be here shortly. He brought his tank."

"Listen. All of you. I need all of you to stay down here and stay silent." Gale felt a sharp pain in his calf as he said this. "Ow! What?" He looked down and saw the tiny Yorkie dancing around his feet. "Jesus, never changes. Damn dog. Sweetie, what happened to your leg?" Gale just noticed the cast.

"Broke it. They casted it in Kazakhstan." Gale just stared at her. "Long story. What's the situation here? House looks shot up. Trouble?"

"Yeah, Iranian soldiers holding the overpass and we've had a couple run ins with 'em. We think there's Russians out on the road and Iranians in the woods." Joey just stared at him, "I know, long story." She unslung the M-4 rifle she carried. He hadn't noticed that either. He hadn't expected to ever see her again. "Look, you can't move well. Stay down here with all the kids and keep them quiet."

"Bullshit! I love you, but I'm not your wife at the moment. I've got these Marines here and more coming. Let's sort this out. Copy?"

"Roger that, Commander." Gale smiled. She was home. He watched as Joey quickly introduced him and the others to the Marines who were bringing in some teenagers. They also carried, with difficulty, an unconscious Pasha and another wounded Marine. They put them on the spare bed in the side room. Joey turned and hopped up the stairs. He followed, still smiling, but that changed quickly.

# FIFTY-FOUR

December 26
6:30pm EST
Joey Washington

Joey stepped out of the basement doorway, Gale followed. She looked around. Robert was by the window with the Corpsman. Lou was with Ahmed, Javad, Simmons and the other Marine. Donneker was putting the fire out. All the candles were out.

"Lou. What's the situation here?"

"It's good to have you home. I'm sure Layla is overjoyed to see you. Shouldn't you be downstairs with Layla. It's probably going to get bad up here." Lou immediately regretted his words. She snapped.

"Look, Lou, I've had a rough couple of days. I'm dizzy. My leg's broken. I was in outer space two days ago and just flew across the Atlantic in a stolen plane full of drugs. Now I'm here and I brought the Marines. Staff Sergeant Simmons and I need to know what the situation is, right now, so cut the shit and spit it out!"

"Sir, Commander Washington is in command of our team." Simmons added. Joey raised an eyebrow at Lou and he nodded respectfully.

"SITREP. Quickly," she ordered.

Lou was about to speak when gunfire echoed through the woods behind the house. They all hit the floor. Joey knew it was close.

"Iranians and Russians. Hopefully shooting at each other at the moment, Joey," Gale said.

"Well, they know where we are. Wood smoke from the fire and those headlights in the court. No one turned them off. The whole place is lit up," Javad said.

"Shit, we're sitting ducks in this house. I'll go kill the lights," Simmons said.

"No, I've got it. I just need y'all to cover me." Donneker said and was out the front door before anyone could object.

"Dammit! Robert, Corpsman, cover him. Simmons, get on that radio and let the others know we're going to need them ASAP."

The gunfire out back wasn't aimed at them. It was becoming more sporadic. She didn't know if that was good or bad. Simmons went to the open front door and crouched behind Robert. He spoke into the radio, giving location and situation, but all he got back was bits and pieces of broken speech.

"Commander, I don't know if they got it. Those lights! We're all lit up targets here. My bad. Didn't know we were walking into this," Simmons said.

"Movement in the woods out back," the Marine at the window over the kitchen sink whispered. "They're coming. Don't know who or how many, but they're out there."

Joey and Gale went to the front room. Donneker was in the headlights now, running to the Humvee.

CRACK!

Donneker stopped in the front yard and fell forward, face first into the snow.

"Contact front!" Simmons yelled. "He's hit and down! We're screwed here. Bullets are gonna shred this house."

"Yes, we know. Nowhere else to go. Find your spot and cover your area." Ahmed said.

"Commander! We need to get people out and around the other houses to cover this one or we won't make it," Simmons growled.

"Big Man, Lou, Corporal, the four of us are going to make a run to the other houses. Try to move around their flank," Simmons said as more gunfire erupted out back. Some rounds punched through the walls and everyone flinched as drywall and dust again filled the room.

"Go. We'll hold here," Javad said. "Go, my friend."

He punched Ahmed in the arm and waved him out as Simmons knelt in the doorway, scanning around the Humvee with his rifle. Then he steadied the weapon and fired.

BOOM! BOOM!

Both headlights exploded.

"Go! Go!" Simmons yelled. He and the other three darted out into the heavily falling snow. Dark had returned without the headlights.

"Gale, tell the girls and everyone downstairs what's happening," Joey said.

She trained her M-4 out the bay window, wincing as she leaned against a wall. Gale grabbed her shoulder and squeezed, then headed around the wall to the basement door and went down.

❋ ❋ ❋

Gale jumped the last three steps to the carpeted floor of the main room in the basement. Layla met him, eyes wide.

"Layla, bad guys are here. Some of us are upstairs, some went out to cover the house. Here, take this." He pulled his pistol from the holster and held it out to his daughter. She took it with shaking hands.

"Dad…"

"Listen, last resort, okay? You remember how to use it?"

She pulled the slide back a little, ensuring a round was chambered and pointed the weapon at the floor in both hands. Gale smiled and hugged her. He looked around the room. Bibi, Mama, Susan, Brook, Alex, and Sara. The two elderly ladies both had shotguns. Mimi looked fearsome.

"Safety is on. Remember to flick it off, if you need to use it. Finger off the trigger until you're going to kill something? You can do this." Gale assured her.

"You all get ready. I don't know what's gonna happen, but if anyone you don't know or who isn't a U.S. Marine comes down those stairs, you shoot 'em. Clear?" They all nodded as he looked around. There were boxes from Ahmed's and Floyd's piled up around the room, Sara was rummaging through one in the corner as Alex slumped in the same corner with the pug. Chewie was barking at him. He kissed Layla on the forehead and ran back up the stairs.

❋ ❋ ❋

Ivan lay prone in the snow covered woods. Most of his men had been wounded or killed. Vans shot up on the road. He didn't know where the rest of his men were. He'd seen five of them as he sprinted into the woods for cover. Whoever had shot up his people, also had people in the woods in front of him. The cold was seeping into the front of his clothes as he lay still on the ground, falling snow slowly concealing him in the dark. Some of his men to his right engaged, but hadn't survived the return fire. He'd decided against this course of action. All he could do was watch.

There were houses where the woods stopped. More shots pierced the woods. Muzzle flashes briefly lit up the trees here and there. Too many. At least a dozen men in front of him in the woods. There had been light in one of the houses a moment ago, but darkness had returned with several gunshots followed by another volley of fire from the woods. They were firing into all the houses.

**⁂**

"Marine!" Joey yelled from the hallway to the Lance Corporal that was hunkered down in the kitchen by the back door. Gale crawled around the wall next to her.

"Here, Commander!"

"Is that grenade launcher on your M-4?"

"Affirmative."

"Well, why don't you put some rounds into the woods. Buy us some time."

"Yes Ma'am!"

The young Marine rolled over to the back door, opening it enough to get some room to fire. She watched as he aimed into the woods and pulled the trigger on the launcher attached under his rifle.

WHOOMPF!

The explosion halfway to the main road lit the entire area behind the houses as the light reflected off the new fallen snow. Gale appeared next to her again.

"Again!" Joey yelled.

WHOOMPF!

Another grenade left the kitchen door and another explosion reported in the woods. Joey looked around. Robert was prone, aiming his shotgun out the open front door. The old Iranian was covering the Marine at the back door. She had no idea who this old man was, but he seemed calm and steady.

The last grenade explosion in the woods had lit up the kitchen. He didn't seem bothered by bullets and explosions.

"Grenade! Cover!" the Marine yelled, and slammed the back door, rolling away.

The old man was lightning fast as he grabbed her and Gale, pulling them from the wall and into the dining room for cover as the back door blew into the kitchen. All the windows in the door and over the kitchen sink shattered. Shards of glass and shrapnel shot everywhere. Joey's ears rang, but she didn't think she was hit.

"Marine!" she yelled. No response.

"Gale!"

"Good, I think."

"I'm hit." The old man said next to her. "My back." He squeezed his eyes shut in pain.

"Everyone downstairs, quick." Gale wiggled around the wall on his stomach and opened the basement door. "Layla, we're coming down!"

She got the old man and started to drag him. He'd shielded them from the blast. Then Gale was there.

"Go, Joey! Drag him down there with you. Get them ready." Gale said and turned, rifle aimed at the back door.

"Gale, they're gonna get in here. I'm staying put. This is my fucking home. You go on down. Keep 'em safe. I'll do what I can here." Robert said.

Bullets ripped through the first floor above their heads. Drywall, wood, and pictures that had been hanging on the walls went flying in the darkness, glass crashing. It seemed like forever, but seconds later the firing stopped.

"Missed me, you bastards! I'm still here and still fabulous!" Robert yelled out the front door. There was nothing else to do. Gale rolled awkwardly through the basement door, pulling it shut behind him.

"Joey, I'm coming down!"

# FIFTY-FIVE

Ahmed, Simmons, Lou, and the other Marine made their way in the darkness around the houses and out into the woods. Explosions ripped through the trees just ahead of them about thirty yards. They flattened themselves against the ground in a line perpendicular to the men they saw lit up by the grenades. Several of those men had been flung like ragdolls. Ahmed scanned the woods ahead, AK-47 trained in front of him. There was movement. He widened his eyes to see in the darkness when an explosion hit the back of Lou's house.

"Jesus Christ!" Lou said.

"There! Pick your targets and engage." Simmons said. Multiple figures were silhouetted in the woods by the grenade's light.

Simmons and his Marine fired first, then Lou. Ahmed picked his target and fired one round at a time for accuracy. After the first few volleys, Simmons stood and took cover behind a tree and kept firing. Ahmed did the same, picking a large tree next to him. He'd just leaned out to fire when a bullet bit into the wood next to his head. He flinched and ducked back behind the tree. Close.

"Sergeant! Are more Marines coming soon?" Lou asked.

"Hopefully!" The Sergeant replied. "Meantime lets clear these woods." That was all Ahmed needed to hear. Hopefully wouldn't cut it. He stepped from behind the tree and stalked into the woods picking targets and destroying them, one round at a time.

\* \* \*

An and Alice tore into the neighborhood from the two-lane road where they'd left their pursuers either dead or dying in the snow. He didn't like what he saw. Through is night vision there was a line of figures at the entrance to the cul-de-sac where his parents lived. He'd gotten a broken communication from Simmons. All he'd heard was "under fire" and "house next to the Commander's" before it broke off. Fletch pushed Alice as fast as he could without sliding off the road. She was tracked, but at speed could still slip and slide in this heavy snow. They were stopped a hundred yards down a straight residential street. No houses here. His parent's cul-de-sac was a bit off to itself, separated from the rest of the neighborhood by streams and woods. The whole area was in complete darkness and a bit away from the main highway. The street he was on ran parallel to the road that led to an overpass and the main highway. He sent the LAV to the overpass for access to the main highway. They'd deploy there and come in behind his parent's house in the woods.

He didn't know the situation, but those dozen or so figures lit up in his optics were firing into the court. They weren't his guys, cause he hadn't sent that many. They wouldn't hear them coming over their volume of fire. Didn't call the M1A1 whispering death for nothing.

"Driver! See the line of men?"

"Roger!"

\* \* \*

Lou was behind the other three in the woods. He couldn't see any more targets, but they were out there because they were still taking fire. He emptied his magazine, released it, inserted another in one smooth motion. He realized that the rounds weren't so much coming from the woods as they were from the court passing by his house and hitting trees above them. He moved. The others could deal with what was left out here. Robert and the rest needed help. He hit the ground and crawled the rest of the way to the front corner of his house.

He buried his head in the snow as rounds beat themselves into the front of his house. Raising his head, he inched around the last bush and saw flashes from multiple rifles out by the entrance to the court. Shit! That was a lot of men. He couldn't do anything. The rounds kept him down. Too many. It was so loud. He watched helplessly, infuriated. What the…? Something appeared to the left of the rifle flashes and swiftly rolled into and over them. One at a time. Then it was out of sight. The firing had stopped. His mouth hung open.

❋ ❋ ❋

"I ain't cleaning that shit out of the tracks. Nope. Not it. That's nasty." Stewie said in disgust.

An ignored his loader and traversed the turret and main gun toward the court. His thermal showed several figures firing into the house next to his parent's home and then the image flared white. Grenade. Shit! He couldn't engage. He didn't know where the friendlies were.

"Driver, turn into the court. To those houses at the end."

"Zombie Six, Recon!" An's radio crackled.

"Recon, Zombie Six Actual, Go."

"We're engaged with unknown targets and gun emplacements on the overpass. There's a large force here." It was Buford.

"Copy Recon! Close and destroy. We've got bad guys here too."

❋ ❋ ❋

Javad covered his face with his arms as the drywall in the ceiling of the basement fell in on him. He was laying on the floor, where Gale had dragged him. That had to be a grenade on the main level. He watched a blond woman, Susan he thought, usher his mother, the other older woman, and the pregnant woman into one of the rooms off this main room. There were boxes and supplies stacked all around. The light from the oil lamp danced. The commander and her husband had their rifles aimed at the stairs. He saw Sara with two other girls in the corner. He'd brought this horror to her. She looked so much like her mother. She looked like his sister. It couldn't end like this. It couldn't. He coughed. Tasted blood. Not good, he thought. He had his .45 pistol in his right hand resting on his chest. Sara pulled something from the box next to her. The oil-fueled lamp light reflected off the shiny steel. There was etching on it. A knife. Sara held it tightly in her fist and looked over at him then squeezed her eyes shut.

He knew that knife. The knife Hafez used to kill his sister!. Memories flooded him. Ahmed must have kept it. Why would he keep that thing? Movement on the stairs pulled his attention back to the present. Robert fell onto the basement floor at the last step, his shotgun thumped on the floor next to him. Sara screamed. He looked at her, locking eyes with her. He put a finger to his lips and she quieted. Gale stepped in front of the girls, aiming his rifle at the stairs. The blond girl was holding a fat dog, sitting in the corner behind the others. The last girl had a pistol. She was crouched behind Gale. Last stand then. Everyone fights. He felt a tug at his leg and found a small, furry dog biting and pulling at his pants, growling. He smiled at the absurdity of it. Then something hit the floor next to Robert.

A loud bang and white flash filled the room. He was blind and deaf momentarily. Flash bang grenade. This was it. Standing in the room at his feet, staring down at him was a figure. He tried to raise his pistol, but the figure knocked it easily away. He saw another man, rifle aimed at the others while a third man yanked the rifle out of the commander's hands and pushed her to the floor. Gale already lay on the floor next to his wife. Helpless, Javad heard a laugh.

"Little Lion Cub? Is that you?" Javad's heart sank. "You were our mysterious passenger then." Javad looked up at the man standing at his feet pointing a rifle at his face. Hafez!

"Bastard!" Was all Javad could muster. How had it come to this again?

"No one to save you this time, Lion Cub," Hafez spat.

"Say hello to your sister when you see her again."

Hafez aimed his rifle at Javad's head. A flash of movement by Hafez's feet caught Javad's eye and Hafez looked down at that tiny, ferocious dog. It was attacking his calf.

BOOM! BOOM! BOOM!

The soldier next to Hafez flew forward from the blast of Robert's shotgun. The man wasn't dead. The other soldier crumpled against the other room's open doorway. He'd found death from the old women and their shotguns. Javad reached for his pistol, but it was too far. Hafez kicked the dog from his leg and turned to engage this new threat.

"No!" In Javad's peripheral vision, Sara darted from the corner and plunged the knife into Hafez's neck. He spun and aimed his rifle at her, but several blasts took him down before he could fire, falling on top of Javad. He looked over at the doorway and saw his mother, Bibi standing there with her shotgun. She slumped back against the shelves behind her.

"For my daughter!" Javad heard her say as he turned to find Layla screaming, smoke drifting from her pistol. Everyone fights, he thought. Javad looked at the face that was mere inches from his own. Hafez coughed and his body jerked from the effort, but his eyes met Javad's.

"I will see you in hell. But not just yet." Javad whispered to Hafez with a twisted smile.

* * *

Lou descended the basement stairs. Joey watched him step over Robert, shotgun clutched in his hand, at the bottom step. Blood soaking the carpet around him. Lou turned into the main room, scanning for threats, rifle to his shoulder.

"Sound off! Anyone hurt?"

"Only the bad guys, Lou. And the old man." Joey yelled. Christopher jumped from Alex's trembling arms and ran to Robert and then turned, jumping up to paw at Lou's legs, whimpering. Footfalls on the stairs caused Lou to turn, weapon ready.

"Don't shoot!" Ahmed yelled from the stairs as he reached the bottom. Joey exhaled and reached for Layla who laid her pistol on the floor and embraced her. Joey watched Lou kneel next to Robert. He felt for a pulse, then shook with sobs, stroking Robert's hair. Oh no. She watched the room fill up. Simmons knelt by Lou, saying something in his ear, hand on his shoulder. The Gunny came down. They were safe.

"Mom! Brook! Where—" Mimi came out of the side room and An engulfed his mom in a hug.

"Everyone, let's get upstairs and check everyone over. The corpsman will look at any wounds. My men are wiping the rest of these people off the overpass, so stay alert. There could be more around, but I don't think they want to tangle with us anymore," Simmons said.

"Help! In here." Susan yelled from the other room.

Joey watched Ahmed pick up the corpse lying on top of the old man and heave it over to an empty space by the wall, like it weighed nothing. The body landed with a thud, discarded like trash. Ahmed knelt as Sara crawled across the floor to him. Then Bibi was there as well. Sara let out a wail and buried her head in the old man's chest. His arm moved and a bloody hand stroked Sara's hair.

"Sara, I'm still here, for now at least."

"Hey! Who is this?" Joey asked.

"I am Sara's father, Javad." He coughed violently and blood sprayed onto his face.

"Corpsman!" Simmons yelled.

"Yeah, I'm gonna need him as well." Susan said, rushing out of the side room.

"Who's hit in there?" Joey asked.

"No one's wounded, except for the two that came in that way." Susan thumbed over her shoulder at the Marine and Pasha, still unconscious. "Baby's coming!"

❋ ❋ ❋

Joey winced. Gale grabbed her hand. They were sitting on the couch, next to the bar in the main room. The fire was going again. Gale didn't remember who started it, but it was warm and welcome. He was okay, just shaken a bit, with a large, bloody gash across his left eye and cheek where the butt of a rifle had connected. He looked at his girls. They were together and alive.

"I've never seen one up close. Show me." Gale said.

"Layla, stay with your dad. Get some clean water from the pot in the kitchen and help him clean the wound some more."

Layla nodded. Joey grabbed the crutch she tossed before the fire fight. Gale watched her limp to the front door. She turned and stepped aside, waving her arm out the door. He winked at her and nodded. They'd nicknamed it Alice. He could see one the crew halfway out of one of the hatches, scanning with his machine gun. The sight filled him with a sense of safety.

"Marines coming in!" Joey turned her head to the corner of the house as several Marines came from around the back.

"All clear in the woods and on the overpass," one of them said to Joey as he stepped into the kitchen from the back door.

Her shoulders slumped, she turned to sit next to Gale on the couch, laying the crutch on the arm. He stopped his daughter from her cleaning as Joey took his hand and put her other arm around Layla and they all squeezed.

"I didn't think I'd see you guys again. I love you both. More than anything," Joey said softly.

"Love you too, honey. Hey, how was your trip?" Gale chuckled. "Ahh. My face hurts."

"Yeah, right. Was rough. Had to leave Tavis in Scotland to look for his family. But, I want to know what happened here before I got back."

"Well, I managed to get through all this without firing a shot. Can you believe that," Gale said. He pulled Layla into him and squeezed her hard.

"I'm sorry you had to pull the trigger. You did the right thing. You have nothing to feel bad about. You protected all of us." Joey said and joined the hug.

"I'm just happy you're both here." Layla said tears streamed down her face as Chewie came bounding up from the floor.

"Who's the good girl? You got that bad man, didn't you?" Gale said as he scratched the dog behind the ears and pulled his ladies in even closer.

# FIFTY-SIX

December 27
8:00am GMT
Tavis Kinley

He glanced down and behind him from his spot in the small turret. His wife, Moira, and his three kids, Maighen, Dougal, and Duncan were amusing themselves with various items they found in the small troop compartment. His luck was holding, for now.

After he bid farewell to Joey and Pasha, he packed his gear and grabbed the L1A1 semi-automatic rifle that Alfie had produced for him. Where the old man got it was a mystery to Tavis and Alfie wouldn't say, except that it had been gathering dust under a floorboard for decades. These weapons were illegal in Britain. Alfie and Owen were veterans of the Falklands war and Tavis assumed one or both of them had sequestered away some other useful items as well.

He had just started out in the golf cart to find his family when a ship's horn sounded in the small bay. His older brother, Tanner, docked the Shark shortly after. Once Tanner heard the story and Tavis' plan, he suggested a different approach.

Which brought him back to watching his family. Tanner next to him in the turret with his young seaman's apprentice, Sammy, driving.

"How ya doin', Meg?" Tavis asked his fifteen-year-old daughter.

She hadn't been more than two feet from him since he found them at their friend's home in Lochgilphead yesterday. They stayed the night there and headed back to Campbelltown this morning.

"Good, now that we're all together. Just watchin' the idiots."

"Language, Meg." Moira said and Tanner chuckled next to him.

"Boys, put that stuff away. Try an find a first-aid kit, if ya can." Tavis said.

His twin, seventeen-year-old sons, were into every nook and cranny in the troop compartment. He was sure there had to be one in here somewhere. Fate had shined on him, when Tanner told him what was in his ship's open-air hold. Four British Warrior Infantry Fighting Vehicles. He was transporting them to Oman in the Gulf, but turned around when the attack happened. It was challenging getting this thing off the ship, but once they did, it was already fueled and ready to go. It had everything except ammunition for the thirty-millimeter cannon in the turret.

"The ground clouds er out in full force this mornin'," Tanner said.

"The what?" Moira asked as Meg squeezed up with Tavis in his spot to see what her uncle was talking about.

"Sheep, dear. Sheep."

Tavis pointed over to his left as they rolled down the A83 on the northwest coast of the spit to the hills, gently sloping up. They were covered with hundreds of sheep. Their full, fluffy, white coats did indeed make them look as if they were little clouds.

"Ground clouds! Idiot." Moira laughed.

"Mum. Language." Meg said.

They took a left bend in the road heading south past the airport to Campbelltown proper and a warm fire and hot breakfast at his parent's house. Tavis looked out over the fields to the airstrip and saw a Gulfstream jet parked on the runway.

"Sammy! Taking a detour. Turn off the road and head to the airport. Looks like Joey's back. Damn! They didn't make it. Get over there quick." Tavis said.

In short order, Tavis knew something was wrong. It wasn't the same plane they were rolling up on and it was surrounded by armed men. As they closed the distance, he recognized one of them.

"Tanner, these aren't good guys. It's not Joey's plane. You see that one there? Standing next to the woman?"

"Aye,"

"That's who we stole Joey's plane from."

"Well, this is awkward, isn't it? Looks like he followed ya'," Tanner said.

"Wonder how long they've been here? Doesn't matter. Meg, get down there with your Mum. Moira, you and the kids stay inside and stay quiet, no matter what?" Tavis said.

"We will. Meg, come 'ere next to me," Moira said.

"Sammy, stop just short of that group in front of the plane. Tanner, train the main gun on the airplane."

"We got no ammo, Tav."

"They don't know it, now do they?"

Sammy slowed the armored fighting vehicle's tracks to a stop fifty feet in front of the executive jet. Tavis stuck his head out of his hatch, while Tanner's was shut tight and locked. The turret traversed so the canon was aimed at the cockpit. There were ten armed men on the runway spreading around their vehicle. He focused his attention on the man, standing next to the blond-haired woman.

"Good to see you again, Boris," Tavis said flatly.

"Tavis Kinley! You shouldn't have taken my plane." Boris the Wolf replied.

"Aye, we wronged you after you got us out. Grateful for that. Had to get home, you see. Your plane's not here, if that's what you're lookin' for." Tavis saw a piece of paper in Boris' hand and a phone in the other.

"I had nice conversation with your parents at their home this morning. I know where my plane went. I wasn't expecting you though. Is lucky for me." Boris raised the piece of paper, then the men around the vehicle started moving in, rifles raised.

"Stop! I will shred your plane and your men if you come closer!" He said, lowering himself slightly in the hatch, ready to shut it.

Boris was about to tell his men to attack when the woman next to him snapped at him in Russian. The Wolf turned to her and they had a heated exchange that Tavis didn't understand, but she turned and walked up the stairs into the plane.

"Seems you are lucky one today," Boris waved his arm and the men retreated to the plane after the woman. "We leave now. Hope our paths do not cross again, for your sake." He boarded the plane and Tavis told Sammy to get back on the road and to his parent's home as fast as he could.

"Jesus, Mary, and Joseph! Ya pissed that Russian off somethin' fierce," Tanner said.

A few minutes later Tavis opened the door to his parent's house and they were there sitting in front of the fire.

"You two alright?" He asked a little louder than he meant to. The rest of his family filled the room behind him.

"Havin' tea, Tav. We're okay, why?" His father asked, now standing, giving a hug to Meg.

"There were men in a plane—"

"Boris! He was nice. Not at all like you described him. Didn't yell or anythin'. Said he was tryin' to find your friend, Pasha. Shared tea with him just a bit ago. He took the note Joey left ya with her address." his mom said.

"Your friend, Joey, writes hard. Left an imprint in the pad. Copied it for ya," his dad said with a wink.

"Oh, fer fook's sake!" Tavis said and wrapped his parents in a hug. The sound of the Gulfstream taking off over them shook the house and he looked over his shoulder at his brother.

"Tanner, what's the range on that ship of yours?"

# FIFTY-SEVEN

Ahmed was standing in the cul-de-sac near the massive Alice. Sergeant Simmons was next to him. They were talking over plans when Layla, Sara, and Alex approached.

Alex walked past them to the tank, the rotund Christopher wobbling along beside her. Sara stopped next to Ahmed and said, "Alex would like to paint. It's how she deals with things."

"Paint what, where?" Ahmed asked, putting an arm around his niece.

"Excuse me?" Alex called up to Stewie, who was smoking a cigarette in his hatch.

"What can I do for ya, ma'am?" Stewie asked in his southern drawl.

"They said her name is Alice. I'd like to paint on her." Alex said, her voice quiet, but determined. She carried a sort of open tackle box, but it was filled with paint brushes, paint bottles, and spray paint cans. Stewie looked around, probably for his boss, Ahmed thought.

"I don't think she's asking Corporal. Go ahead, Alex." Simmons said.

The Marines and Ahmed watched in some amazement at the skill Alex was applying to the form coming to life on the side of the tank's turret. Sara and Layla were up there with her. The fat pug was snoring on the warm engine compartment, never far from Alex. Chewie was bouncing around on top of the tank, growling at Stewie, who'd just pulled her up out of the hatch and plopped her down next to him. They adopted her as sort of a mascot, ferocious as she was.

"Who took a dump in my tank! Fucking rat dog! Aw...shit's on my boot, man," Jones yelled from inside. Ahmed smiled and Stewie laughed, cigarette smoke clouding his face.

"Oorah, little Marine," Stewie whispered, giving the small, bouncy dog scratches behind her ears.

"Uncle Ahmed, she's finished! What do you think?" Ahmed surveyed the scene. Alex, poor Alex. She'd been through the most out of the three girls. He stepped forward with Simmons to get a better look.

"Perfect! Love it, girl!" Simmons commended Alex. "Hey, you paint clowns?"

"I suppose I could. It would clash with this though." Alex gestured to her creation.

"Oh, not on the tank. Got the perfect place though." Simmons winked at Stewie.

Ahmed studied the figure on the side of the desert brown turret. The figure was dressed in a short camouflage skirt. Her graveyard gray hair up in a pony tail on top of her head, except for several strands that covered one eye socket. Instead of the pretty little faeries he remembered from children's stories, the arms and legs were skeletal, wings in tatters, with the face a hauntingly angry skull. One skeletal hand held a bloodied knife. The figure stood barefoot on a bed of skulls as if she was crushing them with "Sic Semper Tyrannis" written through the image. Ahmed's heart filled with sadness and regret for Alex. She was a brilliant artist. He considered the three girls. They were the same age now that Javad's sister had been when she'd been murdered. Such innocence lost.

\* \* \*

An stood in the doorway of the spare room in the basement. The dead had been moved outside with the rest two days ago. Pasha and Javad lay on the queen-sized bed next to each other, both sleeping. They'd been lucky. There was an intravenous line in each of their arms connected to two bags of fluids nailed to the wall above them.

"How are they?" he asked Susan.

"They'll make it. Both of them. Thanks to you and your men and their scrounging abilities. Finding the doctor was lucky. I'm just a vet."

She pulled her blond hair back into a ponytail and checked Javad's pulse.

The wounded Marine was on the couch in the main room behind him. After the firefight, Susan had gone with his men in the LAV to her practice. It was in the neighborhood about a mile away. The sound of the LAV and all the fighting had brought people out of their homes on the other side of the neighborhood. One had been a doctor. They raided all the supplies they needed from Susan's vet clinic and the local pharmacy. They found more supplies and drugs, although, people had already been through it a few times.

"Val. Nina. How you two doing? Need anything?" An asked the two Russian teenagers. They were sitting in chairs on Pasha's side of the bed. They hadn't really moved. Nina was holding Pasha's hand. A little, round panda-shaped plushy toy rested on his chest.

"No, thank you. We're good for now." Valeri said.

An nodded and went back upstairs. The main room had been swept of dust, drywall and shell casings. A fire was crackling and Bibi and Mama were playing with the little ones, Carly and Stevie. Although, they were much more interested in the bundle that Brook held in the chair, next to the roaring fire.

"How's he doing?" An bent over and kissed the newborn on the forehead.

"Sleeping and eating." She looked exhausted. Her eyes were red from crying. "Tell me again, An."

"I didn't see him hit. He was in one of the LAVs. We had a convoy of tanks and LAVs. If anyone could fight their way out of that, Bao could. The more I think about it, the more I believe he's alive and fighting. We'll get to him.

"How long do you think?"

"Some of my men are staying here with you, the doctor, and the rest of the neighborhood. I think the local threat has subsided. I've got to get Gale and Javad to Mt. Weather. After that, we're going to find your husband. He's stubborn, Brook. You know this." She smiled and kissed the baby. She wouldn't name him until An got Bao back and they could decide together.

"How long, An?"

"A week, maybe two." An didn't know, but he smiled to reassure her.

❈ ❈ ❈

Gale and Joey were packing what he'd need for his journey west. They had buried Floyd, Robert and Dennis behind Lou's house near the woods and stream. The ground was hard to dig in, but the Marines had the duty and made quick work of it. The graves were shallow, but it was a good place.

"What are the girls doing out there?" Gale asked Joey. She joined him at the window, slipping an arm around his waist, just above his holster that held the pistol that he hadn't used once during this whole thing, although Layla had. Doubt crept back into his mind as he thought of what he did over the last couple of days. With the exception of saving Dennis on the road and putting together a better picture of what had happened to the world, he was fairly useless in protecting his daughter or his wife.

"Unknown." Joey said.

They watched all three girls sitting on top of the engine compartment focusing on something on the side of tank's turret. One of the crew was watching from his hatch, smoking a cigarette. Sergeant Simmons and Ahmed were standing next to the tank in conversation. She left him to head back to the kitchen table and sat down, writing on a pad of paper.

"What's that?" Gale asked as he followed her into the kitchen.

"It's a note for Tavis Kinley. It explains what happened here and what we know. I left him our address here when we left him in Scotland. I know I'm staying here with Layla and the group, but I wanted to get all this down. Just in case. Maybe he'll make it here, maybe not. I hope they will. By they, I mean I hope he's found his family by now. I think they'll stay there. It's their home. But who knows? It's a long shot, but leaving a note just in case."

"That's a big long shot now. I do hope that he's found his family. I really like Tavis. If anyone can get it done, it's him."

"Where are the winter gloves and hats?" Joey asked. He and Layla had theirs, but she was in space so they hadn't gotten hers out for the season.

"Upstairs in our walk-in closet. Yeah, you'll probably need that stuff."

She hopped over to him and gave him a long kiss. It was unbelievable that she'd made it back. He wrapped her in his arms and vowed to himself never to let her out of his sight again. Well, except for this short trip west and back again. He looked out the back window over the sink to see a Marine stepping up onto the deck. He recognized him as Sergeant Buford. A sniper rifle slung on his back with his M-4 in his hands.

"I wonder what he's doing?" Gale said as Joey opened the back door.

"Why don't you ask him. I'm going to get my hat and gloves and see what those girls are doing to Alice," she said and climbed the stairs out of his sight.

"What's up, Sergeant?" Gale asked.

"Just walking the perimeter and found a set of tracks from the woods out back to your deck. You all been out there?" Buford replied, looking around.

"Gale!" Joey's scream from upstairs wasn't playful. He heard thuds on the floor above him. He rushed to the stairs, Buford behind him. He pulled the pistol from its holster and flipped the safety off as he climbed. He heard struggling in their bedroom. He entered the room with his pistol aimed in front of him. Joey was wrapped up in one arm of a tall, blond man in military fatigues. He was pointing a gun at her head. Gale took aim, finger on the trigger.

"Stop. No harm will come to her. Where are Yerik and Tatyana?"

Gale took him in. At the top of his military jacket Gale saw his shirt underneath. It was white and blue striped. Spetznaz. Shit.

"Who are you?" Gale asked.

"The one who will kill her if you don't answer my question. Where are they?"

The Russian's eyes were alternating between Gale and to the door. Buford.

"Dead. Outside on the side of the house across the way." Gale replied.

"In that case, you will bring me Alexandra. Quietly, or I will kill her." Joey stopped struggling.

"Alex? Why Alex?" Gale asked.

The man took a deep breath.

"My name is Ivan and Alexandra is my daughter. My wife and I gave her up to the state, although, not so willingly, when she was just a baby. Yerik and Tatyana are not her birth parents. Bring her to me now and we'll go on our way. She will want her real family now that the only family she's ever known are dead."

Joey turned her head into the man's elbow and pushed up, sliding her head down and through. She moved just enough to the side.

The sound of the gunshot was deafening in the enclosed space. Two more shots filled the room from Buford's M-4. Ivan dropped backwards to the floor.

"Gale! He's dead."

Buford moved in front of him now to check the Russian. Joey's hand came to rest on Gale's arm, lightly pushing down so the smoking pistol was aimed at the floor. He looked at her and holstered it. She put her arms around him and they stepped back from the body as they heard the front door bang open.

"Up here! All clear!" Buford yelled.

"What the hell? Y'all good?" Simmons said.

"Who's that?" Ahmed said. Gale looked at Joey and knew what she was thinking.

"We don't know. He was hiding out in here and grabbed Joey. I shot him." Gale said.

"He said some things in Russian. We couldn't understand him. From the shirt, I'd say he was Russian Spetznaz." Joey said.

"I'd suggest clearing the rest of these houses, Sergeant. Who knows who's hiding in here." Gale and Joey left the room and headed outside to hug Layla and Alex.

# FIFTY-EIGHT

December 28
Panama Canal Zone

Captain Zhou was about at the end of his patience and comfort. He'd lost track of how long they'd been on the ship, but it was about two weeks, he thought. His rank allowed him daily visits to the bridge, where he could at least see the sun, or moon, depending. His men were not as lucky, nor was he allowed to switch places with them. Orders.

At least they knew where they were going. Once they'd been well out to sea, all the officers were briefed on the mission. He then briefed his men. The mission was not Taiwan as he'd thought. It was the Eastern Coast of the United States.

Over the last three days, there were regular briefings. The news was actually fairly positive, but of course it would be. His division wasn't in the fight yet, so telling them bad news wasn't going to happen. He stepped out onto the wing of the bridge and scanned the body of water they were travelling through and up to the banks. They were about to enter the northern locks of the Panama Canal that emptied into the Caribbean Sea. The Chinese flag flew at multiple places within the small city and airport they were approaching next to the locks. Paratroopers had taken the city and airport here and the other locations at the southern locks days prior. Passenger aircraft brought in the rest of the occupying troops to secure the canal for their passage.

Smoke rose in several spots and there was sporadic gunfire that pulled his attention to the forest south of the airport. They were told of light resistance, but he knew that it was early in the campaign. It would get worse, before it got better, if it did. He thought about their mission and if they would encounter the same. There was fighting here in Central America. The Americans would surely not be happy to see them when they arrived. They wouldn't be fighting civilians or militia, like here. They were to land in North and South Carolina. Their job was to destroy the U.S. Marine garrison at Camp Lejeune then move to Fort Bragg, then up into Virginia.

He was under no illusion that the Americans would allow them an easy go of it, but he and his men didn't care at this point. They just wanted off this ship. He looked aft of the massive container ship he was on to the long line of other converted container ships and cruise ships carrying men, weapons, supplies, and armored vehicles. There were dozens of them. He hoped it was enough.

Engine noise made him look up to see what he thought was a Chinese bomber, followed by another, coming in low for a landing at the approaching airport. He watched them descend and touch down. That must have been a grueling flight across the Pacific.

* * *

He had to urinate. The last hour of the flight was challenging due to that fact. Major Tang brought his bomber in for landing at the airport at the Panamanian city of Colon at the northern end of the canal. There were container and passenger ships lined up to the south as far as he could see. These are the men he and his wingman, Captain Liu were here to support. They were the only two strategic bombers command could release for this mission due to the unexpected resistance by the Indians. They expected the American assets in the South Pacific and Indian Ocean to be tough to defeat, but they hadn't counted on the Indians to pre-emptively strike Pakistan, freeing their forces up to challenge the Chinese in the region. Someone had tipped them off, he though.

The bomber's wheels hit the runway harder than he wanted them to, but he really had to empty his bladder and he wasn't going to wait for a facility to go in. At least there would be no more long flights like this one from across the Pacific. His next waypoint was Guantanamo Bay Naval Base in Cuba. Once the war had started, there was no longer the threat of retaliation from the Americans. At least not much. The Cuban army had attacked the base on Christmas morning from both sides with nearly three times the number of troops the Americans had. He was told before he left that the Americans didn't surrender. Fought to the last man, taking nearly ten thousand Cubans with them.

He stopped the bomber at the end of the runway and moved it off to make room for Captain Liu. There he parked it and unstrapped as did his crew. They scrambled out of the plane and were hit with eight-five degrees and a breeze. Lovely, he thought, as he and his crew lined up in front of the bomber and unceremoniously urinated in unison on the grass just off the runway. As they finished, a truck with soldiers sped down the runway from the terminal buildings and stopped next to them. The troops jumped out and fanned out toward the treeline about a hundred meters distant, while one soldier trained a machine gun in the same direction.

Tang turned to greet a sergeant who was yelling at his men to spread out. He was about to speak when the machine gunner opened up into the treeline and everyone hit the pavement. Tang heard bangs as rounds hit the side of his aircraft. Shit! There were two thuds behind them from the terminal buildings and then a whistling sound as mortar shells exploded among the trees. Silence returned and after a few seconds, he looked up. Boots were next to his head. He quickly stood and looked into the face of the sergeant.

"You fucking idiots! This is a war zone. We still have infiltrators. You could have been killed, or worse, gotten my men killed. Police up your aircraft and move them over to the terminals. We'll provide cover for you while you move or taxi them, whatever. Now!" Tang stood shocked at the man's tone, but then he moved as the sergeant completely ignored him after that and took up position next to his men on the grass.

Tang turned and Captain Liu was standing there looking at the treeline. He walked up and Liu saw him and slowly shook his head at Tang.

"Remind me to find that sergeant later to apologize and thank him. Let's not do that again." He whispered in Liu's ear.

"Yeah, I like it better in the air, Major."

Tang and Liu moved their planes as Tang continued to think about his own mortality and that he'd need to check his planes for bullet holes. If this thing wasn't personal before, it was now.

# FIFTY-NINE

Commander Blackstone sat in his tight quarters at the desk, his bunk directly behind him. Only the small light on the bulkhead lit his desk and the letter that sat on it. He rubbed his face and read it for what seemed the hundredth time. It was short and to the point, as it should be. He was never supposed to read this. It was one of four identical letters that sat in the Commander's safe on board each of the United Kingdom's four Vanguard class Ballistic Missile Submarines, and his being the only one left. He had thought it appropriate to open the letter with his Executive Officer or XO so there could be some semblance of transparency for the crew.

It was hand written in flowing cursive. The penmanship was perfect. It was a copy obviously as the original sat with the writer of the letter, the Prime Minister, who he must assume was dead at this point or incapable of communications. Each of the other copies of this letter were ash now just like the submarines they resided in at Faslane, Scotland. They were aware of the nuclear strike there. They were also aware of a nuclear strike on Brest, France, where the four French Ballistic Missile Submarines were home ported. Three of those were also ash. The fourth of their *Triomphant* class, *Le Terrible*, was running about five hundred yards a port of his boat at the moment.

The had met up several days after Christmas right where they were supposed to if something like this were to occur. In the deep near the Canary Islands just off the coast of Morocco in North Africa. Two days prior, Blackstone and his boat had sat for a hour just off the coast of France, near Brest, surveying the damage through their periscope. The thick black smoke that blanketed the coast like a burial shroud was enough of a sign. They had to stay silent, like a hole in the water, as they were likely being hunted, so no going home. They'd be waiting for him. It's what he'd do initially if he were them.

The other submarine running about a thousand yards aft of the two Ballistic Missile Submarines was the *USS Virginia*, a fast-attack submarine, which was able to shadow them until the two came to periscope depth to communicate. They were taken aback as the *Virginia* had also raised its periscope with them. For all of their advanced technology, they hadn't known she was there, but she was a welcome addition to their "fleet." The *Virginia* was now their security as they counted down and prepared to run. Between the three of them, listening to the airwaves, had collected data via their individual means. They determined a course of action and based on the letter in front of him.

All three commanders agreed. Based on the data they collected, and the fact that there was nothing transmitting from Europe, BBC Radio 4 was off-line, and no Emergency Action Messages from any of the three countries, that there had indeed been some kind of nuclear strike in conjunction with an EMP event or attack. They were getting plenty of traffic south of their position, and from the Middle East they were receiving short wave and low frequency transmissions. The reports they received via unencrypted ELF, or Extremely Low Frequency, broadcast from India, the only other country aside from the US and Russia to have the capability, was disturbing and rage-inducing. Apparently, the Indians were dealing with their own issues as well. So, their small fleet, here and now, could certainly take care of one cancer, but the other was problematic as they didn't want to cause a misinterpretation of actions and unnecessarily escalate hostilities.

He looked at the letter again and read it for the final time.

> *Commander, if you are reading this, then the worst has occurred and you have lost contact with the British Government. The government, myself, and even the country may no longer be here. You are on your own. I do not envy your situation or the decisions you must now make. I will attempt to ease this decision-making process for you, but in the end, the decision you make is yours alone.*

1.  *Retaliate with Nuclear Weapons against the aggressor or aggressors,*
2.  *Do not retaliate,*
3.  *Use your own judgement,*
4.  *OR, put yourself and your boat under the command of the United States, if She is still there,*
5.  *Go to Australia or New Zealand*

*The course is yours, Commander.*

*For Queen and Country.*
*God Speed.*

He looked at the signature at the bottom of the letter and knew, in that moment, whether the Prime Minister was alive or not, he had made his decision and the Commander on *Le Terrible* had concurred and was even more willing than he. The U.S. Commander was in concurrence as well, as he needed to be now that he was part of their little fleet. If he had not concurred, he could have very well stopped them with little effort. There was a knock on the door.

"Enter."

His XO stuck his head in the small room.

"It's time, Captain."

Blackstone was a Commander in the Royal Navy, but on this boat, he was Captain.

"All warheads are dialed down in yield as we discussed, except the one? I don't want to do more damage than absolutely necessary."

"Aye, Captain. All dialed down and targeting packages selected for military targets only, except the one."

"Right. Go to Action Stations Missile. I will be there directly."

The XO acknowledged and closed the door. Blackstone stood, took a deep breath, and looked at the ship's crest that hung on the bulkhead over his desk. He studied it. He loved this boat and the crew, but more than that, he loved his family, who were probably dead or soon to be. The decision wasn't as difficult as he thought it would be. He made for the door, turning back once more to click the light off. He took in the crest of his ship that hung above his desk one last time. At the bottom was the boat's name, appropriately, *HMS Vengeance*.

❋ ❋ ❋

Alarms sounded in the Operations Center deep under the Ural Mountains. The Russian duty officer silenced the alarms and put his screen up on the big screen at the front of the room where everyone could see what he was seeing, including the Defense Minister, who appeared by his side quietly.

"The satellites are picking up launch blooms near the Canary Islands off Portugal." The duty officer stated flatly trying to keep his nerves in check. He was trained for this, but to actually see nuclear missiles launched in anger, perhaps at them, was horrifying.

"Da, I can see this. Where are they headed? How many are there? What are we looking at in terms of warheads?"

"One moment, Minister. Trajectory is coming up. There are six missiles from two submarines. Depending on which countries the subs belong to, there could be between one and five warheads for Britain and France or up to ten for the Americans."

There was a long pause as all thirty or so personnel in the room held their collective breath and let those numbers sink in.

"Terminal points coming up on the screen now, Sir."

The whole room watched the digital map on the big screen populate with large red circles where each of the missiles was heading. Those circles would turn into smaller, solid red dots when the independent warheads separated from the host missile on re-entry into the atmosphere, breaking off to their specific targets.

"That's it? No other missiles?"

"No other missiles, Sir. We are not targeted."

Everyone in the room exhaled as one. There were even some cheers and clapping as the tension released, like a taught rubber band being pulled tight and then letting it snap back.

"Admiral, surge our attack subs in the Mediterranean and Atlantic and sink them."

"Do we warn them?" This came from one of the junior officers at another station who wasn't privy to the strategic plan, so it was an innocent and altogether human question.

"Nyet. They can do nothing. It is better this way. There are only seconds left anyway."

The defense minister pointed up at the screen as each of the six trajectories broke into five separate and distinct warhead tracks covering nearly the entire country of Iran, but not the population centers, except the one. Everyone in the room watched silently, no longer cheering or clapping, as each track disappeared with a solid white circle indicating a detonation on the ground. One loose end tied off.

## The End of the Beginning

# ACKNOWLEDGEMENTS

(This is the not made-up part)

Without Shannon, my best friend and love of my life, I'd never have gotten this finished. For taking over all the weekends and handling all the routine and not-so-routine things so that I could write is worth its weight in gold or silver (she likes silver). That's a lot of silver. She also made me stop dreaming and start doing. For that, I'll love you forever. I mean, I would anyway, but this is extra! And thanks to my three kids, also known as the Minions or Siblets, who kept me completely grounded while I wrote this by frequently telling me "you're not published yet, Dad!"

I grew up the son of a children's librarian. So, I had all the books. I read all the books. Books were always there. Thanks, Mom, for bringing the books, instilling my love of reading, and the spaghetti.

My aunt, Sally, who over the years has supported me in one way or another and who told me more than once that many Sibley's before me wanted to be writers, but they were better procrastinators. That stuck with me and I applied my ass to the seat and my nubs to the keys.

I used two editors for this book. The first was Norah Vawter, who was my developmental editor. She was just amazing. More than anything she did, which was a lot, she told me that I'd written a book, after reading my first draft. It kept me going, even though her next statement was that I had a lot of work to do, which was also true. My copy editor was Brittnee Strachan, who sorted me out early on with a bit of realism and then got down to telling me "dude, find better adjectives!" I can't thank either of you enough. Also, a big shout out to Greg for using his network to put me in touch with Norah.

Huge thank you to Katie Hagaman for my swanky logo and for recommending Anuschka Roberts for the cover. Nush is an amazing graphic designer. She brought Alice to life! On that note, amazing work from Paul Blake at Vengeful Lemon for the book trailer! Thanks, mate.

During the writing of this story, which includes U.S. Marines and a main battle tank in it, I had to do a great deal of research. I'm not a Marine, nor did I ever serve in the military. Therefore, I sought out great people that were. Five Marines, two Army, and one Navy. Two of them are pilots and one was a tanker. I can't thank you all enough for the ground truth and answering my quirky questions, when you didn't have context. In no particular order: Dan, Jim, Amy and Jeff (who fought over the one copy I sent them), Kevin, Lee, and Tim. Thank you all for your service and for sorting me out. Yes, I know...Marines is capitalized!

A big thanks to John, whom I've known over thirty years, for spotting some stupid word issues (its steel, not steal!). It pains me to list him here as it will go to his head, but credit where due. You are awesome.

Finally, I'd like to thank the Internet! Much Google-Fu was required in the writing of this story. Also, all the fabulous authors in the Writing Community on Twitter. It's not the dumpster fire the rest of the site is, except for, well, the late Friday "dumpster fire" threads that were so much fun and caused the delay of many an author's book, I'm sure. If I had to thank one person on Twitter, it would be Dzintra Sullivan, International Best-Selling Author and writer lifter-upper! She makes Twitter, and the world, a better place for indie authors. Follow her. Buy her books. Trust me.

These peeps are great and I highly recommend them if you're in need of their services:

Norah Vawter, Editor and Author, norahvawter.com
Katie Hagaman, Graphic Designer and Author,
    katiehagaman.wixsite.com/mysite-1
Anuschka Roberts, Graphic Designer/Artist, Twitter @NushDraws
Paul Blake, Book Trailers and Author, vengefullemon.wordpress.com
Melinda Martin, Martin Publishing Services, https://melindamartin.me

# ABOUT THE AUTHOR

Mark Sibley

Mark Sibley is a corporate crisis manager and war gamer. He's developed and facilitated over a hundred war games for various organizations over the years and managed as many real-world crises for those organizations. This experience, along with a life-long dream of writing a novel, provided him fertile ground for pulling together all the aspects of this story and developing them into what became Mongol Moon. If you tell a war gamer that a particular bad thing can't happen, that war gamer will come up with a plausible scenario to prove you wrong…eventually.

He is a life-long Virginian and lives in the Commonwealth with his wife, three kids, and current pack of female terriers, two Boston Terriers, Izzy (our Queen) and Dobby (the Dumb-Dumb), and the ever ferocious Chewie the Wookie, a five-pound Yorkshire Terrier with one fang. If you've gotten this far, you know her pretty well by now. Christopher (Fat-Body), the neurotic Pug who's a complete mess, is also written in as I fondly remember him from thirty years ago. He made an impression on me, obviously. He was a good boy. At any given time, there is also a foster dog at our house, rounding out our pack.

Made in the USA
Coppell, TX
19 June 2021

57712619R00184